To Anna + Wade
Best wishes —
[signature]
7/d8

The Red Spoke

George D. N. Coletti, DMD

First Edition-2015
Stone Mountain, Georgia

DISCLAIMER: This book is a work of fiction. Names, places, characters and incidents are either the product of the author's imagination or are used fictitiously. Any resemblance to actual persons, living or dead, events or locations, with the exception of historical persons and events, is entirely coincidental.

Editor-in-Chief: Nancy Knight
Manuscript Editors: Susan Coletti and Charlie Hooper
Historical accuracy Editor: Joey Sequin
Storyline Editor: Lynne Dundon

Cover Design and Title: Susan Spickerman Coletti

Special thanks to Ms. Angelia Gibbs for her motivating contributions.

Summary: This novel, set in the little hamlet of Stone Mountain, Georgia, occurs just before, during and after the Civil War. The story revolves around a fictitious family, the Jernigans. Buck Jernigan and his freed slave, Isaac, become stealth abolitionists utilizing the Underground Railroad as a means to emancipate slaves from their environs.

ISBN-978-0-9890002-3-9

Dedication

This book is dedicated to the past, present and
future abolitionists around the world, who have served,
are serving and will serve to free those who are enslaved.

Table of Contents

Table of Contents Cont'd

PROLOGUE

On August 20, 1619, the arrival of the some twenty African captives aboard the Dutch ship, *Man of War,* historically marks the beginning of the African plight in America. The ship's cargo hold is empty and the captain exchanges the captured Africans for food from a Spanish vessel then sets sail.

It is clear that the Africans were considered indentured servants. An indentured servant would be required to work a set amount of time, then granted freedom.

Records of 1623 and 1624 list them as servants, and indeed later records show increasing numbers of free blacks, some of whom were assigned land.

In 1640, at least one African had been declared a slave. This African was ordered by the court "to serve his said master or his assigns for the time of his natural life here or elsewhere."

All thirteen of the original colonies were slave-holding colonies at the time of the signing of the Declaration of Independence. When the United States Government was formed and later, slavery still existed in every state in the union. There was an "Expressed" consent when the Constitution was written that slavery would not go into the territories. However, slavery was distinctly recognized in the Constitution and its legality was reinforced by the Supreme Court's decision in Dred Scott v. Sanford, which stated that slaves were private property, giving owners the right to carry slaves into any part of the United States or her territories.

This decision would lead to an "implied" consent for the abolitionists, and the North to disregard the Fugitive Slave Act of 1793 and the Law of 1850.

On these two separate occasions, Congress enacted legislation regarding fugitive slaves. The Fugitive Slave Act of 1793 required the return of runaway slaves to their owners. This Act was rarely enforced by northern states, which led to the more direct Fugitive Slave Law of

1850. Under this law, all United States Marshals and other Federal officers were required to aid in the capture and return of a fugitive slave or face penalties.

Every Act of Congress and every decision of the Supreme Court had sustained the rights of citizens to own slaves. Additionally, the Senate of the United States adopted a resolution that "all of the states were sovereign and equal," and that Negro slaves were property. Therefore, Congress had no right to interfere with this kind of property in the territories, and each state had the sole right to legislate on the subject.

Another factor leading to the War Between the States was the arguments for and against full state, rights, which means that the rights of states to decide whether or not to accept certain federal Acts and/or rule them unconstitutional.

The Federalist Party had opposed the adoption of the Constitution on the grounds that, under it the powers of the central government were too limited and those of the states were too broad. Justice Marshall, by judicial construction, constantly amplified the powers of the Federal Government, and at same time, restricted those of the states.

The coalition of the old Abolition or Free-soil Party had existed since the establishment of the Union. The Free-Soil Party was perhaps being more threatening because it was sincere in its fanatical desire to abolish Negro slavery.

This coalition was a small but militant fragment of the old Federalist Party made up of aristocrats who favored a strong central government.

The growth of the abolition movement was brought about mainly from the Dred Scott case, John Brown's Raid and the passage of the Fugitive Slave Act.

Another coalition was the northern wing of the old Whig Party, which believed in protective tariffs and a national bank.

The last and most formidable factor in this coalition was made up of the army of manufacturers located in the middle and eastern states. The shipbuilders and the fishermen had for many decades fattened themselves on subsidies, bounties and protective tariffs, all at the expense of the people of all other sections of the Union.

The fight for and against slavery into the territories actually went against the "expressed" consent not to allow slavery into any of the territories. This included the Louisiana Purchase, the Mexican War, the Kansas-Nebraska Act and The Missouri Compromise.

The Republican Party and the election of Abraham Lincoln as President in 1860, served to increase the agitation by seemingly trampling upon the Constitution, nullifying the Acts of Congress and defying the Supreme Court. It was not a party of fixed and well-defined principles but rather was believed to be a coalition of these several parties and fragments of dead parties organized in its day to combat the principles of the party of Thomas Jefferson.

South Carolina seceded from the Union on December 20, 1860, and the American War between the States, begins.

Abraham Lincoln

For your own eyes only

Springfield, Illinois
December 22, 1860

Hon. A. H. Stephens

My dear Sir,

Your obliging answer to my short note is just received, and for which please accept my thanks. I fully appreciate the present peril the country is in, and the weight of responsibility on me.

Do the people of the South really entertain fears that a Republican administration would, *directly, or indirectly*, interfere with their slaves, or with them, about their slaves? If they do, I wish to assure you, as once a friend, and still, I hope, not an enemy, that there is no cause for such fears.

The South would be in no more danger in this respect, than it was in the days of Washington. I suppose, however, this does not meet the case. You think slavery is *right* and ought to be extended; while we think it is *wrong* and ought to be restricted. That, I suppose, is the rub. It certainly is the only substantial difference between us.

Yours very truly
A. LINCOLN

Chapter One
Surreptitious

Buck Jernigan and Isaac are picking up supplies at the local Stone Mountain General Store. Hill, a slave from the Cedar Plantation, is also gathering supplies at the store. Buck makes a motion with his head, and Isaac subtly changes his direction to pass closer to the wagon the slave is loading. He doesn't speak, but nods in greeting when he walks by.

Hill had contacted a freeman in Canada, via word of mouth, that he wanted to escape. Although he had no other communication with his friend, he was awaiting instructions for where and when to meet his "conductor" of the Underground Railroad. Because of the highly charged atmosphere of suspicion these days, he is trying very hard to appear normal. He wants to draw no attention to himself. His master is an intolerant man who punishes his slaves severely for even the slightest infraction of his rules. Seeking freedom would likely result in his death or, at the very least, being whipped and chained.

His head and chest, and indeed his entire stature, as solid as a rock, indicates that he is physically no ordinary man; and not being under the influence of the spirit of "non-resistance," he has occasionally been found to be a rather formidable customer.

For five or six years, the greater part of Hill's time was occupied by trying to escape and being in prison and for sale. All of these were punishments for his running away. If he doesn't succeed this time, he fears the worst.

His mechanical genius is excellent, so were his

geographical abilities. He can make shoes or do carpenter's work very handily, though he has never had the formal training. As to traveling by night or day, he is always road-ready, has an uncommon memory and can give exceedingly good accounts of what he sees.

After returning with his last load of supplies, he climbs aboard his wagon. As he picks up the reins, he notices a very small and scrappy piece of paper with a drawing on it. He bends over as if he's tying his shoe and snatches the paper. Upon examination, he sees a drawing of a cross. He immediately knows what this drawing indicates. He looks around and sees no one to whom he can attribute the drawing to unless it could be Mr. Buck or Isaac. He squeezes the small drawing tightly in his hand, snaps the reins and heads out of town.

Once out of sight, he stops to more closely examine the drawing. The code, a coded message from an abolitionist "Shepherd," appears before his eyes. His planned escape from slavery is falling into place.

The message is in the form of a drawing of a Presbyterian Church cross, which means the "station" is the church closest to Hill's plantation. In the center of the cross is the number 2. This means only two slaves can come. The cross also has three arms, which indicates to arrive at the destination at 3 AM.

The future runaway becomes very excited, yet very anxious. He takes the note, stuffs it in his mouth, chews it and then swallows it. There will be no evidence that he has either contacted the Underground Railroad or that he has received any type of communication from them.

Upon his arrival at the plantation, he unloads his cargo under the direction of his foreman, finishes his chores and heads to his cabin to join his wife, Lizzie, for supper.

Lizzie watches him closely, seeming puzzled by his behavior. "Whatsa matter? You nervous as a fat dog in a briar patch."

"Shhh!" He takes her hand, opens his cabin door and peers around to ascertain that no one is nearby.

Hill leads her to a chair as he takes one opposite her and holds her hands. "I got de sign."

The surprise in her face is unmistakable. "You got .
. ."

"Yes. I got a paper, jus' a bitty piece." He glances around and listens intently for a moment to make sure nobody is approaching their cabin. "We gon' leave tonight."

In a whisper, he relates what has happened that day. Her eyes become bold. Joy and fear all mixed into one play across her face. "Merciful Lawd."

They know they must have their freedom. Hill begins to go over the plan; he leans in and tells her that from the moment they leave the plantation she must be disguised as a man and to understand that there is danger ahead. The desire to be free is very powerful and Lizzie agrees to everything that Hill lays out. For the precious jewel of freedom, they are willing to make any sacrifice, or to endure any amount of suffering.

This Presbyterian Church is near the Yellow River, normally about one hour walk from the plantation. At a safe time they depart the plantation and stealthy make their way to the "station" arriving around 2 AM and hide in the crawl space under the church floor. Before long their "Shepherd" appears, and their journey begins.

Because of the danger involved, the Shepherd only knows his "Station" and the location of the next one. All other aspects are kept secret, so that, even under torture, nobody can give away much information.

Early the next morning Buck Jernigan and his "Slave", Isaac, are up early getting the mule and wagon ready for a trip to town. They begin a discussion about the message to Hill left by Isaac. Buck and Isaac are secret abolitionists. Neither of their wives is aware of their activities with the Underground Railroad.

Years ago, Buck, on a trip to Philadelphia, met an African-American abolitionist named William Still. Mr. Still is a conductor on the Underground Railroad and the chairman of the Vigilance Committee of the Pennsylvania Anti-Slavery Society. At the time of the meeting, Buck was already an abolitionist at heart. After several meetings with Mr. Still, Buck devised a plan where he and Isaac could assist in freeing slaves.

Buck and his wife Betty Gail acquired Sally and Isaac when they were toddlers. Sally's and Isaac's parents were close friends. They were slaves of Buck's older cousin, Henry, and his wife Shannon. One fateful afternoon, Sally's parents went fishing on The Yellow River with Isaac's parents. Isaac's mother accidentally slid off the bank and was carried off by the rapids. In an effort to save his wife, Isaac's father jumped into the raging river. Sally's mother and father hung on to a tree branch just over the river trying to reach their beloved friends but the branch gave way to the heavy load and in less than three minutes all four had succumbed to the force of the water. There were no survivors.

Henry's wife, Shannon, had since passed away and he was beginning to liquidate his farm and move to his old childhood home in Philadelphia. Henry offered orphaned Sally and Isaac to Buck to simply get them off of his hands. Buck and Betty Gail took the kids and raised them along with their two children, Mia and Norman, educating them on the basics of reading, writing and 'rithmatic. When Sally and Isaac were older, Buck and Betty Gail gave them chores on the farm and paid them a fair wage. Buck gave Isaac and Sally their freedom when they turned eighteen and they married shortly thereafter. Isaac and Sally elected to stay with Buck and Betty Gail out of their love and respect for each other, and, although they would not be slaves in Canada or in a Free State, they would still be discriminated against, and making a decent living would be very difficult. In addition, they were afraid of being kidnapped along the way and sold into slavery. For special reasons, Buck and Isaac were able to convince Sally and Betty Gail not to disclose to anyone that they were free.

As Buck and Isaac are bringing the mule and buggy out of the barn they see horsemen heading their way. It's the slave hunters. They stop and firmly question Buck and Isaac about any suspicious Negroes passing through the area. Isaac acts like a slave and takes off his hat as the slave hunters question Buck. They tell Buck there is a $300.00 reward for the Negro woman Lizzie and her husband Hill. The horsemen get into the description of Hill and Lizzie, both about twenty-eight years old; she is medium sized, dark complexion, good-looking. When spoken to, she replies quickly. Last seen she was neatly dressed, wearing a red and green blanket shawl, and most likely was carrying a variety of clothing with her. They suspect that she ran off in company with her husband, Hill, who is about 6 feet in height, with slight impediment in his speech, dark chestnut color, and a large scar on the side of his neck.

With no leads from Buck, the slave hunters depart. Isaac tells Buck that he imagines those two names will appear in the local newspaper with the other runaways. Buck smiles and tells Isaac, "That makes another one for us now, Isaac.

After one week of hazardous traveling with various conductors of the Underground Railroad, Hill and Lizzie reach Savannah, GA.

They are to meet up with Captain James from Wilmington, Delaware. He was at the helm of a schooner named *Liberty Bell* and their voyage extended to Philadelphia. Captain James was true to freedom, the sea was his only address, he was the right man in the right place, and very well understood his business as a "Conductor" in charge of their new "Station".

They knew when the *Liberty Bell* would begin her voyage and that she was loaded with tar, rosin, and spirits of turpentine. Captain James was to hide Hill and Lizzie in a safe place in the ship that wouldn't be "smoked." The slaveholders of North Carolina had a law enacted requiring all vessels coming north to be smoked to expose runaway slaves who might be stowed away on a vessel.

To survive the smoking, the inventive genius of Hill and Lizzie soon lent itself to devising a safeguard. The safeguard consisted of silk and oil-cloth shrouds, made large, with drawing strings, which, when pulled over their heads, would be drawn very tightly around their waists. A bladder of water and towels were provided. The towels were to be wetted and held to their nostrils. They had determined to struggle against death for liberty.

The hour approached for being at the wharf. At the appointed time, they were on hand ready to go on the boat; Captain James stowed them away. They were ready to run the risk of being smoked to death; but as good luck would have it, the law was not carried into effect in this instance, so that the smell of smoke was not upon them. The effect of the turpentine, however, of the nature of which they were totally ignorant, was worse, if possible, than the smoke would have been. The blood was literally drawn from them at every pore in frightful quantities. But as heroes of the bravest type, they resolved to continue steadfast as long as a pulse continued to beat, and thus they finally conquered.

The invigorating northern air and the kind treatment of the Vigilance Committee which met them at the dock, acted like a charm upon them. They improved very rapidly from their exhaustive and heavy loss of blood. Desiring to retain some memorial of them, a member of the Committee begged for one of their silk shrouds, and likewise procured an artist to take the photograph of them; for years to come, these keepsakes were valued very highly. In the regular order of arrangements, the wants of Hill and Lizzie were duly met by the Committee, financially and otherwise. After a week, they were forwarded to Canada. After their safe arrival in Canada, Hill addressed a member of the Committee:

KINGSTON,
MR. WILLIAM STILL—*Dear Friend*:—I take the

opportunity of writing a few lines to let you know that we air all in good health hoping those few lines may find you and your family enjoying the same blessing. We arrived in King all safe Canada West I goes to work this morning at $1.75 per day and Lizzie is at work for Mr. George Mink and I will open a shop for myself in a few days.

      Yours with Respect,
      Hill

Chapter Two

All that Glistens is not Golden (Meeting the New Sheriff)

Several weeks later as the early morning sun eases through the window on a clear and crisp day, Norman rubs his eyes and throws his sheets back. The aroma of breakfast and his mother's and father's voices inform him that the world is ready and a waiting the arrival of his enthusiasm. The seven-year-old leaps from his bed, presses his nose against the window and peers out to check his rabbit box in the small garden near the house. The trap is still open, but there are plenty of rabbits nearby and one will soon become either a pet or a meal.

"Wee-Bean!" calls his father, using the nickname Uncle Isaac gave him years before. "It's time to eat. We gotta go to the new sheriff's swearing-in ceremony today. Your mama is fixing rabbit stew for the affair."

Norman smiles, slips his straps over his shoulders and heads for the kitchen. Mia is helping their mother gather the plates and serving utensils for the trip to City Hall. The family sits down for breakfast, and Buck leads the family blessing. "God, we ask you to direct the new sheriff in all matters to relieve this place of the toxic consequences of the quarry workers round the mountain. Eliminate their toxic qualities of drinking, fighting and womanizing. Amen."

After finishing breakfast, Uncle Isaac hitches Jack to the wagon. Like most mules, Jack is a stout and headstrong animal. The only person he allows on his back is Wee-Bean, whom he takes to school 'most every day. Anyone else attempting to ride on Jack is thrown instantly. Uncle

Isaac has readied the horse and buggy for the trip and the festivities of the day. Everyone dresses in their Sunday best, though Betty Gail had to force Wee-Bean into his dress clothes. Mia was up early heating the irons on the stove so that his collar would be smooth and stiff. Wee-Bean dislikes dressing up as much as his father but takes the challenge with his well-known smile and humor, declaring,

"Even the bluebirds are gonna laugh at me, Mama, with this here blue shirt on."

"Just you never mind," Betty Gail says. "You look fine. It's time to go." Everyone loads into the wagon and off they go in a cheerful mood.

The journey to town on the narrow trail is uneventful except for the few rabbits and squirrels skirting around. Main Street is crowded with horses and buggies. A festive mood prevails. Sniffing the air, Buck asks, "Smell that roasted deer, barbecued pork and beef."

Wee-Bean nods vigorously. "I sure can. I can't wait." Mia stands and holds to the back of the buggy seat and looks around at the festive scene. "Look at those cow brains, corn bread and biscuits."

"Look, Ma. There's Mr. Maguire from the Promised Land Plantation.

I hope he's brought me a fresh apple like he always does. His wagon is loaded with his corn, peas, beans, fried okra, and squash. Hello, Mr. Maguire!" shouts Wee-Bean as he rushes over to greet their friend from Lithonia.

Mr. Maguire reaches into a basket and retrieves two large red apples, "Here's an apple for you, Wee-Bean, and one for your teacher tomorrow."

"Thanks."

"How are your studies at the Academy, Wee-Bean? That's the place to be for the best education around these here parts, I hear."

"Making real good grades, so far, Mr. Maguire. Pa said he'd get me a squirrel gun real soon if I keep up the good work."

"Well, you're old enough now to have a squirrel gun, and I know your pa will get you a fine one. Just you be careful."

Wee-Bean moves along, admiring the apple, peach, and pecan pies on the tables being set up for dinner. His eyes are wide open and his mouth is watering to taste whatever fragrant delight is teasing his nostrils. "Mmm. Smells real good."

Buck looks at the crowd gathering for the festivities and excuses himself.

The day is bustling with people, at least two hundred and fifty, there to celebrate the swearing-in ceremony. The new sheriff, Tom Perkerson, is working the crowd, greeting and thanking all the citizens. He seems to enjoy sampling the food before others have the chance. His wide-brim hat complements what appears to be a new, store-bought brown suit. His old brown boots add to the effect. Sheriff Perkerson stands about five feet ten inches tall and has a mustache and small goatee. His coat is open, revealing a pistol on his left side. Just about everyone respects Mr. Perkerson. He opposes drinking and fighting going on with the rough necks from around the mountain quarry. His campaign promise was to "clean up the town."

Shortly before noon, the church bell rings and the citizens gather at the depot to witness Mr. Perkerson taking his oath of office. The city's officials are on the platform adjacent to the depot. The mayor introduces Congressman William B. W. Dent and his wife, Eliza. Sheriff-elect Perkerson had asked his good friend Congressman Dent to administer the oath of office.

Congressman Dent gives Mrs. Perkerson *The Bible* to hold for her husband and asks Sheriff-elect Perkerson to place his left hand on *The Bible*, raise his right hand and to repeat after him:

"I do solemnly swear, before God and the citizens, that I will uphold the laws of the United States, the State of Georgia, the County and the City. I swear that I have not been engaged in a duel, either directly or indirectly, either as a principal or second, or in any character whatsoever in this state so help me God." Sheriff Perkerson finishes his oath, smiles and waves to the crowd.

The Judge takes the Bible from Mrs. Perkerson and hands her the sheriff's new badge. She smiles, takes his coat lapel gently, pins the badge just above his heart and follows with a loving embrace. The crowd cheers and throws their hats into the air.

Sheriff Perkerson finishes his oath, smiles and waves to the cheering crowd. He states a few of his concerns, which are mostly related to apprehending the runaway slaves. "I will do my absolute best to return the runaway Negroes. I will forthright send the slave hunters to apprehend the runaways at the Canadian border before they reach their Promise Land. When they are retuned they can expect full punishment under the law. They need to remember what the preacher said, 'Obey their master.'"

"If you wish to live among great citizens, drink crisp spring water, enjoy a long and healthy life, pray, and be free from crime, you need to live in Stone Mountain. Let the feast begin!"

During the celebration, Isaac engages in quiet conversation with some of the Negro friends.

Thom asks, "Man, I gotta escape. My master goan kill me. He beat me when the wind change direction."

Isaac listens to Wayne express their desires to escape. "I'se waiting for a word from a "Shepherd," too. But you jus' cain't do nothin' stupid."

Warren shakes his head and spits toward the group of white men standing a few feet away. "I ain't waitin' not one minute longer than I has to."

Isaac feels the man's anger and frustration and fears that he might be ready to bolt. "Then you needs to pass the word along yo' kin up north. Mebbe they can hep get you started. But you cain't jus' run."

After the ceremony, Congressman Dent meets up with Buck. "Hello, Buck."

Buck clasps his hand. "Hello, Congressman. We're sure glad you could be with us today."

About that time, Davis Wade approaches Congressman Dent and says, "I hope I am not interrupting, but if you're not real busy at the moment, I need to talk to Congressman Dent about some farm matters." Buck excuses himself and begins looking for Drury Lee and Thomas Maguire.

Finding Thomas, he asks, "Thomas, did you catch those three runaway Negroes?"

"I caught one of them, but the other two got away. The one I caught won't ever try that again."

Buck smiles and excuses himself. He walks over to Aaron Cloud and Thomas Henry and says, "Hello."

They respond to Buck by shaking his hand vigorously and clapping him on the shoulder. They resumed their conversation.

Aaron continues, shaking his head and grimacing. "Bet you're having a problem with the Negroes. They just don't like heights."

"You're right. I have to stay on 'em all the time. Had to give a couple of 'em a taste of my whip."

Aaron laughs. "Just be sure your tower is anchored better than mine was or the wind will make short work of it! I saw yours last week, and everything looks great. The anchors seem to be deep enough in the granite to hold it to the top of the mountain, but you never know."

It's nearing three o'clock when Buck finds his friend Drury Lee, looks around surreptitiously and asks. "Do you have it?"

"It's in my wagon. Picked it up in Decatur the other day. It's mighty fine."

"Great! Let me fetch it and hide it in my wagon." They start out together and Buck pays Drury eight dollars. Once they reach the wagon, Drury reaches in and hands over a squirrel rifle to Buck.

Buck examines it closely. "Mighty fine piece. I think Wee-Bean will like it. Thanks for picking it up for me."

The festivities are coming to an end, and Betty Gail gives Buck that familiar look that says it's time to go home. Before leaving, Buck presses the new sheriff's hands tightly, "Good luck to ya." The Jernigans climb into the buggy and head home around the mountain.

Buck points toward the rolling clouds. "A storm's brewing and we best git."

Wind ruffles the leaves on the trees as they pass, revealing the lighter undersides. The temperature drops suddenly and thunder rumbles in the distance. The wind gains force—thrashing trees like whips.

"Let's git on, Jack, only a half mile to go!" Buck calls out anxiously. Fat raindrops begin to fall. Lightning crackles across black clouds, and thunder booms almost immediately. Hail pelts them as the dirt road turns to mud almost instantly. A bright flash and deafening boom knocks Jack over and carries the buckboard over into the ditch with him. Mia, Betty Gail and Wee-Bean are thrown into the mud. Blinding rain and wind cut into Betty Gail's face as she searches for her children. She hugs them close for a moment before they resume the search for Buck. She hears his cries for help.

Betty Gail clasps her hands to her heart. "Merciful Lord, Buck's trapped under the buckboard."

The muddy deluge floods over him. His shouts become garbled as the sienna colored water flows over his head. Jack lies motionless in the ditch, making no noise.

They rush over to Buck and shield him from the rain and mud.

"Pa!" Wee-Bean scrambles down the bank, fighting a rising panic as he wipes water and mud from his father's pain stricken face.

Betty Gail assesses the situation as quickly as she can. "All right, Wee- Bean, help me lift the buckboard. Mia, help your pa slide out from under."

"No, no," Buck cries. "Don't touch my leg. It's broken!"

"Go get Doctor Hamilton and whoever else you can find to help!" screams Betty Gail to Wee-Bean amidst the chaos and wreckage.

He darts off up the muddy embankment and dashes towards town just as the clouds separate and the wind becomes a little calmer. Still muddy, he reaches the livery stable and throws open the door. Screaming and crying, he calls out frantically, "Lightning struck us, and Pa's trapped under the wagon! We need help!"

"Come here, Norman. Calm down, son. What's happened?" Levi takes Wee-Bean by the hand and tries to settle him down to get more information. Wee-Bean rubs his eyes. "Pa, Ma and Mia are over the crest of the hill and Pa is pinned under the load."

John Beauchamp jumps on his mount and goes for Dr. Hamilton while others gather outside with their horses, wagons and ropes, ready to head toward the scene with Wee-Bean.

The storm disappears almost as quickly as it came. The sun is bright and the sky sparkles blue once again. As the group led by Wee-Bean hurries toward the accident they encounter tree limbs, tin roofing torn from houses and water flowing on the red clay street. As the team tops the hill, Wee-Bean sees the overturned wagon Buck is trapped beneath.

"There it is," he shouts.

Buster Phillips hastens to the Jernigans' aid. The other men remove the harness from Jack. Then they line up on one side, push and return the wagon to the upright position. Wee-Bean scurries to his father's side.

"I'm okay," Buck says calmly. "Go check on Jack."

Wee-Bean, with tears running down his cheeks, slowly approaches poor, mud-covered unconscious Jack. Expecting the worst, Wee-Bean pats poor Jack on the head and then realizes that he is blinking his eyes. "Jack! You're alive!" Wee-Bean scrambles to lift Jack's head from the mud. Buster and his companions pull Buck cautiously from the mud and place him on a waiting wagon.

"Betty Gail, you take Mia and Wee-Bean on home while I go to Dr. Hamilton's and get fixed up right. Isaac, you and Sally go on out to the farm and make sure the place is all right."

As the wagon is about to pull away, Dr. Hamilton rides over the hill. He stops by the wagon, dismounts and begins to examine Buck's leg. "Hello, Buck. Looks like you had a little accident."

"Sure did, Doc. Be careful with this leg. I know it's broken."

Cutting away the cloth of Buck's pants leg, Dr. Hamilton shakes his head. "It's broken all right, but no tears in the skin. That's good news. Take him to my house so I can splint him up!"

"I hate to bother you on such a day, Dr. Hamilton." Buck tries to find a comfortable position.

"No bother on my part at all, Buck. I'm glad I'm here to help."

Jack begins to neigh louder and suddenly rolls over for a brief moment. He kneels and then stands erect while Wee-Bean is holding tightly to the halter.

"Good boy. Good boy, Jack." Wee-Bean hugs and kisses his beloved animal.

Mia hugs Jack and Wee-Bean together, trying to hold back the tears. As Mia turns to look back up the hill, she places her hand upon her chest and inhales quickly and deeply. She taps Wee-Bean gently on his shoulder.

Wee-Bean turns. "What, Mia?"

With a grin and giggle, Mia answers, "Look at Jack's tail!"

Wee-Bean stares, speechless, eyes and mouth open wide. Finally, he mutters, "His tail. It's standin' straight up . . like a pole!" About the same time, Jack turns his head and flicks his tail but only the tip flickers in response to his attempts to place it in the inferior position. After their shock subsides, Mia and Wee-Bean walk Jack for a bit to check for other injuries.

Buster Phillips returns from Dr. Hamilton's with news for the twins and their mother. "The doc's splintin' yo pa's leg. Said he be good in 'bout six weeks. De men will bring him home soon," he says as he dismounts. Mia points to Jack's tail. Buster turns and asks with amazement, "W'at happened?"

"I guess it's still got lightning in it!" replies Wee-Bean.

The group begins to gather the remnants of the cargo. Mia, while surveying the scene, realizes that the birds are out singing again. It makes the drudgery of their work slightly more pleasant. All of the dry goods are now the color of the clay as are the garments she is wearing.

The seeds and feed in the burlap are also wet. They load what they can salvage, and Buster hooks his horse to the wagon. Wee-Bean sits on the back of the wagon and holds Jack's harness tightly. The odd-looking animal trails behind.

When they stop at the farm, Betty Gail jumps from the wagon and looks around. "What happened here, Isaac?"

Isaac points toward the hen house. Still shaken, he says, "Miz Betty Gail, we's lost da hen house en some shingles on the 'zebo."

Betty Gail scans the farms, but nothing else seems amiss. "Looks like everything else is okay. No real damage."

Isaac looks at Norman and points at the mule's tail. "What's the matter wit Jack's tail?"

Wee-Bean replies anxiously, "Still got lightning in it!"

Uncle Isaac mutters, "Probly so! Probly so!" He begins to unload the now-wobbly wagon. "Got ter fix this 'un 'fore we uses it again."

Darkness is approaching as friends bring Buck home.

"Pa! You're home!" shouts Wee-Bean excitedly, rounding the corner of the house.

"Yep, everything's gonna be all right, son," Buck assures Wee-Bean.

Mia chimes in, "Pa, you got home just in time. Sally has fresh rabbit stew for us. It's on the table and waiting, so let's eat!"

Wee-Bean places a stool for his father to rest his broken leg on and they all gather for supper. Buck says, "Need to say a blessing." As the aroma of the rabbit stew fills the air, the family joins hands and Buck bestows a gracious thanks to God.

With supper over, Wee-Bean and Mia assist their pa to his chair nearest the small fire to warm him from the spring chill and dampness in the house. The events of the afternoon move from a formal discussion to humor. Wee-Bean tells his pa the story about the effects of the lightning on the mule. "How long is the lightning gonna stay in Jack's tail?"

Buck laughs, imagining the sight. "Now that's what

you call a real hair-raising experience! I have no idea how much longer that lightning's gonna stay in it, but what a sight he must be!"

The next day, Buck gets the squirrel rifle from the buggy. He's on the front porch spitting tobacco and reading the newspaper when Wee-Bean comes around the corner. "Hi, Pa! That was a great picnic. Do you want me to feed the chickens now?"

Buck motions for Wee-Bean to come sit next to him. "I know you and your friends have been playing army and fighting the Indians and the British. So I got you a squirrel rifle so you can learn to shoot for real."

Wee-Bean looks down so as not to appear to be afraid. "Pa, that there squirrel gun might kick me clean to the ground."

"Don't worry none about that. This squirrel rifle carries a light charge and isn't that rough on you," Buck reassures him.

"I just don't think I'm ready to shoot it yet, Pa." Wee-Bean's eyes reveal the fear of disappointment that all young boys have when they feel they haven't lived up to their father's expectations.

Buck pauses for a few seconds and inhales on his pipe. "Now suppose you're out in the woods and a bear is a coming on you. Tell me what you'd do."

Wee-Bean looks back at his pa as he answers, "I'll just run and climb a tree!"

Buck shakes his head and places his hand on the gun, aiming it toward the fresh plowed yet barren planting fields. "Well, son, that's a fine idea except a bear can out-climb all of us. Now, what if you're out in the corn field, no trees around, and a bear comes at you. What will you do then?"

Wee-Bean places his hand across his mouth and rubs his bottom lip, then looks his pa directly in the eye and declares, "Well, Pa, I guess heaven ain't so bad!"

Buck lets out a loud howl, smacks Wee-Bean on the back and places the squirrel gun against the wall. He spits out the remainder of the tobacco and says, "Let's go feed the chickens!"

Buck is at the depot delivering the last bales of cotton of the season. "Have either you or Betty Gail seen today's newspaper?" asks James Goldsmith.

"No, just fixin' to buy one."

"Don't know if you folks have heard or not, but Congressman Dent passed away. His funeral was a couple of days ago."

"I hate to hear that. I heard a while back that he was not doing too well, but figured it was just a temporary sickness." Buck gives James five cents and picks up a newspaper.

Across the top the headlines read: "Congressman William Barton Wade Dent Dies March 3, 1855 at the age of forty-nine."

James replies, "By the way, more news. George W. Latham came by today. He's getting ready to start construction on the Stone Mountain Seminary here by the railroad. He's going to be the principal and Judge Smith's wife is going to teach music, embroidery, ornamental needlework, and wax work."

Betty Gail looks in the direction of the building site. "Really."

"Miss Sayer's the assistant teacher in charge of the English Department. When do they expect the Seminary to open?" asks Betty Gail.

"Mr. Latham thinks the first session will be in January of 1858."

"I'll have to look into that for Mia. We best get back home and write a letter of condolence to Mrs. Dent and her children. I hope you have a good day, James, and keep those trains on schedule." Buck mounts his wagon and he and Betty Gail head home.

Chapter Three
Five Years Later—A Quest for the Best

On a cold January day in 1860 Buck and Wee-Bean are on the porch discussing the up-coming planting season when Uncle Isaac returns from town and delivers the newspaper to Buck. He nods at Wee-Bean and smiles. Taking a break in their discussion, Buck scans the front page. "I see the Georgia Military Institute in Marietta is capturing the headlines again. It says here, 'The state-owned Institute has a new Superintendent and Commandant. The State is offering school grants to admirable and worthy individuals. One student from each Congressional District and two from the State at large may receive the grants. The individuals receiving scholarships will be required to teach in Georgia for at least two years upon graduation.' Sounds good to me. What do you think, Wee-Bean? You talk about wanting to be a General someday."

Norman quickly answers, "Yes, sir. That sounds good to me!"

"Why don't we all take the train up to Marietta in a couple of weeks and check the Institute out? The whole family should go."

"Okay, Pa," replies his excited, maturing, fourteen-year-old son.

"Well then, that settles it then. I'll write a letter to the new superintendent for an appointment to visit the campus. Says here his name is Major Francis W. Capers and he helped found the South Carolina Military Academy in

Charleston."

In March of 1860 Buck and his excited family arrive in Marietta, board a carriage and head to the Georgia Military Institute College located on College Hill on Powder Springs Road. As the carriage approaches the one hundred-ten acre campus, Buck and Betty Gail smile as Wee-Bean and Mia show signs of being awestruck.

On the narrow road to College Hill, Buck notices the peaks of four mountains. From here, he can see that they're nestled in a valley made by the surrounding Lost, Brush, Blackjack and Kennesaw Mountains. Massive trees dot the campus, casting an intricate pattern of sunlight and shadow. The carriage passes through the entrance to the campus itself. Buck marvels at the lush landscaping.

"I never saw so many pretty roses and flowers before." He points at a bed of brilliant flowers. He leans forward and taps the driver. "Tell us about these buildings."

The carriage driver points out various buildings on the campus. "That two-story building is the classroom building, and those fourteen over there are the one-story barrack buildings, each having two rooms. Each barrack has an adjacent steward's quarters with six rooms, a dining room, a kitchen and a gun house."

They approach Major Frances W. Capers' quarters, a grandiose three-story, columned building, which proudly flies a gigantic United States Garrison Flag. He then reins the horse to a stop slowly. Two servants present themselves. "Yous is the Jernigans?" asks one of the servants.

"Yes, we are," replies Buck.

"We been 'specting you. Major Capers will be back shortly. Please come inside." The servants assist Betty Gail and Mia from the carriage as Buck and Norman follow behind. One of the servants escorts the Jernigans to Major Caper's secretary, who cordially introduces himself.

He welcomes the Jernigans. "Would you like some

lemonade?"

"Thank you." Buck and his family readily accept the cool drink.

The waiting room's appointments consist of paintings and some fine china. A painting over the secretary's desk is of General Washington crossing the Delaware River on Christmas night in 1776. There's a large painting depicting the Battle of Bunker Hill. Buck points out to Norman, "That's one of the first battles of the Revolution." Another great oil illustrates General Cornwallis having General Charles O'Harn surrendering his sword in his behalf after the English defeat in 1781 at Yorktown. Buck proudly points to this picture. "This was the final battle for our independence and your great-grandfather was there."

Before they can finish looking at the décor, Major Capers opens the mahogany door to his office, steps in and introduces himself. "Welcome. I am Major Capers. I've been expecting you."

Buck introduces his family. Major Capers invites them into his office, gesturing for them to sit. "How was your train ride from Stone Mountain?"

"Not too bad. The sky was a little cloudy, but not too much humidity, making for a mighty pleasant trip," replies Buck with a nod.

"Norman, I understand that you might have an interest in coming to GMI. We have a very regimented program here and expect a lot of studying and dedication to learn military tactics. This institution follows the same academic and military criteria as West Point Military Academy. You must be willing to devote your mind and body to the principle of the Georgia Military Institute and the principles of leadership and knowledge. Would you be willing to do this, Norman?"

"Yes, sir. My pa lost his fingers in the Mexican War and my great grandfather fought in the American Revolution. They fought for our freedom and our homes and I want to be just like them. I want to be a leader."

Major Capers smiles, stands and extends his hand to Buck. "I'm pleased to know you're a veteran and survived your wound." Then he extends his hand to Norman as he invites the family on a tour of the campus. "Captain McGill, our Commandant of Cadets, is waiting for you in the reception area. He is also our professor of Engineering and acting- Professor of Drawing. He is going to be your escort for the campus tour."

They leave the Major's office and return to the reception area. Captain McGill introduces himself. As they begin their tour, Buck says, "The newspapers say the United States government gave the school a hundred and twenty short muskets, sixteen small swords, and a battery composing of four brass six-pounder field pieces. Also, the State Arsenal at Milledgeville issues muskets to the school, is that true?"

"Sure is. We also get tents from the Chatham Artillery, the Savannah Guards and the Republican Blues. Although the muskets are old, without these supplies, the Institution could not operate in the customary military environment. Let's visit one of the barracks first."

They enter one of the rooms of the barracks. "Each room is about eighty square feet. In your room you can have an iron bedstead, pine table, looking glass, foot tub, wash basin, water bucket and dipper, broom, washstand and a candlestick."

"How about playing chess or backgammon?" asks Norman.

Placing his hand on Norman's shoulder, Captain McGill says "Sorry, but it is against GMI rules for cadets to play chess, backgammon, cards, or read any novel, poem, pamphlet or book that is not a part of their studies. No horse, mule, dog or waiter either. You just will not have time. At all times you'll keep your quarters clean and neat. Let's head for the kitchen and Old Abe."

Buck takes Betty Gail by the arm as Mia walks along. Norman follows close to Captain McGill.

Standing outside, Captain McGill explains, "The kitchen and dining room are attachments to the steward's quarters as is the gun house. This is 'Old Abe.' He is the steward in charge of these quarters." Betty Gail questions the steward about the meals. Old Abe shows her the storage room containing vast amounts of canned goods and cured meats. "We gits lots of fresh vegetables from what we grow an' meat from town. We git plenty good eats."

Buck ponders to himself to ask if Old Abe and the other two servants are held in bondage. Because of the highly charged emotions most people feel about slavery, Buck never discusses the subject. Maybe, at some time in the future, he can ask the servants if he has an opportunity to speak to them in private. If he didn't have a family to worry about, he wouldn't have to be quite so secretive and didn't dare express his feelings.

"I'll take you to the two-story classroom building next," says Captain McGill as they depart the steward's quarters. "We follow the academics of the United States Military Academy at West Point as closely as possible. Freshmen and sophomores are on the second floor. In these classrooms, freshmen begin their studies with arithmetic, algebra, French, English grammar, literature and geography." The Captain escorts them to the next set of classrooms. "These classrooms are for sophomores. They study geometry, more French, rhetoric and drawing. As you can see, the classrooms have all of the equipment and books necessary for teaching and learning. Let's go downstairs now for the junior and senior classrooms.

"The juniors' studies include calculus, science, history and drawing and are conducted in these classrooms. Down the hall, the seniors study engineering, architecture, mineralogy, geology, ethics, philosophy, rhetoric and military tactics. We keep them mighty busy and expect their minds and bodies to become a proud part of GMI's soul."

"Everybody likes a parade. When do you have parades?" asks Buck.

"It is 3 p.m. now. The cadets have a dress parade at 4 p.m. every day, except Saturday and Sunday. Let's go by Old Abe's quarters. He is preparing an early supper for you before the parade begins."

"What time do the cadets get up every morning?" asks Norman. "Reveille sounds at 6:30. Then we have morning prayers and the policing of quarters. This is when we inspect your room for orderliness and cleanliness. Finally, breakfast before classes, which begin at 8 in the morning and end at 4 o'clock in the evening. At 4 o'clock in the evening, just like today, the cadets have a dress parade. After supper you're expected to go to your room and study. There's always a professor available to assist you if you have a problem. When taps sounds at 10:30, you'll extinguish all lights and go to bed. This ends the day."

When they arrive at Old Abe's, there's a spread of fresh corn, beets, green beans and pork chops, ice tea and lemonade with apple pie for desert. "Hopes ye like me cooking," says Old Abe.

"He has to go now to prepare for the parade with the cadets. Old Abe is one of the drummers," says Captain McGill as he joins the Jernigans for the meal. "What do you think so far, Norman?"

"I like this place. I can't wait to see the cadets on parade. Like my pa said, I guess everybody likes a parade."

After they finish the sample meal, Captain McGill escorts them to the parade ground. "Sit under this big oak. This gives one of the best views of the cadets. I'll visit with you again after the parade."

Several locals begin approaching the parade grounds. Norman sees all of the beautiful young girls gathering round, but stays quiet. Some drive up in their buggies while others walk, all looking for shady spots. Many of the locals come in full dress, complete with servants to hold their umbrellas.

As 4 p.m. approaches, more carriages, buggies and young girls line up to view the grandeur of the parade and handsome cadets. Many of them introduce themselves to the Jernigans and conversations begin about how proud Marietta is of GMI. Several of the spectators ask Norman if he is planning on attending. He simply smiles and says, "Maybe!"

The parade begins sharply at 4. Old Abe is there with another drummer and a fife player. The cadets establish their ranks facing the viewing crowd and commanders of the Cadet Corp. The Cadet Commander barks a series of orders. "Order arms!"

The entire Corps demonstrates the precision of moving their muskets from their shoulder to the ground, as if they were one. "Present arms!" Again, the cadets bring their muskets in a position in front of their breasts. "Present colors!" The Color Guard marches forward and renders the flags. Appropriate music plays. Everyone stands. All the men take off their hats, placing them over their hearts, while the women do the same with their hands. The crowd turns as one to face the flag quietly. This moment is for remembering the sacrifices of the past and the hopes for the future. With a resounding "BOOM," the two brass cannons fire, echoing the unsuccessful shelling of Fort McHenry on September 13, 1814, at the end of the War of 1812.

As the music ends, the Cadet Commander orders, "Reduce arms!" and the cadets bring the muskets' butts to the ground again. The colors march to a position to lead the parade with the accompanying drummers and fifer. "Shoulder arms!" Again the cadets perform in unison and bring the muskets to their respective shoulders. "Pass in review!" The Cadet Commander and his staff position themselves in front of the Cadet Corps and the march in review begins. The cadet commander and his staff lead the parade formation passing in front of the reviewing followed by the other companies in formation. As each company passes the reviewing stand, the cadet officers raise their sabers to a salute position, turn their heads to the right recognizing the GMI Superintendent, the Commandant and GMI Professors. At the same time, the Gideon Bearer lowers the Company flag to a horizontal position.

"What an incredible sight! Look at those uniforms, shiny buttons and shining emblems on their hats. Their uniforms are perfect! I stand here looking at our future soldiers, the defenders of America and freedom!" exclaims Betty Gail.

Buck puts his arm around Norman's shoulders. "Well, what do you think, Norman? Would you like to become a part of the Georgia Military Institute, the West Point of Georgia?"

Norman looks up at his father and smiles. "Yes, Pa, I'd like it!" Last in the parade order are the two brass cannons.

"Look at the two saddle horses! Solid limbs, full firm chest and sure-footed. They appear to have a good disposition," Mia says as she points to the horses.

"Those are the exact qualities the saddle horse needs to lead the team. See the riders? Look at their inside leg when they pass." Buck nods as he looks appreciatively at the horses. "They have a metal shield to protect their leg from sustaining an injury from the limber. Now look closely, again. That four-wheel wagon is really two, two-wheeled wagons."

"What do you mean a two-wheeled wagon, Pa?" asks Norman.

"See the limber is the front wagon which holds one ammunition chest. A two-wheel caisson wagon hooks to the back of the limber wagon and also carries two additional chests of ammunition."

"I got it," replies Norman.

The parade lasts about forty-five minutes. The Jernigans are talking with some of the locals when Captain McGill returns. "Well, the decision is yours, Norman. Here is a petition for the admission examination." He hands it to Norman, who happily accepts the petition.

"Thanks, Captain McGill."

"You're quite welcome, Norman. Now, Mr. and Mrs. Jernigan, do you have any other questions for me or Major Capers?"

"Not right now. We want to thank you for the tour and hospitality. Our train leaves at
7 p.m. so we must get to the train station," says Buck.

Captain McGill shakes hands with Buck and Norman and touches his fingers to his cap. He thanks them for their interest in GMI.

"My carriage is waiting," says Captain McGill. "I'll direct the driver to take you to the station. If you have any questions, telegraph or write to me or Major Capers. Have a safe trip home to Stone Mountain and may God bless you."

The sun has long been down and the moon is peering over the mountain on this spring night as the train pulls into Stone Mountain Station. Mr. Goldsmith is still in his office at the depot. He waves to the Jernigans as he delivers a sack of mail to the mail car. The Jernigans walk over to the stable.

"I gots you buggy ready, Mars Jernigan," says the stable hand as he hurries to bring it forward. They climb onto the buggy and head round the mountain.

Everyone is exhausted from the exciting day. Buck yawns. "Bed time, I reckon." After his prayer, Norman climbs into bed. GMI, the boom of the six-pounders, and his papa's stories are in his dreams.

When everyone is in bed, Buck looks for Isaac. The man summons Buck to the barn. There, Isaac hands Buck a letter from Jerry Jackson (his code name for William Still). Buck opens the letter. It states that he and his friends drank from the "River Jordan" (Ohio River) with the help of the big dipper. Buck shakes Isaac's hand and tells him. "That makes about thirty now. He then burns the letter. "The Presbyterian Church and the small hidden cave on the Yellow River are great stations. It took Buck and Isaac almost a year and a half to build the cave. They hauled the extra dirt back to the farm to use it as topsoil.

"I wonder how many of that thirty actually made it to their destination." Isaac asks.

"Some of them are bound to have been captured and re-sold or returned to their owners. Some could've gotten sick while hiding out in the cold wilderness." Buck sighed, hoping that none of the slaves he'd helped had fallen victim to those fates. "I guess we'll never know, especially since none of them knew we were involved in their escape."

Buck removes the petition for the admission examination papers given to him by Major Capers at Georgia Military Institute. After supper, the family settles in to fill out the petition for the admission examination. Previous and current education experiences are important. Proudly they list the Stone Mountain Academy as Norman's background for education.

"Listing Stone Mountain Academy should be in your favor, Wee-Bean. Now, here it says that you must take the standing examination at the Institute on May 10th. It begins at one o'clock in the afternoon and lasts about two and one-half hours. It also says that you must come alone."

The following day in Mr. Latham's offices, Betty Gail and Mia complete the petition for enrollment in Stone Mountain Seminary. Mrs. George K. Smith greets them and assures Mia, "Graduating from Stone Mountain Academy will make your studies here a lot easier. So far everyone who has come from the Academy has done very well. We look forward to having you as a student."

Mr. Latham continues, "The first class begins on June 18. Each class lasts twenty-two weeks. The first class studies will include the Alphabet, Orthography, which is the art of spelling, and Orthoepy, which is the study of correct pronunciation. You will also take Reading, Oral Arithmetic, Numbers, Tables, Weights and Measurements along with Mental Arithmetic and Penmanship. Penmanship is taught by the Hammond and Potter's System. During the course of each class, we will have guest lecturers and instruction in Vocal Music.

Mrs. Smith gives Mia a box of books. "These are your books for the First Class. The embroidery, fancy needle work, wax work, including the stock, will be kept at the Seminary."

"I'm excited about starting," replies Mia.

Betty Gail opens her small purse, "Here is the $12.00 for the First Class and the extra $8.00 for the embroidery and other materials. Buck and I are so glad the Seminary is in Stone Mountain. We thank you for accepting Mia's petition for admission."

Chapter Four
Endearment, Advancement and Progress

In June of 1860, Norman grows anxious for GMI's decision. Whenever a family member returns from the post office, he would ask, "Any mail from GMI?"

"No news yet. Just have to wait till they make up their minds," becomes the monotonous response.

Finally, in the middle of June, Mia picks up the mail and there is a letter from the Georgia Military Institute. Although filled with excitement, Mia dares not open the letter. She runs outside and holds it up to the light, hoping to get a glimpse of the messages inside. No luck! Mia exclaims excitedly, "Look Uncle Isaac, a letter from the Georgia Military Institute for Wee-Bean! Let's get on home so Wee-Bean can open it and read what it says!"

Uncle Isaac whips the horses along at a trot, stirring up plenty of dust as they head round the mountain. Betty Gail and Sally are shelling peas on the porch as the buggy makes the turn into the yard. Mia raises her hand holding the letter high in the air. "Ma! Wee-Bean has a letter from the Institute!"

Uncle Isaac pulls the horses in to a walk and then to a halt. Mia jumps from the buggy as her mother meets her about half way. With a broad smile, Mia asks, "Where is Pa and Wee-Bean?"

"They're still in the field gathering the spring crops with a couple of Buster's darkies. Let's just wait and surprise them both at supper tonight. Now, Isaac, you and Sally keep quiet about all this. I just know his acceptance is in this letter. They know his pa and grandpa were soldiers and they know Norman will make a great soldier and military leader, too. We'll give Wee-Bean the letter from GMI with his dessert."

"Great idea, Ma!" exclaims Mia.

Betty Gail continues with the plan. "We still have some of that deer Wee-Bean shot. It's in the meat house. Your pa and Wee-Bean would rather eat good, mild and tender venison than lamb or pork. We'll have fresh corn, squash, and the butter beans Sally just got through shelling. Isaac, go and get me enough venison to make four big steaks for supper and whatever you and Sally can eat."

Full of excitement, Betty Gail, Mia, Isaac and Sally start preparing the fabulous supper in the outside kitchen. While Sally and Isaac are preparing the meal, Betty Gail and Mia set the table, complete with a fresh apple pie in the center. Still warm, the aroma of the pie fills the room. "That's a happy smell, Ma. Wee-Bean and Pa will catch that scent before they even open the door. You wait. When they come in, they'll say, 'Where's that pie?' And we'll say, there on the table. Put the letter from the Institute under the pie."

Soon, ol' Charlie starts barking, a sure sign somebody is coming. Rushing to the window, Mia and Betty Gail peer out only to see two stray cows cutting across the near pasture. Somewhat let down, they return to the dining room and decide to shell the rest of the butter beans while Sally and Isaac finish up the supper. Betty Gail is pondering her children's futures and asks casually, "How much do you like Buster Phillips, Mia?"

"I like him fine, Ma, but he is our neighbor and he is more like a big brother. Ma, I've known Legare for several years. Every time he comes by, we go riding or have a picnic by the creek or climb the mountain and talk. He's . . more like me. Not that there's anything wrong with Buster, it's just that he's not my type."

"He's going to make somebody a good husband someday and your pa and I would kinda like it be you."

"I know, Ma, he has a good farm and he's always been good to us. I just like him for a neighbor and friend. That's all.

There goes ol' Charlie again. Maybe it's them this time!" Mia runs to the window and sure enough Norman and Buck are heading toward the house from the barn. Mia confirms, " They must have come in the back way this time. I guess they got the horses put up and the darkies are taking care of the harvest. Looks like one of those afternoon showers forming up over the mountain. The sky is getting cloudy. Let's sit back down and pretend to be shelling those butter beans."

While Norman is outside, Betty Gail and Mia show Buck the letter from the Institute. "It came today?" Buck asks, surprised.

"Yes, Pa. It was at the post office this morning. Uncle Isaac and I came on home right away. Ma and I made it a surprise for you and Wee-Bean. Now, how about we put this letter under the apple pie plate? When supper is over, you ask Wee-Bean to pass the dessert and he'll find it. No telling what his reaction will be when he sees this letter!"

Buck walks closer to Mia. "Let me have the letter." Mia hands it to him. He glances at the return address and places the light brown envelope under the pie plate. A loud clap of thunder breaks the excitement. "Looks like a good shower is coming and it might stay for a bit. How long before supper is ready? I can hardly wait to have Wee-Bean open that letter."

The back door bursts open and Norman enters. Taking off his hat, he slaps it on the side of his pants in an attempt to remove some of the rain water.

Those are mighty thick clouds. Rain might stay a while. Best light those lanterns. We need to be able to see our supper," Buck tells Mia as he winks and finishes lighting the lanterns.

About the time the last lantern is glowing at its brightest, Sally and Isaac open the back door and start to bring in the special meal. "Cookin' that deer of yours, Master Norman! Gots fresh corn and squash to eats too," explains Sally happily.

Once the meal is on the table, the Jernigans take their usual seats. Everyone joins hands and Buck offers grace. Buck says, "Wee-Bean, you gets the first cut of deer, then pass it to your Ma and Mia."

"You, Ma and Mia usually go first." "You go first tonight, son."

Betty Gail interjects, "It's your night."

"Well, thank you, but I still need to hear from GMI,"

Buck redirects the conversation. "Sounds like the rain has settled down quite a bit."

Mia struggles to keep up the act and manages to ask, "Will you please pass that corn along with the butter beans and squash?"

As the last bit of gravy is soaked up, Norman grins and asks, "What about that apple pie, Ma? I'm ready for some!"

"Well, son, it's right in front of you. Have a slice and then pass the plate to your Pa!" Norman pulls the pie plate toward him but doesn't notice the envelope on the far side. He takes a slice of the pie and places it on his dish. "Sure does smell mighty good!" Norman utters as he samples the remnants on his fork. Mia, Betty Gail and Buck look at each other in amazement. How could he miss the envelope? Everyone is silent. Norman notices the awkward moment and asks, "What's the matter? Did I do something wrong?"

Buck asks instantly, "Are you going to eat all the pie yourself or are you going to pass it on to me?"

"Sorry, Pa. It's just so good and you know it's my favorite. In fact, the piece I just cut was really for the rest of you. What's left in the pie pan is mine!"

Everyone laughs. Norman picks up the pie to pass it to his father and finally notices the envelope. After handing his father the pie plate, Norman turns his head to get a good look at the address on the envelope.

Developing a serious look on his face, Norman picks up the envelope and says, "What's this? Oh gosh! It's a letter from GMI!" He leaps to his feet with excitement, his chair tumbling behind him as he grasps his table knife and breaks the seal. Everyone jumps up and surrounds him as Sally and Isaac come rushing over. Norman hurriedly takes out the letter and reads it to himself, "Yeah, yeah!"

"What does it say? Read it out loud, Wee-Bean,

read it out loud!" his father demands.

"Okay, okay! Let me get my breath." He pauses for a moment and begins, "June 12, 1860, Master Norman Jernigan Post Office, Stone Mountain, Georgia—"

"We know that part! Read the rest!" Mia urges nervously as Norman continues.

"Dear Master Jernigan, this is to inform you that your application for admissions to Georgia Military Institute has been reviewed by our Board of Governors. This review consisted of your scholastic record and the character recommendation from Congressman Joshua Hill.

"I have been directed by the Board of Governors to inform you that the Board of Governors is granting you admission to Georgia Military Institute. Congratulations! You, and you only, are to report to my office at the Institute on the second Monday in July. Follow the rules in the Institute catalogue regarding allowable personal items. Your obedient servant, Frances W. Capers, Major Superintendent."

With a big "Whoop-pee!," Norman throws his head back and tosses the letter in the air. His mother hugs him tightly. Soon, they are all holding hands and dancing around the table. After a few minutes, civility returns.

"Now, where's the apple pie?" Buck asks.

"Who put the letter under the pie plate? That was a bona fide surprise, sure enough!"

"Not knowing is part of the surprise, Wee-Bean!" responds Mia.

The rain stops. The family settles on the front porch and can see the half-moon peeking through the separating clouds. Somewhat calmer, Norman reflects, "When I went to GMI in May to take my examination, I had a good feeling that my score would be satisfactory."

"Must have been. We are all very proud of you, Norman. We know you'll make a great cadet and soldier." Buck looks at his only son, pride shinning in his eyes. "Several days ago I read where Governor Brown spoke at the

GMI Commencement. He said he is recommending an increase in the number of cadets by admitting one from each county. The governor went on to say that this would supply our people with a large number of highly trained Southern born teachers who have too often been abolition emissaries in disguise."

Full of excitement, Norman rises early, the hot July sun already making sweat beads across his brow. The aroma of his favorite breakfast is drifting under the door of his room. Betty Gail and Mia are preparing his favorite French toast and maple syrup along with hot cakes and fresh sausage. Norman is eager to head to the train station, but realizes his own personal need to hurry won't rush the train schedule.

Anxious though he is, he sighs and glances around his room. He double checks his personal items, packing only the items allowed by the Institute rules. Some belongings are in a leather trunk while the smaller items fit nicely into his soft bag. Norman closes the trunk and ties the mattress to the trunk. Last he securely ties the bedstead with twine.

Mia walks to the kitchen door and calls, "Breakfast is ready, Norman." "Coming." He opens his bedroom door and hurries into the dining room, smiling with his cache of GMI household requirements. Uncle Isaac and Aunt Sally are setting the table for breakfast. Buck looks at his children, realizing how quickly they're growing up.

"Let's all sit for breakfast. This is a great day for the Jernigan family. We are going to see a future general board the train today for GMI." Buck's broad smile expresses his pride.

Betty Gail takes the biscuits from the oven as Norman heads to the table. Mia grabs Buck by the hand as they find their familiar seats round the table. "Sally, you and Isaac come and sit with us this morning."

Sally and Isaac gladly pull up two more chairs to the large round table and sit silently.

"Let's pray. Dear Lord, today is a special day for our family. Guide Wee-Bean, I mean our young man, Norman, to follow your commandments. Guide him to become a leader among his peers. Protect him from evil and grant him good health. We ask this in God's name. Amen."

Everyone lifts their heads. "You start out passing the food, Norman," says Buck. "It's going to be four months before you get your Ma's cooking again." "Okay, Pa." The clattering of the dishes, butter and jelly on the biscuits, sweet smelling French toast and fresh maple syrup covering the hot cakes make it a breakfast feast fit for any young fellow heading off to Georgia Military Institute.

"Are you sure you want to go alone to Marietta, Norman?" whispers Betty Gail.

"Yes, ma'am. That was the rule. I need to show up by myself. I can get settled quicker this way when I get to the college."

After breakfast, Isaac goes outside and brings the carriage to the front of the house. Mia helps Norman bring out his belongings and Isaac places them on the carriage. Norman walks over toward his pet mule, grabbing an apple for him along the way. Jack meets him at the fence and takes the tasty morsel. Norman pats Jack's head and says, "See you in four months, ol' buddy!" He turns and gives Sally and Isaac a big hug. "Don't forget the rabbit box, Uncle Isaac! I'll see you around the end of November, Aunt Sally." Norman's voice has a slight quiver and he clears his throat to mask his emotion. Buck, Mia and Betty Gail are already on the carriage as Norman steps up and sits between his mother and sister.

"Gitty-up!" commands Buck and the horses pull away from the farm.

As they arrive at the station, Norman jumps off of the carriage and ties the horses to the hitching post. He gives his hand to his mother and sister as they step down while Buck eases off the other side. They all go inside.

James Goldsmith, the railroad agent, sees Norman. "Today is a big day for you, Norman. We are all proud of you. Everyone knows you'll do well at GMI."

As he hands Norman his ticket for the train ride to Marietta, Buck gives him the one dollar to cover the cost of two tickets.

"Thank you, Mr. Goldsmith. I am going to do my best," replies Norman. Soon, he hears the train whistle coming from the direction of Lithonia.

"Well, I guess it's time." Norman timidly turns to his family. Tears begin to flow from all of their eyes as they hug each other without saying a word. The scene of the pure bond of a family could never be more profound. Mr. Goldsmith watches with tears rolling down his cheeks as well.

"I love you, Wee-Bean," whispers Mia.

"I love you, son." cries Betty Gail.

Buck looks sternly at Wee-Bean. "I love you son. Take care."

"Thanks, Pa. I love you, too." Norman tries desperately to hold back tears. He releases his grasp slowly, straightens his shoulder's resolutely, turns and boards the train. He takes a seat next to an open window on the side where he can see his family. The sun glistens over the depot, reflecting in the shiny windows and polished brass hand rails. He sees his leather trunk and bedstead going to the baggage car. The porter lifts and pushes them inside. Mia and his mother clutch their handkerchiefs and his father lowers his head slightly, placing his hand in his pocket.

The train whistle blows, startling the solemn family. "Last call! All aboard!" shouts the conductor. He waits one minute, picks up the easy step, and waves to the engineer. They hear the straining of the initial start on the engine, followed by a series of short bursts of smoke and then the train jerks into motion. It pulls away slowly. Norman smiles and waves. As the train becomes more distant from Stone Mountain depot, he leans out of the window to catch one more glimpse of his family. Suddenly, the clack-k-de-clack of the rail and the surrounding wilderness are his only companions. He watches as the granite sentinel that has been a part of his life as long as he can remember slowly disappears behind a thick growth of trees.

Settling back into his seat, he holds on to his belongings as if he is holding on to his family. His mind begins to vacillate slowly between Stone Mountain and

GMI. After the train departs the Atlanta mile-post one, Norman decides to eat the lunch his ma made for him. The first item that meets his fancy is a large apple from one of their trees. Biting into the apple reminds Norman of the smell of that fresh apple pie and the placing of the acceptance letter from GMI. With each bite, he laughs as he remembers that great evening and how everybody danced around the table. After the apple, Norman eats his turkey biscuit. Finally, he indulges in the homemade cookies. Content with a final thirst-quenching drink from his canteen, he sits back and waits for the next twenty minutes or so to pass. *After these next few minutes, my life will be forever changed. I'm no longer just a kid by the name of Wee-Bean. From now on I'm Norman Jernigan.*

For the first time in his life, he is thinking of himself as a man. He considers that for a moment and smiles, visualizing himself sitting on the porch with his pa and his friends. He laughs out loud, causing a woman two seats ahead of him to turn and glare briefly. He tries to act with more decorum, as befits a young man in his position, but can't as he continues to reflect on the fun times with his family.

Shortly, the train slows, as it takes a long curve before entering the straight-of-way into the Marietta station. The whistle sounds with a loud burst of steam and the train cars bump and jerk, coming to a sudden stop on the Western and Atlantic railroad track. The front of the now familiar train depot reads "Marietta, Georgia." Several wagons and carriages are parked at the passenger platform. A sign which reads "GMI cadets report here" catches his eye. Norman takes his cache of goods and exits the train. Approaching the GMI carriage, he recognizes Charlie. "Hello, Charlie."

"Hello, Mars Norman. I think you're the last one due from the south part. Lemme fetch your trunk 'n' mattress an' take you on in."

While Charlie is locating the trunk and bedstead, Norman climbs onto the carriage, stands and stretches a bit while looking around. Charlie soon returns. After loading

Norman's required household items, Charlie unties the reins from the hitching post. He climbs aboard and orders the horses on toward Capitol Hill, just on the outskirts of town. "Yo books is already in yo room. Once ya register at Major Caper's office, de board of inspectors will guide you through da rest."

"Thanks, Charlie. I'm ready to start." Pulling up to Major Capers office, Norman sees several other cadets are departing to the barracks. Norman is greeted as soon as he jumps from the carriage.

"I'm Major Black and you are?" "My name is Norman Jernigan, Sir."

"Charlie, take his trunk to Company B. His roommate is going to be Cadet Paul T. Goldsmith. I'll have him sign in."

"Goldsmith? I wonder if he is any kin to J. W. in Stone Mountain." Norman wonders aloud.

"Follow me, Cadet Jernigan," orders Major Black. Upon completing Norman's registration, Major Black and the new Cadet Norman Jernigan proceed to the barracks.

Once there, Norman meets his roommate. His items are being checked by another inspector. "Hello, my name is Norman Jernigan."

"Nice meeting you. My name is Paul Goldsmith. I hear we are going to be roommates."

"Looks that way. It's going to be a real adventure."

Norman and Paul head to the commissary, continuing to get to know each other. "I'm from Stone Mountain, Paul. Where are you from?"

"Just north of here in Cass County, but I was born in South Carolina."

"In Stone Mountain, our railroad agent's name is James W. Goldsmith.

He runs the depot. Any kin to you?"

"I hear we have some distant relatives down your way, but I'm not sure if he is or not. Most likely is, since there are not too many Goldsmiths around. I'll check with my ma and pa and let you know."

Peering down the hall toward the day room, Norman

sees some of the cadets beginning to assemble. He and Paul head down the hall to meet some of them. Sam Goode, Edward Jordan, T. J. Hunt, G. A. and W. F. Patillo are a few. A general discussion begins. *Where you from? Do you know ..? No messing around here. Food sure is good. Rooms are a little small, makes it easier to keep orderly. Know any good jokes? Gonna really get busy tomorrow. I have a cousin living there. How big is your family farm? How many slaves? Gotta girlfriend? Like hunting and fishing? Ever been to ..* Bonding was superb among the cadets as the first day comes to a close. The bugler sounds Tattoo and fifteen minutes later signals lights out, then candles out.

"All present and accounted for," the sentry on duty shouts.

Chapter Five

Honor and Trust

The first Saturday in October, Congressman Hill invites Buck to the hotel for a political discussion on secession. On the way to the meeting they pass the burned down Stone Mountain House.

Buck says, "Not much left of the place. Even the brick walls are ready to fall down. Mr. Alexander was in partnership with Josiah Clark from Social Circle. Lost it all."

"I'm afraid we all stand to lose a lot more, Buck, if we secede," replies Congressman Hill.

Politics is the all-absorbing topic of the day. Fierce discussions have, at times, ended in deadly duels fought in some secluded spot. Usually one of the hotheaded disputants stains the ground with his heart's blood, and forfeits a life of which his country might prove to have sore need. Some such discussion is in progress as Buck and Congressman Hill dismount their horses and fling the reins to a waiting stableman. Buck looks at the new hotel, then climbs the steps to the porch. To his neighbors' surprise, Buck joins the audience. He disapproves of the newcomers and is deeply hostile to their invasion into the simple life of his community. He generally shuns all relationships with them.

The principal speaker, Congressman Lucius J. Gartrell, is a stately man of the planter class, a lawyer by profession and well known throughout the state. He rises to address the attentive listeners, and seems, indeed, to be carried forward rather by the impetuous current of his own thoughts than consciously addressing his remarks to any audience. Congressman Hill seats himself beside

Buck, whose keen eyes become riveted upon the speaker.

"It is not of one aggression, or of many aggressions, that we complain," begins Congressman Gartrell, "but of a long series of aggressions, extending from the very founding of this government. We entered this Union with a full understanding that all our rights, including the right to hold slaves, would be respected. Who has profited more by the institution of slavery than the people of the New England States?"

"Nobody but the Yanks," shouts a man Buck doesn't know.

"Who is more largely responsible for it? Did they not have for many years a monopoly of the slave trade?"

"Absolutely," yell several others. Buck turns to see who was yelling, but fails to discover who they were.

"Did they not sell their slaves to Southern planters when they ceased to be profitable for themselves?"

"Yeah, we got cotton ground and they ain't."

"In spite of constitutional guaranties, compacts and those so-called compromises, by excluding slavery from the territories, the North seeks to deprive us of the fruits of Southern statesmanship and valor. The vast territory of this country comes from the political wisdom of Jefferson and to the favorable issue of the Mexican War. That war was fought mainly by Southern soldiers under Southern leaders."

"That's true, Congressman Gartrell." Red-faced James Gozz stands with his fist in the air. Tis to the South that the country is beholden for them territories. But what about that John Brown fellow?"

"The North dignifies John Brown by the name of martyr," answers Congressman Gartrell. "Yet his hands are red with the blood of his fellow-citizens in Kansas."

"Good thing he done dead," shouts James Elliott, another angry spectator. "Also, in the name of humanity, John Brown has sought to deliver ourselves and daughters to the brutal fury of a Negro insurrection."

"Only if they want to die," can be heard among the louder shouts.

"When heavily burdened with a protective tariff

imposed just for the benefit of Northern factories, South Carolina declared nullification. Then, the North re-echoes with the cry of treason! Now the followers of this red-handed fanatic are protected by Northern governors who disregard the laws of the general government. When these fanatics proclaim that they live under a higher law than the constitution, does the North cry treason? Nary time!" shouts the Colonel with his fist high in the air. "All the traitors the North knows are south of Mason and Dixon's line."

"They best stay north of that line and live than come south and die," yells John Holmes.

"We, of the South," the Gartrell goes on, "are by force of circumstances an agricultural people, and agricultural we must, for the most part, remain. Ever since I could remember I have heard the institution of slavery referred to in the pulpit and in religious conversations. Although not so much as a fact that might be proved to be holy, but which was incontestably divine in its origin and character. Just as much as marriage or any other Christian institution. As sovereign states, we entered the Union. As sovereign states let us depart, peaceably if we may, forcibly if we must."

Buck angrily jumps to his feet. "Secession's a mighty bad remedy, Congressman," he shouts while giving his quid a turn in his capacious jaw and sending a stream of amber over the railing. "A mighty bad remedy. I'd think a powerful long time before I'd say secede. I'm not a denyin' as how the facts are like you say, matter-of-fact they never make a right but two wrongs don't make a right. I'm clean against secession. If we can't get our rights in the Union in respect to those territories you're talking about, then we can't get them out of the Union except by fighting for them. As to the blackies, we hang the abolitionist fools now what circulates that poison among them and we can't ever do any more. Suppose we secede and have a Northern and a Southern Union. Then there might be another split and we'll have an Eastern and a Western Union. Where does it stop?"

There's mumbling among the crowd, some booing and some agreeing. Buck listens and decides the crowd is about evenly divided. "Then you propose to vote for Bell and

Everett?" asks Congressman Gartrell. "That's what I plan to do. The constitution of the country, the union of the States and the enforcement of the laws is a good enough platform for any man to stand on. Human nature is a sullen, obstinate, unreasonable brute. But it always has its own way with all of us and the results most always are disappointing."

"Mr. Jernigan is right." Judge George K. Smith rises and nods to Buck. "It is the fatal split in the Democratic Party that is about to ruin us. Oh, for a leader with the broad statesmanship and true patriotism of Washington, and the eloquence of Patrick Henry! You are hotheaded people, making the mistake of considering a fanatical minority to be the Northern people. The great majority of the thinking people of the North and South are opposed to extreme measures."

Congressman Hill stands and the crowd gradually gets quiet. "Allow me to explain how the Northerner and Southerner view one-another." He walks sedately to the podium. Most of the crowd sits back down. "The North and the South are two households living under one roof. Two nations under one name. The intellectual, moral, and social life of each has been utterly distinct and separate from that of the other. We do not understand or appreciate each other's feelings or development. It is true we speak the same language, use the same governmental forms, and most unfortunately, think we comprehend each other's ideas."

The spectators become quieter still listening for a key point. Buck leans back against his chair, glad for so gifted a speaker to have the floor.

"Each of us thinks we know the thoughts and purposes of the other better than the thinker knows his own. The Northern man despises his Southern fellow-citizen in bulk. The Northern man views the Southern fellow as a good-natured bragger, mindful of his own ease, fond of power and display, and with no animating principle which can in any manner interfere with his interest. Now most of the Southern men simply despise their Northerner as cold-blooded, selfish, hypocritical, cowardly and envious."

"That there's a real definition for a Yankee," spouts John Holmes with several others in agreement. A few men chuckle at his assessment.

"This is how the North and the South play at cross-purposes, each thinking that he knows the other's heart far better than he seeks to know his own. That's all I have to say. Thank you, Judge Smith, for allowing me to speak."

There's a little mumbling and Congressman Hill takes his seat.

Judge Smith hesitates briefly. "You are most welcome, Congressman Hill. All the political conditions of today point to a like result. Let but this new party find its Cromwell, who under the pretext of war will set aside the Constitution to advance party interests. Then the parallel will be complete. The cry of a violated Constitution will unite the South; the cry of a broken Union will unite the North. When I contemplate our situation," continues Judge Smith in a more somber voice, "I think I see the green fields of our land stained red with blood, and the very flower of our young Southern manhood festering upon the hillside where the flowers of spring are happy today." The crowd becomes somewhat quieter. "Yes, the blood of our best and dearest, and what reparation could ever wash that stain away?" Judge Smith trembles with emotion, and puts his hands over his eyes, as if to shut out the crimson vision. His audience is visibly impressed.

Then the hot-headed unknown spectator who, through it all is chewing vigorously and expectorating on the floor, missing the spittoon until a filthy puddle forms a malodorous puddle at his feet, leaps to his feet and exclaims, "Blood, did you say, Jedge? I'll drink all the blood that's spilt. Them fellers haven't got no fight in 'em. They're jest a blusterin' a little to let themselves down easy."

Judge Smith sternly replies, "Such unthinking men as you, sir, are the cause of these sad conditions. I heard you say you would drink all the blood that is spilled, but you're not willing to give of your own blood. However, sir, you're not willing to shed your own blood to save your slaves. You treat your livestock better than your Negroes. You are more than willing to beat the blood from the bodies of your slaves to save your property or to tame the Negroes. When the armies of the North and South stand face to face, you and those like you will not be found upon the battlefield."

"That's an insult I'd not take from a younger man." Red-faced the unknown spectator raises his fist as he walks toward Judge Smith.

"I am always responsible for my words," replies Judge Smith evenly, "and at your service any time." Judge Smith bids the stranger and the gathering a courteous good-bye, exits the building, mounts his already saddled horse, and canters away. The angry John spits out more of his tobacco, eyeing the Judge until he is some distance away.

That night, Congressman Hill and Buck sit together on the veranda, chairs tilted back to a comfortable angle, their feet upon the gallery railing. Congressman Hill takes up the thread of the morning's conversation. "I have just come from Washington. If the South secedes, there will be war. Apart from mere sentiment about the breaking of the Union, of which there's no lack, the South has too much to lose in a business way. The South is a great and wealthy portion of the Union, and the North is dependent upon us for products. The North must have our cotton for their factories. With secession, all the present business conditions will be changed."

Buck responds, "Business reasons lie at the bottom of most wars."

"It's true. That topic does not find its way into spread-eagle speeches, but down deep in the hearts of nations, the thought is there."

"In reality there is one of four modes by which the issue of slavery can be solved. The first and safest mode is the voluntary emancipation on the part of the slave owner and that is not about to take place."

"You're right, Buck. What do you feel would be the second choice?"

"Political action in the exercise of assumed, not to say, usurped, legislative authority."

Joshua is quiet for a moment while he ponders that

point. Then he leans forward in his chair, looks directly into Buck's eyes and tells him, "Jefferson and Madison were against slavery, but in order to form our Union, Jefferson and Madison presented as part of the Federal Constitution the Fugitive Slave law. Along with this came the right to exclude slavery in any of the territories or future states. These provisions were universally accepted by all of the signers of the Federal Constitution."

Buck listens intently as Congressman Hill leans back in his chair and continues, "The Fugitive Slave Law became nullified with the acquisition of the territories of Louisiana, Florida and Texas because this gave the Union nine more slave-holding states. This left the Free States without the shadow of a political obligation to deliver up fugitive slaves. This is what has strengthened the abolitionist because the pact formed by the founding fathers has been abandoned."

Buck leans over and spits his tobacco over the porch rail and onto the pine needles on the ground. "What you are saying is true and leaves only two other options."

"What might they be, Buck?"

"The third mode is servile insurrection and war or the fourth, which appears to be where our country is heading, political disunion and civil war."

Buck looks sternly at Joshua and asks, "And what chance has the South to win?"

"My own conclusion is against a population of twenty million in the North and set against nine million in the South with four million of our population slaves, and therefore noncombatants, we don't stand a chance of winning a war. The North has nine billion dollars of estimated wealth. We in the South have less than three billion dollars in total wealth, of which two billion dollars of our wealth is in slaves. Give the North the world for a recruiting office, the navy to blockade all Southern ports and the better part of our military stores. I want to know what heroism could win against such odds."

Buck breaks the long silence on a somber note, saying, "No heroism, just big egos. The true winners will be the freed slaves by way of abolitionists or otherwise."

The day after Election Day November 6, 1860, Buck is among a large crowd gathering at the depot to get the latest news. Late in the afternoon a telegram comes through. "LINCOLN WINS! Lincoln,180 electoral votes: California, Connecticut, Illinois, Indiana, Iowa, Maine, Massachusetts, Michigan, Minnesota, New Hampshire, New York, Ohio, Oregon, Pennsylvania, Rhode Island, Vermont, and Wisconsin. Stephen Douglas (Northern Democratic), 12 Electoral Votes: Missouri, and New Jersey. John Breckinridge (Southern Democratic), 72 Electoral Votes: Maryland, Delaware, North and South Carolina, Georgia, Florida, Alabama, Mississippi, Arkansas, Louisiana, and Texas. John Bell (Constitutional Union), 39 Electoral Votes: Tennessee, Kentucky and Virginia."

"We're in trouble now! Governor Brown is going to take us out of the Union!" says Buck. Most of the citizens agree and the look of worry and concern is evident on the faces of most of the crowd.

Buck shakes his head wearily. "This is a sad day in America. We are in for hard times and a long and bloody civil war."

On Thursday November 8th Governor Brown in his annual message to the legislature states, "The organization of several volunteer corps is now complete. These volunteer corps is now commanded by young gentlemen educated at the Military Institute in Marietta. These young commanders reflect great credit upon the Institute. The ranks of the Marietta Rifles, the Kennesaw Dragoons with the appointment of Captain Capers, and the McDonald Guards are filling up with volunteers from area alumni, current and former GMI faculty."

The following Tuesday November 13th Robert Toombs and Alexander Stephens have been invited to address the Georgia General Assembly. Toombs for secession and Stephens against.

"Honorable Robert Toombs rises to the podium. "GENTLEMEN OF THE GENERAL ASSEMBLY:

"I very much regret, in appearing before you at your request, to address you on the present state of the country, and the prospect before us, that I can bring you no good tidings. . ."

In closing, he says, "My countrymen, if you have nature in you, bear it not. Withdraw your- selves from such a confederacy of the Union; it is your right to do so—your duty to do so. I know not why the abolitionists should object to it, unless they want to torture and plunder you. If they resist this great sovereign right, make another war of independence, for that then will be the question; fight its battles over again—reconquer liberty and independence. As for me, I'll take any place in the great conflict for rights which you may assign. I will take none in the Federal Government during Mr. Lincoln's administration." Robert Toombs takes his seat.

Upon arriving at the depot in Milledgeville, Buck, William Sheppard and Jesse Lanford take a carriage to the Capitol building. "Look, there's James Simmons from Gwinnett County."

The three men walk over to talk with James, who is in a discussion with some of the legislature. He sees Buck approaching and acknowledges him with a nod and raising his hand indicating he will be with them in a minute. Buck, Jesse and William continue to talk while James finishes his conversation.

"Hello, gentlemen, I'm glad you are able to come to the Session Convention. It's been interesting so far."

Jesse gazes at James. "What did Senator Toombs have to offer?"

"Well, he's one hundred percent for secession. He's always been hot-headed. Said he would not serve under Lincoln and for us to appoint someone else in his place."

Buck responds, "Sounds unreasonable to me. As smart as he is, he should know the South will be destroyed if we secede. There will be war. He has everything to lose . . all his wealth, land, and fame. The Union should stand."

Interjecting into the conversation, William states, "He

always acts like a spoiled child when he can't have his way. Mule-headed fits his temperament. Georgia will be better off without him in the Senate."

James Simmons smiles to his friends, "I feel like Congressman Stephens will counter Senator Toombs' arguments tomorrow night. Right now I'm hungry. Let's go get something to eat."

The next day Buck, William and Jesse take a chilly November evening walk to the capitol building. A number of spectators are in the balcony to observe the speeches and debate, but they are able to find three seats together.

Congressman Stephens walks to the podium to address the State legislature at the Capitol in Milledgeville. The Chamber of the State House becomes quiet as Congressman Stephens stands before the podium.

Congressman Stephens begins, "Fellow citizens: I appear before you tonight at the request of Members of the legislature and others, to speak of matters of the deepest interest that can possibly concern us all, of an earthly character. . .

"My object is not to stir up strife, but to allay it; not to appeal to your passions, but to your reason. Let us, therefore, reason together . . There is with me no intention to irritate or offend.

"I say to you, you have no power so to act. You must refer this question to the people. We, the people, are sovereign. I am one of them and have a right to be heard; and so has every other citizen of the State. You legislators—I speak it respectfully—are but our servants. You are the servants of the people and not their masters. Power resides with the people in this country . . Our Constitutions, State and Federal, came from the people. They made both and they alone can rightfully unmake either.

"I am for exhausting all that patriotism demands, before taking the last step of secession. I would invite, therefore, South Carolina to a conference. I would ask the same of all the other Southern States, so that if the evil has got beyond our control . . which God in his mercy grant may not be the case, we may not be divided among ourselves."

This time there are cheers of approval along with applause.

Congressman Stephens returns to his seat as the legislature stands, giving him a loud and long applause of appreciation.

Buck slaps his knee wearily. "These two speeches are only the beginning. I guarantee you Congressman Stephens's views have the support of Joshua Hill, former Governor Herschel Johnson and Benjamin Hill and you know Thomas Cobb and Governor Brown support the views of Robert Toombs."

Chapter Six
A Secret Passage

Upon returning to Stone Mountain, Buck receives a letter from his cousin Henry in Philadelphia. He tells Buck that good mules are used like horses and corn seed is hard to come by. Henry asks Buck to purchase three mules along with two bushels of corn seed and bring them to Philadelphia. He would gladly pay the expenses. Buck responds that he and Isaac could deliver the mules and seed.

Buck and Isaac talk in the garden and make plans to "Shepherd" three slaves from the Honey Creek Plantation. The three Negroes are Thom, Wayne and Warren. The trio has asked relatives to help them escape to the Promise Land. Thom, Wayne and Warren regularly come to town early on Wednesdays to get supplies for the plantation.

Buck arranges for a livestock boxcar to be on the side track in Stone Mountain. He requests a separate boxcar for the mules to avoid other livestock in order to prevent shipping fever. He also makes his contacts for the date of the escape and their drop-off point.

Thom has already received a message from a Negro named Willie from another farm and that Willie would be their Shepherd. Buck and Isaac are aware of Willie, but Willie is not aware of them.

Buck notifies Willie through his contacts, and Willie notifies Thom, Wayne and Warren of the plan. The Trio is to depart as usual before daylight for their weekly trip to

Stone Mountain. However, they are to leave the wagon and horses in the woods and hightail it to the depot while it is still dark. There should only be one boxcar with a manifest attached stating that three mules, four sacks of corn seed and twenty bales. Get inside and box yourself in with the bales of hay and wait. Food and water will be there for all of you.

It is Wednesday and most people will be in church that evening so the missing Trio (Thom, Wayne and Warren) will not be noticed until late that night.

Just as the sun breaks the darkness, Buck and Isaac arrive with the three mules and sacks of corn seed. The doors to the livestock boxcar are opened. Buck and Isaac lead the mules into the boxcar, place each one in a stall, load the corn seed and await the northbound train. Levi at the livery stable knows to pick up their mule and wagon later that morning.

At seven o'clock the train arrives. With a few simple maneuvers the boxcar is hooked to the rear. Buck enters the passenger car and Isaac will ride in the boxcar as usual. The train heads north with short stops in Decatur and Atlanta. When the train departs Marietta, darkness has set in and Isaac calls to Thom, Wayne and Warren that it is safe to come out from hiding. They answer and cautiously make themselves known. "I hope we had enough food for you."

They look around and see Isaac's outline in the dark. "What is your name?" Thom asks.

Isaac replies, "Just call me your Shepherd. Here is what you will do. As the train slows down outside of Cassville, I will crack the door and you jump out when I say. You will head toward the only nearby spot lantern. There will be a conductor waiting for you there and he will transfer you on North."

"What if he is not there?" asks Wayne.

Isaac replies, "No worry. A conductor never misses his appointment.

Soon the train begins to slow down. Isaac cracks the door and peers for the spot lantern. He points it out to the trio and they thank him for his aid. Swiftly, they all jump and are swallowed up in the darkness.

The rest of the trip is pleasantly non-eventful. When they reach Philadelphia, Henry greets them at the depot. He and Buck meet Isaac at the stock car. The train yardmen have placed the ramps to unload the mules.

The next morning, Buck and Isaac are dropped off at the depot. Buck tells Henry that he is going to do a little shopping for Betty Gail before the train arrives and not to wait around for him and Isaac. Henry bids them farewell and heads back to his farm West of Philadelphia.

Buck and Isaac stop at a dry goods store and purchase a few gifts of fabric and notions for their wives. They then head for an appointment with Mr. Still at his residence. The pair announces their presence with a simple door knock. In a matter of a few seconds the door opens and Mr. Still smiles, extends his hand. "Good morning, Buck. Good morning, Isaac. Please come in."

While escorting Buck and Isaac to the parlor, he asks, "How was your trip to Philadelphia?"

"Close call at one point. A posse was checking train cars at the depot just after the Negroes jumped. Otherwise, it was smooth.

"That was a close call." Mr. Still has fresh coffee and breakfast confectionaries for his two guests. Mr. Still, Isaac and Buck begin discussing the details of their latest foray on the train ride.

As the three partake of their confections, Isaac says, "We didn't know the three Negroes were in the boxcar until I summoned them just before they leaped out at Cassville."

Mr. Still greets Isaac's answer with a broad smile. "There are only a few basic escape methods. First is on horseback or on foot—which is the worst method."

Buck nods and sips his coffee. "But that's the one they most often try."

Mr. Still agrees. "You're right. The second way is hiding in a wagon and it is the next worse, third, is by train with a conductor is a better way. But, the best way is by boat since the boat can take a runaway North to Free States and Canada, or South to Mexico, Cuba, or some other country."

Buck finishes his pastry. "No matter what way you choose to travel, to go under the cover of night is a wise move."

The hinges on the parlor door give a muffled squeak as it opens and a petite, Negro woman appears. Mr. Still stands followed by Buck and Isaac. Mr. Still then begins his introduction. The three men stand. "Gentlemen, it is my pleasure to introduce the 'Moses' of the abolitionists, Mrs. Harriet Tubman.

Isaac and Buck look at each other, then at Harriet and back to one another. They are awe-struck by her strong, peaceful presence. Finally they walk over to Harriet. Embracing her together, they both had "sweat" in their eyes. Buck's raw emotions settle down, and everyone returns to normal. They focus their attention on the problems at hand as they sit around the table and the conversation erupts.

Harriet reaches across the small round table and places her hands on Buck's. "Thank you, gentlemen, for your acute, secretive and dedicated efforts to assist in freeing those held in bondage either by Negro or white masters. This dangerous work required tremendous ingenuity. I admired your courage for being a part of this movement."

Mr. Still injects, "Harriet figures that the slave owners stay indoors more often during the winter months, when the nights are long, cold and dark. This presents the slaves with a slight, but greater advantage to complete their escape. Once she makes contact with escaping slaves, they leave town on Saturday evenings, since newspapers won't print runaway notices until Monday morning. You two keep these tips in mind."

Buck smiles appreciatively, "Isaac and I really are eager to help in any way we can."

Mr. Still relates, "Harriet's journeys into the land of

slavery put her at tremendous risk, and she used a variety of subterfuges to avoid detection."

Buck and Isaac lean back and listen to every word Harriett speaks. "I once disguised myself with a bonnet and carried two live chickens to give the appearance of running errands."

Isaac smiles as the image of this prim woman carrying chickens comes clearly into his mind. She has a very likeable way about her.

"I suddenly found myself walking toward a former owner in Dorchester County. Acting on impulse, she yanked the strings holding the birds' legs, and their agitation allowed her to avoid eye contact."

"Good move," replies Buck.

Harriett takes a sip of coffee. "At another time I recognized a fellow train passenger as yet another former master. To avoid his glare, I snatched a nearby newspaper and pretended to read. Fortunately it was not upside down since I am known to be illiterate. Luckily, the man passed me by not taking any notice of me at all."

"You have a quick mind, Miss Tubman. That is why you've been so successful in the abolitionist movement and the Underground." Buck nods with respect. He looks at the mantel clock and stands. "Unfortunately, the time has come for us to depart. Our train leaves shortly. Thank you, Mr. Still, for giving me and Isaac this great opportunity to meet Mrs. Tubman."

Isaac walks over to Harriett. "Mind if I give you a big hug?"

Harriett smiles and with her arms open, invites Isaac and Buck into her loving embrace.

Mr. Still escorts Buck and Isaac to an awaiting carriage. He tips his hat. "Farewell and God speed to both of you."

Isaac says, "Buck, I didn't think I could be more energized than I was until I met Moses . . Mrs. Tubman."

"Yep. She's an exceptional person . . . a real heroine."

Chapter Seven
Joe Brown Draws the Sword

Buck keeps close eyes and ears to the regular 1860-1861 Georgia legislative session in Milledgeville, anxious to find out what the state government's reaction is going to be to Mr. Lincoln's election to the presidency. Picking up the *Decatur Watchman* at the depot, Buck reads the headlines and rushes over to Liberty Hall for coffee with Sheriff Perkerson and some other friends. Most of the men are sitting around the pot-belly stove talking about the same subject.

Buck and Sheriff Perkerson rush inside. Buck shouts out, "Hey, guys, the legislature is having a special session January 16. And listen to this! Joe Brown has issued a proclamation. Everybody turns their head toward Buck. Some of the men take their pipes out of their mouths, while others spit tobacco into the bucket next to the stove.

"Read it, Buck!" anxiously responds Jesse Lanford.

"Executive Department Milledgeville, Georgia
November 21st 1860
A PROCLAMATION
By Joseph E. Brown, Governor of Georgia

The General Assembly of the State of Georgia, now in session, has passed unanimously an Act in the following words:
"Whereas, The present crisis in our national affairs, in the judgment of this General Assembly, demands resistance; and

"Whereas, It is the privilege and right of the sovereign people to determine upon the mode, measure and time of such resistance.

"Section 1. Therefore, the General Assembly do enact, That upon the passage of this Act, his Excellency, the Governor, be, and he is hereby required to issue his proclamation, ordering an election to be held in each and every county in this State, on the first Wednesday in January, eighteen hundred and sixty-one, for Delegates to a Convention of the People of this State, to convene at the seat of government, on the sixteenth day of January, eighteen hundred and sixty-one.

"Section 2. That said election for delegates shall be held and conducted in the same manner and at the same places as elections for members of the General Assembly are held in this State; and all returns of such elections shall be in the same manner forwarded to the Governor of this State, who shall furnish each delegate chosen with a certificate of his election.

"Section 3. That the counties entitled under the Last Act of Apportionment to two members in the House of Representatives, shall be entitled each to three delegates to said Convention; and the counties entitled under said apportionment to one Representative, shall elect each two delegates to said Convention.

"Section 4. That said Convention when assembled, may consider all grievances impairing or affecting the equality and rights of the State of Georgia as a member of the United States, and determine the mode, measure and time of redress.

"Section 5. That the members of said Convention of the people of Georgia shall be entitled to the same mileage and per diem pay received by the members of the present General

Assembly, and said Convention shall, by vote, fix the pay of all their officers, and of any delegate or delegates they may appoint to any other Convention, Congress or Embassy; and shall provide for all other expenses incurred by said Convention.

"Section 6. That said Convention shall have the power to elect all officers necessary to the organization, and to do all things needful to carry out the true intent and meaning of this Act, and the Acts and purposes of said Convention.

"Therefore, I, Joseph E. Brown, Governor of Georgia, in obedience to the requirements of said Act, do issue this my Proclamation, ordering said election for delegates to said Convention, to be held in conformity to said Act; and requiring the managers of elections for delegates in the several counties of this State to certify and send up to this Department all returns of said elections, as in case of elections for members of the General Assembly.

"And I do further require all delegates elected to said Convention to meet at the Capitol, in Milledgeville, on the sixteenth day of January, 1861, to consider of the mode, measure and time of resistance.

"Given under my hand and the Seal of the Executive Department, at the Capitol, in Milledgeville, this 21st day of November, in the year of our Lord eighteen hundred and sixty.

"Joseph E. Brown By the Governor:
H. I. G. Williams, Sec'y. Ex. Dept."

"Let me see that thar newspaper, Buck," insists Malcom Hamby.

Buck hands the newspaper to him. "Read it for yourself. We've got to elect delegates on January 1. I guess

Judge Smith and Charles Murphy will be on the ballot." Raising his fist in the air, Buck emphasizes his words, "That's who I'm gonna vote for! We know them both and they are against secession. Judge Smith once served as our seventh Postmaster. Charles Murphy had been our state representative. He is currently our state senator as well as the Judge of our Inferior Court. They both are pro-union. I'll bet James Simmons is going to be a representative for Gwinnett County."

Upon returning home, Buck hurries into the house, removing his hat as he goes through the door. "Betty Gail, all of the people I have talked to are going to vote for Smith and Murphy."

"I hope they win," she says and sighs. "All this talk of secession scares me, Buck."

He slides his arm around her waist and hugs her close. "Let's don't borrow trouble, Betty Gail."

On Monday January 7, 1861 a snowy, winter day, Buck and Betty Gail take Mia to the Stone Mountain Seminary to begin her second Class. Mia sits between her mother and father on the journey. "We are very proud of the grades you received on the First Class examination," Buck says. "You and your brother are very bright, and we're very excited that you're entering the Second Class."

"The First Class was not bad except for the mental arithmetic problems. Once I caught on, they became simple for me. Some of my First Class instruction is going to continue with the Second Class. I'll pick up my books when you drop me off at the seminary."

Betty Gail and Buck hug their daughter tightly. "Do you have the twenty-dollar gold piece we gave you to pay the tuition and supply fees?"

"Yes, Mama, I do. Right here in my pocket."

When the Jernigans reach the seminary, Mia gives her mother and father a hug and leaps from the wagon. Buck tells Mia, "We'll pick you up after school. I hope the snow will end before the day is out."

Inside the warm seminary building, Mia reports to

Mrs. Smith to get her books and schedule.

"We're so glad to have you back, Mia. You are a wonderful student and set a good example for study habits for your classmates."

"Thank you, Mrs. Smith. I am anxious to get back to the studies. I really enjoyed my First Class."

"How did your brother do at GMI?"

"Very well, thank you, and he loves it. Mr. Goldsmith's cousin is his roommate. They have become close friends."

"I'm glad to hear that news."

Later on in January, as the secession Convention draws near, Buck sits by the fireplace, tastes his hot coffee and begins to read. "Dang-it-again! Betty Gail, listen to this." Betty Gail comes to his side as Buck reads, "Senator Murphy died on us just when the state special session is about to begin. Paper says he died of pneumonia shortly after his election this month. He had said many times during the campaign that he prayed he never would live to see Georgia leave the Union. I reckon his prayer has been answered," Buck mutters to himself with disgust.

Betty Gail picks up the paper and reads a few lines. She sighs and shakes her head sadly. "Another strike against Georgia for staying in the Union."

The day the convention begins arrives. The delegates are divided sharply over the issue of secession. United States Senator Robert Toombs and former United States Secretary of the Treasury Howell Cobb and his brother, Thomas R. R. Cobb, along with Governor Brown, favor immediate secession from the Union. Congressman Stephens, a close friend of President Lincoln, argues that his election should not by itself harm Georgia.

Alexander Stephens stares at the men gathered around. "Lincoln's election could not harm Georgia and as Georgians, we should be patient and observe what Lincoln will do as president before pursuing any dangerous course."

Buck heads back to Milledgeville again to sit in on the Secession Convention of the legislature. He, William

Sheppard, Marvin Minor, and Mark Beauchamp, having arrived on the Central of Georgia train, are anxious to hear Congressman Stephens' speech, speculating openly about what may happen.

William Sheppard says, "It is a singular fact, however, and as true as it is singular, the Northern conscience never became quickened to a realization of the enormity of slavery until after the Northern slaveholders had converted their own slaves into gold. Then the gold found a lodgment deep down in their pockets and the abolitionists changed the name of the Jefferson Party to the Republican Party."

"I agree," replies Marvin. "The Republican Party has declared 'a higher law' than the Constitution and denounces the Union as 'a covenant with hell' and the Constitution as 'a league with death' and who derisively points to the flag of the Union as 'a flaunting lie.'"

Mark Beauchamp jumps into the conversation. "Yeah, you're right. It's the triumph of this coalition which is denying the Southern people equal rights in the Union and heaping upon us insult after insult with the objective to humiliate and destroy three thousand million dollars, worth of our accumulated wealth which is invested in slaves."

Buck has listened quietly until now. "Yep, and many of the slaves were bought from the people of the States now waging this political war against us."

In their seats in the balcony of the State Capitol, Buck, Marvin and Mark listen to the last plea from Congressman Stephens. He concludes, "We should wait and see what Lincoln does as president before we take any drastic action such as secession."

Buck leans over and whispers to Marvin, "Mr. Stephens' views do not have the support of former Governor Herschel Johnson or Benjamin Hill. Remember former Governor Johnson and Benjamin Hill ran against Joseph Brown for Governor."

On Saturday the 19th of January, the vote for secession is taken at the Capitol in Milledgeville. By a vote of the delegates, a resolution at the convention appoints Peter Fite Hoyle, a physician from Decatur, to fill the vacancy of the late Senator Murphy. Dr. Hoyle arrives several days after the Ordinance for Secession is adopted, but is given permission after he arrives to sign the document. Dr. Hoyle officially registers his nay vote. George Smith also votes against the Ordinance for Secession. The vote is 208 to 89 in favor of secession.

Outraged, Buck exclaims, "I can't believe we have 208 idiots in the Georgia Legislature! This is the end for Georgia. The South will never survive a war. We will be demolished by the demons of war. The three disgusted men head back to Stone Mountain.

The next day the headlines read:

"AN ORDINANCE
TO DISSOLVE THE UNION BETWEEN THE STATE OF GEORGIA AND OTHER STATES UNITED WITH HER UNDER A COMPACT OF GOVERNMENT ENTITLED, "THE CONSTITUTION OF THE UNITED STATES OF AMERICA,

"WE, THE PEOPLE OF THE State of Georgia in Convention assembled do declare and ordain, and it is hereby declared and ordained,

"That the ordinance adopted by the people of the State of Georgia in Convention on the second day of January, in the year of our Lord seventeen hundred and eighty-eight, whereby the Constitution of the United States of America was assented to, ratified and adopted; and also all Acts and parts of Acts of the General Assembly of this State ratifying and adopting amendments of the said Constitution, are hereby repealed, rescinded and abrogated.

"We do further declare and ordain, That the Union now subsisting between the State of Georgia and other States, under the name of the "United States of America," is hereby dissolved, and that the State of Georgia is in the full possession and exercise of all those rights of

sovereignty which belong and appertain to a free and independent State.

"GEORGE W. CRAWFORD, PRESIDENT
Attest: A. R. Lamar, Secretary Passed January 19, 1861"

Mid-March, Norman writes home.
"Dear Ma and Pa,

"There is great anticipation on campus about war with the North. We read about the secession vote. Although a lot of the cadets may be leaving to join the service or to become drillmasters, the faculty is advising us to stay and train the different units as they organize. Until then, our studies and drills go on."

During assembly on March 23, Captain McGill stands before the Corps. With his waiter, Jake, by his side with a wheel-barrow full of newspapers. Captain McGill orders each Company Commander forward and instructs them to ensure each cadet receives a copy. "This is a historical speech by Confederate Vice President Alexander Stephens, and each of you must read and understand the concepts set forth."

Upon dismissal, each Company Commander has each squad leader secure enough copies for distribution. Norman and Paul take their copies and read the headlines before class begins:

"On March 21, 1861, Confederate Vice-President Alexander Stephens, of Georgia, gives an extemporaneous speech at the Athenaeum in Savannah."

Sitting in front of the fireplace, Buck reads the newspaper to Betty Gail. "Let's read what our Vice-President has to say."

Buck suddenly realizes that there are really two separate nations in America: The United States of America and the Confederate States of America. He looks over the top of his newspaper at Betty Gail and shakes his head. He sighs and continues to read.

"At half past seven o'clock on Thursday evening, March 21, 1861, The Honorable Alexander Stephens addresses the largest audience ever assembled at the Savannah Athenaeum. They were waiting in the house, waiting most impatiently for the appearance of the orator of the evening, Hon. A. H. Stephens, Vice President of the Confederate States of America. The committee, with invited guests, was seated on the stage, when, at the appointed hour, the Hon. Charles C. Jones, Mayor, and the speaker, entered and were greeted by the immense assemblage with deafening rounds of applause.

"The Mayor then, in a few pertinent remarks, introduced Mr. Stephens, stating that at the request of a number of the members of the convention and citizens of Savannah and the State of Georgia now here; he had consented to address them upon the present state of public affairs.

"Mr. Stephens rose and spoke as follows:

"Mr. Mayor and Gentlemen of the Committee and Fellow-Citizens: For this reception you will please accept my most profound and sincere thanks. We are in the midst of one of the greatest epochs in our history. The last ninety days will mark one of the most memorable eras in the history of modern civilization.

"A general call arose from the outside of the building for the speaker to go out. There were more outside than in. The Mayor rose and requested silence at the doors and stated that Mr. Stephens' health would not permit him to speak in the open air.

"After the momentary disruption, Vice-President Stephens resumes his speech, "Seven States have within the last three months thrown off an old government and formed a new. This revolution has been signally marked, up to this time, by the fact of its having been accomplished without the loss of a single drop of blood.

"This new constitution or form of government

constitutes the subject to which your attention will be partly invited. In reference to it, I make this first general remark: it amply secures all our ancient rights, franchises, and liberties. All the great principles of Magna Carta are retained in it. No citizen is deprived of life, liberty, or property, but by the judgment of his peers under the laws of the land. The great principle of religious liberty, which was the honor and pride of the old constitution, is still maintained and secured. All the essentials of the old constitution, which have endeared it to the hearts of the American people, have been preserved and perpetuated.

"Another change in the constitution relates to the length of the tenure of the presidential office. In the new constitution it is six years instead of four, and the President rendered ineligible for a re-election . . The new constitution has put at rest, forever, all the agitating questions relating to our peculiar institution—African slavery as it exists amongst us—the proper status of the Negro in our form of civilization. This was the immediate cause of the late rupture and present revolution. Jefferson in his forecast had anticipated this as the 'rock upon which the old Union would split,' He was right. What was conjecture with him is now a realized fact. But, whether he fully comprehended the great truth upon which that rock stood and stands may be doubted. The prevailing ideas entertained by him and most of the leading statesmen at the time of the formation of the old constitution were that the enslavement of the African was in violation of the laws of nature; that it was wrong in principle, socially, morally, and politically. It was an evil they knew not well how to deal with, but the general opinion of the men of that day was that, somehow or other in the order of Providence, the institution would be evanescent and pass away . . They rested upon the assumption of the equality of races. This was an error. It was a sandy foundation, and the government built upon it fell when the 'storm came and the wind blew.'

"Our new government is founded upon exactly the opposite idea; its foundations are laid, its cornerstone rests upon the great truth that the Negro is not equal to the white man; that slavery—subordination to the superior race—is his natural and normal condition. This, our new government, is the first in the history of the world, based upon this great physical, philosophical and moral truth . . They were attempting to make things equal which the Creator had made unequal. In the conflict thus far, success has been on our side . . It is upon this, as I have stated, our social fabric is firmly planted; and I cannot permit myself to doubt the ultimate success of a full recognition of this principle throughout the civilized and enlightened world.

"As I have stated, the truth of this principle may be slow in development, as all truths are and ever have been, in the various branches of science . . It was so with Harvey, and his theory of the circulation of the blood. It is stated that not a single one of the medical profession, living at the time of the announcement of the truths made by him, admitted them. Now, they are universally acknowledged . . It is the first government ever instituted upon the principles in strict conformity to nature, and the ordination of Providence, in furnishing the materials of human society. Many governments have been founded upon the principle of the subordination and serfdom of certain classes of the same race; such were and are in violation of the laws of nature. Our system commits no such violation of nature's laws. With us, all of the white race, however high or low, rich or poor, are equal in the eye of the law. Not so with the Negro. Subordination is his place. He, by nature, or by the curse against Canaan, is fitted for the condition which he occupies in our system . . It is not for us to inquire into the wisdom of His ordinances, or to question them. For His own purposes, He has made one race to differ from another, as He has made "one star to differ from another star in glory. The great objects of humanity are best attained when there's conformity to His laws and decrees, in the formation of governments as well as in all things else. Our Confederacy is founded upon principles in strict conformity with these laws. This stone which was rejected by the first builders 'is become the chief of the corner'—the real 'cornerstone'—in our new edifice . . We hear much of the civilization and Christianization of the barbarous tribes of Africa. In my judgment, those ends will never be attained, but by first teaching them the lesson taught to Adam, that 'in the sweat of his brow he should eat his bread,' and teaching them to work, and feed, and clothe themselves."

"At the conclusion, Vice-President Stephens takes his seat amid a burst of enthusiasm and applause, such as the Athenaeum has ever displayed within its walls, within the recollection of the oldest inhabitants."

"Wow! This is some speech! I knew all along the Confederacy meant business, but this truly means war!" exclaims Buck. He stands and approaches Betty Gail with the newspaper in his hand.

"Give me about five more minutes to finish and I probably will give you two Wows!" Buck takes his seat at his desk and combs over some particular parts of the speech. Buck finds the "peculiar institution" portion the most interesting and he takes his pencil and underlines that section of the speech.

"What do you think about African slavery being named the 'peculiar institution,' Betty Gail?" asks Buck.

Betty Gail pauses for a moment then replies, "It is a peculiar institution of repression in order to perpetuate greed and dehumanized individuals. In other words, slavery. What else can it be called?"

"No doubt! It's like Vice-President Stephens said, President Jefferson forecasted and anticipated. Slavery is the rock upon which the old Union would split."

On January 23, 1861, Congressman Hill refuses to withdraw from the United States House as directed by the Georgia Convention. Instead, he regretfully submits his letter of resignation from the United States Congress to the Speaker of the House of Representatives.

Chapter Eight
The Saber Strikes

On April 12, 1861, Governor Brown issues the first call for volunteers to assemble no later than April 22 for training. From every corner of the state, Georgia patriots report to Camp Brown. Under orders from the Governor, GMI faculty and cadets train the volunteers.

The first Confederate recruits assemble for training on April 23rd at Camp Brown. Major Capers gathers the GMI staff in his conference room. Once everyone is seated, he opens the letter and sums up the details to the staff,

"We have orders from Governor Brown to train volunteers at Camp Brown, four miles south of Marietta. The officers and non-commissioned officers of Phillip's Brigade are already regularly encamped for some weeks. All ranks are surrendered. I am in command, and the cadets acting in such capacity as he assigns them. Our general schedule will be: One day is sufficed to fix the separate company ground and train them to assembly. The second day the organization is in one company with the cadets acting as commissioned and non-commissioned officers. For several days afterwards the main instruction will be in guard duty. After the first week, the encampment is by battalion. The drills are in different arms, infantry, artillery and cavalry. The officers of the various regiments, then forming or formed, shall find a place in ranks and profit by the practical instruction and the drills of the encampment."

"On April 30, 1861, Governor Brown went up to review the training of the Phillip's Brigade at GMI." Buck shows the newspaper article to Mia and Betty Gail. "Read this about GMI and what the Governor has to say about the training."

Taking the newspaper, Mia reads, "Major Capers, elegant in his manners and thoroughly fitted for his duties, aided by his cadets as they are detailed by him to drill the various squads, prove the absolute need in times such as these of military educated men." She turns to the next page, "Here's another article on GMI." She begins reading out loud.

"The GMI cadets vote to recognize the Phillip's Brigade as GMI's first contribution to the training of Georgia's army. For this occasion, the cadets elect to present the 'Stars and Bars' given to them by the Marietta ladies to the Phillip's Brigade."

That night, Paul tells Norman, "Chills raced up and down my spine when I heard the new words to the Star Spangled Banner. It was as if I was listening to the soul of the Union and the spirit of the Confederacy."

Norman continues the conversation, "I found myself speechless as well. The men of Phillip's Brigade came here ready to fight, but know very little about tactic. Some think fighting a war is like hunting squirrels . . not much to it. Now Phillip's Brigade knows discipline and tactics."

"I only hope they are all successful and return home safely."

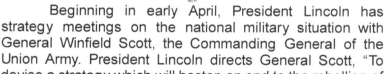

Beginning in early April, President Lincoln has strategy meetings on the national military situation with General Winfield Scott, the Commanding General of the Union Army. President Lincoln directs General Scott, "To devise a strategy which will hasten an end to the rebellion of the Southern States and bring the Southern States back into the Union."

President Lincoln orders a blockade of the South on April 19, six days after the fall of Fort Sumter. The job of creating and maintaining a true blockade of the South falls on the shoulders of Secretary of the Navy, Gideon Welles.

He informs his naval commanders, "To meet this new challenge the navy must begin a massive expansion of its fleet. The Union as well as the South is aware the most strategically important coastal region is Hampton Roads in Virginia where the wide mouth of the James River pours into the Chesapeake Bay. For the North, Hampton Roads is our doorway to the Confederate capitol at Richmond. For the South, this is the passage to the sea and potential European allies. Fort Monroe, the massive stone fortress that guards the inward approaches to Hampton Roads, is solidly in our hands. We must ensure that Fort Monroe remains in Union control. It is key to Union expeditions into the South, as well as an anchor for the blockade of the Atlantic coast." In the spring of 1861, the navy consisted of eighty-two largely obsolete ships.

In response to General Scott's Anaconda Plan, General Robert E. Lee and President Jefferson Davis meet to determine the effect of General Scott's naval blockade and conclude, "That all of the forts along the coast are beyond the reaches of the federal artillery."

Since secession, former United States Congressman and now Colonel Lucius J. Gartrell, is a fiery advocate for war. He prides himself with military ado and hastens to organize the Seventh Regiment, Georgia Volunteer Infantry in May. Colonel Gartrell plans to be among the first to take the field against the North. The fall of Sumter early in the spring sends an electric thrill through North and South and from both sections come the call to arms.

Chapter Nine
Proposal by Buster

On a beautiful sunny day on the first of June, Buster Phillips' acres are blooming with fresh crops. His farm adjoins the Jernigan farm. The Jernigans consider Buster well-to-do, good-looking, and above all else, kind. According to Buck, Buster is a most desirable match from every standpoint for Mia. Therefore, when Buster set his eyes upon Mia, Buck and Betty Gail gave a glad consent. Buster finishes his regular Saturday night supper with the Jernigans and invites Mia to sit outside with him.

"Mia, 'afore my very eyes you're a fadin' from me, an' it looks like unless you marry me, I must jest stand by and see you die. Let's fix the wedding day. Mia, please give the man what's loves you the right to care fer you until death."

As Buster speaks, he takes her hand in his and presses tenderly. She does not encourage his grasp. Instead she allows her hand to lie unresisting in Buster's. "Your pa's mighty stirred over politics these days. He reckons how there's gonna be great trouble in the land. It 'pears he's about right. Who'll protect you then, Mia, like a husband can? Let da preacher marry us right away, an' give the old folks another son to lean on."

As Buster continues speaking, Mia's gaze roams listlessly over the lovely scene before her. She hears Buster's voice as one hears in a dream, wishing that it were the voice of Legare. She sees the frantic struggles of a brilliant butterfly entangled in the lace-like meshes of a spider's web. Her feeling prompts her to remove her hand from Buster's clasp and go to the assistance of the insect. However, she does not yield to the impulse. She leaves her hand hidden in the Buster's unwanted grip. She, too, is tangled in a mesh much like the poor insect, which circumstances are weaving around her. She sees her struggle as unable to break the silken threads of the web of Buster's love.

"Speak, Mia," says Buster. "Shall I tell your ma an' pa we've set da day?"

Mia is confused because of her love for Legare. She knows her parents favor Buster. They've both are gone out of their way to let her know they expect her to marry Buster. A tear slides down her cheek. Yet, not desiring to offend Buster or her parents, she murmurs, "Yes."

It is now August and Mia is up early on her way to start her Third Class in the Seminary. Her ma, pa, Isaac and Sally wave to her as she takes the horse and wagon, heading towards town.

Mia is excited to be trusted for the first time to drive herself to school. She takes care not to over-tax the horse as she reaches the edge of town. Proud of herself, she drops the horse and wagon by the stable and dashes to school.

"Good morning, Mr. Latham."

"Good morning, Mia. I see you're ready to start your Third Class."

"Yes, sir." Mia reaches in her purse and takes out a twenty-dollar gold piece. "Here's the twenty dollars for my Third Class tuition and supply fees."

"Thank you, Mia. Your books are in Mrs. Smith's room. I believe you already have a list of the courses, but here is another one for you. You were among the top of your class again. Congratulations!"

"Thank you, Mr. Latham. I really like the Seminary." Mia takes the list and reads it over: Advance studies in Penmanship, Arithmetic, Mensuration, Composition, and English Grammar. New studies include Bookkeeping, Plane Trigonometry, logarithms, Physical Geography, Physiology and Botany.

That afternoon on the way home, Mia stops and buys a newspaper for her father.

"Looks like salt might get scarce. A lot of speculating going on. Isaac and I have been working on the ginny today making sure all of the wheels are greased and ready for the cotton crop. Been reading the paper. Didn't realize so many of our boys have gone off to the war." Buck hands Betty Gail the newspaper. "Looks like about seventeen of our locals have enlisted."

Betty Gail puts the paper down and stares straight ahead. Buck watches her for a moment. "Are you all right?"

"All right?" Betty Gail echoes. "I don't think so, Buck." "Tell me what's wrong. Are you hurtin' somewhere Betty Gail?"

She sinks into a chair and shakes her head. "No, Buck. I don't think I am." She turns suddenly as if coming out of a dream. "Oh, I'm not in physical pain."

"Then what is it?" Concern scores Buck's forehead with wrinkles. "Talk to me. You got me worried."

"It's all true, Buck." Betty Gail closes her eyes briefly as if in prayer. "We're at war, really at war.

Chapter Ten
November Elopement

Legare and his father arrive by train to Stone Mountain. Congressman Hill has some business to attend to with the Dents concerning the new furnishings in the hotel. Legare and his father go inside the depot while waiting for their baggage.

"Good day!" exclaims James Goldsmith, the station agent, as he waves to the Hills. James asks, "Have you heard the news?"

"What news, James?" asks Congressman Hill.

"The news about Mia and Buster. They are to be married."

"Well, I'm proud for them. I'm sure we have an invitation at home. We've been staying between Atlanta and Milledgeville most of the time, trying to deal with this terrible war. I know Buck and Betty Gail are very proud and happy."

The news of Mia's approaching marriage to Buster Phillips is not what Legare wants to hear. His face flushes angrily and the blood receding leaves it deadly pale. He's just returned from a trip to Milledgeville with his father and came to Stone Mountain to visit Mia.

As Congressman Hill and Legare pass by the Jernigan's farm they see Buck in the distance. Buck waves for them to come over. Congressman Hill and Legare are always welcome with the Jernigans, as well as every Stone Mountain home.

The small farmers of the district and the wealthy owners of broad plantations appreciate the work their congressman has done. In particular, the Hills are frequently seen at the Jernigan's. Old Uncle Isaac's never failing, "Howdy, Mars' Hill and Mars' Legare."

Buck greets the Hills. "Did you hear about General Winfield Scott? Everybody knows he was the most able general in our country's history with the exception of George Washington."

"I understand congratulations are in order for an upcoming wedding." Buck smiles. "Yep, coming up soon, Mia and Buster."

Buck and Joshua have engaged in many long and anxious talks about the political questions of the day and today is no exception. The mutterings of the coming storm of civil war is disturbing to even this secluded spot.

Mia, always sweet and gentle, seems to be avoiding Legare. She flushes and pales beneath his inviting and loving gaze. During each warm summer day, Mia has been drooping like a wilted flower and goes listlessly about her household tasks.

Buck walks down the steps and shakes Congressman Hill's hand. "What brings you and Legare to these parts today?"

"Gotta meet with Eliza and Hugh Dent at their new hotel on the mountain. Had a little work done on the hotel and I need to pay my part of the bills. Business is getting slow though and all of us have concern for keeping it open."

Buck admires the horse Legare is riding. He dismounts and hands the reins to Uncle Isaac. Buck takes Legare's hand. "Good to see you, son. Mighty fine mount you got there."

"Thank you, sir.." He smiles at Buck's words. Legare closes his eyes briefly and imagines himself sitting with the Jernigan family—as a real part of the family. He can hardly breathe for a moment. If only that were possible. Nothing could make him happier.

"Legare and I better mosey along to the hotel before dark. Have a good evening."

Legare takes to his mount and his father to the carriage. Buck tips his hat and, reining the horses, Legare and his father canter the horses up the mountain.

As Buck turns to go into the house, he sees Mia sitting on the porch like a wilted flower, not caring about her household tasks. He can't figure out why Mia is so temperamental. He asks himself what ails the girl. *She gets punier and punier every day. Must be the birds and the bees. So long as it's Buster bee, that's okay.*

As they ride to the front entrance of the hotel, the odor of fresh paint overpowers the sweet smells of the forest. The building stands resplendent in a fresh coat of white paint with crimson facings. The green shutters compliment the changing forest leaves. John and Hugh Dent are on the veranda talking with some of the guests when Congressman Hill and Legare arrive. The Dents are delighted and eager to visit them. Hugh and John jump from the porch to greet their friends, taking the reins and securing the horses.

"Hello, Congressman Hill, Legare. I hope your trip was good," says John with a smile. Hugh summons one of the stablemen over to take the horses as Congressman Hill and Legare dismount from the buggy.

"Glad to see both of you." Hugh extends his hand. "I hope you like the new paint job on the hotel. It was almost too late in the year to paint but the weather has been warmer than usual."

He gestures at the hotel edifice. "Brightens the place up a lot and the color of the shutters really makes the hotel stand out. How is your mother?"

"She is just fine and making sure supper is ready for the guests and us."

"Of course. There are a few guests, men from the neighboring city, playing cards. They hope to make expenses by fleecing the inexperienced gentlemen from the plantations."

"Most of the plantation owners have great self-confidence. The gamblers will bet against the plantation owners' inexperience and self-confidence. I hope you make them check their guns when they arrive."

They both laugh. Some of the guests recognize Congressman Hill and engage him in a conversation about the war effort. Congressman Hill gladly shares what he knows and then moves inside to visit with Eliza Dent.

"It's good to see you, Joshua." Eliza approaches, wiping her hands on her apron. "Where is Legare?"

"He's outside talking to John. They are catching up."

Eliza and Joshua make their way to the sitting room, take comfortable chairs and continue their conversation. "And Emily, how is she? I was hoping she would come along and stay a few days."

"We still have five children at home younger than Legare. Keeps her plenty busy. I figured you would have the boys looking after the place."

"I just came up a couple of days ago to see how they were doing with the paint job. I plan on departing tomorrow or the next day."

"Well, after supper we can talk about how much money I owe for the expenses of the hotel."

"It's not very much. Hugh keeps a good set of books and watches the money closely. Just not many visitors this summer like last year. The war and all, you know. If it doesn't do better next year, we probably should close the hotel down for a while."

"Hugh has good business sense like his father. Whatever the two of you decide will be satisfactory with me. Let's hope the war is over by then and peace returns to our country."

"Amen to that."

After supper, Legare excuses himself and strolls out into the moonlight. He looks toward the mountaintop, now bathed in a flood of silver light. Far down below, Legare sees the twinkling of a light in Mia's house. He wonders if she is still awake. Thinking of his love, the one woman whom the wide world holds for him, Legare drops onto the bare rock, still warm from the sun, and buries his face in his hands. Honor forbade him to interfere with her upcoming marriage. Prudence whispers that their social spheres are different. At the close of every one of Legare's arguments, Mia's radiant face smiles at him. Her lovely brown eyes seem to shower love into his own. Words are not necessary, although he has not spoken a syllable which could betray his feelings. Legare knows Mia loves him. All he needs to do is figure out how to get her to admit it and break her engagement.

Exhausted from his sleepless night on the mountain, Legare finally lays his head upon the warm granite with his last thought. "Come what may, Mia shall be mine." And then he falls asleep. Strange fancies vex his slumber, the outcome, no doubt, of the depressing events of the past days and his hope for the future. So realistic is the dream that it lingers in his mind long after he awakens. Legare arrives at the hotel as daylight is peaking on the eastern horizon with a pink and gold sunrise.

Sitting on the porch, Joshua watches his son approach from the mountain path. "Where were you last night, son?"

"Took a walk and fell asleep on the mountain," answers Legare. Even though he and his father are close, he doesn't feel he can discuss his feelings about Mia.

"You have been mighty quiet since we arrived in Stone Mountain. Is something bothering you?"

"Nothing I can't handle, Father."

"Anything I can help you with?"

Legare looks at his father. "No, sir, this problem is all mine to solve."

Legare goes to his hotel room to take a short nap. After awakening, he spends the day with John and Hugh. They climb the mountain together and gaze out over the beautiful forest, joking and laughing, but Legare's thoughts are focused on Mia as he sees her little farm house in the distance. The fall colors are exceptionally bright and fill his mind with the grandeur and beauty of nature as well as his love. He won't soon forget these moments on the mountain, thinking of Mia.

Supper is a jovial occasion with his friends, but Legare feels he has to get away alone. He waits for an opportunity and then steals away from the hotel. He wanders onto a path through the woods and surprises a fox along the way. Lost in the tranquility of the evening, he is all the more eager to find a way out of his dilemma. He's wandering where his feet lead him when he reaches a crystal clear creek at the base of the mountain. He sits quietly and, after a while, stretches himself full length upon its mossy bank, imagining what life with Mia might be like. Closing his eyes, he tries to shape some kind of plan for him and Mia. He comes to no definite conclusion, but realizes he must see her. He feels an urge to follow a tugging at his heartstrings and walks in the direction of the Jernigans' farmhouse. As Legare begins walking the path from the creek, their favorite picnic spot, to his surprise he finds Mia standing on the other side of the creek.

His heart pounds as he leaps the small creek and rushes to her side. Now that he's with her, he has no idea what to say. Finally, he manages to speak. "Some kind angel must have sent you here in answer to my prayers."

"I've just come from a neighbor's." She takes his out-stretched hand and looks at him with her beautiful, but sad, brown eyes. "Have you heard the news about my wedding?"

"Yes, Mia," he answers with a low voice. "Shall I congratulate you?

Mia's lips turn down and start to tremble. She takes a deep breath and tears begin to flow, glistening on her cheeks in the moonlight.

"If you love Buster and wish to marry him, I'll leave Stone Mountain tomorrow morning." Legare musters all his courage and takes her hand. "But something tells me—something here." He places his and Mia's hand upon his heart. "Oh, Mia, don't you know how much I love you! Can't you tell when you look into my eyes?" He gathers her into his arms as her tears turn into an uncontrollable weeping. She rests her head on his chest in silent acknowledgement of their love for one another.

Legare's heart breaks to see her in such distress. Their situation seems hopeless. The honorable approach would be for him to escort her home safely, wish her happiness on her upcoming marriage and walk out of her life—forever. He simply cannot do that. His own heart is breaking and he knows hers must be. But to act any differently would bring shame to both families.

He looks down at her and lifts her chin. In the soft moonlight, she stares up at him, her love apparent in her gaze. "Mia, I consider myself an honorable man, but I cannot just wish you well and walk away. I adore you and would have you rip my still-beating heart from my chest before I would see you marry another."

Mia reaches up and caresses his cheek. "Oh, Legare . . what answer is there for two people in our situation? What can we do?"

Sobs wrack her cheeks as she buries her face against his chest. "Shhh . . Mia, my love. We will be together. I have a plan."

All of the emotional obstacles evaporate. Mia regains her composure and the two sit on the mossy creek bank. She wipes away her tears. "Legare, what will Pa and Ma say if I let them know I don't want to marry Buster?"

He rises and walks a few steps away. The anguish in her voice is enough to break his heart. She has always been a good daughter and what he's asking of her will make her view herself otherwise. But to ignore their feelings is something he cannot do. He returns to her side, takes her hand and helps her to rise. They walk slowly through the woods, fearful yet solemnly discussing their dilemma as they approach her home. Together, they stand on the edge of a clearing under a wide-spreading oak, sheltered by beautiful fall leaves. Moonlight drifts through the falling leaves as he kisses her an enduring kiss that holds promises of more.

"Good-night, my darling Mia. Bring your necessities, dress as a boy and meet me here tomorrow at midnight." They embrace again, much longer this time, with a kiss full of fire. Reluctantly, he releases her and watches her graceful form until she enters her father's gate. With the heart of a cupid, Legare sprints like a deer up the mountain, scurrying back to the hotel to make final preparations.

The following morning, Congressman Hill finds Legare on the porch, deep in thought. "I am departing for

Atlanta and will return sometime tomorrow. You're welcome to come along or stay in Stone Mountain to visit with your friends."

Unable to believe his luck, Legare replies hastily, "I'll stay!"

Around midnight, Mia and Legare approach the small one-room log cabin of Uncle Isaac and Aunt Sally. Uncle Isaac and Aunt Sally are awakened by a quiet knocking on their windowpane. Uncle Isaac jumps up, lights his candle and rushes to the window. Seeing Mia, he opens his window and places a stick to hold the window in place. "Mia, what is you doing up dis late?"

"Uncle Isaac, I'm running away with Legare. I have loved him from the moment I first laid my eyes on him. I just want you and Aunt Sally to know that I am all right. I know Ma, Pa and Norman will worry, but I hold your word not to speak a word to them or anybody else about this." Aunt Sally looks on and Uncle Isaac tells Mia with a loving smile, "O, Lordy, me know'd all 'long 'bout des. What took you so long? Now jus' git. Wes ain't saw nuffin! God bless you!" Mia reaches through the small window and hugs and kisses Uncle Isaac and Aunt Sally good-bye. Legare grasps Uncle Isaac and Aunt Sally's hands and squeezes them gently. Then, without saying another word, Legare and Mia, holding hands, slip off into the dark.

As they approach Legare's horse, Mia turns to view the dark outline of her home and begins to weep. She takes a last look of the surrounds of her happy childhood and family, then Legare whispers, "Come, dearest, we've got to ride, or we'll miss the train. You'll see them all again another day, I promise."

Mia sobs quietly. "Never again. Ma and Pa will be changed, or they will be indifferent to me." Legare places her gently in the saddle, climbs on himself, and the horse soon takes them out of sight.

Finally, they reach the stables near the depot. Legare leaves a note on the horse for Mr. Levi. "Please deliver the horse to my father when he returns to town. Legare Hill." They hurry toward the depot where the train is waiting to depart. It is late and no one is at the ticket window.

Mia, dressed in her "young man outfit," and Legare board the train. They should be in Augusta by morning.

Legare hands Mia some money. "When the conductor asks you for your ticket, just give him two dollars and just say, 'Augusta please.'"

"I have money. Hold on to yours."

There are only a few other passengers on board, so Mia and Legare take separate seats across from each other. Soon the conductor gives the lantern signal to the engineer that all are on board. With several strong chugs from the engine boiler, the train eases from the depot, on its familiar journey to Augusta.

Once the trip is under way, the conductor passes through the car and asks Mia, "Where to young man?"

Mia hesitates for a moment and says in her deepest voice, "Augusta." "That will be seven dollars and seventy-five cents please, sir." Mia hands the conductor a ten-dollar gold piece. He gives her change and a paid ticket to Augusta. "My name is Allen; if you need anything just let me know."

Mia smiles and nods her head. She smiles and gives Legare a little wink. They begin their lives together, a daring chapter of love and adventure. Mia knows the future holds a reckoning ahead for her. One day, she and Legare will have to face their parents. But, for now, life is wonderful and exciting—and full of promise.

Chapter Eleven
Rage and Disappointment

The Jernigan family is astir early in the morning. Around 9:00, Buck is excited about the day's events and is anxious to see his daughter. "Why is Mia sleeping so late?"

"Let the child alone," replies Betty Gail. "I'll wake her shortly."

Soon Sally has breakfast on the table, and Betty Gail goes to Mia's room and taps on the door. There's no answer. She taps again a little louder and calls, "Mia, breakfast is ready. Remember Buster is coming over to have breakfast with us this morning." Still no answer. Suspiciously, she opens the door and peeks inside. She does not see Mia, but the bed is made. Betty Gail throws open the door and shouts for Buck. "Come quick! Mia's gone."

Anguish and surprise render Buck speechless. Uncle Isaac and Aunt Sally stay quiet in the kitchen. Almost at the same time, Buster knocks at the front door. Uncle Isaac answers the door and Aunt Sally is standing still and quiet in the dining room.

Buster, not taking notice of their stoical posture, smilingly says, "Good morning, Uncle Isaac and Aunt Sally. Mighty fine day. Where is everybody?" "'orning, Mars Buster," replies Uncle Isaac while pointing to the back of the house. Looking in the direction which Uncle Isaac has just pointed, Buster sees Buck come rushing to the kitchen with Betty Gail not far behind. Standing still, Buster examines their faces and takes in the situation at a glance.

"Whoever he is, and I think I know," Buck shouts,

shaking his fist in the air. "Let him take my curse and as for this unthankful and disobedient daughter—"

"Oh, no! No! Mars' Buck," cries Uncle Isaac, "Don't curse da little gal. Me carried in these ol' arm."

Betty Gail puts her hand upon his lips to keep back the dreadful words, and weeps aloud.

Shocked and pale, Buster screams, "If he's wronged her, if he wronged de gal I love and we live to meet, one of us will die!"

Aunt Sally and Uncle Isaac look at each other sadly. Uncle Isaac says nervously, "Vengeance belongeth to de Lord. You turn de other cheek, Mars' Buster."

Immediately Buck takes his rifle, mounts his horse and gallops up toward the hotel. At the front entrance, Buck dismounts and spots Hugh Dent on the verandah. "Where's Legare Hill? Is he with Mia?"

Mrs. Dent hears the commotion from the hotel study where she is examining the day's receipts and rushes onto the porch. "What's troubling you, Buck?"

"Mia's missing. Not home all night. I think she and Legare done run off somewhere!"

"Legare was not here all night. His father is in Atlanta, and we expect him back sometime today to finish up some business here. I'll tell Joshua you need to see him as soon as he returns."

"Do that for me, Mrs. Dent. Much obliged to y'all. If you see my daughter or Legare, best warn them I'm a disturbed man!" Buck turns his mount and heads down the mountain, still in search of his daughter and Legare. "Hugh, you best high tail it to the depot and wait for Joshua. Let him know what's happening. Mr. Jernigan is not a happy man right now."

Hugh is waiting at the depot as the afternoon train arrives in Stone Mountain. He sees Congressman Hill standing in the passenger car and greets him as he steps from the train. Looking somewhat puzzled, Congressman Hill asks, "Hello, Hugh, what brings you here? Is something wrong? Is everyone all right?"

"Well, sir, as far as I know everyone is all right, but Mr. Jernigan came to the hotel this morning. Looks like Mia and Legare ran off sometimes during the night. Mr. Jernigan is mighty upset. You probably should stop by his farm. He wants to see you as soon as you arrive."

"I was afraid something like this was going to happen. Legare has loved Mia since he first laid eyes on her. Let me fetch my buggy and try and smooth Buck's feathers a bit. I know he and Betty Gail are, or were, excited about Mia and Buster's upcoming wedding. "

Congressman Hill and Hugh rush to the Jernigan farm. Buck sees the dust from the buggy and steps from the porch as Congressman Hill pulls to a stop. Hugh takes the reins as Joshua steps down from the carriage. "I hear we are missing two young 'uns."

Looking sternly at Joshua, Buck replies, "Yep, ran off during the night. I've searched these woods, been all over the mountain and creeks. Not a sight or sound of them anywhere."

"I am heartily sorry and share the strain and anxiety caused by the actions of these two children. If we all think about it, we all have been bearing witness to the romantic looks Mia and Legare have given each other."

"If your son has violated my daughter, he is going to be full of buck- shot!" replies Buck with Betty Gail austerely gazing at Joshua and Hugh.

Joshua, in a neighborly manner looks straight at Buck. "Buck, my son would not violate your daughter, for he has the utmost respect for her as well as respect for you and Betty Gail. There's no telling where they are right now. They are going to have to show up sooner or later and face the consequences. I'll share with you any information I obtain and will count on you to do the same."

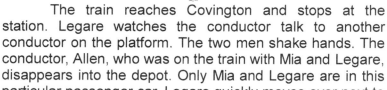

The train reaches Covington and stops at the station. Legare watches the conductor talk to another conductor on the platform. The two men shake hands. The conductor, Allen, who was on the train with Mia and Legare, disappears into the depot. Only Mia and Legare are in this particular passenger car. Legare quickly moves over next to her. "Let your hair down now. A new conductor is coming on board."

Mia removes her straw hat quickly. She then removes the hairpins and her beautiful long hair cascades down to her back. Now Legare and Mia are sitting next to each other as the new conductor, Chip, waves the lantern to the engineer. As the train departs, Legare holds Mia's hand, looks her directly in the eyes and declares, "Mia, I'll always love you!"

"I have loved you from the moment I first laid eyes upon you, Legare." As the train continues toward Augusta, the monotonous clickety-click of the train wheels passing over the track produces a hypnotic effect. Holding each other's hands, Mia and Legare fall asleep with her head resting on his shoulder.

The jerking of the train stopping in Augusta suddenly awakens the two lovers. Legare opens his eyes. "Looks like we are in Augusta, Mia."

She raises her head up, places her hand over her mouth, and yawns. She stands up and stretches her arms upward and out to relieve their bodies from the stiffness of their sleep. Placing her hands on the window sill, she peers outside into the morning sun to investigate their Augusta surroundings.

Legare takes her arm and, picking up the luggage, they move to the back of the passenger car and descend the steps. At the doorway they face a chilly Augusta morning. Chip, the conductor, assists Mia as she places her foot on the ladies, step and onto the station platform. Mia tightens her coat to keep the brisk morning air from filtering through her clothes to her warm body.

As she studies the crowd, Mia sees young couples probably the same age as she and Legare. She wonders if any of those young couples are eloping. If they are, she hopes they love each other as much as she and Legare. Legare steps from the train with a broad smile and takes Mia's hand. "There are several hotels on Broad Street. The best one is the Augusta Hotel. Augusta has private baths and running hot water. We'll stop by there first and, if you like it, we'll stay there. If not, we'll find a hotel you like. Then, we will find the local Baptist preacher and get married! How does that sound to you, Mia?"

She blushes. "Let's go take a look at the Augusta. I need to freshen up a bit before our wedding."

"The hotel is a couple of blocks from here. We probably can walk just about as fast as waiting to get a carriage. What do you want to do, Mia?"

Mia takes his hand and glances at their strange surroundings. A sense of adventure fills her and she can't wait for events to unfold. "Let's walk. The fresh cool air feels good and will help wake us up."

Legare picks up their luggage and they depart the Georgia Railroad platform and head for the hotel. As they stroll down Broad Street, the city is still quiet. Tall, stone buildings line both sides of the street, some probably five stories in height.

"People say that Broad Street is the widest street in all of America."

"Well, it is plenty wide for sure. Nothing like it in Atlanta!" replies Mia. They pass by the principle office building for the cotton merchants.

The banks have not opened. Several darkies are out early sweeping the sidewalks in front of various buildings. As Mia and Legare pass by, they render a good morning to each other. The theater marquee displays the latest stage production, a concert featuring many of Mozart's works.

"Here's the Georgia Railroad Bank Building. My father owns stock in the Georgia Railroad. Look at the twin stone columns on each side." Legare stops and glances around. "Here we are. Let's see if you like it or not."

Mia looks at the stately exterior as they climb the several steps to the entrance. As they reach the door, a butler wearing a red velvet coat and top hat opens the door for them. "Good morning."

Mia and Legare exchange greetings with him and enter the lobby. The lobby has marble floors covered with oriental rugs. Grand gas light chandeliers sway from the ceiling. The walls have large beautiful oils depicting scenes of early America, early Augusta and Georgia. Legare and Mia approach the front desk and observe paintings of Washington and Jefferson hanging on the wall behind the desk.

"May I help you, sir?" asks the clerk.

"Yes," replies Legare. "My wife and I would like to view one of your suites if possible." Mia turns her head toward Legare, smiles and takes his hand.

"Yes, sir. Just give me a moment while I look over the room list. There's one on the second floor with a private bath and hot water. Here is the key, sir. The stairs to the right will take you to the second floor. Then turn right. The suite is the last room."

Taking the key, Legare asks the clerk, "May I leave my luggage here?"

"That will be fine, sir."

"Thank you. We will be back in a few minutes."

Mia and Legare climb the marble staircase to the second floor, turn right and find the suite. He unlocks the door and allows her to enter first. The suite is large, probably twenty by thirty with the bath additional. The bathtub is copper and has a little side-arm gas furnace attached at one end. It has the shape of a shoe like the French and English models. The water in the tub flows and circulates backwards until the entire bath is heated to satisfaction.

There's a table and four chairs, two comfortable cushioned chairs, a coffee table and a large wardrobe. The headboard of the bed is massive with beautiful designs and constructed from maple. The wooden floors are accented with small oriental rugs. Legare walks with Mia and they open the tall blue cotton draperies partially covering a large window. The view overlooks the Savannah River and the many steamers full of cotton.

"I like the suite, Legare. Let's take it."

He kisses her. "I'll go down, check us in and bring the baggage up." Legare dashes downstairs and informs the clerk that the suite is satisfactory. He signs the registration card.

A bellman approaches. "Would you like for me to

assist you with the luggage sir?"

"Please." Picking up the luggage, Legare and the bellman go to the room. Legare is a little embarrassed. He knocks on the door. Mia opens it and smiles. "I left the key in the room by mistake."

The bellman places the luggage on racks. "Is there anything else I can assist you with, sir?"

Legare hands the bellman a tip. "Thank you. That will be all for now." The bellman departs. "Mia, while you freshen up, I'll go down the hall to the common bath to shave and wash up."

"I'll see you in a few minutes." They kiss lingeringly, and Legare leaves the room. He hastens down the hall to the common bath to bathe.

Returning to the room, Legare finds Mia combing her hair. "Almost ready, Legare, just a few more strokes."

Legare approaches Mia from behind and places his arms tightly around her waist. Pushing her hair away from her cheek he kisses her and whispers, "I love you, Mia Jernigan, and I'm hungry and we need to get a set of rings and we need to find a preacher—straight away."

"Straight away is the word of the day! Let's get started!" She kisses Legare again.

They go to the hotel dining area. The hostess escorts them to a table near a window. "Is this satisfactory, sir?"

"All right with you, Mia?"

"Fine, thank you."

After breakfast, they walk down Broad Street looking for a jewelry store. Not too far away, they find a small one with a window displaying a large assortment of engagement rings and wedding bands. They study the display and Legare hugs her close. "Do you see a wedding band you like?"

Mia tucks her hand in his. "This is a gift from you. You pick. You're a gift to me and I'll pick your wedding band. How does that sound?"

"Well, Mia, you already have me wrapped around your finger for life. A wedding ring you pick out for me will give me two beautiful objects to look at and cherish for the rest of my life." He hugs her, tasting her hot breath, feeling her soft body nestled in his arm, her heartbeat strong and fast. With a smile he opens the door for her and follows her in.

A well-dressed gentleman pops out of a door in back. "Good morning to my first customers of the day. What can I do for you?"

Legare and Mia respond, "Good morning, sir!"

Legare continues, "We're getting married today and would like to purchase a set of wedding bands."

Looking at them, the salesman smiles. "You are a beautiful couple. I think I can help you. Follow me down to the other display case." Upon reaching the display case, the jeweler removes several trays of wedding bands. "Now you take your time deciding. You'll have to wear these for the rest of your lives, so I want you to be happy with your decision."

Legare and Mia pick up and examine several different styles while the jeweler silently attends to some of his paper work. Soon Mia finds a ring she feels suitable for Legare. "I have chosen this gold ring for you, Legare. See it has a bold gold ridge border around both edges. To me the ridges represent your sound and honest character."

Legare examines the ring and tries it on. "I love it. I picked the ring I like for you immediately. This one stood out like it was calling me to pick it up." Legare hands Mia the gold band. "See how the exceptional width magnifies the beautiful and strong design of the band and at the same time compliments your strengths and beauty. This is why I chose this band for you."

Mia slides the ring on and gazes at it for a moment. "Fits perfectly." Mia admires her ring with a broad smile. "We've made our choices, sir, and are ready to settle up."

The jeweler comes over and takes the two rings. "Beautiful choices. You both have good taste."

"How much do we owe you?" asks Legare.

"Six dollars each."

Mia looks at the jeweler. "He'll pay for mine, and I'll pay for his. That way they are gifts from each of us and we never can ask for them back."

The jeweler nods his head in agreement. "May your life be filled with happiness, success and good health. God bless you both." Legare shakes hands with the jeweler, thanks him for his kind words, and they depart.

Outside, Augusta seems to have come to life. Horses and carriages are moving along Broad Street, and pedestrians are becoming more apparent. "It's around 10:30, Mia, and the Baptist preacher should be up and about by now. The church is on Green Street. Let's take a carriage there."

Shortly, a carriage passes in their direction and Legare waves to the driver. "Are you for hire?" asks Legare.

"Yes, sir. Where would you like to go?"

"Take us to the Baptist Church on Green Street." After a short ride, they arrive. Standing in front of the rectory, they read a plaque; On May 8-12, 1845, the Southern Baptist Convention was founded at this Church. Its first president was William B. Johnson. The mission of the Southern Baptist Convention was to preserve the religious foundation for human slavery.

"Well, looks like we are getting married in a historical place," says Legare. "Our historical moment in a historical place."

Mia smiles shyly, realizing that in a few moments, she and Legare will be husband and wife. "I'm so happy, Legare. I wish . . I wish everybody could be as happy as we are today.

Legare replies, "We both know that our love will carry us over any mountain across any ocean and always to each others arms. "

Legare takes Mia's hand as they enter the rectory. "May I help you?" asks a lady sitting at a desk. Legare hugs Mia and nods. "Yes, we would like to know if the pastor is available to marry us this morning."

"Why, I'm sure he'll be delighted to marry such a lovely couple. Just give me a moment and I'll locate him for you. His name is Rev. A. J. Huntington. Have a seat if you would like."

In a few minutes, Rev. Huntington appears and the

receptionist introduces him to Mia and Legare. "My receptionist has notified me you would like to be married this morning."

"Yes, sir, we would," replies Legare.

"Are any family members coming? Do you have a best man and maid of honor?"

"No, sir, just me and Mia," Legare informs the pastor laughingly. "I'm the Best Man. That's why Mia is marrying me and Mia is the maid of honor and that's why I'm marrying her!"

Rev. Huntington and his secretary laugh at Legare's comments. "I guess you're right on that matter, son. If you would please give us your names and addresses so your marriage can be placed in the Church Records."

"My name is Hugh Legare Hill. I'm from Madison."

"My name is Mia Jernigan. I'm from Stone Mountain."

Rev. Huntington studies Legare for a moment. "You wouldn't be kin to Congressman Hill, would you, son?"

"Yes, sir. He's my father. Mia and I are eloping."

"Your father is a courageous man, and so are you. Well, let's go into the Chapel for the wedding ceremony. If it is all right, I'll have my secretary as the witness to your marriage."

"It will be a pleasure to have your secretary as our witness."

The four enter the Chapel and approach the altar. The sun shines brightly through the windows of the chapel, producing a very enlightening atmosphere. Rev. Huntington starts the wedding ceremony with a prayer. Mia and Legare bow their heads. As Rev. Huntington prays, Mia's wish is her Ma, Pa and Norman, and Legare's family, could be here and be happy for them. She silently prays they will forgive her for running away to be married.

Tears begin to flow down Mia's cheeks as Rev. Huntington ends the prayer. Seeing Mia's tears, Rev. Huntington, asks, "Are you all right, Mia?"

"Yes, sir, one eye is shedding tears of joy, and the other eye is shedding tears of sadness, for I wish our families were here with us."

Legare wipes away Mia's tears. Teary eyed and yet smiling, they stand hand in hand placing rings on each other's fingers. Repeating the eternal love vows, Mia and Legare end with, "to love and to cherish till death do us part."

Then they seal their vows with a kiss.

Legare thanks Rev. Huntington and his secretary and offers to pay the minister, but he refuses to accept any money. "It is my gift to you for being the son of a great statesman."

Thanking the Rev. Huntington, Mia and Legare depart the chapel and begin walking back to the hotel, hoping to wave down a passing carriage. When they reach Broad Street, Augusta has turned into a busy town.

Passing by a cafe, Legare suggests to Mia, "It's dinner time, Mia. I think we should eat before returning to the hotel."

Smiling, Mia takes Legare's arm and pulls him closer. "Yes, I want a full meal, because I doubt if we get any supper."

Following their dinner, they decide to walk the four blocks to the hotel. They arrive around three o'clock and Legare goes to the front desk and orders two steak suppers with champagne to be delivered to their room around 7:30. They go up the stairs and he unlocks the door. He picks her up in his arms. She smiles and places one arm around his neck and one hand on his shoulder as they enter their honeymoon suite. He closes the door with his foot and carries her to the bed. Gently laying Mia on the bed, he kisses her with deep emotion and passion.

"I'll be back in a moment." Mia gets up and goes to her luggage. "I have a special gown I want to wear for our honeymoon." Mia turns and enters the separate room with the claw foot bathtub.

Legare takes his fresh clothes from the luggage and departs for the common bath area down the hall. In a few moments, he returns to the room and awaits Mia.

As Mia emerges from the dressing room, Legare takes her hand. "Mia, I love you. Our life together will now begin."

Legare gently takes her hand, looking down into

her face. They embrace and touch their lips together, melting their souls together in their first real kiss as a married couple.

"You are mine, Legare, and I am yours." Mia snuggles closer to him than she has ever been.

"Forever, Mia." Legare inhales the soft, sweet scent of her hair. "We have a lifetime before us. This moment is just the first of many beautiful memories we will make together."

Throughout the night, Mia and Legare, share themselves in the dreamy state of their wedding night until the sunlight beckons them to rise. They awaken to an Augusta that has already begun its day. From the hotel window, Legare sees the four-hundred-ton steamer *Talamicco* at the docks on the Savannah River. "Mia, let's take that steamer rather than the train to Savannah. The trips on the river are very scenic, even this time of year. We probably can eat on the steamer as well."

Chapter Twelve
Savannah Bound

They walk down to the dock and seek out the captain, Captain C. R. Powell. "Sir, my wife and I would like to purchase a ticket to Savannah if you have room on board."

"Why sure, there are ten cabins for guests. Most of them are empty this time of year. Take cabin number five. The keys should be in the door. It has a private bath and is the largest cabin on the steamer. We make a couple of stops and should arrive in Savannah about this time tomorrow. We serve hot meals and have plenty of duck right now."

Legare gazes at Mia who nods. "That sounds fine, sir. When do we board?"

"The Petersburg boats are docking and we have several hundred more bales of cotton to load, so if you want to come back in about an hour we'll be ready to depart. I'll give three long blasts of the horn to let you know the steamer will be leaving in fifteen minutes."

"Thank you, sir."

"Leave your luggage with me for now. You can put it in the cabin when you board."

Legare hands over the luggage to the Captain. "Thanks again, sir."

After the newlyweds leave their belongings on the steamer, they walk along the riverfront. "See those long, open-face boats, Mia? They are the Petersburg boats. From what I understand, the Petersburg boats transport the cotton from farther up the river. The Savannah River is navigable for shallow draft and barge traffic from its mouth to Augusta but ocean vessels can only travel five miles above Savannah,"

"I've heard of the Petersburg boats, but never even seen a drawing of one."

"It's kind of slow on the river and the wharf right now, being it's winter. Even the cotton warehouses are not weighing much cotton. There go the three long horn blast. We best go ahead and board."

He takes her hand and they walk onto the gangplank. The side rails are solid, but the gangplank shakes a little as they walk to the main deck. They take their baggage and locate cabin five.

"Watch your step, Mia. There's a high ledge under the door. Helps keep the rain water on the deck from entering the cabin." She steps into the cabin and is surprised at the small fixtures and furniture.

"This almost looks like a doll house! It's so cute and quaint and really pretty." She walks over to the porthole and peers to the other side of the river. She decides to have a seat at the small table in the cabin. When she sits down, she attempts to move the table a bit and finds that it is bolted to the floor. "Why is the table bolted to the floor, Legare?"

"Everything on board a ship is secured in case of a storm." He takes her hand. "Come over here. Try to open this drawer." She rises, walks to Legare, places her hand on the drawer handle and pulls, but to no avail.

"Lift up the drawer handle and then pull."

Mia follows his instructions. The drawer opens easily. "Pretty good trick! Come over here and sit with me a minute, Legare. I need to talk to you." She takes his hand and they sit on the side of the small bed. "Where are we going to live?"

"My mother and father have a beautiful home on the river in Savannah. I thought we could live there."

"Think about it, Legare. We are in a pickle. There's no telling what is going on in Stone Mountain and Madison. Might even be a lynch mob looking for both of us. Now I love your mother and father, but we have just eloped. You're taking me to live in your parents' river house without their permission. I don't think that is a wise move. I feel that we would be insulting your family if we did that. Moving there without their permission would not make them at all happy. Think about it for a moment. I have all my money with me. We need to find our own place to live."

Legare is silent for a few seconds. "You're absolutely right, Mia. We will stay at the Pulaski Hotel, if you like it, in Savannah until we rent our own place. I have money in the bank in Savannah from my working with Uncle Richard every summer. He always told me to save my money for a rainy day. So that's what we will do." Legare pulls Mia close, feeling her warm body against his as he hugs her tightly and kisses her lips.

"I love you, Legare, but we best get breakfast before we have dessert! I'm starving."

Still holding Mia, Legare whispers in her ear. "I love you, too, Mia. Let's go to the cafe across the street from the docks. It looks like a popular place to eat."

Just as Legare is paying for the breakfast, Mia turns her head toward the wharf. "Is that the steamer's signal?"

"Yep, that's our fifteen minutes call to board."

Standing on the main deck of the steamer, Mia and Legare watch the shore man release the large ropes from the cleats on the pier. The deck hands draw in the heavy rope and stow it in a designated area. The paddle wheel slowly begins to turn, moving the giant ship from the pier as if she were a baby.

"This is going to be a beautiful day, Mia. We should see some grand sights on the river."

The steamer picks up speed as she slowly moves away from the congested area of the docks. Most of the crew is engaged in the routine duties of maintaining the equipment and cargo. Standing at the rear of the steamer, Mia and Legare watch the paddle wheel push the boat farther from Augusta until Augusta disappears into the mist almost as if by magic. Now, only a few Petersburg boats and small boats with fishermen can be seen on the river.

Yawning and taking a deep breath, Mia whispers, "I need to take a nap. Let's go to the cabin." Holding hands, they stride to their cabin as the November sun begins to break through the mist. Once inside the cabin, Legare hears the inarticulate sound of the machinery operating the paddle wheels. The sound flows like a sleepy hum throughout the cabin. Legare places his hand near the radiator, "This radiator sure makes a comfortable cabin."

Mia acknowledges Legare with a sweet smile as she closes the curtain over the porthole. Then they undress and pull the covers back from the bed. Mia eases in between the warm wool covers. Legare lies next to Mia and they draw as close as possible to one-another, embrace and kiss. Exhausted and in love, they fall asleep in each other arms.

A loud blast from the steamer's horn five hours later instantaneously awakens them. They are in the same embrace as they were upon falling into their idyllic sleep. They dare not move, fearing that they'll lose their ideal and romantic embrace. Mia and Legare spontaneously enter into an amorous and blissful state, repeating the rapture of the honeymoon and then fall back into a peaceful slumber. Later a strong wave from a passing ship startles and awakens them again. Legare sits up and pulls back the curtains. The bright sun causes him to shield his eyes for a moment.

Mia kisses Legare's hand. "I'm hungry again. It must almost be dinner time."

Departing the room for dinner, Mia and Legare seek out a deck hand.

"Where can we find some food?"

"Down those stairs over there. That will take you to the captain's mess. Just let the cook know what you would like for dinner. I know we have some fresh roast duck and roast vegetables. The cook makes a great wine sauce to go with the duck for our guests."

"That's what Captain Powell said to us earlier. Want to try the duck, Mia?"

"I'm so hungry I could eat the feathers and the quack right now! Thanks for the recommendation. We are going to try the duck—quack and all!" The deck hand laughs and nods his head.

Mia and Legare locate the Captain's mess. Inside there are several waiters. One of them approaches. "I assume you're the passengers in cabin five?"

"Yes, we are," replies Legare. "How did you know?"

"You're the only passengers on board today! You can sit anywhere you like, but I recommend the table by the window."

Taking their seats, Legare informs the waiter, "Thank you. We already know what we would like for dinner. The roast vegetables and the roast duck cooked in the wine sauce everyone has been telling us about. Also, two glasses of red wine with the entree, please."

After dinner, Mia and Legare stroll the main deck observing the ship's cargo. They eventually make their way to the helm of the boat. Captain Powell is steering the steamer as she gently runs the Savannah River.

"Are the two of you going any place else after you get to Savannah?" asks Captain Powell.

"No, sir, that is our final destination," replies Legare. "My Uncle Richard owns the Magnolia Plantation in Savannah. I believe your steamer has carried his cargo before."

"Oh sure, I know Richard. I've hauled cotton and rice for him on many a trip. He's a really nice man."

"Thank you, sir," replies Legare.

"The duck you recommended for dinner was splendid. I would like to have the recipe for the wine sauce before we leave the ship, if that's possible," asks Mia.

"It's really a very simple wine sauce. I'll write the recipe down for you and leave it on your door when my relief for the wheel arrives."

"Thanks, Captain Powell," replies Mia.

Legare adds, "We are going to check out the bow. I'm sure we will see you again."

Finding a comfortable seat at the bow of the boat, Mia and Legare get a first-hand look at Mother Nature on the river. Turtles are sunning on the logs along the river. Frightened by the steamer, alligators plunge into the water and disappear only to surface in a moment to study the intruder. Kingfisher birds fly by, plucking small fish and salamanders from the water. A bald eagle departs his high perch and dives into the water. Grasping a large fish in his talons, he flaps his wings gracefully to gain speed and altitude. Soon the majestic bird is over the tree line, heading for his nesting site.

The river banks are scattered with woolly-headed darkies with their cane poles, fishing for the large river cats. Their clothing is constructed from patches of every color of cloth available to them. The women sit, smiling and playing with the children in their sack-like apparel. The women adorn themselves with beads and dress their heads with handkerchiefs.

As the sun begins to set and the evening gets cooler, Mia and Legare return to the cabin. On the door is the recipe for the wine sauce.

"This recipe is simple. I can make this for you whenever you want, and we can recall our first boat ride as husband and wife." Once inside the cabin, Mia and Legare lie facing each other on the bed. "What are we going to do in Savannah to make a living, Mr. Hill?"

"I have worked for Uncle Richard during the past two summers overseeing the darkies and managing three hundred acres of cotton. I hope when we see Uncle Richard and Aunt Josephine, he'll still allow me to work on the plantation. If he doesn't, I'll get employment at either a bank or as a clerk in one of the courts. I want to study law but that might have to wait until the war is over. Don't you worry, I'm not concerned about employment." Leaning closer to Mia, he kisses her gently on the forehead. "I know I have skills that can be useful to someone."

"I can work, too, teach school maybe, Legare. I have some gold with me from home. We'll be able to make it, I'm sure. Just might take a while. So long as we are together, we will be all right. We just need to get to Savannah and settle down."

"We'll be there tomorrow and start our new life together. Of course, we may not live in splendor for a while."

Mia interrupts. "I've never lived in splendor. You know what a modest home I come from, so don't think I'm in a rush, honey. A hayloft with you is just fine for me. The Augusta

Hotel was like a palace, but my splendor is being with you."

"What makes you happy, makes me happy, too." Holding each other tenderly, they drift into a slumber until the steamer's horn awakens the two lovers once again. "Look! It's dark already! We must have slept for a couple of hours. Let's freshen up and get some supper. I could really eat a steak! How about you, Mia?"

"Steak and wine. I wonder if they have any muscadine wine."

After dinner Mia and Legare meander around the main deck in the fresh river air. She pulls her shawl tightly around her shoulders and arms and Legare is wearing a light jacket. They find the seat at the bow of the boat. Peering into the night sky, as the quarter moon rises over the horizon, they talk about the wonder of the universe. "What do you think is really out there?" asks Mia.

"That's hard for us to know. I'd like to meet the Creator and have at least a thirty-minute conversation with Him to find out."

"That would be a most interesting conversation all right!" Mia laughs and shrugs. "What would be your first question?"

Studying the star silently for a moment, Legare takes Mia's hand. "I would ask Him where He came from."

"Mighty good question. And your second question?"

"Depends on how he answered the first one!" Legare wrinkles his forehead.

"Mighty good answer." Mia kisses Legare sweetly on the cheek and whispers in his ear, "It is getting mighty chilly sitting on the deck. So my next question is, are you ready to go to bed?"

"You bet." The newlyweds enter their cabin and light a candle. Soon the warm glow fills the room. They prepare for another night filled with the bliss of love.

The next day, following their mid-morning breakfast, they stand on the main deck. "Look, Mia, the Savannah docks are in sight."

Shading her eyes with her hand, Mia looks in the direction the boat is heading. "Yes, I can see the outline of the buildings. How far is your father's river house from the docks?"

"Only a mile or so. We'll take a carriage to Antonio's for dinner and then to the Pulaski Hotel."

The stores and warehouses on the riverfront grow larger. The tall masts of large sailing ships and paddle wheels of steamers come into view as they approach the docks.

"I never knew this many ships could be in one place. Look at all of this cotton! What's in those large sacks over there?" asks Mia.

"Those are sacks of rice. It would be hard to calculate how much cotton and rice are in the warehouses and aboard the ships. There's no way to export the cotton and rice from here anymore. The Yankees have all of our water routes in and out of Savannah blocked. The last time my father and I saw Uncle Richard, he told us that he has been transporting rice by train to other Southern cities, but the cotton stays here."

Captain Powell steers the steamer cautiously towards the dock. At the appropriate moment, the crew throws the large tie, down ropes to men on the dock. Slowly the steamer draws next to the dock and the paddle wheel stops. The crew lowers the gangplank to the awaiting hands. The dockhands secure the gangplank and the captain gives the go-ahead for disembarking. After thanking the captain for providing them passage to Savannah, Mia and Legare disembark.

Taking her by her hand, Legare leads her down the gangplank onto the dock. She is amazed at the number of ships on one side and the large cotton and rice warehouses on the other side of the riverfront. It is a busy place. Men are moving the large bales of cotton to the warehouses for sorting and grading.

Chapter Thirteen
In Search of a Home

Strolling up the steps to Bay Street, Mia observes the granite steps, "This rock looks like Stone Mountain granite." She stops, kneels and runs her hands over the granite steps. "Feel, Legare, what do you think?"

Legare kneels next to Mia and feels the stone. "I think you could be right. The mica pattern is the same. We can always come here and visit when we miss the mountain. Look, there's a carriage." Picking up their baggage, they rush up the steps. They wave at the driver to get his attention. The horse and carriage stop. Legare helps her climb aboard and asks, "We haven't eaten since breakfast. How about some dinner?"

"I'm hungry all right!"

"Wehr fuh go suh?" ["Where to go sir?"] asks the carriage driver.

"Let's go to the Pirates' House. You'll like this place, Mia. My family eats there when they are in town."

Puzzled by the carriage driver's dialect, Mia asks, "What language did the carriage driver speak?"

"Oh, that's the Gullah dialect. You'll catch on to it fast."

"I thought you said we were going to Antonio's."

"We are. Antonio is the owner of the Pirates' House." Legare and Mia sit close to one another, holding hands and exchanging an occasional kiss with murmurs of a tender "I love you."

All the while, Mia studies the landscape. "What are all those gray, stringy plants hanging from those willow leaf and oak trees?"

"It's Spanish moss. Almost like mistletoe, but it's not a parasite and isn't attached to the tree. Spanish moss has air roots that pick up moisture from the air. The city of Savannah's an old place. Look at the houses. Most of them are brick or frame structures."

"We studied Savannah in Seminary. I know Savannah is larger than Atlanta and its streets are laid out nice and square. Atlanta's streets are more like cow paths. Look at the large yards and beautiful ornamental shrubbery and at this time of the year."

They pass several parks on their way to dinner. "These city parks are absolutely gorgeous. Look at the beautiful trees and statues and the mansions surrounding the squares."

"One day soon, we'll tour all of the parks in town."

"Yah de Pirates House Mistuh." [Here is the Pirate's House, Mister.] Legare reaches into his pocket and hands the driver ten cents.

"If you don't mind waiting until we finish dinner, I would like to ride down to the shore before going to the Pulaski Hotel. Of course I'll pay you for your wait as well."

"Happy fur suh." [Happy to, sir.]

Legare assists Mia from the carriage. He places his arm around her waist and they go into the Pirates' House.

Antonio recognizes his old friend as they enter. "Hello, Legare." Shaking hands, Antonio continues, "Glad to see you. And who might this beautiful young lady be?"

"Antonio, you have the pleasure of being the first person I know to meet my wife, Mia."

Smiling, Antonio takes Mia's hand and kisses it. "My dear lady, it is a great pleasure to meet you and have you dine at my establishment. You have married a wonderful young man." Looking to Legare, he inquires, "What do you mean I am the first person you have introduced your lovely wife to?"

"We eloped two days ago."

Clasping his hand and with a broad smile, Antonio looks at the newlyweds and declare, "Love is mighty powerful. Only those truly in love know how deep and boundless it can be. May your life forever be wonderful! I am honored to be the first to meet your wife. You're always welcome here."

Legare takes Mia's hand. She smiles and holds back her tears of appreciation as she says, "Thank you, Antonio." Sensing her sincerity, Antonio gives the couple a good Italian hug. "Dinner is on me today! Follow me to my most special table." Seating the newlyweds, Antonio lights the candle in the center of the table. "I'll order for both of you."

"Thank you again, Antonio. I did not expect this, but thank you.

"You are very welcome, my friends." Soon Antonio returns with a bottle of white wine. "From my family vineyard in Italy, comes this wine that I share with the two of you." Removing the cork, Antonio pours three glasses and offers a toast. Legare pushes his chair back and stands while holding Mia's hand. "Long life, love forever, healthy children and prosperity, I toast to Legare and Mia." The three glasses click.

"Thank you, Antonio." Mia wipes her tearful, yet happy eyes.

Legare shakes Antonio's hand. "Thank you so much, Antonio. Your toast will always be true for us."

A familiar voice from across the room asks, "Is that you, Legare?" Legare turns and sees a family friend and neighbor, Mrs. Turner, sitting at a nearby table. "Excuse me a minute, Mia, while I speak to Mrs. Turner. She is widowed. She owns the house next to us on the river." Legare excuses himself and heads over to Mrs. Turner's table. He takes her hand, leans over and gives her a tender hug around her neck. "I have a surprise and good news to tell you, Mrs. Turner. First, are you eating alone today?"

"Why, yes I am."

"Then please come over and join us. I want you to meet someone special."

"Well, that's mighty nice of you, darling. I would love to meet that beautiful, young lady sitting with you. Are you sure she won't mind?" "Not at all, Mrs. Turner." Legare assists Mrs. Turner from her seat and escorts her over to their table. "Mrs. Turner, I want you to have the pleasure of meeting my wife, Mia."

"Well, my-oh-my. Darling, it is a real pleasure to meet you." Mrs. Turner looks at Mia, smiles and extends her hand. "I'm Katherine Turner. A good friend of the Hills."

"Thank you, Mrs. Turner. It is a pleasure to meet you as well."

"When did this happy event take place?"

"Just two days ago."

"A big wedding I hope. But Legare, darling, I'm disappointed that I didn't receive an invitation."

"Don't feel badly. There were only four invitations. One to Mia. One to me. One to Pastor Huntington, in Augusta and one to his secretary, our witness. We eloped!"

Being caught completely by surprise, Mrs. Turner places her hand on her chest, "Well! My-oh-my, darling, you could not have picked a more beautiful bride. But why did you elope?"

"To make a long story short, it was love at first sight and to prevent an unfortunate event from occurring, we decided to elope."

"What unfortunate event could cause you to do such a thing?"

"Mia's upcoming marriage to another man."

Mrs. Turner laughs and hugs Mia. "Well, well, my dears . . I'll wager that put the tongues to wagging."

Mia blushes, but can't help smiling at the affable woman. "We didn't stay around long enough to find out, but I'm sure it did."

"When did you arrive in Savannah?"

"About an hour or so ago."

"And are you going to stay at your father's house?"

"Oh, no. We are staying in the Pulaski Hotel until we find our own place."

"Darling, Legare, you must have really stirred the embers when you ran away."

"Probably so, Mrs. Turner," responds Legare.

"To say the least," says Mia with a chuckle.

"What does your family do, Mia, darling? Oh, and where

are you from?"

"My folks have around three hundred acres of farmland in Stone Mountain, raising cotton, corn, hogs, and a few dairy cows. I have a twin brother, Norman, who is enrolled at the Georgia Military Institute in Marietta."

"Have you been to Savannah before, Mia, darling?"

"No, Ma'am. This is the farthest I've ever been from Stone Mountain."

"Are you glad you ran away to get married?"

"I could not be happier if I had the wedding equal to that of the Queen of England. I love Legare. A wedding would have been nice with our families and friends there. Having the blessing of our families is important, but . . I hope . . I know that will come later. The circumstances just did not permit that to happen."

"Is there some kind of a family scrap going on, darling?"

"No, Ma'am. My folks had their heart set on me marrying our neighbor, but I never had my heart set on marrying him. The first time I saw Legare, I knew he was the man I was to love forever."

"I like you, Mia, darling. You don't put on any airs! You are a very honest person and that look in your eyes when you glance at Legare lets me know you really love him."

Mia smiles and blushes at the same time. "Thank you, Mrs. Turner."

Hesitating for a moment, Mrs. Turner continues, "Not going to move in your father's place, right?" Mia and Legare nod in agreement. "Truly an act of good judgment and respect. I have known you all of your life, Legare. I am concerned about this war. My boys, 'Cannon Ball' Connon and Christopher Richard, are in the Union Navy."

"What about Stephen Charles? Is he staying in Savannah to practice medicine?"

"No, Stephen Charles is a medical doctor in Nassau now. None of us is sure what's going to happen to Savannah, being it's such an important port. Mia, my husband was a very successful cotton broker. He built us a place in Nassau several years ago and I have decided to move there. In fact, my trunks are on the ship already."

"When do you expect to leave for Nassau?" asks Mia.

"Probably in a day or two. The captain suggested that I stay at the Pulaski Hotel so as not to delay the ship's departure." Taking Legare and Mia's hands, she winks conspiratorially. "So here is my wedding present for both of you. I have put my river house up for sale, furniture and all. Mia the same builder constructed your in-laws' house and my house."

Mia smiles and looks at Mrs. Turner. "How interesting."

"Well, dear Mia, they are nearly the same style and plan. My banker has all of the papers at his office to handle the transfer." Mia and Legare look at each other as if to ask "What is Mrs. Turner talking about?" Reaching into her purse, Mrs. Turner pulls out her set of keys.

"Here are keys to the house. Take Mia over there and spend the night. I'll go by and tell my banker you're staying there. A carriage will pick you up at ten o'clock tomorrow morning and take you to the bank. If both of you like the house, it's yours for half of what I'm asking. The other half is your wedding gift."

Totally caught by surprise, Legare squeezes Mrs. Turner's hand. "Mrs. Turner, I can't believe you're making us such a wonderful offer as our wedding gift."

Mia smiles and softly says, "You are very kind, Mrs. Turner, and most generous. This is too good to be true. We will pay you full price for your house if we like it, even if I must work to earn more money."

"A young lady who is not afraid of work. Unusual. I like that. Now both of you listen. It's my house and I can sell it to whomever I want and for whatever price I decide. I won't have to worry about the house that I love. No more discussion. Simply say 'Thank you.'"

Mia becomes teary eyed. "Thank you, Mrs. Turner. This wedding present means more to both of us than you'll ever know. We will be happy to spend our first night together in Savannah at your house."

"Now if you don't like it, Mia, darling, don't let Legare talk you into buying it. All right?"

"Legare and I have pretty much agreed on everything so far. We tend to think alike."

"Good, keep it that way! Just one more matter. While I am alive, you cannot rent the house. If you decide to sell, I must have first refusal to buy it back at the same price plus any major expenses. Deal?"

"Deal," reply Legare and Mia. "Now let's eat!"

The waiter comes from the kitchen with Antonio's famous Italian salad and homemade bread. Another waiter serves a huge platter of beefsteak and potatoes. "This is Mother's recipe for the salad and bread. I leave you to eat and enjoy. Let this be your wedding feast from Antonio."

"We cannot thank you enough for dinner. This truly was our wedding feast and we shall forever remember your friendship and thoughtfulness." Mia concurs. "Thank you, Antonio. You and Mrs. Turner have made this day even more special for us." Antonio and Mrs. Turner walk to the carriage with Legare and Mia.

As the carriage drives away, Antonio waves and shouts, "Bon Voyage!" and Mrs. Turner throws a kiss. Riding out of town, the carriage driver takes the direct road to the beach.

They stop at a large sand dune. Legare holds Mia's arm. "Let's take off our shoes so we can walk on the beach."

They remove their shoes and Legare assists Mia from the carriage. There is somewhat of a chilly breeze as they climb to the top of the sand dune. Mia listens to the murmur of the rippling waves crowned with their whitecaps rushing on each other. The silver sand sparkles against the bright afternoon sun. The happy couple holds hands and stares out at the horizon. As the gentle wind blows and partially releases the ribbon from Mia's hair, it begins to ebb and flow with the changing wind.

"I cannot get over Mrs. Turner, selling us her house."

"There's no doubt that she thinks a lot of you and your family, Legare. It's as if she considers you as part of her own family."

"You're probably right. She's known me from birth

and has always admired my father. I think she secretly loves him! Look over there, Mia. That tall structure is the lighthouse on Tybee Island. It shows ships where the mouth of the Savannah River is located."

Holding hands, they stroll to the ocean's edge. Mia lifts her skirts just in time. A cold wave rushes in and wets their warm feet. They bounce up attempting to avoid the cold seawater. Legare squeezes her hand. "Mighty cold." Sea gulls fly overhead begging for food.

Watching the gulls, Mia notices that some are motionless in the air, moving neither forward nor sideways. "Look, Legare." They watch the gulls for a moment before movement in the water catches their attention.

Mullet dash along in the shallow water. Occasionally, one springs into the air as another fish follows in pursuit. Fiddler crabs dart in and out of their boroughs. Mia stops on several occasions to pick up various seashells. She places the prettiest ones in her jacket pocket. Returning to the carriage, Legare gives the driver directions and the carriage pulls away from the beach.

A few moments later, Legare taps the driver on the shoulder. "Stop here, driver. Mia we must get groceries for the house. I almost forgot we'd need food." They step down from the carriage and enter the grocery store. He finds the clerk. "Do you have a chicken you can kill and dress?"

"Yes, sir. How many do you want?" asks the clerk.

"Just one," replies Legare.

Mia is fascinated with the grocery store. Stone Mountain has market days, but not a store with fresh provisions like this one. The General Store has hardware and household items, but not fresh food.

They gather various food items including bacon, eggs, bread, grits, fresh greens, wine and butter along with the fresh chicken. After paying for the goods, Mia and Legare are again on their way to the river house.

"There's the river house, straight ahead on the right! Do you see it?" Holding onto Legare, Mia stands up in the moving carriage.

Smiling and full of excitement, she says, "Yes, I see the house. It's beautiful! I had no idea how nice this would be!"

Mia and Legare remain standing as the horse and carriage stops in front of Mrs. Turner's river house. He jumps from the carriage out stretching his arm to his new wife. She hesitates for a moment while the jumps into Legare's waiting embrace, admires the beautiful house and the surrounding gardens, which will be their first home. The carriage driver, having already tied the horse to the hitching post, removes the groceries and luggage from the carriage.

"Just place the groceries and baggage on the steps." Legare settles his debt with the driver. Soon the carriage is out of sight and the only sound is the mild cool breeze migrating through the trees surrounding the house. "Mia, you wait here while I open the door. I must carry you over the threshold and into our new life." They hug and kiss lingeringly.

Legare climbs the stairs to the front door. Searching his pocket, he finds the key and anxiously slips it into the lock. He turns the key several times but the latch does not release. As his heart races, he realizes that he is trying the key to the back door instead of the key to the front door. He hastily places the second key into the lock and it releases. Legare turns the doorknob opening the door and leaves it slightly ajar while he returns to his wife. "Are you ready?"

Mia kisses Legare and places one arm around his neck.

He bends over, placing one hand behind her knees and the other arm to support her back. As he lifts Mia to the level of his chest, she chuckles and gives him a sweet kiss on the cheek. When they reach the door, he pushes it open with his foot and steps across the threshold. He carries her to the bedroom and gently lays her on the bed. He lies next to Mia and they embrace passionately as the joy of the moment rushes over them. Their warmth is eventually compromised by the cooling temperatures in the house.

"Go ahead and put up the groceries while I get the fires started." The fireplaces and stoves had been cleaned and made ready. Legare lights the fire in the parlor and the stoves in the bedroom and the bathtub room. Lastly,

Legare goes out to a storeroom on the side of the house where the water heater is located. Here he lights the charcoal underneath the huge boiler sitting high off the ground. Gravity sends hot water to the bathtub room and kitchen. Mrs. Turner's room has an English tub similar to the one at the Augusta Hotel.

Returning to the kitchen, Legare finds the chill in the river house is subsiding. "Come, Mia, let me show you our new home." Taking her by the hand, he begins the tour. "Of course, this is the kitchen."

Mia studies the kitchen layout. "Very similar to my home with the high hearth and fireplace."

"Outside there's a cookhouse, carriage house and two cabins for the servants."

Entering the parlor, Mia observes the beautiful Oriental rug on the floor and the rosewood table with eight beautiful chairs. She rubs her hand across the table and then observes, "Look, Legare, how the drapery blends with the Oriental rug, wing back chairs and sofa."

"It is very elegant, Mia."

She then looks at the chandelier hanging above the dining room table and walks over to one of the tables next to the sofa and chairs. She picks up a candleholder. "That four-branch oil chandelier matches these beautiful crystal candleholders." She feels the cuts in the crystal and then gently returns it to the table. She then turns her attention to the wallpaper. She runs her hand over the scene of well-dressed, polite society riding through the woods in beautiful carriages. Legare is still silent as Mia continues to take in the luxurious decor of the house. With Legare by her side and holding her hand, she silently studies a large oil painting of a Savannah Plantation hanging over the rosewood sideboard. Sconces hang from the wall with beautiful figurines resting on their pedestals.

"Let's go upstairs, Mia. I think you will find the view beautiful from the cupola." Still holding hands, they climb the stairs to the second bedroom. "This is one of the guest rooms. It also has a bath."

"A high post bed, Legare. I've always admired

how pretty they are. This one is perfect for this room." Resting at the foot of the bed is a large steamer trunk. "Look, Legare, a slipper chair. I have my grandmother's in my bedroom in Stone Mountain. She releases his hand and gently sits in the slipper chair. "Sits just like my grandmother's. You sit in the armchair and let me know how you like it." Legare sits in it and leans over the inlaid table separating them.

"This chair is as comfortable as you are beautiful, Mia."

She gets up, crosses to Legare, sits in his lap and kisses him. "I love you, Legare. You make my life beautiful."

They tour the remaining two bedrooms. Mia stands in the last guest bedroom for a moment at the edge of the ornate Oriental rug, smiles back at Legare and takes a step. The plush carpet cushions her steps as she strides to the trestle table. She rubs her hand across the gleaming mahogany surface, noticing her reflection in the lustrous finish.

"Now, Mia, for one of my favorite spots. The cupola."

"I heard you say that earlier. I'm not sure what that is."

"The cupola. The little house on top. Follow me." They climb the narrow staircase to a trap door. Lifting the trap door, Legare takes hold of the handrail in the cupola. He reaches for Mia's hand as she climbs onto the platform to join him. Standing in the cupola, she is amazed at the view across the river.

"It's beautiful up here. You can see the ocean, the river, and some of the city, the forest and even the universe."

"Over in that direction is Fort Pulaski."

"I've studied about General Pulaski."

"Look out toward the river. We have a small dock to fish from. There's a rowboat that we take out in the summertime, but it's too cold to get on the river now."

Mia looks into her husband's eyes and smiles. "We're already in a boat! Or maybe in a pickled boat, but as long as I am in the boat with you, I really don't care about the season." She kisses Legare, and he draws her close and tight. She embraces him passionately. With her arms still around him, Mia peers over his shoulder. "The sunsets and sunrises must be beautiful from up here."

"There are some mighty striking ones, especially in the early spring and fall. We'll come back up here and check out the view at sunset." Now standing next to each other, he stares out across the river, suddenly thinking of his family back home. "Like my father's property next door, this property is about three acres on the river. Over there's the barn for the carriages and horses. Father's horses are kept at Uncle Richard's. Jesse and Al are the darkies that care for our horses, and Tot is our cook, but they stay at Uncle Richard's as well. We bring the horses and darkies over here when we're in town."

Descending the stairs from the cupola, Legare asks, "Well, what do you think, Mia?"

"Mrs. Turner has to be an angel. Who could not love this place? To me, this house is a palace. I promise I'll take good care of it."

"You just take care of me. Let the servants take care of the rest!"

Mia smiles. "I have nearly $325 in gold remaining. I wonder how much Mrs. Turner is going to ask us to pay."

"Don't really know, but I think I have enough in the Bank in Savannah to pay her if it's not over $2,900 Right now, let's get a bite to eat and then go back to the cupola and watch our first sunset together in our magnificent new home."

"Let's have cornbread, chicken, greens, rice and tea for supper."

"Great, I'll get the fire going in the wood stove and high hearth kitchen fireplace."

Mia removes the whole chicken and cuts it into sections. "Legare, you like your chicken battered, or roasted over the open fire?"

"Let's cook the chicken over the open fire. I saw the skewers on the high hearth over the kitchen fireplace." Legare grabs the skewers and hands them to her.

"You skewer the chicken and start cooking it and I'll prepare the rest." He places the skewered chicken on the rack over the hot coals in the kitchen fireplace and watches the process of the chicken roasting. He rotates each skewer occasionally to ensure the chicken is cooked thoroughly. Soon the house is alive with the aroma of fresh-cooked food. They place their supper on the table and gaze lovingly at each other.

"This is our first official home-cooked meal together in our new home, Mia, I'll remember this moment and how it came about."

Taking her hand, he prays, "Thank you, God, for protecting and delivering us together. Always be assured that the love Mia and I share is enduring and everlasting . . and by all means, thank you for giving Mrs. Turner a heart of kindness, love and generosity. Protect her and grant her a long and happy life. Bless our families and may we be joined again someday soon. Please bless and protect our soldiers. Amen."

With misty tears in her eyes, she squeezes Legare's hand and hugs him tightly. "I love you more than you'll ever know. You are my heart and soul."

Legare draws Mia around to his lap and kisses her sweetly.

She snuggles against her husband's chest for a moment before returning to her own chair. "You are my heart and soul too, Mia. We are going to be very happy together."

After supper, Mia clears the table. "Legare, I'll clean the dishes if you get the heater going in the tub and light the fireplace in the bedroom."

"I'll do that. Are you sure you don't need help with those dishes?"

"No, I don't mind at all." She busies herself scrubbing the dishes and hums to herself. She can't remember ever being this happy.

Returning from the bedroom, Legare watches her for a moment. "Mrs. Turner is right. She left everything. All of the towels, soap, washcloths and robes are in the bathtub room. All of the sheets, blankets and pillowcases are in the bedroom chest of drawers. The house is completely furnished."

"I'm just about finished with the dishes. Is the water in

the tub hot?"

"It's beginning to warm up. I think we have time to see the sunset."

Mia folds the dishcloth and turns. Legare takes her hand as they climb the stairs to the cupola. They walk to the side which faces the river. Although the sun is not setting directly along the river, the red sky reflects in the rippling waters. The sky darkens and the beauty of the full moon averts total darkness. The moonbeams turn the ripples of the dark river into a sparkling mirror. Occasionally, a distant splash is seen in the river as a fish attempts to escape a pursuer. A cool November breeze carries the sound of an owl declaring his territory, completing a beautiful first evening in their new home.

"The bath water should be hot by now, Mia. Let's go down and I'll get more wood for the fireplace while you bathe."

She returns to the warm bathtub room, undresses and steps into the comfortable tub of hot water. Legare finds a hefty mound of coal and decides to burn it rather than wood. As he places the large lump of coal in the parlor fireplace, Mia calls out, "Legare this tub is large enough for the two of us!"

Legare hurries to the bathtub room. He opens the door and leans in. "Are you inviting me to bathe with you or do you just need someone to scrub your back?"

"Why don't you come on in and find out?" responds Mia as she spreads her arms to invite him to join her. He closes the door and then sits on the rounded lip of the tub and begins disrobing. She has a washcloth in her hand and stirs the water. Then she soaps the cloth and begins to wash Legare's back as he slides backwards into the tub. He takes his hands and splashes his face and head.

"Turn around and I'll wash your handsome face and chest for you."

He turns to see Mia's radiant smile that takes over the commands of his emotions. Silently she washes his face, shoulders, chest and arms.

"Turn around, Mia; I need to hold you tight against my body."

With her back to Legare as he places his arms under her breasts and draws her soft derriere tightly against his body.

Legare holds her tenderly and kisses her warm neck. "I love you, Mia."

"And I love you, Legare." They stay motionless, comfortable together as they enjoy these quiet moments. "Let's go to the parlor, Legare. I'll get the blankets and pillows and have a cozy spot ready in just a few minutes."

Slowly they stand together. Mia's wet body drips upon Legare, her breath reaches the lips of her lover. Forcing himself to move, he steps from the bathtub and secures towels and robes for the two of them. "I'll be waiting for you in the parlor or we may never leave this bath."

Grinning broadly while retrieving her towel and robe, Mia taunts Legare. "I'll be in front of the fireplace before you have the blankets and pillows on the floor."

Legare gathers the quilts and pillows from the bed and takes them to the parlor. Then he removes several other quilts from the trunk at the end of the bed and places these along with the other quilts on the floor. Spotting the half full bottle of wine from dinner, he swiftly picks up two glasses and begins pouring wine as Mia enters the parlor. She walks up behind him and places her arms around his waist.

"I won, I beat you to the fireside bed! Plus I have two glasses of wine." He turns and gives her one of the glasses of wine.

She offers a toast. "With you, Legare, I'll always be a winner and my love for you . . I don't know how it can grow to any greater heights than heaven."

"You're already my Goddess." As they sip their wine together, taking off their robes, they lie on the quilts in front of the warm fire and let the heat of the fire dry their hair as they lazily finish the wine.

The next morning, they're watching from the parlor window as the carriage arrives at their door at the appointed time of ten o'clock. They ride to the bank in the carriage sent by Mrs. Turner. Apprehensively Legare looks at his wife and says, "I hope we can afford this house, Mia."

The twenty-minute ride seems like an eternity. The driver stops the horse and carriage in front of the bank and Mia and Legare get out. Taking a deep breath, Mia looks around as if to get a sign from his countenance that everything is going be all right. All that is visible is the clear, November sky and a few birds soaring high above the trees. Other citizens walk by unaware of what the future might hold for Mia and Legare as they enter the bank.

"Come on in, you two!" Legare and Mia turn around and see Mrs. Turner standing in the open bank door. She takes Mia by the hand. "Well, Mia darling, how did you like my little house on the river?"

"To be honest, Mrs. Turner, I am reluctant to tell you."

Looking somewhat bewildered, she leans back and stares. "Darling, what is it you don't like about the house?"

Legare also stares at Mia in amazement.

"Because if I told you how much Legare and I truly fancy your house, you would no doubt double the price."

"Oh, darling, I thought for a moment . . you simply had me scared blue." She turns to Legare. "Legare, darling, I consider myself a good judge of character. Your wife has a confident mind and a quick wit about her. She sets the example of a beautiful, independent, Southern countrywoman! You best hold on to her. I knew from the first time I met her she was a special person. Come on inside and let's close this deal. The captain informed me that the boat leaves for Nassau in about an hour."

They walk into the bank president's office. He rises and extends his hand to Legare. "How are you today, Legare?"

Legare shakes his hand firmly. "Fine, thank you, Mr. Lilly. This is my wife, Mia."

"How do you do, Mrs. Hill? I'm Donald Lilly. It is a pleasure to meet you. Please, let's all take a seat at the conference table. Mrs. Turner directed me to draw the deed on her river house for you. I put Legare's name on the deed. Is that the way you wish to have it?"

"Yes, please." He looks to Mrs. Turner, "I am almost

embarrassed to inquire how much are you asking for your house? Mia and I need to know the price."

"Well, darling Legare, how much money do you have in the bank here?"

"I have about $3,000." He glances at Mia and squeezes her hand.

"And I have about three hundred twenty-five dollars in gold with me, Mrs. Turner."

Smiling, Mrs. Turner takes and holds Mia and Legare's hands. Love is worth much more than gold. Legare, you have always been like a son to me, and I have always loved and admired your mother and father . . and Mia, you would make me a wonderful daughter. You are unassuming, very intelligent, although it is somewhat masked by your accent, and you're very beautiful."

Mia blushes. "Thank you, Mrs. Turner, for the compliment."

"The house is yours for nineteen hundred dollars."

Mia and Legare are unable to suppress their stunned emotions and indisputable gratitude to Mrs. Turner. A huge lump forms in Legare's throat as tears of appreciation flood from Mia's eyes.

"Now, now. I've already signed the necessary papers and Mr. Lilly will transfer the money to my account. The ship is waiting and so is my carriage. I know you two will always be happy. God bless you, both."

Mia and Legare, almost unable to speak, stand and hug Mrs. Turner together. Finally Legare and Mia are able to say their good-byes as they escort Mrs. Turner to her carriage. "Your thankful tears mean more to me than all the words in the dictionary." Boarding the carriage, Mrs. Turner directs the driver to the dock where her journey will begin.

Mia and Legare return to Mr. Lilly's office and finalize the deed. Then Legare has the money transferred from his account to Mrs. Turner's. "Mr. Lilly, I may be in need of employment. I don't know if my Uncle Richard will hire me to work the darkies in the cotton fields as he has in the past."

"Well, as a matter of fact I can use you part-time.

Your family banks with me and I always like to help my clients. I need a teller three days a week since one of my employees takes vacation this time of year. Probably for two months, maybe three. Could you start next week?"

"I'll go ahead and say yes! Cotton field work doesn't start until February. I'll see you on Monday at nine o'clock." Legare stands and shakes the hand of his new boss. "We need to buy two horses. Is there a stable still nearby?"

"Yes, and he has some quality carriage horses. I'll get my carriage driver to take you there."

"Thank you, sir."

After procuring two horses, Mia and Legare ask Mr. Lilly's driver to take them to their new home on the river. They sit very close to one another. Mia is still full of emotion and gratitude for Mrs. Turner. "I still cannot believe that Mrs. Turner sold us her house for nineteen hundred dollars. It is a dream come true. Just think, this will be our sanctuary. We will raise our children and grandchildren there."

Legare smiles at Mia's enthusiasm. "Yes, Mia. We'll grow old together there."

Chapter Fourteen
The Governor's Call to Muster

Legare picks up a newspaper and reads the following:
"Executive Department Nov 9 1861
Milledgeville, Ga. Proclamation
"To the Volunteer Military Companies of the State: The invaders having landed a force upon the soil our sister State of South Carolina near the borders of Georgia, where they now hold position and menace the City of Savannah; and it being thought advisable to increase our force for the defense of the coast, I issue this my Proclamation, giving notice that I'll accept, in addition to the number of volunteers already accepted, the services of the thirty companies which will first tender their services and report to me their readiness to march. These companies will be received for six months, unless sooner discharged. Each Company, to be accepted, must consist of not less than fifty nor more than eighty members, rank and file, unless the statute shall, in the meantime, be changed so as to permit a greater number to compose a company. Each man in each company must be armed with a good country rifle or double-barrel shotgun, or with a good military gun, fit for immediate use. It will also be necessary for each volunteer armed with a country rifle to carry with him his bullet molds, pouch and powder horn or flask; and those armed

with double-barrel shotguns must each take with him a powder horn or flask.

"As our homes are in danger, it is hoped that no citizen of the State having a good gun will hesitate a moment to carry or send it into the service.

"Given under my hand and Seal of the Executive Department the 9th day of November A.D. 1861.

James E. Brown"

Phillip Buford McCurdy mustered in on the sixteenth of November. Phillip is commissioned First **Lieutenant** of militia for the Stone Mountain district.[120] One week after his friend Phillip McCurdy musters, Buster decides to follow the example of his neighbors and proceed to the seat of war. Buster has come to spend this last evening with his dearest friends, Buck and Betty Gail. During supper, Buster seems unsettled and his attitude toward life is much more morose.

After eating, he hands a letter to Buck. "This here gives you power o'er my property, Buck."

Buck opens the letter and reads. "*I hereby entrust all of my worldly property to Buck Jernigan which includes my six slaves, Irene and Harvey and their seven year old daughter, Luci. Also my Negroes, Jacob and Ellen, and their fifteen- year-old son, Mark until my return.*"

Buck passes the letter to Betty Gail, "We expect you to come back home when the war is over . . just like we look for Norman to return home. There's to be no worry on your part. We will care for your place as if it is ours."

Standing sternly and with a serious, yet stoic expression, Buster says, "Look after de place since I ain't here to tend to it myself—an' if I never comes back hit's your'n— leastways, hit's your'n in trust fer Mia. Keep my place till she comes a creepin' home in shame . . fer the one what loved her best. An' tell her . . tell her . . how much I cared fer her, an' dat I never blamed her when she chose another—an' don't be hard on her, fur my sake, don't be hard on her."

Buck's eyes meet Betty Gail's as Buster speaks his confused thoughts. A painful silence follows the reading of Buster's letter and hearing his verbal wishes. Betty Gail wipes her moist eyes with the corner of her apron. Buck clears his throat, acting as if the evening air suddenly affects his voice. Gathering his composure, Buck stretches his hand to Buster and with a warm clasp, seals the unspoken compact.

In truth, Buck is thinking about Mia, about how she has broken his heart. Pain seizes his chest and he can hardly breathe as he recalls her innocent, girlish face. For just a moment, he would give anything to see her, but the shame of her action rushes over him like a tidal wave.

"Good night," says Buster. "I must go to bed. I gonna be a stirrin' by daylight tomorrow mornin'." He strides rapidly outside, toward his farmhouse. Buck and Betty Gail walk out to the porch and stand together for some minutes, gazing at Buster until he disappears into the darkness.

Concerned about Buster's mental state, Betty Gail rises at dawn and hurries down the path to his house. She knocks gently and a servant soon opens the door. "Mornin' Miss Betty Gail. Mars Buster still sleeps."

Betty Gail quietly enters Buster's abode and pauses irresolutely before his sleeping form. Buster's damp locks have fallen back from his broad forehead, revealing a look of peace and dignity. Her heart aches from the thought that she must rouse this dear son of her adoption from his peaceful sleep and send him forth, perhaps to death.

"Wake up, Buster, wake up! The day is here!" Sitting on the bedside, Betty Gail burst into tears. He opens his eyes and takes her hand.

"I am de one who needs to cry, fer I am 'parting my parents, and maybe dis here life. Thank you fer coming to wake me, fer I must depart soon."

"You will always be in our prayers, Buster. May God protect you and send you back to us." Kissing Buster on the cheek, Betty Gail tearfully departs.

Buck and Betty Gail travel to town to see Buster off. A large crowd is assembled at the depot to bid farewell to the departing troops. Mothers, sisters, wives and sweethearts struggle vainly to repress all signs of grief so they can give their heroes a brave send-off. A small band composed of town folks and children from the Academy and the Seminary make the great rock echo with martial strains. At length the music of the fife, flute, and drums play a soft and familiar tune. Suddenly, all is quiet until the long roll of the drum thunders through the hearts of everyone. The women draw their veils more closely over their tear-stained faces.

Buster notices Betty Gail and Buck. He nods solemnly as he joins the other men.

"Fall in!" calls the sergeant. Each soldier takes his assigned spot in the formation. The long gray line blends with the backdrop of the gray mountain in the distance. The roll is called. The sergeant turns and salutes his captain. "All present or accounted for, sir!"

Captain Johnson returns the sergeant's salute and the former takes his place at the head of the column. The parting moment has come. "Right face! Forward, march!" and onto the waiting train, whose smoke seems to be anxious to carry these brave men north.

The little band plays again.

Over the course of the next several days , Buck and Isaac talk about Buster's slaves. Buck tells Isaac, "I have somewhat of a mental battle going on between my conscience and my loyalty to Buster. However, I have decided to take sides with my conscience and help his Negroes go free."

Isaac suggests, "Treat them like you do me and Sally and let them have twenty-five percent from the sales of food, cotton and livestock."

"That's a good idea. If Buster says anything about it, I'll tell him that they work hard and I just let them keep them money instead of keeping it for them." Buck adds, "When you get the chance, Isaac, talk to Harvey about the Underground Railroad. You can be the shepherd."

"I'll tell Harvey that after the cotton is harvested would be a good time to start planning an escape."

While Isaac and Harvey are taking a trip to town, Isaac asks Harvey, "Have you thought any more about running away with Irene and Luci?"

Harvey looks a bit surprised, but continues the conversation. "My imagination of freedom has always been a part of my life."

Isaac replies, "Imagination can lead to knowledge and I have some knowledge to help you escape. I might know someone who knows a conductor in the Underground Railroad.

Harvey pulls the wagon to the side of the road. "Do you 'ave any idea how dangerous trying to run away would be? If'n we got caught we would be chained and whipped, even my little girl.

Isaac replies, "You must conquer your fear in order to carry out any plan. You must not hesitate once you make your decision for me to help you and your family run away."

Harvey asks, "How does you know so much bout the Underground Railroad? Have you helped our people run away before?

Isaac hesitates before answering. "You know, as I know, that many of our kind have disappeared around here and only a few were caught. The ones that were captured went on their own instead of using the Underground Railroad. We are like animals in the same cage and we accept that circumstance when in reality we really want to roam the earth."

Harvey sits thoughtfully for a moment. "Remember when Sue Lee disappeared? She was light-skinned. Mr. Buster bought her when she was fourteen for his housekeeper. Sometimes in de mornings and sometimes in de evening she would 'ome out crying. We's know what he was having her do. One day when Buster was in town, Sue Lee came out and got on a horse. She said a neighbor came by and told her some of de cattle were out on de back side of de farm and she was 'oing to herd 'em back. When Mr. Buster came home he found her missing and asked us where she was. We told him the story and he hurried to the back land. He found her horse tied to a fence post. He threatened to whip us if'n we not tell him who told her about the cattle. We told him and he tied me to a post anyway, hit me many times and fer some reason cut me loose. He check with all of de neighbors and put a reward add in de paper."

"I remember her escaping, but Buck and I never knew of the other or he never would have allowed Buster to court Mia," Isaac sadly replies.

Harvey continues to question Isaac, "Why ain't you and Sally run away from the Jernigan's?"

"We have no relatives any place else. Mr. Buck and Ms. Betty Gail treat us well, pay us well and give us a nice cabin to live in. They taught us to read and write. We are happy here and I know you are not. Mr. Buster treats you more as property than he does as a human. Right?"

"Right," exclaims Harvey with a snap of the reins and a loud whistle.

"He pays us a little, but he keeps the money. Gives it to us if'n we need clothes or shoes.

Silence follows and Isaac can tell Harvey is in deep thought. He hopes Harvey will come to a decision soon.

During breakfast on a cold January morning in 1862, Legare thinks about the day and glances at his wife. He can hardly keep the smile from his face, knowing that every time someone mentions her name he breaks into a broad grin. He's more in love than he ever thought possible. "Mia, the bank is closing at noon for a Board of Directors meeting. Mr. Lilly told me I didn't have to stay after closing, so I think I'll go over to Uncle Richard's and Aunt Josephine's. My visit should be a surprise since they don't know I am, or rather we are in Savannah."

"What are you going to say to them?"

"Probably that I have someone special I want them to meet. I'm not going to let the cat out of the bag regarding our marriage and Mrs. Turner's gift. We can surprise my cousins by divulging those details when I take you over to meet the family."

Mia walks out to the carriage in front of the house with him. He gives her a loving embrace before he boards and heads for the bank.

After a short day of work and a short surprise visit with his family, Legare returns to his new wife and home. "Well, how did your visit go with your family today?"

"Only Uncle was home. So I got to visit and we had dinner together. He wanted to know what I was doing in Savannah."

"And?"

"I just told him I was checking on some business matters for my pa. As I was leaving I told him that I had someone special I wanted him, Aunt Josephine and my cousins to meet. Of course I had taken off my wedding band. He tried to pull more information from me, but I told him that he would just have to wait."

"Then what?"

"He got enough to know that there's a special girl in my life and invited us over for supper tomorrow. He also seemed excited about meeting you. Then he asked me where we're staying."

Mia takes his hand. "How did you answer that question?"

"That also was a surprise."

"So you didn't tell him we eloped?"

"No. I didn't say much else except that he'll be impressed when he meets you tomorrow evening." Legare kisses her and she smiles.

"I'm looking forward to meeting your Savannah family. Did you tell me they have seven children?"

"Yes, but only four will be with us for supper. Jordan and Matthew are in England studying to be mercantile brokers in Europe. Marcelle is there studying medicine."

"Why do you call your cousins, Uncle and Aunt?"

"I guess because they're so much older than I am. I was taught to address them as Aunt and Uncle at an early age. Let me warn you, Aunt Josephine can be curt at times. She's like a big rock in the road. You can't change the position of the rock, so you just have to go around it. Enough about them for now."

"I've been promising to buy us a couple of guns so I bought two pistols today. They're the new Colt revolving type. Got some cartridges so we can practice." Legare pulls out an article that is included with the pistols and holsters. "This article is real interesting. It's the history about Samuel Colt and how he came up with the idea for a revolver."

Legare hands Mia the article. "It's interesting. You might want to read it later."

Mia glances at the article and places it in her pocket. "I'll will. Let's shoot."

"Right now?"

"Yep."

"Have you shot a pistol before, Mia?"

"Why, of course. Simply place a paper wrapped cartridge in each of the six cylinders." Legare watches intensley as Mia continues, "then pull the loading lever each time to ram the ball home. When this is finished place a percussion cap on the cone at the rear of each cylinder like this. Now I am ready pull the hammer back and aim. See that stump over there, Legare?"

"That small one by the barn?"

"That's the one. Watch now." Mia pulls the hammer back and gently squeezes the triger.

Legare is surprised because she is not hesitant in showing her skill with a pistol. He backs away. Mia takes the pistol aims quickly and fires once, twice, three times.

"Hit it three out of three." She lays the pistol on the ground. Smiling she turns to her astonished husband. "It's your turn now, honey."

The next evening, Mia and Legare depart for Uncle Richard's and Aunt Josephine's. The ride is a leisurely twenty minutes. They soon pass a long row of fencing. "This is one corner of Uncle Richard's property. This tract extends about one mile square. He has another larger tract near the river for flooding the rice fields."

Mia looks amazed as she views the grounds, although barren in the winter, she can visualize the tall corn and the cotton growing as far as one can see. "How many slaves does your Uncle Richard have?"

"Not real sure, but probably around a hundred or so."

"This plantation is enormous. Larger than the Johnson's. How many acres are here?"

"Covers some six thousand acres."

"Is Uncle Richard or Aunt Josephine your blood kin?"

"Uncle Richard is a relative on my mother's side of the family. My Aunt Josephine is from England. That's why my cousins are in England studying."

"Is this the only place they have?"

"No, they have a home in Florida as well. Since my childhood, we've always visited Aunt Josephine and Uncle Richard. For the last two years, I worked on the plantation learning to manage one of the cotton sections. Uncle Richard paid me good wages."

"So what are your other cousins like?"

"Let's see." Legare grins at her. "There are seven children: Trina-Marie, Claire, Ian, Jordan, Matthew, Marcelle and Keaton. Ian is closest to my age and Uncle Richard used to take us hunting and fishing when all of our work was completed. During the first summer, Uncle Richard taught me the techniques of the daily business of planting and cultivating, grading, and ginning cotton."

"Did Ian help you?"

"No, Uncle Richard put him to work with the darkies so he could learn about rice cultivation." He points at a stately mansion. "There's the big house." They turn onto a lengthy dirt trail. A wooden, split-rail fencing lines both sides of the trail. She sees a scattering of cattle on one side and the open winter fields to the other.

"What a beautiful house."

"It is a three-story Savannah type. See it sits around fifteen feet above the ground and has the typical large, wide stairs ascending to the porch."

Although the plants are dormant, Mia visualizes the landscape is full of beautiful azaleas, numerous varieties of roses, camellia, the yellow flowers of Chinese juniper plant, perennial iris flowers in white, blue, violet, and purple.

"Look, honey, there's a witch hazel plant. Ma and

Aunt Sally use the bark, leaves, and twigs once they're distilled in alcohol and water. It makes an all-purpose astringent for use on bruises and swellings." She passes the gardens and feels as if she is a humming bird, observing and studying the details of each flower that is yet to bloom.

"The porch, look how wide it is and you can walk around the whole house just like Ma's and Pa's in Stone Mountain. I'm kinda scared about meeting your family in such a grand place. It's so overpowering."

"Just think of this place as if you were at home. You will be fine," Legare reassures her.

At the instant the carriage pulls in front of the mansion, an elderly stable hand appears and takes the reins of the horse. "'Ello, Mistuh Legare!"

"Hello, Jesse! Mia, this is Jesse. Remember, I told you about him?" Jumping from the carriage, Legare shakes Jesse's hand. "Jesse, this is my wife, Mia, from Stone Mountain."

Jesse removes his hat and nods his head. "Ya'as, Ma'am."

Mia and Legare walk up the wide stairs to the large front door. A shiny, brass plate about two inches long and one inch wide protrudes from the front of the door. Legare twists the plate several times. A bell rings on the other side of the door each time Legare turns the brass plate. "Oh, my! Let me try it!" Legare smiles and removes his fingers and Mia takes her turn and twists the bell plate. Almost at that instant, the knob turns and the door opens. "'Ello, Mistuh Legare!"

"Hello, Jemima!" Legare and Jemima hug each other. He whispers to Jemima, "This is my wife, Mia, we want to surprise Aunt Josephine and Uncle Richard." Jemima giggles and renders a slight bow to Mia.

"Nice to meet you, Jemima."

Uncle Richard sees Legare and Mia at the front door and hurries down the hall to greet them. "Hello, Legare, and who might this young lady be?"

"This is the special person I was telling you about. Are you ready?"

"I certainly am."

"This is my wife, Mia! We eloped to Augusta in November."

"Well, congratulations to both of you! You certainly picked a beautiful young lady to marry. Come on into the back study. I think everyone is there. I just happened to see you in the hall."

Richard leads the way, and Legare places his arm around Mia's waist as they follow him to the back study. Richard enters the mahogany-paneled study where the family is gathered. Some are standing and talking. Two of the younger children are playing a game of checkers, and Josephine is talking to Trina-Marie. Richard steps forward, "Guess who I found at the front door?" Everyone becomes silent and looks as Legare and Mia enter the study.

The eyes of each family member fall on Mia with her small, delicate features. Her sweet, morbidezza appearance is that of a pure Southern beauty and is so perilously fascinating that everyone is clearly in awe of her. The kids jump up and run over to Legare, giving their usual Southern hugs, followed by Josephine. Mia stands quietly by as Josephine approaches. Legare takes Mia's hand. "Everyone listen. I want to introduce someone special to the family. This is my wife, Mia!"

Taking a deep breath and placing her hand on her large bosoms, Josephine appears almost faint. "Well, mercy me! When did all this take place?" The rest of the family is somewhat shocked as well and a silence temporarily comes over the room.

Uncle Richard instructs the butler. "Bring in champagne for everyone. We must toast the newlywed couple."

"Aunt Josephine, Mia and I eloped in November and were married in Augusta."

Recovering from the shock and excitement of the news, the children come over and begin welcoming Mia to the family.

"I'm Trina-Marie."

"I'm Claire."

"I'm Ian."

"I'm Keaton."

Talking all at once, the excited children begin to ask questions.

"Now, now children. I've got to meet the beautiful blushing bride." Josephine strolls over to Mia and extends her hand. "I'm Legare's Aunt Josephine, but really, I'm Legare's cousin by marriage."

"It's nice to meet you." Mia's polite yet deep Southern accent causes Aunt Josephine's eyes to widen in shock.

"It's nice to meet you as well, Mia. Welcome to the family. Excuse me while I go and check on supper."

The servant comes in with the champagne and pours everyone a glass. Uncle Richard begins a toast but notices Josephine is missing. "Hold on a minute and let me find Mother." He goes to the kitchen and finds Josephine talking to one of the cooks. "Josephine, come back to the study, I am giving a toast to Legare and Mia."

"I can't right now, Richard. That girl scared me to death when she opened her mouth with that accent! Just let me get my breath. I can't believe poor Legare would marry someone who talks like that."

"Now, Josephine. She is purely Southern and has a beautiful accent! Pull yourself together and come in the study so we can toast and have supper."

Josephine begrudgingly returns to the study and takes a glass of champagne. Richard raises his glass and everyone else also lifts their glass. "To the health and happiness of Mia and Legare. May their lives be long, full of love and prosperity." Everyone, including Josephine, clicks their glasses against Mia's and Legare's. During supper, Mia displays her simple social graces as she and Legare disclose how they met, fell in love, eloped, and ran into Mrs. Turner. "Then we returned to Augusta and spent Christmas Eve and Christmas on a steamer."

Claire walks over to Mia and Legare. "If there was ever a true love story, this has to be one of the best, certainly the best I ever heard. I think you should write a book."

After dinner, Mia and the children tell stories and laugh genuinely. Trina-Marie leans toward Mia with a warm smile. "I love your accent. Listening to Gullah all the time dilutes our Southern accent. It just sort of begins to blend together. It's great to hear pure Southern again."

Aunt Josephine turns a deaf ear on the children's conversation. At the evening's end, the children and Uncle Richard have accepted Mia, but Aunt Josephine is unable to see how Mia will fit in with her social groups. In her own fashion, she welcomes her nonetheless.

On the way home, Legare tells Mia, "Uncle Richard is allowing us to use Tot, Al, and Jesse."

"Doesn't he need them to work in the fields?"

"He says they are getting too old to do any field work and they'll be coming over in a couple of days."

"What about Tot?"

"According to Uncle Richard, Tot is going to be permanent while Al and Jesse will switch off every three days."

"Well, can we just buy Tot from Uncle Richard?"

"I offered to buy Tot and Al, but Uncle Richard said they are too old to sell and, if the truth is told, I believe he's too fond of them. They've been with him for a long time. If you don't care for them after a few days, we can send them back."

"We'll see."

"So, how do you like my cousins?"

"You have a great family. All of your cousins are wonderful. I just love them, especially Marie. I hope I get to visit with them often. And what a beautiful home! I should say what a beautiful castle. I've only seen drawings of homes so lovely."

"It is spectacular in its own way."

"I bet the flower gardens are spectacular in the spring and summer. I can't wait to see them in full bloom."

Chapter Fifteen
Valentine's Day Surprise

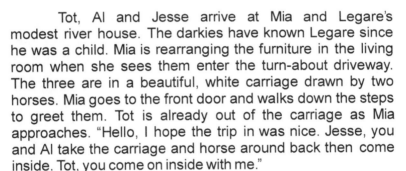

Tot, Al and Jesse arrive at Mia and Legare's modest river house. The darkies have known Legare since he was a child. Mia is rearranging the furniture in the living room when she sees them enter the turn-about driveway. The three are in a beautiful, white carriage drawn by two horses. Mia goes to the front door and walks down the steps to greet them. Tot is already out of the carriage as Mia approaches. "Hello, I hope the trip in was nice. Jesse, you and Al take the carriage and horse around back then come inside. Tot, you come on inside with me."

"Yas'um."

Mia has some hot water boiling for tea. She pours a cup of water for the two of them. "Have a cup of tea with me, Tot, so we can get a little better acquainted." Mia notices that Tot is a little hesitant. "It's all right, Tot, come on and sit down. Have some tea."

Tot pulls the chair from around the table and has a seat across from Mia. She is slender, has a strong mind and has always been a very capable servant. "Have you always lived in Savannah, Tot?"

"No, Ma'am, I's traded from a man in Decatur fuh two cows and a mule when I's fourteen. Had to leave my fambly. That nigh onto thirty-five years. I's part Cherokee Indian and part Negro."

"How about Jesse and Al. Where are they from?"

"Dey two fum Suhwannuh. Jesse 'n' Al wuk fuh Massuh Richud 'n' Congressman Hill." [They both are from Savannah. Jesse and Al both work for Mars Richard and Congressman Hill.]

Al and Jesse enter through the back door directly to the kitchen. They take off their stocking caps and stand in the kitchen silently. "Al, you and Jesse can come and sit down with me and Tot. I just want to find out about you and what you usually do around the river house."

Tot turns and with a diminutive smile, looks at Jesse and Al signaling all is well. With great humility, Al and Jesse walk over to the table and take a seat as they continue to clutch their stocking caps.

"Tot informs me that both of you are from Savannah." Al and Jesse look at each other.

Jesse squeezes his hat in his hands. "Yas'um we two bin bohn on Massuh Richard plantashun. We duh brudduh." [Yas'm both of us born on Mars Richards' plantation. We are brothers.]

"What are your duties at Congressman Hill's house?"

This time Al answers. "We keep de groun' 'n' de flouwuhs. We clean de stall 'n' pretty up de 'n' feed haws' when deh deh yah. Sumtym' we ketch fish fuh Tot fuh cook. We help inside we deh need we. We keep de two wadduh tank full. We keep de fuh on de one tank gwoin for de hot wadduh. We do wha' ebbuh else de tell we fuh do." [We keep the grounds and flowers. We clean the stalls and groom and feed the horses when they are here. Sometimes we catch fish for Tot to cook. We help inside when we are needed. We keep the two water tanks full. We keep the fire on one tank going for the hot water. We do whatever else you tell us to do.]

Mia turns her attention to Jesse. "How many horses are generally kept there?"

"Shree haws 'n' two carriage, Ma'am." [Three horses and two carriages, ma'am.] Mia is satisfied with her new servants and asks Tot to start supper while Al and Jesse help relocate furniture. Like a good wife, Mia hopes to have the house neat and supper on the table when her husband arrives home.

Mia smiles. She likes all three of her new servants and hopes that at some point, Uncle Richard will either give them or sell them to Legare. Remembering their conversation at the church when they married, she knows that Legare will free them.

On Valentine's Day, Mia is settling into her home in Savannah and is comfortable with her role as Legare's wife. For the past few weeks she has been feeling very tired and suspects she might be with child. She has confided in Tot about her changing feelings.

Mia wakes up before Legare with a "butterfly" feeling in her stomach. She places the palm of her hand against her belly in anticipation of feeling the life which she and Legare have created. She kisses her dear husband on the cheek and awakens him with her heart bursting with love. "Legare, dear, happy Valentine's Day."

Legare enjoys a last moment of drowsiness and then opens his eyes. He can't resist teasing her a bit. "Good morning, darling. Is it really Valentine's Day?"

Mia is too excited to rise to his jibe. "I have something important to tell you. Something very important."

He snakes his arm around her, pulls her close and kisses her. "And, what, dear Mia, could be more important than the two of us . . snuggled up together in bed on this fine morning?"

"Legare! Stop teasing me. This is important."

"Nothing is more important than kissing my wife good morning."

She pokes him in the ribs. "Legare, listen to me for just a moment and then—"

"And, then?" he asks suggestively.

"Oh, you. You're incorrigible." She turns aside in mock anger. "Maybe I should just keep my secret."

Legare laughs, pulls her back into his arms and gazes into her eyes, observing the sparkle and adoration so evident there. "Mia, I adore you. It's a beautiful morning and I can't resist teasing you." He kisses the top of her head and assumes a serious demeanor. "Now, what's so important that can't wait?" He turns her onto her back and raises his upper torso above her so he's looking down into her eyes again. "I demand that you tell me now, temptress, or I'll devise—"

"Oh, Legare . . I do love you." She kisses him and then lies back on the bed to look into his eyes. "I'm so happy and need to tell you our exciting news. We are going to be parents!"

Speechless for a moment, he stares at her, trying to comprehend what he's just heard. His eyes widen with excitement and his smile beams from ear to ear. He wraps Mia in his arms. "Mia, darling, how wonderful! I love you. This is the best Valentine's news I have ever received, or ever could receive. When did you find out? Tell me the details."

"I have suspected I was with child for the last couple of weeks and dear Tot confirmed that the dream of bearing your child has now come true."

Chapter Sixteen
Panic in the Streets

The tranquility of the early morning of April 10, 1862 is shattered with a series of loud blasts. Mia opens her eyes wide and her hearing becomes keener. She wonders if she is awakening from a dream. Suddenly a second blast is heard from the direction of Fort Pulaski. Nervously she throws her cover back, scrambles into her robe and dashes into the hall to see what is happening. "Legare!" At 8:15 a.m. Captain Quincy Gillmore, a brilliant engineering officer, gave the order to open fire on Fort Pulaski.

Since February, he has been devising a plan to capture the fort. During the months of February and March 1862, he hid his operation on Tybee Island, operating only during darkness and utilizing the deep grass and bushes for concealment. Without detection, he transported thirty-six siege guns and mortars, weighing a total of eight and one-half tons, into position on the north shore of the island. He is discharging the new rifled guns and the new high-speed conical shells used by the Union onto Fort Pulaski.

Legare rushes to Mia just as she is coming out of the bedroom. Another huge blast causes a vase to crawl from the sideboard and smash to the floor. Windows rattle and a mirror in the dining room crashes. The shelling is relentless. For a moment, Mia fights the panic rising in her. "Tot, secure the other mirrors. And glassware. What's happening, Legare?"

"Sounds like it's coming from Fort Pulaski. Let's go up to the cupola, Mia." With Mia still in her robe, Legare practically drags her up to the cupola. "Damnation! The Yankees are shelling the fort."

The scene is both grand and awful. From every sound of the cannon, a white curl of smoke floats high in the air, forming countless smoky ribbons and rings. In moments, the acrid smell of the smoke reaches them.

Holding Legare tightly around his waist, she nervously stares at the evidence that the war has, at last, come to Savannah. "Seems those rumors we've been hearing must be true. Those Yankee ships been sitting on the river since December."

"Listen, Mia, do you hear that strange noise?"

"Yes I do. It sounds like some sort of a crowd or something."

Mia looks slightly in the other direction. She claps her hand over her mouth and grabs Legare with the other. "Oh my, look there in the distance."

At first, they have to strain to see the throngs of people pouring through the streets, a stampede of panic-stricken humanity. Legare shakes his head sadly. "It seems nobody knows where they're going; they're just running from the danger they perceive."

They watch in silent awe as mothers drag screaming children along behind them, slaves run with dogs on leashes and others shove people to one side in their haste to leave. Yet others pull carts of household goods. Some, on horseback, seemingly with no remorse, trample through the crowd, leaving injured and dead in their wake. Hysteria rules Savannah.

Appalled by the sight of a mob where yesterday there had been only peace and tranquility, Mia dashes down to the bedroom. Legare follows close behind. "Legare, I had best get dressed in case there is trouble. Maybe you'd better check the pistols and be sure they are loaded. See to it that Tot is safe."

"Calm down, Mia. We are safe here."

She rips her nightgown over her head and stares at Legare. "I'm as calm as you are, honey. Just wanna be ready in case trouble comes around." He nods and leaves the room to do as she asks. Her hand flutters to her abdomen protectively. "You're safe, little one. Never fear. You have a mother and a fine father to take care of you."

Legare soon returns. "Tot's just fine. She's taken down the rest of the mirrors, but the one over the buffet is in shards as we suspected. She's going to clean that up and then start dinner. Let's go back to the cupola and have another look around."

From the cupola Mia looks at the countryside and town. "Honey, the shelling is still going on but looks like the crowds are beginning to diminish. I guess everyone got to where they were going."

"These people should stay home and guard their belongings in times like this. Seems like the Yanks are only after Pulaski."

When they return from the cupola, Tot is in the kitchen preparing dinner, and Mia inhales the aroma. "What's for dinner, Tot?"

"Cornbread, fish, rice and spring greens, Ma'am Mia."

As suddenly as the ruckus from the streets began, it ends and the city is eerily quiet. Mia and Legare are preparing to sit for dinner, when there's a sudden, loud knock on the door. Between this loud knock and the resumption of the shelling, Mia's nerves are jolted more than before. She and Legare jump from the table. Without a word, they rush to the desk and take the pistols from the drawer.

"Stand back, Mia." He peeks through the side of the curtain. With an audible sigh of relief, he holds up his hand. "It is Aunt Josephine and Uncle Richard."

Richard spots Legare and waves frantically. Let us in! We've come to check on you."

Mia unlocks the door. "Come in, come in."

Uncle Richard stops just inside the door. "Put the pistol down, you're safe for the time being. The Yankees are shelling Fort Pulaski." He pauses and asks, "You wouldn't really shoot anyone would you, Mia?"

She responds with a look of firm conviction. "In the blink of an eye!"

Aunt Josephine appears nervous. She changes the subject quickly. "We're preparing to depart if conditions continue to deteriorate. The slaves are packing our silverware, clothing, food and other necessities of the moment. If the Yankees invade Savannah, we will certainly leave."

Mia asks, "Why are the Yankees shelling Fort Pulaski?"

Richard glances at Legare and then grimaces. "It guards the river's entrance to the ports of Savannah. Without the river available, we cannot ship our cotton to Europe or receive supplies. We have a smaller plantation further south and will be leaving tomorrow afternoon if matters get worse. You're welcome to join us."

Legare ponders his uncle's invitation but does not answer immediately. He eyes Mia for a moment. "Uncle, I feel that I must remain here, but Mia cannot. Her condition . . well, I must think of our child. Mia will go with you."

Mia jumps to her feet. "No, Legare. No, of course, I can't leave you."

Aunt Josephine rises and puts her arms around Mia. "Now, dear, you must listen to Legare. He's right. You must think of your child."

Mia gazes for a moment at Aunt Josephine and then turns back to Legare. "If you stay in Savannah, I will too! You cannot force me to leave." She shifts her gaze back to Aunt Josephine. "I have a responsibility to my husband and to my home. I . . Do what you must, Aunt Josephine, but do not expect me to leave without Legare."

Legare opens his mouth to speak, but, seeing the determination in his wife's eyes, decides that the discussion has—for the moment—ended. Perhaps he can reason with her later, but he's well-acquainted with her stubborn resolve. For her safety and that of their child, he would prefer her to go, but for his own comfort, Legare wants nothing more than to have her at his side. He is a man at a crossroads and paralyzed with conflicting desires. He needs time to think . . and time is the one commodity which may not be afforded him.

Later in the afternoon, Uncle Richard and Legare climb back into the cupola. The firing hasn't abated in the least. Smoke rises from the Union cannons on the north side of Tybee Island. Shells strike the walls of Fort Pulaski, which is only one mile away. Shouting down into the house, Uncle Richard calls, "Josephine, you and Mia come up and look at the battle. The Union must have some type of new cannon. Every shell is hitting the fort."

Aunt Josephine and Mia scurry up to the cupola and watch the continuing bombardment. Uncle Richard gestures widely, indicating the area near the fort and the river. "I don't see any troop vessels, so I don't think the Yankees are going to try and take Savannah. Probably just going to starve us out if they are successful in taking the fort."

"From what I can see, Uncle Richard, our cannon fire is not making any marks on the Yankees on Tybee. Looks like the Yankees are better shots than we are. Pray our troops are all safe." Mia closes her eyes briefly and utters a silent prayer while Legare squeezes her hand gently.

Uncle Richard tries to comfort the ladies, but can say little to achieve that. "I've been counting the cannon shots. They are averaging seven shots a minute. That's around four hundred shots each hour. I don't see how the fort can stand much longer."

Looking around from the cupola, Legare sees the streets are still crowded with people moving in all directions, but the initial panic seems to be subsiding. "Everyone seems a little more at ease since there are no troop ships in sight."

The shelling progresses through the day but begins to slacken at nightfall. Only periodic shelling continues during the night. Mia sits in her comfortable chair in front of the fireplace and falls asleep, while Aunt Josephine follows suit on the sofa. Legare bids Uncle Richard goodnight as he departs quietly for the plantation. Al and Jesse watch for activity outside while Tot stays half-awake to ensure no one tries to break into the house.

Before sunrise the next morning, Mia awakens to the

enticing aroma of brewing coffee. Upon opening her eyes, she is almost unaware of where she is. She realizes she slept in the chair all night. She stands and stretches, noticing Aunt Josephine sleeping on the sofa. Mia smiles as Aunt Josephine grunts an occasional snore. Tot is in the kitchen having a cup of fresh coffee and greets Mia as she walks in.

"I hab some fres' coffee mek. Would ya wantuh, Ma'am?" asks Tot.

"Sure smells good," comments Mia as Tot pours her a cup and gives her a warm muffin. Mia takes her cup of coffee to the bedroom and sits next to Legare on the bed. She rubs his back gently. He awakens and rolls over. "Good morning, honey. I had a sleepless night without you next to me."

He places his arms around her thickening waist. "You looked so peaceful sleeping in the chair, I would have felt guilty to awaken you just to have you by my side."

"I missed you, too. Maybe Tot's coffee will warm your spirits a bit." Mia holds the coffee cup as Legare sits up. She places it to his lips and he takes a long sip. He and Mia share a good-morning kiss and briefly escape the chaos that surrounds them. Once out of bed, he leads her to the front door. He opens the door slowly and visually investigates the misty morning. No sooner than the door opens, than the shelling begins again. Aunt Josephine awakens and looks around, startled as if she isn't certain where she is. Legare closes the door quickly.

Unaware that Aunt Josephine is awake, Mia looks out a window as Tot refills the cup. "The streets are quiet. I bet most everyone has already scattered from town. Just a few stragglers and lots of litter is all that's left. Look, the police and militia are making rounds."

Aunt Josephine yawns, stretches her arms and looks around to let everyone know she is awake. "Oh my goodness! I fell asleep on your sofa. Just look at me! I am mess!" She begins to straighten her clothing and hair, obviously embarrassed to be caught with her appearance so disheveled.

"Aunt Josephine, you're welcome to use our wash basin in the guest room to freshen up. Tot has some hot tea waiting for you. Legare and I are going to the cupola to see what else is going on."

"Thank you, darling, but where's Richard?"

"He went to the plantation last night to check on the children but will be back soon to pick you up." Legare smiles at his aunt. He's seldom seen her in such disarray. "He didn't have the heart to awaken you."

Appearing somewhat disgusted, Aunt Josephine goes to the guest room to gather herself a bit before breakfast.

When she returns, Tot asks, "Wantuh some breckwas?"

"Yes, Tot, eggs, grits, cured ham and muffin with hot tea."

"Yas, Ma'am." Tot turns and heads to the kitchen.

Shortly, Mia and Legare return from the cupola. He reaches down and plants a soft kiss on her cheek and simultaneously touches her belly where his son or daughter rests.

"What time did Richard leave last night?" Josephine asks.

"A little after dark. He said he'd be back for you around noon. The shelling is still around seven rounds per minute like Uncle counted yesterday. Still no signs of any Yankee troop ships."

Mia, Legare and Josephine take seats at the table. "Is Tot preparing your breakfast, Aunt Josephine?"

"Oh yes, my standard muffin, tea, eggs, grits and cured ham."

The smell of the ham fills the air as Tot serves the steaming breakfast. Aunt Josephine inhales the aroma briefly before attacking the ham with gusto. Mia meets Legare's eyes and both smile. After eating, they return to the cupola to witness the continuation of the shelling.

As she studies the area, Aunt Josephine recognizes her husband's carriage. "Look, there comes Richard. Let's see what he has found out."

Legare and Mia follow Aunt Josephine down into the parlor. As Josephine and Mia rush to the door and swing it open, the shelling stops. All three look at each other in amazement. Mia says, "First this morning, we open the door and the shelling begins. Now, we open the door and the shelling stops! Is this some kind of magic door?" They laugh as Uncle Richard walks up to the house.

Josephine, unhappy, glares at her husband. "Why did you leave me here last night to sleep on the sofa?"

He smiles. "Because that's the quietest and most peaceful I've seen you in ages."

Mia and Legare turn their heads to hide their amusement at Uncle Richard's humor.

Aunt Josephine retorts, "Rubbish!"

Richard notes the sudden end of the shelling and suggests a trip back to the cupola. Once there, silence falls over the group. "Look there," shouts Legare as he points in the direction of Pulaski. "There's a white flag flying over the fort."

Uncle Richard cocks his head slightly and turns an ear toward Fort Pulaski. "Listen. Be quiet. Can you hear those faint cheers? Must be the Yankees on Tybee." Uncle Richard reflects quietly on the sad situation. "Colonel Charles Olmstead is a friend of mind. He told me the story of when he and General Lee met in November of last year at Fort Pulaski. They stood together there on a rampart. General Lee told Charles, 'Upon graduating from West Point in 1829, due to my high standing in my class, I qualified for the highest rated branch of service in the military—the Corps of Engineers.' His first assignment was to build the dikes and a drainage canal for the future site of Fort Pulaski. He assured Charles that, 'The Union guns could not breach the seven-foot thick walls from Tybee. Fort Pulaski is the strongest point to control access to the port of Savannah. Looks like Lee was wrong."

After standing silently for a few moments, they descend from the cupola and gather in the parlor. Quiet, order and stillness return to the town. Legare and Uncle Richard begin discussing what they believe will happen.

Aunt Josephine, on the other hand, seems to want some type of diversion, as if she can't stand to think about the war. "So, dear Mia, what are you going to name your child?"

Mia wrenches her attention from the discussion of the war and stares at Aunt Josephine. "Pardon?"

"I asked what you're going to name your child."

"Name . . oh. We haven't decided." She glances back at Legare. "Nonsense. You must begin thinking about it right away. A name is awfully important to a child. For instance—"

Aunt Josephine's words are cut off by a commotion in the street. All of them rise and dash to peer out the window. Legare is the first to react. "Looks like a messenger."

He rushes to the door and flings it open. "Hello! You, there. What news do you bring?"

Winded, the young man stops and faces the doorway where Legare stands. "Morning, sir. Fort Pulaski has fallen, but the Yankees are not attacking the town. Yet."

Nodding, Legare waves the messenger on. "Thank you. Continue on your journey. God-speed."

Uncle Richard expresses his disgust about the war. "Mia, the South entered this conflict because it allowed emotion to override logic. We must be prepared for defeat." He turns his attention to Aunt Josephine. "I am going to continue gathering most of the valuables and have them transported to the smaller plantation in Florida. They'll be safer there. We need to head home now."

With a sense of foreboding, the families hug. Aunt Josephine and Uncle Richard hurry out to the carriage and leave. Mia and Legare watch until the carriage is out of sight. For a long moment, they stand arm-in- arm on the verandah, looking up and down the street.

Legare hugs her close and sighs. "Mia, dearest Mia. What am I going to do with you? You must—"

"Stop right there!" Mia pulls out of his embrace and gazes up at him. Tears rim her eyes and begin to slide down her cheeks. "I know what you're going to say, Legare. You must believe me when I tell you that I have thought of nothing else since the shelling began. I will not leave you and our home to the ravages of war. Fort Pulaski may have fallen, but the Hill family will stand united against those Yankee invaders. We will fight them together or flee together, but I will not ever leave you."

Chapter Seventeen
Stealth at Work

Harvey visits Isaac in the field where he is plowing. Isaac sees his friend and pulls the mule to a halt.

Buck is sowing seed and noticed Harvey approaching Isaac. Harvey glances around to see if anyone else is nearby. "We have decided to trust you to shepherd us to begin our trip to the River Jordan. (Ohio River as known to the slaves.)

"That's good news." Isaac claps his friend on the shoulder. "Let me make some contacts and you will hear from somebody sooner than later."

The two shake hands and Harvey nervously departs. Isaac snaps the reins with a "Giddyap, mule."

Later that afternoon, Buck meets Isaac in the barn. "I saw you talking to Harvey. I'm assuming he said he was ready to leave."

"Yes, but I can tell you that he is frightened."

Buck smiles. "That's pretty normal. We're going to take care of him and his family. Get a dozen eggs ready to take to Reverend Moss."

Isaac confers with Buck concerning Harvey's decision to head to the "River Jordan. Buck gathers the usual dozen eggs for Reverend Moss, the Presbyterian Minister. Isaac makes the usual delivery. "We got a family of three from Buster's farm that want to go to the 'River Jordan.'"

Reverend Moss asks their names.

"Harvey, Irene and Luci."

"Tell Buck I will notify Mr. Still and he should be getting a message soon."

Isaac and Reverend Moss shake hands and Isaac returns to the farm.

Several weeks later Reverend Moss stops by and seeks Isaac to "check his horse's hooves. Buck joins the pair. Reverend Moss explains that Buck will receive a letter from a Mr. Paul Spain, requesting that Harvey, Irene and Luci come and visit a dying relative by the name of William. Also, Harvey and Irene are not to know that Buck is involved in any way except that he has been asked to deliver them to Mr. Spain. Impress on them that Luci should only know they are going to visit a sick cousin whom she has not met before, only that William is their cousin and had requested they visit with him. In two weeks from today you are to take the train to Ringgold. When you get off, look for a wagon with a partly painted red spoke on the right rear wheel. This will identify Mr. Spain as their conductor. Let him introduce himself first. He will say, "Rains a-coming. You will reply, "Makes the grass green. Mr. Spain will then counter Buck's reply with, "Most of the time." The threesome is to depart with him to his place outside of Ringgold. Then Reverend Moss departs.

At the appointed early morning time, Buck, Betty Gail, Isaac, Harvey, Irene and Luci board the train in Stone Mountain and head toward Ringgold. The Negroes all board the last car. Of course to stay stealth, Buck asks no special seating for Isaac as he boards with the other Negroes. Betty Gail is very excited because she will depart the train in Marietta to visit with their son Norman and his roommate Paul Goldsmith. Paul is actually a cousin of James Goldsmith, the depot agent in Stone Mountain. She has a box of homemade delights for the two soldier boys. Buck and Betty Gail had received a letter from Norman stating that the GMI corps will return to campus in Marietta that week. Buck and Isaac will join her on their return trip from Ringgold.

The day is a beautiful spring day. Bright sun, light breeze and no flies or other insects buzzing around to annoy them. The train stops at Decatur, Atlanta, and then Marietta station. Buck escorts Betty Gail to the door of the coach and, with a big smile, gives her a peck on the cheek. She departs the Pullman and stands on the platform and waves to Buck and Isaac as the train chugs out.

Kennesaw and Acworth are uneventful. The train stops at Cartersville for water and wood for the engine and departs. All of the passengers have their food and enjoy the delights which they have brought. Isaac notices how quiet Harvey and Irene are and begins a conversation with them about the upcoming planting season.

When the train stops in Adairsville, a young Negro girl with a basket of early vegetables boards and sits across from Isaac. Shortly she offers him and his group some of the fresh greens, which they sample with a "Thank you."

As the train approaches the platform in Calhoun, Buck notices a sheriff with five deputies standing by. When the train stops, the sheriff and deputies jump into all the cars and announce to the white folks, "All of you who have Negroes in the last car get off and stand on the platform."

The deputy in the Negro car screams out, "All of you Negroes get out and stand by your owners".

Isaac, Harvey, Irene and Luci, nervously depart the train and seek out Buck and stand by him. All of a sudden a simply dressed young Negro girl with the basket of spring produce comes and stands alongside of them. Isaac, Harvey, and Irene look at each other and their unexpected guest. The sheriff stands in the door of one of the cars and shouts, "Has anybody seen a Negro boy who is not with anyone? He is a runaway and there is a reward for him."

A man down the way shouts back and points toward Buck, "Over there!"

Buck's heart jumps into his throat, his eyes become wide and his breathing deeper. Isaac and the other "four" stare at each other with similar feelings.

Then, the man shouts again, "A Negro boy just took

off from behind that man and ran around the corner of the depot.

At that point the sheriff and his deputies take off after the escaping youth as the passengers follow them with their eyes. A conductor climbs onto the Pullman car platform and shouts, "All aboard" and the passengers begin to board the train as they continue to look toward the chase. Buck looks at the Negro girl and quietly tells Isaac, "I almost messed in my pants!"

Isaac responds, " I think I might have!" Buck cracks a small smile. Harvey, Irene and Isaac look up with relief as if to say thanks to the Lord.

Everyone is quiet for the short trip to Dalton. The train makes a short stop and the Negro girl prepares to depart. She leans over to Isaac and whispers, "Thank you for the train fare and not giving my identity away. I am the boy the sheriff was looking for!"

She/he departs and rushes to a waiting wagon at the end of the depot with a Negro driver and the pair quietly ride away from the depot at a normal pace.

At Ringgold, Buck departs from the Pullman and awaits Isaac and his group. Still emotionally recovering from the near disaster in Calhoun, Buck looks for the wagon with the partially painted red spoke on the right rear wheel. Shortly, Isaac spots the wagon and points it out to Buck.

The group walks over and Mr. Spain says, "Hi, Buck, Rains a-coming."

Buck replies with a sly smile, "Makes the grass green.

Mr. Spain counters with his reply, "Most of the time."

The pair shakes hands. Isaac shakes Harvey's hand, and helps Irene and Luci get on board. Without any further conversation the wagon departs with the conductor as Buck and Isaac await the train heading south to Marietta.

Buck and Isaac sit outside the depot and talk about

the spring planting. They make it a point never to discuss their Underground Railroad activities away from the farm. Soon the train whistle is heard and it arrives to pick up the passengers heading south.

Upon arriving in Marietta, Buck summons a horse and buggy to transfer them to the GMI Campus. They arrive at the parade ground just as Ol' Abe , the drummer and the fife, begins the cadet parade. Buck and Isaac seek out Betty Gail. She sees the two approaching and waves for them to head her way.

The cadets establish their ranks facing the viewing crowd and commanders of the Cadet Corps. The Cadet Commander begins barking a series of orders, "Order arms!" The entire Corps demonstrates the precision of moving their muskets from their shoulder to the ground, as if they were one. "Present arms!" Again, the cadets in unison bring their muskets to a position in front of their breasts. "Present colors!" The Color Guard marches forward and renders the flags. Appropriate music begins to play.

"What an incredible sight! Look." as Buck points. There's Norman. Look at his uniform, the shiny buttons and shining emblems on his hat. All of their uniforms are perfect! I stand here looking at our future soldiers, the defenders of liberty, for America and freedom."

At the conclusion of the parade, Norman and his roommate Paul Goldsmith hurry to Buck, Betty Gail and Isaac. Buck salutes Norman and Paul. They return his salute with a broad smile.

Norman and Paul have permission to visit with Norman's family off campus for supper. Norman tells his dad, "The governor sends orders to close Camp Brown and establish a larger camp at Big Shanty in order, address the growing army's requirements for a larger training area."

Paul states, "With the increase in volunteers, a larger camp, which can accommodate a brigade, becomes a necessity."

"So now you are at Camp McDonald. We saw it from the train when we came through Big Shanty. I believe I read the camp is named in honor of former Governor Charles J. McDonald."

Norman says, "Big Shanty is such a good location for a training camp: plenty of fresh water and the Western and Atlanta Road."

Paul adds, "Yea and General William Phillips of the Georgia Militia is the commander of the camp and treats the cadets as if they, too, are generals. Norman and I inspect the camp together."

Betty Gail jumps into the conversation, "Looks like everyone lives in tents. Those must be the two parade grounds over there, Norman."

"That's right, ma."

Excited about their role in training the recruits, Norman continues, "There's room for infantry, cavalry, and artillery training. "No contact with the outside world is allowed. There's no telegraph although the camp surrounds the depot."

Buck, Betty Gail and Isaac continue to listen to the pair as they proudly detail the events. "There are more spectators on Sundays to view the drills, dress parades and mock battles than there were at GMI. During the mock battles, there are at least 5000 spectators to see how the military conducts war. These simulated battles are our payment for our instruction and furnish us with an objective lesson in the evolution of troops in line of battle. We could never hope to have seen this elsewhere."

After dinner the group makes their way to the depot and the waiting train to take Buck, Betty Gail and Isaac back to Stone Mountain. Buck again salutes Norman and Paul, Betty Gail gives them both a hug and the two cadets shake hands with Isaac. Buck, Betty Gail and Isaac board the train.

As the train departs the depot, Norman sees Buck give him a huge big smile. Soon Norman and Paul are out of sight and Buck sits down quietly for a few minutes and listens to Betty Gail describing her exciting visit minute by minute with the two young men.

Buck takes Betty Gail's hand and gives it a tight squeeze as he begins to reflect and give his overall analysis of the state of affairs. "Your and my forefathers fought for the Union. We are flying the American flag not the Confederate National flag over our property. I guess you could call us, especially me, a protagonist in regards to the Union. Betty Gail sits quietly and listens intently as Buck gathers his thoughts. "I believe the Confederacy is going to fail, especially since President Lincoln has instituted a blockade against Southern ports. In July of last year, General Jackson defeated the Union Army under General McDowell. The defeat was at Bull, which is about twenty-five miles southwest of Washington. The Union troops fell back to Washington over a stone bridge, which was finally blown up by the Confederates. The newspaper stated the Union forces looked like 'a rain soaked mob.' President Lincoln realizes the war will be long commenting. He even said 'It's damned bad.' So, President Lincoln appoints General McClellan as Commander of the Department of the Potomac and relieves General McDowell.

"Then, last September General Fremont issues a proclamation of emancipation in Missouri, which by the way was a brave and great move on his part as a protagonist, but the president revokes it and replaces him with General Hunter."

Betty Gail shakes her head. "This is awful. What else?"

"In November of last year, General Winfield Scott, one of the Union's great generals, resigns and the President appoints General McClellan to take his place. During the same month, the beginning of an international diplomatic crisis for President Lincoln occurred as two Confederate officials were sailing toward England and are seized by the U.S. Navy. England, the leading world power, demands their release, threatening war. Lincoln eventually gives in and orders their release in December. Lincoln said, "One war at a time."

Betty Gail continues to look on solemnly and holds Buck's hand as he continues. "So finally, this past February, there is a dim light at the end of the tunnel for the Union when General Grant captures Fort Henry and Fort Donaldson. But last month the Confederate Ironclad, *Merrimac*, sinks two wooden Union ships then battles the Union Ironclad *Monitor* to a draw. I guess these ironclads will change naval warfare forever. Wooden ships probably will become obsolete. The test-firing of the new breech-loading cannon on the Mountain last year changed my disposition from the old me to an unhappy new me."

"Now we have a son in a Confederate Military Institute and a son-in-law who will be old enough to either join the Confederate army or be conscripted. With the casualty rate as high as it is so far, we stand to lose either one or both. I know Congressman Hill is pro-Union. His son must be also. Therefore, the members of our family are not fighting a war we favor. I will not lose faith in the Union, but the Confederate antagonists are ahead in the game right now.

Betty Gail concludes the conversation, "Remember what Shakespeare once said, 'This above all: to thine ownself be true, and it must follow, as the night the day, ..

We both need rest after this long day."

After arriving in Stone Mountain, they go by the livery stable and get their mule and wagon. Betty Gail has a burning question which she must ask of Buck. She takes the reins from his hands and pulls and stops the wagon.

"What's going on, Betty Gail?' asks Buck.

She takes Buck's face in her hands and turns it toward her face. "I have a question that has been bothering me all day and I need to know the answer."

Buck looks somewhat surprised, "What's on your mind, Betty Gail?"

Silent for a moment , Betty Gail continues. "What was the real reason you took Harvey, Irene and Luci to

Ringgold?"

Without hesitation Buck responds, "You read the letter. Their dying cousin wanted them by his bedside when he passes."

Betty Gail continues, "Are they going to return to Stone Mountain after he passes?"

"Time will tell," answers Buck, even though he knows the former slaves will never return and he hates lying to her. But, he must. She must never know what he and Isaac are doing.

As a sign of approval, Isaac gently elbows Buck in the back.

Betty Gail gently pulls Buck's face to her and gives him a loving kiss on the cheek. "You are a good and brave man, Buck Jernigan. She hands the reins back to him.

He snaps them with a "gitty-up" and they head to their home 'round the Mountain.'

Chapter Eighteen
Double Action:
Medicine, Surgery, Hope and The Texas

In mid-April, the harrowing scenes at Fort Pulaski are somewhat relieved and lightened by the heroic bearing, cheerful resignation, and wonderful fortitude with which the wounded bore up under their afflictions. This is especially conspicuous in the younger soldiers. These mere striplings are wounded badly. Many of the youth are mutilated or mortally injured yet attempt to ignore their pain. The older wounded manifest far greater anxiety toward the character of their injuries, having experienced the sad outcome of comrades wounded in the past.

The wounded men begin appearing at the hospital. Some hobble along while others are brought in the ambulance wagons. Many are stripped nearly naked, displaying the bloody dressing of their wounds. The hospitals rapidly become overcrowded and many who arrive late remain in the wagons exposed to the cold and damp night.

Chief surgeon, Dr. Blair, and the other surgeons work diligently and unrelentingly. By dim lights and in the open air, the surgeons perform countless delicate operations. The air stinks of blood. The halls and rooms are overflowing. Anguish, death, blood and mounds of body parts become a hazard in and around the operating rooms.

A universal spirit of brotherhood and an absence of selfishness are displayed by everyone attending to the wounded and dying. The groans of the suffering and the cries of those undergoing surgery are oppressive. The distinct gurgling sounds of soldiers shot through the lungs, waiting to meet their maker, resonate throughout the compound.

Row after row of soldiers wait for their time on the dreaded operating table. Many are already under the influence of morphine, but still cry out in the agony of life-stealing injuries. The assistant surgeon and Dr. Blair labor intensely with this never-ending chaotic ordeal. As soon as one surgery is complete, another patient is placed on the bloody table. The smell of putrid blood and piles of arms and legs overflowing from baskets near his station greet each new patient. Flies swarm everywhere. The overwhelming presence of hopelessness cannot fail to touch each soldier as he is brought into surgery.

"Doctor, can you save my arm?" The latest young man on the table looks up, his watering eyes imploring.

"I'm afraid not, son," replies Dr. Blair as the chloroform begins to drip on the soft cloth covering the soldier's nose and mouth.

Sleep comes quickly. The assistant surgeon passes Dr. Blair the knife. Grasping the bloodstained tool, Dr. Blair carves away the tissue to the bone, tying off arteries and veins as he goes. Then comes the saw. In a brief moment another arm is thrown upon the pile of lifeless flesh. With a bloody, long and curved needle, the doctor uses horsehair to close the wound. His assistant wipes his hands with a wet towel and takes a three-inch long, straight needle threaded with silk thread, completing the task which but a few hours ago was dreaded. Now, it seems little more than routine, something that must be done to save a life, however distorted it may have become by the war and injury.

The life-altering surgery takes less than twenty minutes to complete. The chloroform stops and the soldier awakens with one limb less than his last memory recalls. His constant companion for the next few days is pain and, if he's fortunate, the nightmares of a morphine-induced trance.

For ten hours, one soldier after another suffers a similar consequence, the amputation of an arm, leg, or finger. When a wound is in the gut, a bare probing finger attempts to find and remove a foreign material from that part of the body. Finally, the long line of soldiers awaiting surgery ends. Exhausted, Dr. Blair and his assistant helps the nurses in making their rounds to the dying, authorizing medication to reduce the pain and suffering. There truly seems to be no rest awaiting those who tend the injured.

The Superintendent at GMI retires early after the excitement of the chase between the stolen General and The Texas. Around midnight on the 13th, the superintendent of the Institute is awakened by a messenger from the Commander of the Confederate provost guards at Big Shanty.

"To: Major John M. Richardson, Superintendent of Georgia Military Institute. Accordingly, four of the Union prisoners are in prison in the Marietta City jail. There's a restless crowd of several hundred gathering about, and I fear an attempt to overtake my guard and render vigilante justice. At all speed, sir, I request that you send cadets with arms to aid in securing the prisoners aforementioned."

Major Richardson hastily scrolls on the bottom of the request and writes, "I'll comply with your request. Major J. T. Richardson." The messenger salutes and takes to his mount and hastily heads toward the jail. Major Richardson wakes up Cornelius. "Play the 'long roll' for assembly."

Upon being awakened by the bugle, Norman tumbles from his bed. "Get up, Paul. Quick. Something serious is going on for Cornelius to call us out at this hour!"

Paul peers out of the window and sees Major Richardson pacing on the assembly ground. In moments, the two cadets are dressed and dash outside. Within ten minutes of the bugle call, the entire cadet corps is in formation with their muskets.

Major Richardson paces the formation as the last cadet joins the others. "The Provost Guard needs our assistance protecting the prisoners at the jail. Your companies are to proceed to the armory and draw ammunition. From there, we will march to the jail and assist the Provost Commander as the need arises." As they procure their weapons, the excitement of the coming action sends the morale high in all the cadets.

Paul glances at Norman with a grin of excitement. "We can keep the order at the jail without any problem."

"Probably a bunch of drunks trying to make trouble. But you can't really blame them too much. After all, those Yanks tried to burn eight bridges between here and the border." Norman can hardly contain his emotions. On the one hand, uncertainty colors his thoughts. But, on the other hand, he realizes that he will, at last, make a contribution to the war effort. He realizes this is only the beginning. For better or worse, the GMI cadets have entered the war.

The Provost Commander sees the cadets as they approach the jail near the depot. He greets Major Richardson, "Take the cadets and have them completely surround the jail. Have them load their weapons and stand tall."

Major Richardson surveys the cadets. "Load weapons!"

The precision movements of loading the weapons are impressive to the mob. The mob's angry shouting lessens as they begin to realize these cadets most probably mean business. After loading is complete, he commands, "Single file around the jail and hold your positions."

Major Richardson and the Commander speak to the crowd in no uncertain terms, "Any person or persons attempting to enter the jail will be shot. The cadets, as well as the provost guards, are armed and ready to respond. We advise you leave the area. Let the courts handle these criminals with true Southern Justice."

The cadet corps maintains a stoic attitude during this "reasoning conversation." The locals are accustomed to the cadets and realize they have been trained to kill or capture. They become very reluctant to challenge them on this issue and the unruly crowd begins to evaporate slowly, easing the tense situation enough for the cadets to settle into a pleasant night of guard duty.

Several days after the capture of Fort Pulaski,

Uncle Richard and Aunt Josephine decide not to depart for Florida, and Mia receives an invitation from Aunt Josephine inviting her to their townhouse near the hospital. After supper, Mia shows Legare the invitation. "I received this from Aunt Josephine today. She has invited me to assist her and her friends in scraping lint, cutting material for bandages and sending culinary delicacies to the hospitals. I would like to help out with the war effort. Would you mind if I accepted the invitation?"

"Why, of course I would not mind. You have a lot to contribute. Your knowledge of herbs would be of great interest to Aunt Josephine and her friends, although most of them are society conscious."

"I'm going on six months with child now. Women generally stay to themselves at this stage, but I would like to go."

"I don't feel Aunt Josephine would send the invitation to embarrass you in front of her friends. Besides, I'm certain most of her friends already know all about us and would love to meet you. So give 'em your best shot, which is better than any of their shots, I promise you that!"

Mia hugs Legare and he pulls her around to his lap. "I sure do love you, Legare!"

"And I sure do love you, Mia!"

The following day, Al takes her to Aunt Josephine's townhouse. Mia is glad to participate in the lint scraping, however, she feels extremely uncomfortable because of the air of a "social occasion" of tea and gossip. Al escorts Mia to the front door and knocks. A house servant opens the door. "'Ello, Al."

"'Ello Jemima. 'Ember Ma'am Mia? Ma'am Josephine is expecting her." "I be back een de carriage hous' wen you ready fuh go, Ma'am Mia." Jemima conducts Mia to the grand sitting room.

Aunt Josephine sees Mia entering and greets her. "I'm glad you could join us today, Mia."

"Thank you for the invitation."

"Come, Mia. I'll introduce you to my friends." Entering the sitting room, she announces, "Ladies, this is my cousin Legare's wife, Mia Hill." Each lady present warmly introduces herself, and Mia acknowledges each introduction with a kind smile and "Nice to meet you as well," then finds a chair. She casually studies the elegant surroundings of the grand room. There are seven marble top tables, beautiful vases and numerous antique lanterns. A thick, bright red and green oriental rug covers the floor.

The drapery is gold in color and ascends to the twelve-foot high ceilings.

The servants serve hot tea, finger biscuits, confections of all sorts, and fresh fruits in a liberal manner. As the servants offer the delicacies, Mia graciously accepts and leaves it to her palate to determine if she'll accept another dose of the same delight. As Mia chooses a piece of fabric to scrape, one of the ladies asks, "Have you scraped lint before, Mia?"

"Many times, ma'am. Why do you ask?"

"Josephine passed on to us that your family only has several hundred acres to farm. So I am curious if you scrape lint at home or if you hired yourself out!"

Mia eyes the lady directly and calms herself before she speaks. This woman is, after all, a friend of Aunt Josephine's and Mia doesn't want to offend her hostess. "I don't hire out and to answer your next question, Legare and I have been married long enough for me to be with child. Do you have any other personal questions?"

Another lady Kelli in the group intercedes, "Pay Jodi no attention, Mia. She is just an ol' nosey gossip. If you're good enough for Legare, you're good enough for me!"

"Why, I did not mean any harm, Mia, I just . ."

"Just be quiet, Jodi, you have said more than enough!" Aunt Josephine cuts off her friend before the situation can escalate.

"No bother, Aunt Josephine, scraping the lint is more important."

The women begin their around-town gossip. Mia is well aware that scraping the lint is secondary to the social gathering. "Aunt Josephine, I will be glad to deliver the lint and bandages to the hospital."

The ladies become very quiet as Mia receives a Victorian stare from the group. Aunt Josephine smiles woodenly. "The hospitals are no place for ladies. The doctors and the nurses will notify us when they need bandages for the patients."

Mia hears the words and knows Aunt Josephine speaks the truth, but Mia is a young woman with a strong sense of duty. "Do y'all not care? If you had a loved one there, you certainly would."

"Yes," replies Kelli. "But we will see them in time and especially when they come home."

Mia offers a simple response. "I see." *What kind of love is this?* She wonders. She simply smiles and continues to scrape lint and partake of the sweet delights, tea and light conversation.

Doctor Samuel Moore, the Chief Medical Officer for the Confederate States, foresees how the shortages in drugs, hospital supplies and medical instruments will present a dilemma to the treatment of patients. He has purchased supplies from Europe and has medical supplies from captured Union hospitals. Dr. Moore also has an indigenous drug manufacturer in Macon. Aunt Josephine has a copy of a book distributed by Dr. Moore. The book details the native herbs and other plants that grow wild in the South. These plants are believed to provide curative qualities to certain ailments and diseases.

Aunt Josephine glances around the room full of ladies. "The newspaper reports show that quinine, morphia(old fashioned term for morphine) and calomel which normally came through New Orleans are no longer as plentiful. Shortages of medicine are already noticeable since the surprise capture of Fort Pulaski. Richard has several of our slaves harvesting as many of the herbs in Dr. Moore's book as they can find."

Aunt Josephine picks up the book and begins showing it to the other ladies. Mia listens eagerly for a moment. "Aunt Josephine, may I take the book home and read it?"

Jodi chimes in again. "My dear child, do you think you can read well enough to understand what the book contains?"

Mia, being of a more gentle and pleasant nature, pauses for a long moment. Knowing herself to be very well read, she replies directly to Jodi. "I'll do my best and surely call upon you or Aunt Josephine for what I can't read and understand."

Another lady, embarrassed by Jodi's comment, interjects, "There you go again, Jodi, minding everyone's business but your own!"

Aunt Josephine hands Mia the book indignantly and continues her conversation with the other ladies. When there's no more lint to scrape or bandages to prepare, Mia bids the ladies farewell, summons Al, and with Dr. Moore's book safely tucked beneath her arm heads home for the evening.

Sitting by the fireplace after supper, Legare wonders why Mia hasn't mentioned her outing today. "How was your day with Aunt Josephine?"

"It went just fine. I met some interesting people and Aunt Josephine gave me Dr. Moore's book on herbs. One of Aunt Josephine's friends by the name of Jodi asked me if I could read."

Looking surprised, he studies his wife a few seconds. "What did you say back to her?"

"Told her if I had any problems I would check with Aunt Josephine and about that time another lady somewhat chastised her for her distasteful comments. Nothing to be concerned about though."

"You're a better person than I am, honey. It's a good thing I wasn't there."

"Thanks, but it's all right. Please forget I mentioned the incident. I know a little about herbs from Mother and Aunt Sally. They were good at identifying and picking the right plants."

"Well, I'm glad you somewhat enjoyed yourself today." Legare places his hand on Mia's enlarged stomach.

She places her hand on top of his. "Feel our baby kicking?"

"Sure do," replies Legare. "Must want out of there!"

"Well he or she is more than half-way to freedom," replies Mia as they snuggle close to one another in front of the fireplace. "When will you see Uncle Richard again?"

"Tomorrow. Why do you ask?"

"I want to talk to him about selecting and collecting herbs with a couple more of the darkies if he can spare them. Ask him when I can meet him."

"I will. This might be the last year for cotton. Uncle Richard said he has word that Governor Brown is going to demand a reduction in cotton production. Food is getting scarce. Corn and syrup are bringing more money than cotton right now."

The next day, Mia reads the book and discusses herbs with Tot. Some of the plants are familiar to both of them. Mia's parents, Tot's parents and Uncle Isaac have used herbs for treatment of their families' ailments for generations. The information has been passed down from generation to generation. "When the blackberries are plentiful we can produce blackberry cordial. This has been recognized as a good treatment for upset stomach. I know painkillers are getting in short supply so we can make some from the jimsonweed also, I see there are a lot dogwood trees in the woods. So we can produce an appetite stimulant or medicine to relieve stomach discomfort from its bark. Willow bark tea is good for aches, pains and fever."

Early the next morning, Mia departs with Tot to seek out Uncle Richard at the plantation. It is planting season and as far as one can see, there are mules and plows working the fields. The slaves are singing a popular Gullah song, *De Fox en de Crow*, all in unison as they plow and plant.

The mid-April day is overcast, relieving much of the sweat and toil of the laborers. Cook stations are abundant and water bearers are running the rows to quench the throats, dry from the dust, hard work and songs.

Mia looks at Uncle Richard and begins to explain

the purpose for her visit. "I think scraping lint and rendering bandages are an important part of the war effort for the ladies, but I feel I can be more useful in gathering herbs."

Uncle Richard listens intensely. "I see. Go on."

Mia continues to present her reasoning. "Throughout my life, my family has relied on herbs for treatment, and I am very familiar with their identification and formulation."

Uncle Richard realizes from his recent conversation with his wife that Mia feels uncomfortable among Josephine's friends. He sincerely comprehends and appreciates Mia for her subtle values, dedication and love to Legare. Without hesitation, he consents to her request. "I'll give you two or three of my older slaves to assist you and Tot with the herbs. Besides, even if we have a good cotton crop this year, I don't see it going any further than the cotton warehouse now that the river is blocked. Probably will have to start planting corn and peas for the soldiers. Come back tomorrow and I'll have my workers who know herbs ready to assist you."

"Thank you, Uncle Richard. You made my day! Just one more request."

"What is it, Mia?"

"Could you set me an appointment with the doctor at Bartow Hospital?"

"I'll be happy to. That would be Dr. Blair."

Mia smiles and gives Uncle Richard a hug before she and Tot depart.

Chapter Nineteen
Back in Stone Mountain

"Ha! Ha! Ha!" Nearly overcome with laughter, Buck gets out of his rocker on the porch. He holds the April 22, 1862 newspaper in his hand and goes to the front door. "Betty Gail, come out here. I want you to hear this!"

"Hear what, Buck?"

"About this double-barrel cannon a dentist in Athens invented!" Betty Gail comes to the front porch and sits next to Buck on the front porch steps.

"Listen to this, 'For a cost of $350 subscription raised by thirty-six interested citizens, the Athens Steam Company cast a double-barrel cannon for John Gilleland, who is a dentist, a builder and mechanic. Thomas Bailey supervised the casting of the cannon. The two barrels have a divergence of three degrees. The cannon is designed to shoot two cannon balls, simultaneously, connected with a chain to mow the enemy down like scythe cuts wheat. The gun is four-feet one-inch long. The bore is three and thirteen-hundredths inches and the gun weighs about thirteen hundred pounds. Each barrel has its own touchhole so it can be fired independent of the other. Then there's a common-touch hole in the center designed to fire both barrels simultaneously. Now this is where the story really gets funny. Are you ready for this, Betty Gail?"

"I'm ready, Buck!"

"The double-barrel cannon was taken out to Newton Bridge Road near Athens for test firing. The test was, to say the least, spectacularly unsuccessful. The cannon was set and aimed at a target of two upright poles. However, when fired, one ball left the muzzle before the other ball and the two balls pursued an erratic circular course. The balls and chain began plowing up an acre of ground, destroying a cornfield and mowing down some saplings before the chain broke.

Then each ball adopted a separate course. One ball killed a cow and the other demolished the chimney on a log cabin, at which point all of the observers scattered in fear of their lives."

Betty Gail chuckles. "I would have liked to have seen that Fourth of July display myself."

"The last sentence says, 'shooting cannon balls connected with a chain is commonly done in naval warfare, but these chain-shots are fired from a single barrel.'"

"I need to get back and finish helping Sally with the washing or whatever it was that I was doing."

Buck kisses Betty Gail and gently wipes the tears of laughter from his eyes. "I'm gonna read the article again. Then I think I'll mail Norman a copy at GMI. Those cadets will really get a kick out of this one!"

Betty Gail goes back inside and Buck returns to his rocker to read the article once again and laughs as he imagines what a sight the firing of the double-barrel cannon must have been.

In early June, Uncle Richard informs Mia of her appointment with Dr. Blair and Madame Cazier at Bartow Hospital. Madame Cazier is the Vice-President of the ladies' State Military Association and the principal lady Manager of the Bartow Hospital. Bartow Hospital is a part of the Oglethorpe Medical College. Madame Cazier is a well-respected homeopathic ladies' physician in Savannah. She and Madam Young are in the process of preparing the hospital in anticipation of the arrival of more wounded troops.

The hospital's location is almost in the center of town. It is an old, Grecian-style building adorned with thirteen columns, each one at least twenty feet tall. Mia enters the foyer, immediately recognizing the odor emitted from mixtures of indigenous herbs. She approaches a slender, sickly young man who is sitting at a desk in the foyer. As she reaches the desk, she notices the clerk has only one arm. She introduces herself politely and tries not to stare. "I am Mrs. Legare Hill and I have an appointment with Dr. Blair and Madame Cazier."

He is stoic and rises slowly from his chair. "Follow me, ma'am. Dr. Blair is expecting you." He escorts Mia to the open ward where there are at least twenty beds lining the walls on each side of the large room. He approaches a middle-age lady. Her face is round and pleasant. She and a gentleman are having a conversation with a patient who is stricken with some type of illness.

Upon Mia's approach, the lady turns and says with a strong French accent, "You must be Mia!"

"I am."

"We can talk about your project in Dr. Blair's office."

The doctor approaches and introduces himself. "Hello, my name is Hugh Blair. I am the Chief Surgeon at Bartow. It is nice to meet you. We have been expecting you. Just give us a moment more and wait for me in my office."

"Follow me, please," says the clerk and he escorts her to an oval table in Dr. Blair's office. Mia notices a stand-on scale as she looks around the office. There is an extension rod that can be extracted in order to measure one's height extending from the scale. In one corner, there's a human skeleton. All bones are intact as it hangs from a slender pole with arched wire at the top attached to the center of the skull.

Lining the walls are several shelves of books that immediately catch Mia's attention, including *Materia Medica* and a copy of the book Dr. Moore has written. Thermometers and a couple of stethoscopes call the mantle home as well.

Soon, Dr. Blair and Madame Cazier enter the room. Dr. Blair is an older man and, like most of the doctors of his era, learned his "science" through an apprenticeship. They take a seat at the oval table with Mia.

Dr. Blair observes her a moment. "We are glad you have come to offer your assistance. Your Uncle Richard is a very close friend of mine and speaks highly of you."

"Thank you for taking your time to talk with me today, Dr. Blair."

"Madame Cazier and I understand you and Tot are familiar with herbs and how to convert them into medicine."

"Yes, sir, Dr. Blair. I learned from my parents. I brought some Rhubarb Syrup and Dogwood Extract for y'all to try." Mia removes a few bottles from her woven basket and places them on the table in front of Dr. Blair and Madame Cazier.

Dr. Blair twists the cork and removes it from the Rhubarb Syrup bottle. He raises the bottle to his nose, sniffing the syrup and samples a small amount of the mixture by using his finger as a spoon. "Mighty good." He passes the bottle to Madame Cazier, smiles and leans back in his chair.

Madame Cazier removes the cork from the Dogwood Extract. Passing the bottle beneath her nostrils, she inhales to detect if the mixture is complete. She places some of the extract on her finger and touches her tongue to it. The three sit quietly for a moment. Madame Cazier stands and locates a spoon on the nearby shelf over the sink. Mia watches patiently as Madame Cazier fills the spoon and swallows a complete dose. She licks her lips and returns to her chair at the small round conference table. "I could not have made it better myself!"

With a warm smile, Mia gives a sigh of relief. "Thank you."

Dr. Blair looks from Madame Cazier to Mia. "The Yankee navy has Pulaski. Lord knows when the ground troops will enter Georgia. I'm afraid the affairs of war are going to involve Savannah. From where the Yankee ground troops will come none of us knows. But when they arrive it will cause chaos all around. There will be an abundance of sickness, disease, death and destruction. For the salvation of the state, it would be better if Governor Brown comes to terms with himself and raises Old Glory again. The impact of the recent blockade on our port is going to prevent medical supplies and food from entering, as well as preventing our crops of rice, cotton and other agricultural commodities from being exported. This will render our economy useless."

Dr. Blair says, "I understand your husband, Legare, is not in uniform yet, and you and your husband are planning on staying in Savannah until the war ends?"

"Yes, sir, that is correct."

"Would you like to go on a tour of the hospital wards and facilities with Madame Cazier?"

"Certainly."

"There are several younger physicians on duty who have been in practice for nearly two years. If you're ready, Madame Cazier, you may take Mia on the hospital tour now."

Madame Cazier and Mia stand as the doctor continues, "I am looking forward to working with you, Mrs. Hill. We are going to need a lot of medicine. The disaster at Fort Pulaski is taxing our ability to care for these brave soldiers."

The last stop on the tour is the operating area. It smells of stale cloth and mildew. Blood stains the floor. They see long, flat tables where the surgeons use the knowledge, skill and instruments available as they try to save lives. Chloroform bottles and small bundles of cloth line the walls. Silk thread and horsehair suture material and a large assortment of needles lie on adjoining shelves, tables and cabinets. There are odd-looking instruments all about the room used for surgery and treating wounds.

Fanning his hand in front of his face, he says, "Flies are a nuisance. Even now, in the early spring, they crave the dried blood and secretions left behind. Sometimes we operate outside because the lighting is better."

Mia absorbs all of the information and feels a bit ill. They return to Dr. Blair's office to talk about compensation for her herbal medicines. Mia takes the conversation back to her herbals. "Payment would be minimal, just for the alcohol, ether and acetone, but in gold coins rather than silver would be ideal. Also, I'll be glad to volunteer in some capacity if you ever need me."

They agree to the terms and Dr. Blair and Madame Cazier bid Mia goodbye. On the way to her carriage, Mia passes the new prison adjacent to the hospital. The prison wagon is parked next to the gate of the stockade. "Go ahead and unload the prisoners." The stockade commander directs the guards. Mia stops to observe the prison induction. As the prisoners climb down from the calaboose wagon, they appear starving, weak and ill from their stay in the overcrowded prisons of Richmond.

Although sobered by the sight, Mia is full of excitement as she boards her carriage. "Jesse, take me by the bank please. I want to give Legare the good news!" Before the carriage comes to a complete stop in front of its destination, Mia hops to the ground and enters the bank with a broad smile. Legare sees Mia and rushes to hug her.

"Good news from Dr. Blair, right, Mia?"

"Yes, Dr. Blair and Madame Cazier seem to be satisfied with my samples. They want me to make more and are willing to pay for them. I told them like you said, I prefer payment in gold and that was all right with them."

"It's just about time for my break. Let me check with Mr. Lilly to see if it's all right for me to leave ten minutes early for lunch." Legare goes to Mr. Lilly's office and returns quickly. "He said I could leave early, but not to be away for more than an hour. How about the Pirates' House?"

Taking Legare's hand, she smiles happily. "Sounds good to me. That seems to be our place for celebrations!"

After lunch and upon arriving at the river house, Mia finds Tot in the kitchen. "Tot, Dr. Blair and Madame Cazier said my herbs were satisfactory and my processing would fill a need for the herbal medicine at the hospital."

"That's all there is to the selection process, honey."

Legare arrives home and walks into the yard. He watches his wife a moment. Her belly is beginning to show her condition. "Mia, dear, I'm concerned about your . . well, your condition."

"My condition? Whatever do you mean?"

"You are carrying our child, Mia." Legare hugs her close and snuggles against her sweet-smelling hair. "Are you sure this is safe?"

"Oh, Legare! Is that it? I am a healthy woman." She places her hands on the bulge on her belly and smiles. "Our child will be fine. In fact, he'll be all the better for having a mother who continued to be active."

Shaking his head, he grins, once again feeling an almost overwhelming pride in his wife. "I must believe you, but you must promise that you will rest if you feel the least bit tired. I am aware of your value to the Confederacy, but I assure you, it is of little consequence when compared to your value as the mother of our child."

Realizing she'll get no work done until he's satisfied, she puts down the bark and slides her arms around his neck. "I promise, Legare. I promise to be as careful of my health as possible. But, you must also promise to be careful of your health. I can't stand the thought of. . Words fail her. Mia simply can't articulate her fears.

He kisses the top of her head, lifts her chin and brushes her lips with his own. "Then don't think about it, Mia. You promise to look after yourself, and I'll promise to look after myself. That's the best we can do, don't you think? We will leave it unspecific. Is that all right?"

Chapter Twenty
The Stork Arrives

Mia is nearing the time for the birth of her child. The Saturday Mid-August day is clear, but sultry with a mild breeze. Mia's pregnancy has produced some back pains and of the usual, "Is this baby coming or not!" emotion. The windows are open in the house to allow the river breeze to afford some additional coolness to the shade trees surrounding the house. Mia and Legare are in the backyard, where Mia has planted her vegetable and herb garden. "Legare, it's hard for me to bend over. Please pick a few of those tomatoes, cucumbers and peppers. Can use them in the dinner salad."

Legare obliges gladly and takes them to Tot.

He returns to Mia and takes her hand, "Honey, it's such a beautiful day. Let's go sit on the pier. You look tired."

They walk hand-in-hand onto the pier. "Legare, the moon is full on Monday. That's when our baby is coming." Reaching the end of the pier, Legare helps Mia sit down so her feet can dangle over the edge. He sits next to her and she takes his hand, placing it on her rounded belly. "Feel our baby, Legare? It's kicking and really wants out to see its wonderful father."

"And more wonderful mother," adds Legare.

"The baby has dropped. See how low the center of my stomach is now. The full moon is gonna push our baby right on out of here.

"You know, Legare, we have written to both sets of parents explaining our marriage, our love for one-another, our whereabouts and how happy we are together. We have waited hopelessly for a letter from either family announcing that they are all well and have found forgiveness in their hearts for our sudden departure and we've heard nothing back."

"I know, Mia. I guess they feel betrayed or something like that . . as close as we were to our parents and all . . I would think they would respect our feelings. I miss my family and yours equally."

"We told them about our coming baby in our letter. I want them to be with us, not just for the baby, but to be together as a family." Pausing for a moment, Mia stares across the river, remembering happy days back in Stone Mountain. "Then again, I don't want to beg them since they have not written. Every girl wants her mother with her at childbirth. I dream of my mother and father often as I work our small vegetable garden to resemble theirs in Stone Mountain. Oh, how I wish for my mother and father to be with us during the birth of their first grandchild."

"Mia, I'll go and telegraph your mama and papa right now and let them know you're about to deliver their first grandchild and we want them here. I'll beg them to come and be with us."

Sitting close to Legare, Mia takes his cheeks between her two hands.

"Having you by my side gives me all the strength that I need. When either your parents or my parents respond to our letters, then we can notify them about the new grandchild. Until then, it's just our baby and us. I just wish they would understand that we are in love." Mia places her head on Legare's chest and begins to sob. He holds her close and begins to cry with her.

With a choking voice, he whispers to his wife, "I'll fulfill your every wish, my love. I know childbirth must be hard physically and emotionally, Mia. We have fared well together, but the love from our families is missing and it hurts deeply. You truly are independent like Mrs. Turner said. You're the brightest example of firmness and courage I have ever known."

Mia becomes restless during the day on Sunday, the 17th of August, the day before the moon will be full.

Nervously, Legare comforts her. He does not allow her to move around the house. Tot encourages her to eat yams and drink as much sassafras tea as possible. In the early evening, Mia holds her stomach with both hands as another small contraction occurs. "Legare, our baby is coming tonight or tomorrow. Please send Al after Madame Cazier."

Legare jumps to his feet. "Yes, darling." He rushes to the back door to locate Al. He dispatches Al to let the midwife know of Mia's condition and ask her to come to their house right away.

Madame Cazier arrives and examines Mia. "Mia, you need to go to the bedroom and make yourself comfortable."

Legare escorts Mia to the bedroom, never leaving her side. Once she is comfortable, Legare encourages her to follow Tot's advice to keep her strength by eating and drinking. He hands another cup of steaming tea to his wife.

Madame Cazier then warns Mia, "You're going to need a lot of strength before the baby arrives. So please eat and drink." Legare is determined on attending to Mia's every need. Peering out of the window, he sees the August moon, full and bright. He sees the drowsy shadows of bats flying through the full moon's outline. The wild shriek of a nearby owl blends with the croaking frogs and chirping crickets.

Endeavoring to divert Mia's attention from the business at hand, Legare asks, "Mia, can you see the moon from your bed? It's so bright! It seems like it's smiling at us."

Mia turns her head toward the window. "It must be beautiful. I can see the bright shadows of the trees from here."

Shortly after midnight Mia cries out, "Legare, our baby is nearing!"

The midwife and Tot are in the bedroom. Tot checks the crib and stacks the extra towels. She brings in extra lanterns, candles and potholders. The midwife places the pans nearby. Some will contain the afterbirth and others will have fresh water for her and the Doctor.

Legare rushes from Mia and goes outside to wake Jesse and Al. He sends Al immediately for the doctor and tells Jesse, "Fetch Aunt Josephine and Uncle Richard after the baby is born."

Tot and the midwife prepare the necessary cloths, water pitcher, and washbasin at Mia's bedside. The two fine silk handkerchiefs are ready as well. It is customary in the Hill family to tie the umbilical cord with two new silk handkerchiefs before separating the new arrival from the mother.

"Breathe through your mouth and push hard," urges the midwife. Mia does her best to comply as tears roll down her delicate cheeks.

How she deeply wishes for her mother and prays for the unborn baby.

After ten hours of labor, Mia is totally exhausted. Her strength has withered and she is able only for one final, almost effortless push. Mia groans while Legare weeps helplessly. Helpless, naked, a new life dashes from its mother's womb and the loud cry can be heard throughout the house. The rooster sounds a shrill clarion of welcome, "Cock-a-doodle-do!" The sun delivers a gloriously bright and beautiful morning through the windows. All nature seems both lovely and joyful. The midwife clears the baby's mouth of fluid. Suddenly, the newborn Hill turns red-faced, begins thrashing at his newfound freedom, and screams even louder.

"Good set of lungs on your baby boy!" says Dr. Blair.

Legare, still holding Mia's hand, now sits next to her. He is dizzy and on the verge of passing out. While the midwife holds the newborn, Dr. Blair picks up the two new silk handkerchiefs from the crib and he firmly ties the umbilical cord. Then he reaches onto the table for the utility scissors and starts a new life by cutting the cord. Unable to speak with tears of joy streaming from his eyes, Legare continues to squeeze Mia's hand.

Dr. Blair smiles as the midwife cleans and wraps the screaming baby Joshua. She places the newborn on Mia's chest. Mia immediately kisses this new life and presses him gently against her breast. Tears continue to roll from her eyes as she softly whispers to their son, "I see your pa, too."

Chapter Twenty-one
Seeking Buster

In early February 1863, Buck leaves the hotel across from the depot as a train heading north pulls into town. The train is loaded with troops, and they appear to be veterans. Upon further observation, Buck recognizes the unit as Buster's. Buck looks among the bronzed faces of the soldiers, the familiar and distinguishing figure of Buster Phillips. John Rankin steps from the train. Several different regiments are returning from Augusta with several boxcar loads of ammunition and new recruits. As the formation is dismissed, Buck rushes to John and catches him by surprise.

"Why, I didn't think you would be here, Buck."

"I just happened to come up for the mail run due on the southbound train. We're waiting to hear from Norman. I wish Betty Gail were here to visit with you, but she stayed at the farm today. You're looking mighty good."

"Been doin' lots' of fightin', Buck. Lots of killin' a goin' on. I'm lucky ta be alive."

Buck claps John on the back, "Got time for something to eat at the hotel across the way? They got some fresh beef in this morning."

"I got thirty minutes."

The two men head across the dirt street. Shaking the dust from his feet on the wooden sidewalk, Buck enters the hotel lobby just ahead of John.

Buck nods thoughtfully. While eating a fresh steak, Buck asks, "Have you seen Buster?"

"Yes, he's at the camp in Augusta now."

"I was hoping he'd be on the train. I would like to have seen him."

"Want me to give him a message?"

"No, nothing urgent. I'll see him soon enough."

Buck takes a sip of cool milk. A long silence follows as the men enjoy their meal.

John finally breaks the silence. "I hope the town survives this war. A lot of our neighbors are getting killed."

"When this war is over I'll be back to start over," John takes the last bite of his meal and pushes from the table.

"Lots of our folks have gone to war, John, some killed, some captured. Got the list posted inside the depot. You know most of them. Let's take a look before you get back on the train."

"Glad to, Buck."

Inside the depot, the list has grown since John's departure over a year ago. There have been 13 more enlistments added, four wounded and three killed since the war started.

"These lists continue to grow, John. Never hope to see anybody else's name here." Suddenly the train's whistle blows. John leaves Buck with a simple handshake. "Good luck to you, John."

"Thanks, Buck." John boards the train and nods at Buck. "Tell all my folks 'hello' for me. I didn't know until this morning that I was headed this way. The train wasn't supposed to stop. Got to get this ammo to the north in a hurry."

A telegraph reaches Stone Mountain in September 17, 1863. Union forces and Confederate forces are facing each other along Chickamauga Creek. Union forces are on the west side. Confederate forces on the east side. For two days, the thick forest conceals the movements of both armies as they attempt to outmaneuver one another. At the end of the struggle, General William Rosecrans seems to have the advantage.

During the next two days, the complete

Confederate army is massing against General George Thomas. He is able to hold firm against the overwhelming Confederate forces, saving the union forces from a bitter defeat. General Thomas retreats through McFarland's Gap to Chattanooga. The Confederates are too exhausted to pursue the enemy. There are more than eighteen thousand Confederates killed and sixteen thousand of the Union. Thus, in reality, the battle is an irresolute success for the Army of Tennessee.

Soon thereafter, the misfortunes of war begin to arrive in Marietta. The civilian population, fleeing from battles, engulfs the city and surely tests its ability to care for them. Many simply pass through on their way to Atlanta. Marietta has sufficient hospitals to care for most of those who are wounded. Then the dead arrive by train and wagons. The cadet corps and the war- weary surviving soldiers are temporarily assigned to bury the dead in the new cemetery across the road from GMI.

Norman writes home in October:

"Thanks for sending me the letter you got from Mia and Legare. It's great to be proud grandparents. I am just as proud to be an uncle. I will write Mia. I'm hoping you and the Hills are going to visit and show them how much you really care for both of them. Leave your feeling for Buster at home. Anyhow, I like Legare better. When you decide to go, give my nephew a big whatever for me! The days are becoming cold and foggy.

"The trees are more beautiful than one can imagine with all of the different colors of autumn. These past two weeks have surely shown us the true and dark side of war. Yet we dream of our chance to prove ourselves in the defense of our homeland. We have been part of the Honor Guard for several Generals who were killed in the battle of

Chickamauga. We lined up with several hundred regulars as the bodies were brought to their final resting place. The caskets are on a horse- drawn bier with one stirrup upon the saddle. The Drummer and Fifer led the funeral brigade. Following the Drummer and Fifer was the Color Guard, then his military unit, usually consisting of about 500 men. And then the casket.

"It is an awesome sight. It seems that the beauty of death is told in nature by the beauty of the colors of the dying leaves on the trees.

"I'm sure you have read about our general, General Benjamin H. Helms, being one of the casualties. General Helms commanded General Breckinridge's third brigade. His wife is Mary Todd Lincoln's sister, making him the brother-in-law of President Lincoln. His brigade was known as the "Orphan Brigade" due to the fact that it is made up of Kentuckians who chose to fight for the Confederacy. The story goes that on Sunday morning, the 20th of September, General Helms was having a difficult time leading his Kentuckians against the Union breastworks of General Thomas when a bullet tore through his right shoulder. He was taken to the field hospital where he later died.

"The Cadet Corps was also part of the Honor Guard for General Preston Smith. He was killed on Saturday the 19th of September. The soldiers who were in the battle said the fighting became so intense in the thick forest that it was difficult to tell friend from foe. The fighting was desperate with hand-to-hand combat. Soldiers screaming with commands as well as screaming from the agony of ghastly wounds.

The third Gen's funeral which Paul and I were part of was for General James Deshler. He was killed on the same day and near the area where General Helms received his mortal wounds. General Deshler was struck directly in the chest by a piece of shrapnel. According to witnesses, the shrapnel ripped his heart completely from his body. What a horrifying sight that must have been. As soon as the roads are passable, General Deshler's body will be sent to Alabama. General Smith's body is to be sent to Memphis, Tennessee, and General Helm's body is to be transported to Kentucky.

"The entire cadet Corps dig graves daily, though not as many now as in the first week after the Battle at Chickamauga. It is now customary when an officer's body is to be honored; the cadet corps provides the Honor Guard.

"I'm worried about Mia. Have you heard anymore from her since the first letter to all of us?"

"I hope everyone is well. Love to All."

Mia rises early on November 11, starting off on a chilly Wednesday morning. The embers in the fireplace are still warm and glowing. Mia eases silently from the side of Legare and places two logs over the warm embers. She opens the door from the bedroom and sees Tot in the kitchen.

"Got de root tea 'n de popcawn cereal ready fuh uh good brekwas fuh you 'n Massuh leGree. Jes' need fuh put de egg on. Got de rice grits fuh de baba. [Got the root tea and the popcorn cereal ready for a good breakfast for you and Mr. Legare. Just need to put the eggs on. Got the rice grits for the baby.]

"That fried ham sure does smell good! Is that part of the pork rump Uncle Richard brought over the other day?"

"Yass, Ma'am!" replies Tot.

"It's still early, so wait a little while longer before putting the eggs on."

Mia enters the bedroom and quietly places a breakfast tray on a table. She sits on the side on the bed next to the sleeping Legare. She whispers gently in his ear, "Wake up, my love." Without moving Legare opens his eyes. "Happy birthday, honey! I have breakfast in bed for you this morning." Legare pulls Mia close to him. He kisses her soft and warm lips, pulling her even closer.

"My life is perfect with you and little Joshua. No man can ask for anything more. I'm living in heaven." After lying together quietly for a few minutes, he looks at Mia. "Not only is today my birthday, but the day I have to volunteer for the army—a double-edged sword." He tightens his grip around her. "Captain Picquet expects me at Thunderbolt before dark. He said I am going to be in Company A of the 63rd Georgia Regiment, doing duty right here in Savannah."

Mia gives him another warm kiss and hugs him dearly. In her heart Mia knows their life is about to change.

Suddenly, little Joshua awakens and stands up in his crib. With his outstretched arms, he calls, "Mama, Pa-pa." Removing the large, warm, down comforter, Legare walks around the bed and takes the little one in his arms. "I don't need to squeeze you too much because you stink! But I can give you a big kiss!" Laughing, Mia places a towel on the bed and the daily routine of the first change of the day is over in a matter of minutes.

"Your breakfast is going to get cold." Mia leans over and lets Legare kiss his son.

"I don't want to eat without you, Mia."

Mia walks to the door. "Tot, bring in my breakfast and the baby's breakfast."

Tot already has the food prepared and brings the tray into the bedroom. "Happy bertday Massuh leGree. 'E uh bootiful 'n sunny day."

"Thanks, Tot!"

Tot departs and proceeds to the cookhouse. She has to prepare for the gathering in the afternoon when Richard and Josephine come over for Legare's birthday. The sun is beginning to shine through the frosty glass, giving a little more warmth to the house. Mia, Legare and little Joshua sit around the table in the bedroom. Little Joshua is in his highchair staring at the food and ready to eat. Legare gives him the first bite of the warm rice grits.

Little Joshua smears his food over his face. Mia feeds him and Legare tries to keep his face clean. Soon Joshua is stuffed and satisfied.

"I've invited Dr. Blair and Madame Cazier over for cake

and hors d'oeuvres this afternoon. It will probably be more like supper, knowing Aunt Josephine. She is making the cake and said it is going to be unusual since flour is hard to come by. Also, I think Mayor and Mrs. Purse and Sara Blake are dropping by for a few minutes."

Legare responds, "I guess we best get moving and get this place in perfect order. You know how Aunt Josephine is about neatness. I wish some of our other friends could be with us, but they are all off fighting. I'm lucky to be able to stay in Savannah. Captain Picquet tells me I'll be close by on Whitemarsh Island some of the time, but furloughs are easy to come by right now."

"Tot has the place clean and neat. How about you, me and Joshua just take a carriage ride through town after it gets a little warmer."

Legare has to enlist today, so he, Mia and little Joshua enjoy the day together having lunch at their favorite restaurant and touring Savannah. Tot and Josephine are preparing to have friends over to Mia and Legare's house for a birthday party before Legare has to go and enlist at Fort Thunderbolt.

When they reach the Savannah River, Legare points to the Confederate Naval yard and tells Mia, "Our navy in the Savannah River is like a mirror of the entire Confederate forces. We do not equal or surpass the Union in any category."

Mia peers down the river front. "I don't think we even have as many naval vessels as the Union."

"Not nearly in number or quality. Since the Federals burned the Norfolk Navy Yard, we won't be building anymore, either."

"What's that we have in Pensacola?"

"That's the naval repair yard in Pensacola." Mia is still looking toward the river. "I feel like those ironclads will change naval warfare forever. That battle between the *Merrimack* and the *Monitor* at the Battle of Hampton Roads proves there will be no more wooden ships for battles at sea."

"That's the way it really looks." Legare takes on a

begrudging tone. "You know our army isn't any better, either. We are outnumbered, out-gunned and out-supplied. Plus, Governor Brown is out of his mind, and I gotta sign up to be a part of this mess today."

"We'll be okay. You're in Savannah and the war is far north of here."

Legare kisses Mia on her cheek.

"Look over there, Legare. There's an old merchant ship that looks like the *Fingal*. Remember the *Atlanta*? I read that it was converted from the *Fingal*, a merchant ship."

"You're right," replies Legare. "The *Atlanta* ran around the Union blockade in June before she had to surrender to the Union Navy. Look over there. There's our 122-foot paddle-wheel boat, the *Everglade*. Poor 'ole navy and poor 'ole Commodore Tattnall. He has the awesome responsibility of ensuring the protection of the converted *Everglade* to the flag ship *Savannah,* sitting right there in the harbor. I assume my duty will include defending the coast and rivers either at Fort Thunderbolt or on one of the islands."

"How many Negroes and whites do you figure have been killed since the first slave was introduced to America?" asks Mia.

"Don't have any idea except there will probably be a million lives lost in this war."

They sit and study the scene quietly for a while. Ready for happier thoughts, Legare says to Jesse, "Let's head to the house. It's nearly two o'clock and the guests will be arriving soon."

"Yaas'suh, Mistuh Legare." Jesse snaps the reins and heads for home.

Mia begins to tickle and play with their precious son on their journey home. Legare joins in just as Mia picks Joshua up to begin narrating the passing scenes. "Look at the big river." Mia
points toward the river. Little Joshua looks for a moment and then turns to his pa.

"Come to your pa." Joshua stretches his arms for

his pa to lift him over to his lap. "Look that way. Look at the big oak trees and there's our house down the road." Little Joshua peers over the front of the carriage while in his pa's lap. "Mia, I find it hard to imagine a better birthday present than spending the day with my beautiful, loving wife and sweet son."

Chapter Twenty-two
A Surprise Package

"Happy birthday, Legare." She kisses Legare and pinches his cheek. "Looks like some of the guests have already arrived," Legare notes as the carriage comes to a stop in front of the house.

"The wooden box of hot rocks is still warm. That was really nice to have. Thanks, Jesse."

Jesse smiles and nods his head toward Legare. Legare jumps to the ground and takes Joshua from Mia as she steps down from the carriage. They see the familiar carriages of Mayor Purse and his niece Sara Blake. Looking somewhat puzzled, Mia sees two carriages that belong to Uncle Richard and comments to Legare, "Why did Uncle Richard bring two carriages?"

Legare shrugs his shoulders and lifts his eyebrows. "Maybe one of them will have to leave early."

Mia opens the door for Legare and Joshua and the three walk into their home. A great surprise causes Mia and Legare to stand completely still and speechless. Tears fill Mia's eyes.

Mia catches her breath and forces her weak legs into motion. She runs with open arms. "Mama! Papa! I can't believe you're here! I've missed you so much and think about you and home all the time."

The reunited trio hugs each other tightly. As Buck squeezes Mia, Betty Gail whispers, "We love you more than you'll ever know."

Simultaneously, Legare is barely able to contain his

emotions and rushes toward his mother and father, grasping them tightly with one arm as he holds onto little Joshua in his other. Tears flow from Mrs. Hill's eyes. She and his father embrace Legare and the grandson they are meeting for the first time. Congressman Hill, like Buck, is quiet. Their actions speak volumes for their feelings.

Mrs. Hill demonstrates her and Congressman Hill's feelings with the embrace only a mother can provide. Tot, Mayor and Mrs. Purse and Jennifer, Uncle Richard and Aunt Josephine are also standing nearby quietly witnessing this emotional reuniting of families. Grandmother Hill takes the baby from Legare's arms. She hugs and kisses him in a manner befitting a new grandson as they walk over to the Jernigans.

She hands the baby to Betty Gail, "I guess it's your turn to kiss this beautiful little cherub."

Betty Gail takes little Joshua and stands next to Buck. Buck still cannot speak, but holds the baby with Betty Gail as they admire him as though to ask for forgiveness for waiting so long to be together.

Without hesitation, Mia goes to Mrs. Hill and Congressman Hill, giving them an embrace without thought of the past and only love for them, her husband, little Joshua and their future.

Legare goes over to Buck. Before he can get close, Buck grabs his hand and in a stern and sincere voice, Says "Legare, please forgive me for doubting your sincerity when you eloped with Mia. We couldn't ask for a better son-in-law or a father for our grandchild."

Legare's heart is swollen with emotion and he can only respond in a whisper. "Thank you, Mr. Jernigan. I love your daughter and your family as much as my own."

Uncle Richard, Aunt Josephine, Tot, Jennifer and Mayor and Mrs. Purse join in the celebration of bonding with everyone. After a while, everyone settles down. Legare is sitting between his mother and Mia as Mia asks her mother, "How'd you get here?"

"We came down with Congressman Hill and Emily two days ago. Richard and Josephine picked us up at the depot and we've had a wonderful visit with them. You see, Emily and I got together not long after you and Legare eloped, trying to figure out what to do next."

Mia starts weeping, wipes her eyes and turns to Mrs. Hill, "I don't know what to say. I am just so happy we are all together."

Legare pulls Mia near. Emily leans forward and takes Mia's hand. "When your mother and father received the letter you and Legare wrote to them as well as to us, we contacted each other."

Excited, Mia asks, "So when did you visit each other?"

"Buck, Joshua, your mother and I have had several visits together."

"So Uncle Richard has been keeping you abreast of our well-being, I guess."

"Oh yes, Richard has been keeping us well informed. It took us, especially your pa, time to get over your running away when you had consented to marry Buster. So when your pa finally swallowed his pride, well, here we are."

"On Legare's birthday no less. What a great birthday present!"

Becoming more somber and lowering her head, Mia tries to regain her composure. "And the day he has to enlist."

Betty Gail takes and holds Mia's hand. "Congressman Hill talked with your father and told him that today is Legare's birthday and he has to enlist so, we all agreed that today would be a good day to surprise the three of you."

"Where is Norman? Why couldn't he come?"

Betty Gail's expression shows her dismay. "We tried to get the school to release Norman for a few days, but they would not because the cadets are training the regular soldiers at Camp McDonald."

"I dearly miss my brother, Ma."

"He couldn't be better. We wrote and told him we were coming to surprise you. These next kisses are from him." Betty Gail gives Mia and little Joshua kisses from Norman. "He loves GMI and, like I told you, they are training the soldiers at Camp McDonald. We don't hear from him that much because paper is getting in short supply. Says he wants to see you and your family badly. He'll send us a telegram to Mr. Goldsmith at the depot. He always asks about his sister."

"And Uncle Isaac and Aunt Sally?"

"They're just fine." Betty Gail hugs Mia and squeezes her three times, cementing their love with tears. "We have been more than anxious to see our wonderful grandson."

Congressman Hill and Buck come over and take seats with the family. Uncle Richard and Aunt Josephine are with their daughters, Trina-Marie and Claire. Mrs. Purse has taken over the care of the baby. Looking around, Legare asks, "Where are Ian and Keaton?"

"Not back from the Florida Plantation," answers Uncle Richard.

Aunt Josephine goes quietly to Tot. "Go to the cook house and bring in the surprise birthday pies." Tot has been keeping the birthday treat warm in the cookhouse away from Legare and Mia. Aunt Josephine then turns and announces, "Gather round, there's a birthday pie coming in the door!"

Everyone jumps to their feet and gathers in the small dining room. The door to the cookhouse opens and Tot enters with two large pies. Legare and Mia stare at the two pies and Legare shouts, "It's a shoo-fly pie! My favorite! "He turns to his mother with a big smile and gives her another hug. "Thanks, Ma."

"I made it fresh this morning." Pointing to the other pie, Mrs. Hill whispers to Mia, "Look, Mia. Guess what your mama has made for you."

Mia leaves Legare's side and moves toward the table. Suddenly, she picks up a familiar sweet fragrance. "Ma, you made me a fresh pecan pie."

Picking up the pecan pie, Mia places it close to her nose and inhales deeply. "Smells just like home! "She rushes over to her mother and father, embracing them both.

Betty Gail smiles and whispers to Mia, "I made it at Richard's and Josephine's but the pecans are fresh from Stone Mountain!"

As if on cue, everyone begins singing, "For he's a Jolly Good Fellow," to Legare, followed by more embraces. Mia takes Legare's hand. "It's time for your spanking, honey.

Bend over."

The entire group bursts into laughter. She takes his hand and places it on the table. "I told you to bend over, honey." He slightly bends and looks over his shoulder. "Not too hard now, Mia."

"I'm giving you the first spank . . the happy one." She spanks him on the fanny once. Everyone applauds.

"I'm next," says his mother, "I'll give you the one to grow on." She also spanks him on the fanny. Uncle Richard walks up with Betty Gail. "Here's the smack for you to eat on," says Uncle Richard.

"Mine is for you to live a long life," says Betty Gail as she renders her spank.

"The last one is from me and Buck," says Congressman Hill. "It's a little late coming, but it's the spanking for marriage." Buck and he walk up behind Legare and each takes his turn in giving him a spank.

Legare laughs. "I bet that relieved a lot of frustration for you, Mr. Jernigan."

"Everything's fine. You got what you deserved—my daughter!"

Everyone applauds again. "And a good marriage it will be. Congressman Hill, I believe it's your turn now."

Congressman Hill smiles. "Now I get to give you the eighteen spanks, one for each year." With each gentle spank his father counts to eighteen.

Standing with a broad smile, Legare tells his family and friends, "Thanks for all your blessed spanks!" The group cheers again. "Time for the shoo-fly pie, Tot."

Tot begins cutting the shoo-fly pie. "Fuss piece ob

shoo-fly is yourn, Mistuh LeGree." Then Trina-Marie and Claire begin cutting and distributing the balance to the guests. Tot cuts a wedge of the fresh pecan pie, "Dis duh yourn ma'am." Before Mia thanks Tot, she nearly ingests the entire wedge in one bite, barely allowing the palate to enjoy the wonderful flavor.

Aunt Josephine turns to the gathering and says, "Don't worry; there are two more of each pie in the cookhouse. Congressman, would you please bless this food so we can get to the pork roast!"

The room becomes silent as Congressman Hill asks the gathering, "Let us hold hands." Each person takes their neighbor's hand and Mia and Legare place their hands tightly together. "Dear Heavenly Father, thank you for this blessed day. A day of rejoicing, a day of families uniting.

"I thank you for giving Legare the constitution to select Mia as his wife and mother of his child and our grandchild. Bless our son, Legare, as he enlists today. Protect and return him to us upon the end of this terrible conflict. Protect our soldiers who stand to protect their family and property against our Union brothers. We beg You to bring reason and fellowship to our leaders of the Confederacy and the Union. And last, God bless the cooks! Amen."

Tot, Jesse, Al, and one of Uncle Richard's servants bring in the birthday feast. Al begins slicing and serving the pork while Jesse serves up the fresh greens and sassafras tea. Soon, the fireplace begins to give more light to the surroundings as the sun creeps behind the crest of the large oak trees. Legare looks at Mia and takes her hand as they stand. Everyone turns their attention to the lovely couple. Legare stands silent for a few seconds. In a quivering voice, Legare says, "Folks, you know what time it is. Mia and I cannot thank you enough for your forgiveness and love. Antonio told Mia and me today that all Friday the 13th's are not bad luck. He's right. Day after tomorrow will be the greatest Friday the 13th on the face of the earth!

"Captain Picquet is expecting me before nightfall at Fort Thunderbolt. It's only about three or four miles from here, so I am going to have Jesse and Al take me there in the carriage. Please, do not make this any harder than necessary. Jesse already has my belongings in the carriage. Captain Picquet said that furloughs are easy to get, especially if you have family in the area, so I hope to be in and out quite frequently."

Tears begin rolling down Mia's cheeks as the entire room swells again with another kind of emotion. The last to embrace Legare is his mother and with "God's speed," he and Mia depart for the awaiting carriage. Standing beside the carriage, Legare holds Mia tightly. "I love you, Mia. There's no soul or heart on earth which could love you more."

Mia responds emotionally, "Only my heart and soul knows how your heart and soul feels."

They embrace tightly and kiss passionately as Al and Jesse reverently observe the farewell of lovers. Legare and Mia slowly separate as he turns and boards the carriage. Soon the carriage turns a corner beyond the house and Mia's tears go from warm to cold as they stream down her soft cheeks.

It's not long before Fort Thunderbolt and the command-center flag are in sight. Fort Thunderbolt and the flag grow larger as the carriage draws closer. Jesse pulls on the reins and the carriage comes to a halt in front of the headquarters building at the entrance of the fort. Al steps down and unloads Legare's satchel.

Legare steps from the carriage and faces Al and Jesse. "Thanks for bringing me to the fort. I hope to see you both again soon." He shakes Al's hand and Jesse leans over and shakes Legare's hand as he passes by the side of the carriage. Taking a deep breath, Legare opens the door at the front building, enters and approaches orderly. "My name is Hugh Legare Hill. Captain Picquet is expecting me before nightfall at Fort Thunderbolt."

"Follow me, Hill. Captain Picquet told me you were

coming in today." He leads Legare to a nearby room. Legare notices the nameplate on the door: Captain Lewis Picquet.

The orderly knocks and Captain Picquet responds, "You may enter." Upon entering, the orderly salutes. "Sir, this is Hugh Legare Hill reporting for muster."

Captain Picquet dismisses the orderly and invites Legare to take a seat. "I see you made it, Legare. Welcome to the 63rd Georgia."

"Thank you, Captain Picquet."

"There are a few papers you need to sign and the oath you need to take. Here is a copy for you to read. Take a few minutes and if you have any questions, please ask me."

Legare takes a few minutes to review the documents. "Everything looks in order to me, sir."

"Good, then let me administer the oath to you. Please stand and raise your right hand and when I finish the oath, you can simply say, 'I do.'"

"I, Hugh Legare Hill, born in Madison in the State of Georgia, aged 18 years and by the occupation a farmer, Do HEREBY ACKNOWLEDGE to serve for the period of THREE YEARS OF THE WAR, unless sooner discharged by competent authority: Do also agree to accept such bounty, pay, rations, and clothing, as or may be established by law. And I, Hugh L. Hill, do solemnly swear, or affirm, that I will bear true allegiance to the State of Georgia, and that I will serve her honestly and faithfully against all her enemies or opposes whomever; and that I will observe and obey the orders of the Governor of the State of Georgia, and the orders of the officers appointed over me according to the Rules and Articles for the government of the armies of Georgia, so long as I remain under the control of Georgia, and should I be transferred by Said State to the Confederacy of States, which have seceded, or may secede from the government of the United States, and may adopt a confederated Government, I will thenceforth, to the end of the term for which I have enlisted, bear like allegiance, and render like services to said Confederacy, by whatsoever name it may be known."

"I do."

"You may lower your hand now, Pvt. Hill." Captain Picquet extends his hand and shakes Legare's hand. Captain Picquet offers Legare a pen, lays the oath on the desk and points with his finger. "Sign here, Pvt. Hill." Legare takes the pen and inks in his name. "Congratulations! You are assigned to Company A of the 63rd Georgia Volunteer Infantry. Major Joseph Allen is the company commander. We will not be issuing you any uniforms for a couple of months. Did you bring extra clothing to wear?"

Yes, sir. I also brought a couple of extra blankets as you suggested."

"Your squad leader will be a fellow called 'Rooster, who is a Sergeant. Rooster is his first and last name."

Legare looks puzzled. "Did you say Rooster is his first and last name, sir?"

"That's right."

"Should I ask how'd that come about, sir?"

"Rooster is from North Georgia. Some hunters found him in a covered wagon asleep when he was a baby. They came upon the wagon with the mules tied to a tree. The front and rear flaps of the wagon were tied closed."

Legare listens intensely. "Really."

"They searched for his parents in the woods and the nearby river, but couldn't find any trace of them. Soon the Sheriff became involved, but nobody could locate his family. There wasn't even a piece of paper in the wagon with any kind of address or name."

Legare appears very concerned. "No trace of his folks at all?"

"None. So one of the hunters and his wife took the baby and raised him to be a fine young man and soldier."

"How did he get the name Rooster?"

"Oh, I almost forgot that part. There was a cage on the side of the wagon with a rooster in it that kept crowing. So they named the baby Rooster. He never took the family name of the folks who cared for him." Captain Piquet looks straight at Legare, "So when he enlisted he had to have a first and last name. So he enlisted as Rooster Rooster."

"What a story. So his family was never found."

"Not a trace of evidence whatsoever as to what happened to them."

"His unit is from North Georgia and he was transferred to Savannah with his unit and some other units. These units were consolidated to form the 63rd. Tomorrow, you'll begin orientation and your drill instructions. Over the next couple of weeks, you will participate in musket drills and artillery drills. Afterwards, you will be assigned to Whitemarsh Island as infantry security. Like I told you, furloughs are easy to come by so long as there's no threat from the Yankees." Captain Picquet leads Legare to the door. "Orderly, escort Pvt. Hill to his quarters."

"Follow me, Pvt. Hill," states the orderly.

Legare picks up his satchel and follows. They go from the headquarters and enter a barracks in the adjacent building. Once inside, Legare sees about fifty beds lining the walls. There are two large stoves, each about a third of the way from each end of the barracks, in the middle of the room. "Sgt. Rooster, here is Pvt. Hill. He mustered a few minutes ago and has been assigned to your squad."

"Welcome to Company A." Rooster extends his hand and he and Legare shake. "Call me Rooster or call me Sergeant, but do not call me sir. What's your full name, Hill?"

"Hugh Legare Hill, but I go by Legare."

"Where you from?"

"I'm from Madison, but my wife, baby, and I have been living in Savannah. Where are you from, Rooster?"

"I'm from the Cassville area of North Georgia. Let me introduce you to a few of the other guys " By now, most of the soldiers in the barracks have gathered around Legare, They all shake hands and introduce themselves to the newest member of their squad.

"I'm Adiel Blanchard. Welcome."

"I'm 7th Corporal Joseph Warren. Glad to have you with us."

"St. John Nimmo is my name. Welcome."

"A. T. Lyon is my name. I'm the Company Bugler."

"Hello, I'm David Blount."

"I'm Pleasant Barnett. Nice to meet up with ya."

"My name is Alonzo W. McCurdy. Welcome aboard."

Shaking hands, Legare looks at A. W. and asks, "Do you have any kin in Stone Mountain?"

"I'm from Madison County, but my uncle Robert McCurdy lives there. Why do you ask?"

"There's a large clan of McCurdys living in Stone Mountain and I am married to a girl from there. Her maiden name is Jernigan."

"I've heard my uncle speak of the Jernigans. Owns a small farm, right?"

"That's them all right!"

"Howdy. My name is John Carroll."

"Hello, my name is Legare Hill. Nice to meet you."

The round of introductions is briefly interrupted when a young gentleman approaches and taps Legare on the shoulder. "Hi, Legare!"

"John Dent! I can't believe it! You're in the 63rd?" John and Legare shake hands again, before sitting in two chairs nearby to talk about their families.

"I hope you're still married to that beautiful Mia!"

"Sure am and we are living in Savannah—just down on the river a short piece from here." The two old friends catch up on old times until the bugler sounds taps.

The following morning at 7:30 a.m. sharp, Sgt. Elijah Stowe sounds *Reveille* with his bugle. Everyone is up and in formation within ten minutes. Rooster pokes his head in. "Just follow along with Pvt. Dent, and after breakfast you'll get your drill instructions and orientation."

After breakfast, Rooster teaches Legare the proper method of military formations and marching. Later in the morning, they discuss the various ranks and the insignia associated with each rank, whom to salute and how to address individuals. He also explains the election process of the officers by the troops. "Got any questions, Pvt. Hill?"

"Not yet. Pretty straightforward," replies Legare.

"Well, Pvt. Lyon will be sounding the bugle for dinner shortly, so take a break. After dinner, you'll meet with Major Allen. He'll give you some history on the 63rd and explain our mission at Fort Thunderbolt."

Following dinner, Rooster walks with Legare over to Major Allen's headquarters. He reminds Legare to "stand at attention" and salute. "Wait until Major Allen returns your salute before returning to attention. Then, remain standing at attention until Major Allen gives you an order otherwise." When they arrive at Major Allen's office, Rooster informs the headquarters clerk that Major Allen is expecting him and Legare.

"I'll tell Major Allen you're here." In a moment the clerk returns. "Major Allen said for you to come into his office."

Rooster and Legare walk to Major Allen's office and knock on the door. "Come In!" They enter, stand at attention and salute. Major Allen returns their salute. "Stand at ease and have a seat. Rooster, if you have something else to do, you may go, and I will send Pvt. Hill to the barracks when I finish with the orientation."

"Yes, sir. There are a few items I need to attend to, sir." Standing, Rooster salutes and departs.

"How has your enlistment been so far, Pvt. Hill?" asks Major Allen.

"Pretty busy, sir, otherwise everything is fine."

"Military clothing is in short supply, but eventually you'll be given some uniforms. This afternoon you'll pick up your musket and accoutrements: knapsack, haversack and canteen. Do you know how to swim?"

"Yes, sir."

"It is important that you know how to swim. We had a soldier drown this past April right here at Thunderbolt. Poor fellow fell out of the boat and never came up. The current was so strong that we never found his body. Probably carried him out to sea." Legare squirms a little in his chair.

"Our main mission is defensive in nature. We guard the coast of Savannah. The entire outside coastal defense batteries were ordered by General Lee to fall back upon the interior forts. For us, that's Thunderbolt and Fort Beulieu. There are two artillery batteries on Whitemarsh Island. The Southern end is Battery Point and there are works at the northeast point."

"What about you, Pvt. Hill? Tell me about yourself. Where are you from?"

"Well, sir, I'm from Madison. My wife and I moved to Savannah about a year ago. We have a house on the river and a son named Joshua. I work for my Uncle Richard on his plantation and with Mr. Lilly at the Bank." Legare thinks it might be best to not give any more details, just in case Major Allen does not like his father's pro-union stand against the war.

"As long as the war is quiet around here, we are pretty liberal about furloughs. However, there are no furloughs while you are in training and furloughs can be stopped at any time. Furloughs help keep more food for the soldiers who have no place to go to for home cooking. If you don't have any questions, Pvt. Hill, you are dismissed. Rooster will give you a tour of the fort."

"Don't have any questions right now, sir."

"Then you are dismissed."

"Thank you, sir." Legare stands, salutes and departs. Returning to the barracks, Legare goes to his cot and finds a haversack.

John Dent sees Legare inspecting his equipment. "Rooster left the haversack, knapsack and canteen for you. The cartridge boxes and musket will be issued to you next week. That's about all you are going to get right now. Supplies are running short."

"Thanks!" says Legare. Opening the haversack, Legare finds a metal plate, fork and knife. The knapsack is empty.

John is sitting on the bunk next to Legare's and watches him as he checks his equipment. "I guess you know you have to provide your own clothing and blankets for now."

Rooster continues giving a tour.

"It's a pretty nice and quiet place. But we keep our eyes toward Wassaw Sound all the time. That's the direction from which the Yankees will attack. I guess you heard about President Davis visiting here last month. He disembarked the *Beauregard* to inspect our unit. He called us the 'Phoenix Riflemen.' He congratulated us for repelling the Yankees on May 19 last year and not losing a single man."

"Personally, I think President Davis makes a good cheerleader. He can really give an encouraging speech," Legare responds.

Soon Rooster returns. "I see you found your gear. Let's move on and take a tour of the fort before dark. Pvt. Harrison, you are the interior quarters guard today, right?"

"That's me, Rooster."

"Okay, Dent, you can come along with us if you like."

John Dent replies, "Should see more action out there than in here!"

The three depart the barracks and approach the highest point on the fort. Rooster points toward the river. "From this position, along this high bluff, we have strategically built earthworks with these mounds, bombproof shelters and cannon emplacements. Now, lean over and look at the river below." Legare leans over as far as he safely can and looks toward the river. "See those large oaks in the river? We put them there as obstacles to slow down enemy ships if they attempt to move up the river towards Savannah."

Colonel Gorgas listens a moment. You've joined a great outfit, Hill. Carry on, Sgt. Rooster."

"Yes, sir, Colonel," and the three come to attention and salute Colonel Gorgas as he departs. "Well, it is almost time for supper. Tomorrow is Sunday and usually preacher Sweat comes and leads us in prayer." Next week, you'll receive your musket training and some more drills and instructions on provost duty, then, you'll get basic training in operating the big guns. When all of your training is complete, you'll be stationed on Whitemarsh in rotation on provost duty around the first week of December. I'm going on furlough this weekend. If I hear any cannon fire I'll return immediately. That is the standing order when you are on furlough. You cannot go out of range of the cannon sound. So, I'll see you Monday."

Legare turns to John, "Let's try to get our provost duty together with Alonzo McCurdy. That way we may be able to have a furlough at the same time and I can take you to our house for supper."

"Mighty generous of you. Rooster can arrange the schedule for us. He's pretty fair about scheduling everyone for furloughs. There are a couple of gals that hang around the fort that provide 'favors' for the soldiers. They're here just about every evening. The guys come and go all night long once their duty is finished for the day!"

"Happy hunting to them! I'm happy to wait for my furlough!"

During the last week of training, Rooster summons John, Alonzo, and Legare for the scheduling. "I have your request for furlough for Christmas and have been reviewing the schedule. Most of the fellows are too far away from home to get furlough for Christmas. If you three are willing to provide provost duty on Whitemarsh from December 10th through the 21st, I can get you a furlough from December 22nd through the 26th. What do you think?"

"I'll be more than glad to serve two weeks on Whitemarsh to be with my family on Christmas," replies Legare.

Chapter Twenty-three
Ignoring the Facts

After returning home from the grand family reunion, Buck heads to town to pick up his mail. He stops by the hotel to get a newspaper and William Sheppard invites him to have coffee with some friends. The conversation generally leads to General Robert E. Lee's June second invasion of the North, heading into Pennsylvania in a campaign leading to Gettysburg. After a couple days of fighting, the tide of war turns against the South as they are defeated at Gettysburg.

Buck interjects, "On July 4th last year the last Confederate stronghold on the Mississippi River surrendered to General Grant after six weeks of battle. I assume you all know that that victory cut the Confederacy in half.

"Yeah, but we will come together again." stubbornly injects James Miliken and he takes a sip of his coffee.

"I don't think so. The South is beginning to lose. Just last week General Grant defeated the siege army of General Bragg at Chattanooga by storming up his impregnable position on the face of Missionary Ridge. The Union is knocking on our door," replies Buck.

"The Union is already set to stop this war. Nobody in the North wants to keep it up. Their morale is really low. Remember this past July when they had those anti-draft riots in New York City where buildings were burned and the blacks were murdered by the poor white immigrants? Why they killed at least 120 people including children.

Should have killed more of those damn blacks like we did at Fort Wagner where half of the Negro troops of the 54th Massachusetts Infantry were killed. Should have killed them all," retorts William.

Buck ponders to himself, what is it going to take for the Union to come to grips with itself? President Lincoln has appointed five Generals to command the Army of the Potomac in less than year. This past May, General Hooker, due to his lack of nerve during the battle, allowed General Lee to whip him with a much smaller force at the battle of Chancellorsville. Then he speaks, "Fellows, don't forget the Emancipation Proclamation freeing all slaves in territories held by Confederates. The President is also emphasizing the enlisting of Negro soldiers in the Union Army. This was to preserve the Union and has also become a revolutionary struggle for the abolition of slavery."

"All those damn Negroes can do is carry hoes and pitchforks. Can't win a war with those. All that Proclamation does is makes us mad and want to fight harder. My Negroes are still working the farm," retorts James while laughing and slamming his fist on the table.

William chimes in, "We need more people around here like William Quantrill where he and 450 proslavery followers raided Lawrence, Kansas, and butchered 182 boys and men."

Buck reminds the group, "Think about it, fellows, right now the whole South is kind of an armed camp. We have police forces, locally and statewide, around that are slave patrols and then there are the bounty hunters. As you know, their job is to watch out on the roads for slaves who were off their farms or plantations for any reason. If very much of our white population is killed, wounded or become missing, and with all of the weapons left behind there could be a servile rebellion. I fear once it starts it will not end peacefully. Get your head out of the sand and think about that outcome, fellows. I suggest you start working more closely with your Negroes. I gotta git home. Good visiting with you."

Buck departs and William tells his buddies,

"Sometimes I think he could be an abolitionist."

James replies, "No he's just acting like a scared puppy with his tail between his legs."

Upon arriving home, Buck summons Betty Gail to tell her they have a letter from Buster. She rushes to his side as Buck opens the letter and begins reading:

"Dear Folks,

"Been doin' lots' of fightin', Buck. Lots of killin' a goin' on. I'm lucky ta be alive. Fur myself I don't take no stock in such talk. But hit do seem powerful good that no bullet nor shell nor nothing never hit me. A many of 'em have come might near!

"With death a starin' me in the face so close? It's strange," says Buster, *"but would you believe instead of seein' the ridge I was on and the long stretch that lay between us and the Yankees, where many of us was expecting to lay down our life . . instead I saw Stone Mountain in her spring green so close, I smelt the honeysuckles on the mountainside. I heard that mockingbird singing among de white blossoms of the dogwood tree. Not fer long, though. Longstreet nodded, and we blasted away at the Yankees. Luck was on my side, an' out of that Hell I survived—how, I never could tell—without a scratch. The next day they retreated, and we buried the Yankee dead with our own.*

"Sometimes I have my misgivings how this here war will end. If the South's whipped, there's no place better than de grave.

"When this war is over, I think about moving to Tennessee. . Sell you my place. Nothin' in Stone Mountain fer me. You have my cousin Michael's address in Tennessee. Enclosed is the deed to my property. Telegraph him three thousand dollars. The slaves probably will be freed by the Proclamation.

Buster"

As Betty Gail wipes the tears from her eyes, Buck hands her the letter and gives her a loving embrace.

Buck locates Isaac and discusses the content of

Buster's letter. "Round up Jacob, Ellen and Mark. Bring them over and let's tell them the news from Buster.

When the trio arrives, they find a shady spot and Buck begins explaining the contents of the letter from Buster. "First, I am going to draw up your freedom papers."

"Did you say freedom papers, Mr. Buck?

"Yes, I did. You will be free to go whenever and where-ever you please. President Lincoln has issued the Emancipation Proclamation and it applies to Georgia as well, but there are no Union troops here to enforce it. So if Georgia does beat the Union you still will be free.

The trio stands and begins shouting, dancing and rushes over to Buck and Isaac giving them huge embraces. Betty Gail and Sally hear all the shouting and come outside to join the group. Buck takes Betty Gail's arm as Isaac takes Sally's and discloses the reason for all of the joy.

Once the emotions settle, Buck advises the trio not to leave the area, but to stay on the farm, work and keep making an income. "Go ahead and move into the big house. And, here's an extra Union flag I have. Take down that Confederate Battle Flag and fly the Union. There are too many soldiers and slave patrols around for you to take a chance on being kidnapped and sold back into slavery. Your chance will come and yes, you are free to go whenever and wherever you want. I will draw up the papers for your freedom as soon as the deed is transferred. Should only be a few days from now.

Holding his hat in one hand, Jacob shakes Buck's hand and tells him, "Mr. Buck, We's don't know 'hat to say."

"Your smile says it all, Jacob. Go home and rest. If I were you I'd keep my freedom quiet because of all the turmoil around here. But you're free to leave whenever you want to," replies Buck. The jubilant trio departs. Isaac and Buck head to the chicken pen.

As Buck is opening the gate, Isaac tells him, "Remember when we helped Sue Lee?"

Buck turns and looks at Isaac, "Sure Do. Why do

you bring her up now?"

"Just found out recently that Buster was using her."

Buck looks astonished at Isaac's revelation, "You mean for sex, Isaac?"

"Yes, sir, I do."

"Damn him . . and he wanted to marry my daughter. Wait until I see him next time! Good for Mia, she is a better judge of character than I am. I owe her a big apology." Much too surprised to say anything else, he and Isaac enter the chicken pen and throw out the feed.

Chapter Twenty-four
Home to Recover

Morning comes early. Mia is awakened by a knock on the back door. "Wake up, Legare. I think Tot needs to come in and prepare breakfast. Did you lock the door last night?"

"Yes, I wanted us to sleep as late as possible. I'll let Tot in." Legare and Mia quickly put on their robes. Mia gathers the quilts and pillows, taking them to the bedroom as Legare goes to the kitchen to open the door for Tot. "Good morning, Tot!"

"Mornin' Mistuh leGree. 'E time fuh yuh brekwas. You haffuh leed d'recly fuh de foht." ["It time for your breakfast. You must leave shortly for the Fort."]

"Mia and I'll have eggs and oatmeal this morning. So long as I leave here by 8:30, I'll be on time." Legare turns and goes to the bedroom. Mia has freshened up and is putting on her clothes. "Come over here, Mia, I didn't give you a good morning kiss."

Mia rushes over. They hug and share a good morning kiss. Mia helps Legare locate his clothes to wear back to Fort Thunderbolt. While Legare is freshening up, Mia lays out the new wool socks, wool gloves, and other clothing Legare is taking to Fort Thunderbolt. "Honey, do you want to take the new boots with you?"

"No, thanks, my old ones are fine for now. Besides, someone would steal them if I did not have them on my feet! Just pack the new gloves and wool socks."

Tot knocks on the bedroom door. "De mush ready, tell me when you want me fuh pit on de egg." ["The oatmeal is ready; tell me when you want me to put on the eggs."]

"Thanks, Tot. I'll let you know in a few minutes," replies Mia.

When Mia and Legare come out for breakfast, Tot looks around and asks, "Weh de baby?"

"Little Joshua spent the night with his grandparents at Uncle Richard's and Aunt Josephine's. I'm going to meet them at the train station in about an hour and bring him home." In no time, Mia and Legare have finished breakfast and Jesse pulls the carriage up in front of the house.

Jesse asks Legare, "Weh yoh bag deh Massuh leGree?"["Where are your bags, Master Legare?"]

"In the bedroom. I think everything is packed. Go ahead and put it on the carriage." Mia and Legare slowly walk outside. The sky is blue and the morning sun's rays are beginning to take the frost from the ground.

Standing next to the carriage, Legare says sadly, "You know I can't get leave for New Year's because I had Christmas leave, but I'll see you a week or so after New Year's." Legare pulls her close in a longing embrace. "I love you, Mia."

"I love you, Legare."

Legare climbs onto the carriage and Mia releases his hand. "Let's go, Jesse. Don't want to be late."

Jesse snaps the whip and the mare moves forward. Legare turns and blows Mia a kiss. She kisses her fingers and sails the kiss off to Legare. Soon the carriage turns and Mia can no longer see his face.

Around 8:30 a.m. on April 23, 1864, there's a knock on Mia's door. Tot responds and opens the door. "Good morning, Mistuh Rooster."

"Good morning, Tot. Is Mia available?"

"Yaas, suh. Muhself git Ma'am Mia." Tot walks through the house and out the back door. Mia is in the backyard with Al starting the fires for preparing herbs for the hospital. "Mistuh Rooster iz har."

Mia gets a worried look on her face. "Tot, watch Joshua." Rooster is still standing on the landing with a serious expression on his face. Mia immediately asks, "Is Legare okay?"

"He's sick with some kind of stomach problem. Been that way for a couple of days. He asked me to get some of your blackberry cordial. He thinks that will clear him up."

"Come on in, Rooster. I've got several bottles ready for the hospital. Let me fetch two and I'll follow you back to Thunderbolt."

"Mia, Legare said for you not to come for two reasons: he's not that sick, and he does not want to give you or Joshua what he has. If he gets any worse I'll come back. He just has a real bad case of dysentery right now."

"Sounds like something he'd say! I really prefer to see him, but I'll do as he wishes. I want to hear from you tomorrow by noon or I'll show up at Thunderbolt. While I have you here, I understand that there's a shortage of blankets for the soldiers and that people are donating carpets to use as replacements. We had these seven rugs washed and rolled up to send down with Legare the next time he comes home, but you can go ahead and take them with you. Several of the larger rugs can be cut up into pieces."

Rooster walks over and examines the rugs. "These are expensive oriental rugs, Mia."

"Legare and I know what they are and we discussed it when he was home in March for Easter. If the 63rd goes to North Georgia this time of year, you will need the blankets. We can buy new carpets after this war is over."

"Well, I know the guys in Company A will appreciate it. We still aren't certain if and when we are going to Dalton. Everything is up in the air with the army in North Georgia right now. The army is low on food and ammo. By the way, those winter greens you have been sending us are really great. Some of the guys tried to plant a small garden at Thunderbolt, but people keep taking the greens before they are ready."

Over the course of the week, Legare improves from

Mia's blackberry Cordial wine and sends a note by Rooster:

"My love,

I am much improved, but lost weight and am still weak from the dysentery. Major Allen tells us the 63rd will be going to Dalton around the 10th or 12th. Major Allen also said I can come home until our departure to get as much rest, strength, and nourishment as possible. Please send Al for me tomorrow around ten o'clock. I will improve greatly when I see your beautiful smile and our wonderful child.

Love, L."

Mia and Tot wake early the next morning to prepare a large pot of chicken soup. When the soup is ready, Mia has Tot fill a glass jar. Then Mia wraps the jar in several towels to keep it hot until she arrives at Fort Thunderbolt. "Tot, keep the house hot. Fill the tub with water and light the heater on it. A good hot bath will relax Legare when we get him home."

At 9:30 a.m., Mia has Al convey her to the fort's front gate. Upon arriving, Mia asks the duty officer, "Please notify my husband, Legare Hill, that I am waiting for him."

"I'll be glad to send for him, Mrs. Hill. He's really had a time with his stomach. Lost some weight from it all. Just wait in the carriage where you'll be comfortable."

In a few short minutes, Mia sees someone that resembles Legare leaving the barracks. Rooster and John are carrying a haversack, knapsack, weapon, and other personal items. Assuming it is Legare whom Rooster and John are accompanying, Mia leaps from the carriage and rushes over to the group. As Mia approaches, she becomes distressed at Legare's appearance. He is bearded, almost skin and bones and looks weak. Mia and Legare have a short embrace.

"How is the love of my life?" asks Legare.

She holds back tears of worry. "The love of your life has some hot chicken soup for you in the carriage and some winter greens for your friends of Company A."

Placing her arm under his, she reaches up and gives him a sweet kiss to the cheek. The group continues to walk to the carriage. John and Rooster assist Legare into the carriage.

She unrolls the towels from around the hot jar of chicken soup and takes the lid off. "Start eating and drinking. I need to fatten you up!"

Legare takes the hot bottle of chicken soup in both hands. Slowly, Mia helps him lift the jar to his lips so he can take a good mouthful. Mia turns to Rooster. "Take the greens out of the back of the carriage, Rooster, so we can be on our way." Rooster and John remove the several bundles of greens.

John walks around to the side of the carriage. "Thanks, Mia. You should get better real fast now, Legare. You have the best nurse anywhere looking after you."

"Thanks for helping bring my gear out to the carriage. Mia is going to stuff me full of food so I should have my strength back in a couple of days." Al snaps the reins, the carriage jerks, and the couple are heading home. Mia pulls Legare's Christmas overcoat tightly around his chest as he takes another mouthful of the hot chicken soup. She removes the scarf from around her neck and places it over his head and around his chin. Sitting as close as possible to him, she assists him in eating and drinking as much as possible.

The day is clear and warmer than usual, yet the morning air is still damp. "This soup is warming my body pretty good."

Mia sits close to her love and places a blanket across his legs and feet to keep him as warm as possible. "Tot should have the tub ready for you when we arrive home. Full of hot water. You can crawl in and relax. I think she might also have a surprise waiting for you when you finish your bath."

"What kind of surprise?" asks Legare.

"If I let on, it won't be a surprise, will it?"

"No, I guess not, but I'm sure whatever it is, I'll like it. Is it something to eat or is it made out of material?"

"I'm not giving out clues. You can guess all you want to, but I'll never give you a clue, even if you come close."

"How is our precious son?"

"Just like his pa. A perfect young man!"

Legare takes Mia's hand. "I miss you and little Joshua every minute I am not with you. I wish we didn't have this war. Life would be perfect for us." Al halts the horse and carriage in the circular drive in front of the house. Mia and Al assist Legare from the carriage. He stands for a moment, looking around the yard and at the house. "Your flowers are mighty beautiful, Mia. Looks as if they might be smiling the way the sun is hitting them."

Mia replies as she supports Legare, "Everything smiles when you're home. Let's get inside and put you in the hot tub." Al and Mia take Legare up the stairs and into the house. "Tot, we're home!" Tot comes from the kitchen and meets the group. "I told Legare you have a special surprise for him when he got home. He kept trying to get me to divulge what it is. Where's the baby?"

"Him sleab."

"Is the tub ready for Legare?" "Yaas, Ma'am."

"Al, get his belongings from the carriage. You and Tot check to see if they need washing while I get him in the tub." Mia helps Legare to the bedroom where Joshua is sound asleep in the crib next to their bed. Legare walks over and admires his son. "He just keeps growing and growing. Look at those rosy cheeks."

"Time for you to get in the tub and soak, Pvt. Hill!" The bathroom is warm from the tub heater. Mia tests the water with her hand. "Perfect."

"Hot and good. I feel better just looking at the tub."

Mia helps him take off his overcoat. Then he sits in a chair while Mia removes his shoes and socks.

"Stand up so I can take off your pants! This time, it's for medicinal purposes only!"

And she and Legare laugh and kiss. When he's standing naked in front of her, Mia sees how much weight he has really lost. She helps him into the tub. "I'll wager you've lost fifteen pounds."

Legare eases down into the water and closes his eyes. "I really need this!" "Soak for a while. When I come back, I'll shave you and trim your hair if you feel like it."

Legare blinks, yawns and closes his eyes. In an instant he is sound asleep. Mia goes to the kitchen and finds the shoofly pie Tot has prepared. She removes a piece and samples it with her finger. "Mighty good, Tot. This will make Legare feel lots better I'm sure. Get Jesse to kill another chicken tonight. Legare will probably eat one whole chicken himself. He looks half-starved."

Mia goes back in the bathtub room to check on the water temperature and tub furnace. After about an hour of rest, little Joshua's movements in his crib awaken Legare. Mia comes in to check on Legare and finds both him and their son awake. She picks up Joshua and whispers, "Your pa is home. Let's go see him. He's taking a bath and has a beard." Mia brings little Joshua into the bathtub room.

Holding out his arms, Legare says, "There's my little man. Come see?" Mia brings Joshua to the tub. Not recognizing his father with a beard, the baby is a little shy at first. Legare reassures him. "It's Papa. Come see Papa."

Joshua recognizes his father's voice. Joshua slurs together "Pa-pa" as he leans over to hug and kiss his father.

"Good medicine," says Legare.

"Do you feel like being shaved, honey?"

"I do now, but I'm glad you didn't ask that an hour ago."

"Let me fetch Tot to take care of Joshua while I get you shaved. Kiss Papa, bye." Mia summons Tot with the servant bell and she comes to the bedroom door.

"Yaas, ma'am, Miss Mia."

Mia hands Joshua to Tot. "Take care of Joshua while I shave Legare. You'll see your Papa after he gets out of the tub."

Joshua tugs his father's beard before kissing and hugging him 'bye. Mia hands Joshua to Tot and then gathers up the razor, shaving brush and soap. Legare has washed his face and hair and looks more refreshed and rested than when he arrived. Mia places a stool next to the tub. She caresses his beard. "Let's see how long it's going to take me to find that good looking face underneath this hair."

"Now don't be in any rush with that razor. I probably can shave myself."

"I know you can, but I want to shave you. Just sit back and don't jump. I don't want to stain the water red!"

"Real funny, honey!" replies Legare, as they pass a kiss.

Mia lathers his beard with the shaving brush. She tilts his head back and begins shaving underneath his chin. Once she has finished shaving and trimming Legare's hair, Mia asks, "Now, how does that feel, honey?" No answer. He has fallen asleep again. Mia leans over and places one hand on each clean-shaven cheek. She gently kisses him on the lips.

Without opening his eyes, Legare gently says, "I know your kiss in my dreams, Mia."

"How do you feel now that you're shaven and your hair is trimmed?"

Legare rubs his face and runs his hands through his shortened hair. "Perfectly wonderful."

Mia reaches to assist him as he stands up in the tub. Using her free hand, she takes a towel and begins drying his lean body. "Tot has your surprise waiting for you. Get your robe on and come to the dining room."

In a weak and low breath, Legare speaks softly, "Mia, I'm still weak, but not nearly as dizzy. The chicken soup must be working already."

"That's good news." Mia takes Legare's robe and holds it open so he can place each arm in the sleeve. She ties the belt around his waist and they walk to the dining room. "I think Joshua is waiting for you at the table."

They take a seat on each side of Joshua. "How is my pal? Do you recognize me now?" Legare asks his boy. Joshua looks at his father and feels his face. He smiles and bounces at his father in affirmation. Legare gives little Joshua a kiss on the top of his head.

"Close your eyes, Legare, and get ready for your surprise." Legare closes his eyes and Mia calls out, "All right, Tot, bring in the surprise." Tot walks in with the large shoo-fly pie and places the sweet and tasty delight in front of Legare. "Now open your eyes."

Legare opens his weary eyes slowly and upon seeing the shoo-fly pie, opens them more widely. "Shoo-fly pie! Just what my doctor Mia ordered." Taking the knife and fork by his plate, Legare cuts himself a large slice and plunks it on his dish. He grabs his fork and begins stuffing himself. Mia and Tot watch happily yet silently as he takes a drink of black tea to wash down the pie and continues the routine of eating and drinking until practically the entire pie is devoured.

"I'm glad you like that pie, honey. Tonight we'll have baked chicken with beets, greens, rice and plenty of parsley. And for tomorrow, we'll have fresh baked fish. "

"Tot, that pie was the best. Thank you so much! Keep feeding me like this, and I'll be back to my normal weight in no time at all."

Mia suggests to Legare, "How about we go in the parlor? You and little Joshua can play by the fire. I need to check with Jesse and Al on the herbs. The pot's boiling with fresh barks and the water's probably ready to be filtered."

Legare goes to the parlor, and Mia brings Joshua. "Tot will stay with you two while I go out back."

Over the course of the next week, Mia slowly nourishes Legare back to strength. Tot is cooking constantly, Mia is feeding constantly and Legare is eating constantly, helping him gain about a half-pound per day. Mia directs Al and Jesse to place a table on the dock so she and Legare can enjoy the warm, spring sun while they dine. She even puts a cot on the deck so Legare can nap outside during warm and sunny days. In the evenings, before supper, they climb up to the cupola to watch the setting sun. The trees and flowers are bursting forth with new growth, and the honeysuckles smell sweet once again. Birds are building their nests energetically while whistling their songs.

"Look there, Mia! I think that's the owl that was hooting the night little Joshua was born. He's roosting in the same tree!"

"I think you're right. Papa told me that owls stay in the same area forever . . however long that is!"

Chapter Twenty-five
Unsettling News

Early Friday morning on May 6, there's a knock on the front door. Legare opens the door to find his friends. "Good morning, Rooster, Wyatt Come on in." The three shake hands and Rooster, and Wyatt enter. Legare calls out, "Mia! Rooster and Wyatt are here! What brings you out so early?"

"I've come to advise you about our new orders." Rooster places his hand on Legare's shoulder. "You sure are looking better. Still a little underweight, but looking good."

"Thanks, Rooster. Feeling better, too."

Mia and Joshua enter the foyer. She smiles. "Good morning, Rooster. Good morning, Wyatt. It's good to see you both. I just about have Legare back to full weight and strength."

"You have done a great job."

"What's the news from the Fort?"

"Well, we came by to let Legare know that our unit is leaving for Dalton on the morning of the ninth. Major Allen said he could just meet us at the depot around 9:30." Looking dismayed, Mia responds, "Well, I'm not exactly happy about that news. Come on in and have breakfast with us. I want to give you a couple of smoked hams to divide up among the company."

The three men watch Mia head toward the back of the house and they go to the parlor. Rooster relates the latest news. Looks like General Sherman is coming on into Georgia. He needs to be stopped."

"If any General can stop Sherman, it's gotta be

General Joseph Johnston. From what I have heard and read, the troops admire him and are glad he replaced General Bragg. He does not take risks with their lives like so many of the generals do. But nonetheless I feel that our 63rd is going to North Georgia sooner or later. The Confederate army is not as large as the Union army," responds Legare. He takes a breath and looking Rooster in the eye says, "Personally, I don't think the South has any more of a chance to win this war now than we did when it started."

Mia goes to the kitchen. "Tot, Rooster and Wyatt are going to join us for breakfast. Make them a good one. The 63rd is going to Dalton in a couple of days. Also, have Jesse bring in two of the largest smoked hams we have in the smoke house. I think there are four left."

Mia joins Rooster, Wyatt and Legare in the parlor and listens to the latest update on the war and Thunderbolt. "Legare told me what went on February 22nd when I heard all that cannon fire around Whitemarsh and Oatland."

Legare stands and leans on the chair back and takes over the story. "The best part is, in their hasty retreat, the Yankees left three excellent surf boats, numerous haversacks, canteens, blankets, Springfield muskets and clothing. Some of the equipment was saturated with blood from their wounded. I found some butter-crackers and meat in one of the haversacks."

"And I found ground coffee in another, and that's about all there was to the skirmish," says Rooster.

"I'm just thankful all of you are safe."

Shortly, the smell of fresh bacon alerts Mia that something good awaits them in the dining room. "From the smell of bacon, I think Tot has breakfast ready, so let's head to the table."

"This looks and smells wonderful, Mia. John and the McCurdy boy will be envious. But they'll get over it when I show them the hams." After finishing breakfast, Rooster and Wyatt shake Legare's hand and bid Mia goodbye. "We'll see you on the ninth at the depot."

Later that afternoon, Legare begins packing his

knapsack and haversack. Mia hands him a blanket for his bedroll and another eight pairs of wool socks. She puts several bars of soap and a couple of washcloths and towels in his knapsack. Last, she places paper and pencil so he can write home. "Here's a new toothbrush for you."

After supper, Tot finishes cleaning the kitchen, and Mia pokes her head in the door. "Be sure we are up at sunrise, Tot. We need to have a good breakfast for Legare before he goes to the depot." She and Legare take turns playing with little Joshua while he bathes. They lie down together with him on their bed. Mia fabricates a bedtime story about a happy soldier going to war for little Joshua. "The soldier has a little boy and the little boy's Mama at home, whom he is going miss dearly. The little boy and the little boy's Mama are going to miss Papa as much as Papa is going to miss them. But everybody knows one day the happy soldier will return home. When the happy soldier returns home, he and the little boy can fish and hunt together. Mama will be happy also. She and the little boy's pa can help the little boy grow up to be a strong and good man. The little boy's mama wants the little boy to grow up to be just like his father, a strong and very loving person who will always look after his family."

Little Joshua falls asleep lying between his mother and father. Legare picks him up gently and places him in his crib. Legare takes Mia's hand and they go to the parlor and sit close together on the sofa in front of the warm and fragrant fire. Holding hands and looking at each other, Legare pulls Mia closer, "This is our last night together for a while, Mia. I hope only for a short while. There are a few items we need to talk about before I leave."

"Yes, I know," she says as a huge lump develops in her throat. "We must talk about the most dreaded scenario of this war, the dreadful possibilities." Holding his hand, she listens and he emotionally proceeds.

"Father went ahead and gave us my share of the stock and bonds in the Georgia Railroad which I would eventually inherit. You know we are getting a good return on that stock and those bonds right now. All of the money goes into our account with Mr. Lilly's bank. I suggest you take some of the money out in gold and hide it here somewhere."

"I know we must discuss these matters, yet no matter how hard I try to understand, this whole thing is like a dream to me . . your leaving, this war, our child, our home. It can never be the same without you here."

The thoughts are too hard to consider, but he knows the rising sun will change everything. "I'll write you every day that I can, however, you may not get any letters for a while. People say the mail is extremely unreliable. If you don't hear from me, please know that I have written. If something awful should happen to me, my father and mother have told me and you that you're a daughter to them. They will endeavor to always fill your every need. I know them well."

Tears stream down Mia's soft cheeks. She inhales deeply, trying vainly to stop her tears. She doesn't want Legare to remember her this way. She offers a warm smile and grasps Legare's hands tightly.

Legare smiles back at her, realizing she's not far from completely breaking down. "In the morning, when I depart for the depot, I want you and little Joshua to follow my carriage to the road and stay there until I am out of sight. This is the image I want to remember, knowing that when I return home, you and our child will be standing there waiting for me. It's going to be hard. I know you want to come to the depot, but I only want this for my selfishness."

In a trembling voice she whispers, "You will return home to me and our child. I'll go outside every day and stand by the carriage hitch and wait for you to appear in the distance. Then little Joshua and I'll run to meet you before you can reach the house!"

Mia and Legare cry and their tears mix as they embrace. Mia wipes her tears away with her hand. "My love, let's not talk of sad things anymore. We know what we both must do. God has taught us how to perform our duty." She thinks frantically for a moment, trying to find a normal activity to relieve the sadness of this night. "Let's walk out on the dock and look at the stars for a while. Maybe they can disclose something about the future for us."

Legare, still unable to speak clearly, nods his head. They go outside and walk to the end of the pier. Upon reaching the end of the dock, they sit down and hang their feet over the edge. Sitting quietly for a while, they listen to the mullet jumping nearby. Then they hear the friendly owl hooting to claim his territory.

"Yep, that's the same owl all right. I would know his voice anywhere!"

Mia looks up into the clear night sky. "What are all of those lights in the heavens? There's the big dipper and the little dipper you showed me. That one next to the new quarter moon is the morning and evening star, right?"

"You never forget, do you? I can tell you something and you always remember."

Mia turns to Legare and holds his dear face between her two hands.

"I love you, Legare Hill, and don't you ever forget that." She kisses him deeply and he almost crushes her in his embrace.

"If only words could describe my love for you. Such a word would cover the entire universe." Legare helps Mia to lie back on the dock. He begins to laugh as they talk about how he felt about her before they ran away together in the dark of the night. Legare and Mia talk about how happy they are about their families' finally accepting and realizing their love and devotion for one another.

"My mere existence here with you and our child is a constant joy. Today the sunshine was brighter and tonight the moonlight is softer. The sky is fairer and the earth more seductive. I notice some of the flowers and trees are blooming and budding at odd times with unwonted richness and profusion. Maybe this is a sign to re-enforce our feeling about the strong common bonds that now unite our families."

Mia becomes quieter as her thoughts turn to the war and how Governor Brown could end this struggle with the stroke of a pen. Feeling a chilling breeze, Mia shivers. "Legare, do you want to go inside? It's getting a little cool out here."

"Yes, and let's sleep in our favorite spot in front of the

fireplace tonight." Legare gives Mia his hand and assists her up from the dock. Together, they walk with their arms around each other to the house. Inside, Legare locks the back door. Mia kisses her husband and begins undressing him.

Legare reciprocates. The fever of their passion for each other begins to rise as the two lovers gather the pillows and blankets and carry them to the parlor. Mia goes to the kitchen and takes a bottle of blackberry cordial and two glasses from the shelf. She brings the glasses and the cordial to the parlor where Legare is lying on the blankets and pillows.

Pouring two large glasses of the cordial, Mia toasts, "This is what got you well, and this is what is going to keep you well. To my dear husband, my lover, and the father of our child. The best there is and ever will be."

They raise their drinks and take a large sip from each other's glass. They sink to the blankets. Sitting adjacent to each other, they watch the fire and slowly finish the cordial. Legare turns and draws Mia nearer. They shut their eyes and enjoy the luxury of lying in each other's arms. At long last they fall asleep.

At sunrise, there's a subtle knock on the door. Mia disentangles herself from Legare's arms and slips from the room to unlock the back door for Tot. "Good morning, Tot."

She and Tot prepare a feast for Legare's breakfast: ho'cakes, eggs, country ham, fresh biscuits, grits and muscadine jelly. By the time they put the food on the table, Legare is in uniform and marches into the dining room with Joshua on his hip. Mia smiles and kisses her two favorite people as they prepare to sit at the table. Mia seats herself, and Tot begins to serve. Mia had Tot to prepare places at the table for Al, Jesse and herself. She wants everyone to have this special breakfast together.

The cheerful mood seems forced as Legare says the blessing. "Bless this family and protect them in thy name." Legare can say no more as tears flow from his eyes.

Mia continues, "Protect and guard over this father and husband. Let him return to us as he leaves us. Amen."

After breakfast, everyone gathers outside next to the carriage. Jesse is driving Legare to the depot. Legare and Mia's expressions speak volumes of love. He hugs Tot, shakes and squeezes Al's hands before turning to Mia and little Joshua. Almost in tears, Legare and Mia press heart to heart and share a loving kiss. Mia clings to him, almost unwilling to relinquish him to the war effort.

"I love you, Mia. I love you, little man."

"We love you, Legare."

Legare turns and boards the carriage. His uniform buttons suddenly glisten brightly in the morning sun. He is wearing one of the new shirts that has his initials and name "H. L. Hill" embroidered on the sleeve. Tot and Al are, now weeping silent tears along with Mia. Jesse snaps the reins as he has for many years, and with the usual jerk, the carriage moves from the circle onto the dirt road that leads to the depot. Legare turns and looks at Mia. Tears quietly slipping down her cheeks, Mia holding little Joshua tightly follow the carriage to the road never taking their eyes off of Legare.

The carriage turns and disappears. Mia stands praying to herself, "Through some miracle, Lord please let me awaken from this nightmare and find Legare and Joshua sleeping next to me."

Chapter Twenty-Six
The Grim Face of War

"HEADQUARTERS MILITARY DIVISION OF THE MISSISSIPPI IN THE FIELD,
TUNNEL HILL, GEORGIA
May 11, 1864-Evening
Major-General McPHERSON, Commanding Army of the Tennessee,
Sugar Valley, Georgia
GENERAL:
　　"The indications are that Johnston is evacuating Dalton. In that event, Howard's corps and the cavalry will pursue; all the rest will follow your route. I will be down early in the morning. Try to strike him if possible about the forks of the road. Hooker must be with you now, and you may send General Garrard by Summerville to threaten Rome and that flank.
　　"It will cause all the lines to be felt at once.
　　W. T. SHERMAN,
　　Major general, Commanding"

Around noon, May 12, the Georgia 63rd arrives at the Dalton depot. Legare peers out of the window. "Well, Rooster, here we are, ready to defend Dalton." Rooster nods. "It's too late in the day to start shooting Yankees!"

　　Legare stares at the flurry of activity surrounding the station. "Let's hope tomorrow is lucky for us and unlucky for them." Colonel George Gordon, the 63rd commanding officer, disembarks and orders the troops to formation. He addresses the regiment, "Men of the 63rd, we are here for only a short break. Gather your equipment and chow down on your rations while I get our orders. Your company commander, Major Allen, will direct you in unloading the supplies from the Augusta arsenal."

Major Allen continues with the instructions, "Maurice Thompson, report to me upon dismissal. Company A, stack your equipment and reassemble at the boxcars in fifteen minutes. Dismissed!"

In the beautiful spring afternoon, Legare, John, Alonzo and Rooster gather their belongings. The trees are just about in full leaf and the aroma of budding flowers fills the cool spring air with a feeling of calm. Finding a nice tree, Legare and Rooster take comfort in its shade. Soon, Maurice Thompson, another member of the 63rd, joins them. "Well, Legare and Rooster, looks like I'm going to be a scout since I know these mountains from one end to the other. They are assigning me to General Wheeler. I'm sure we will see one-another again."

The three exchange handshakes and Legare says, "Good luck, Maurice, and stay clear of the Yankees!" Maurice turns away with a wave of his hand and is shortly out of sight.

Legare and Rooster lay their belongings by the trunk of the large oak tree and stretch out. John Dent and Alonzo McCurdy find a comfortable spot nearby. All four men know they are soon going to have to march somewhere.

The bugle sounds assembly for chow. Beef, early greens and bread are supper for the men.

"Now we are here, men, in Dalton and expecting General Polk's corps from Mississippi to give us reinforcements enabling us to turn the war north. Any questions? If not, take a short break before distributing the ammunition from the train. DISMISSED!"

Major Allen continues to walk and talk with the men, giving more details of recent events.

Somewhat bewildered, Legare asks, "Rooster, do you sense panic in the air?"

Rooster looks around at the other men. "When you're out-numbered three to one, you have two options: first option is to be smarter than the other guy. If that doesn't work, you better run like hell! I'm betting that General Johnston is smarter than General Sherman."

Legare says quietly," Well, it doesn't look like anybody is running!"

As the wagons are being loaded, one of the soldiers taps Rooster on his shoulder. "We're really glad to see this ammunition. This load may keep us going for a few more days. Our artillery batteries are so low on shot and shell that some of the batteries only fire in self-defense."

Around nightfall, all of the freight rail cars are unloaded and the train begins its journey south.

Watching the departure, Legare ponders the sound and sight of the train slowly disappearing into the fading light. It escapes into the forest and around a bend in the track until not even a puff of smoke can be seen. Legare silently thinks, "That train is what brought me here and someday it will take me back home, back to Mia and Joshua."

Just before dawn on Saturday, May 14th, a lone rider on horseback approaches the Georgia Military Institute campus. The cadet sentinel orders him to stop and identify himself. The rider explains that "he has a message from General Henry Wayne for Major Capers." The guards remove the weapons from the rider and escort him to Major Caper's quarters. Upon entering the house, Major Capers recognizes the messenger and has the guards return his weapons before returning to their post. Opening the orders close to the lantern he reads, "The Cadet Corps is to report to General Johnston at Resaca and to hold the corps of Cadets in readiness to obey his orders during the present emergency, whereupon you will receive further orders. The cadets who are of age are to board the first available train to the front. Dated May 12th."

Major Capers orders Cornelius to play the "long

roll" of the drums. Slowly, the cadets awaken by the continuous roll of the drum. Norman and Paul, along with the rest of the cadet corps, spring from their beds. "It's still dark outside. Something important must be happening with the war,"

Paul says as he peers through the window as Norman lights the candles. In full dress with their weapons and gear, the cadets seem to assemble quicker than on most other cool spring mornings. Roll call and the familiar "here and present for duty" response is continuous. Finally "in place rest" the cadets are given five rounds of ammunition each.

Following the issue of the ammunition, the cadet commander shouts, "Attention!"

Major Capers steps forward and reads the order. "The cadets of the Georgia Military Institute who are of proper age are to march to the depot in Marietta and proceed to the front in and around Resaca. The Corps is to report to General Joseph Johnston's headquarters for further orders."

"Hooray! Hooray!" shout the cadets. "We'll show those Yankees a real fight!" yell other cadets. The feeling of invincibility is strong with the cadets at this moment as they swell with pride and readiness.

The 150 or so cadets march down Powder Springs Road and pass the cemetery on their way to the depot. The sick and underage cadets are given orders to stay on campus. Upon arriving at the depot and pitch their tents, the cadets relax and eat some of their rations of bacon and hardtack. Some of the soldiers from Camp McDonald are also at the depot and hear the news that the corps is moving to the front the next morning. They mingle with the cadets. "Give 'em hell, boys," shouts a departing recruit.

"You've been training us so we know you can teach those Yankees a lesson or two!"

Norman is awake early the next morning. He is sitting outside his tent as the sun begins to rise and the morning dew reflects the rays. A whistle is heard. He turns his attention toward the depot as the train approaches and comes to a stop. Suddenly Norman sees the camp come to life as the cadet corps rises apparently full of excitement.

Paul comes out of the tent and sees the steam coming from the engine boiler. "Norman, look at that engine. For some reason that engine reminds me of a tied up hound knowing he is about to be released for a big hunt."

Norman laughs and replies, "It does look fired up all right."

Norman and Paul are among the first cadets to board the train. Cadets Marsh and Hazelhurst seek and receive permission to ride on top of the coaches with several of their fellow cadets. The train pulls away from the depot.

Paul confides in Norman, "Looks like we finally have a chance to fight for Georgia and the Confederacy."

"Yep. I don't know if it is a good idea or not. Let's hope we all make it back."

Later on, the train stops at Big Shanty and the soldiers in the camp see the cadets on top of the coaches. A civilian shouts, "Where are y'all going?"

Marsh shouts back, "Heading to Resaca. We're going to beat you there!"

As the train pulls away from the station, the soldiers at Camp McDonald fire their weapons in the air as a salute to the parting cadet corps. Enthusiastically, Marsh, Hazelhurst and the other cadets on the top of the coaches stand and raise their weapons, showing their determination.

Norman and the cadets inside the coaches wave their hats out of the windows with vigor and excitement as if they have already conquered the Yankees.

Around noon, the cadets arrive at Resaca. There's a fury of activity around the depot. Resaca serves as a staging area for troops which are heading north along the railroad to the battlefields in Tennessee and Virginia. After assembly, Norman asks Marsh, "How did the countryside look from the top of the coach?"

"This whole area is rough and hilly, Norman. All I could see from the top of the train was thick woods and thick underbrush."

Their conversation ends quickly as they hear the thunder of cannon fire in the near distance.

Norman feels a chill over his entire body and becomes more conscious that this is not a game. Norman solemnly turns to his friends, "This is the real thing."

The bugle sounds assembly and the cadet corps takes formation.

The two companies march to the headquarters of General Johnston. Major Capers enters General Johnston's headquarters where he meets Brig. Gen. William Mackall, the Chief of Staff for General Johnston. Major Capers reports to him, "Sir, the cadet corps has arrived and is awaiting your orders."

General Mackall speedily briefs Major Capers, "General Johnston is in conference and disturbing him at this time is not in order. General Johnston has an order for the cadet battalion to be placed under Major Gen. William Walker's division. General Walker's division has orders to prevent a crossing of the Oostanaula River at a location near Resaca. The Cadet Battalion is to form up and march with General Walker's Division to the Oostanaula River near Resaca. Any questions, Major?"

"None, General Mackall. We will report immediately to General Walker's headquarters."

Later in the day, the Cadet Corps moves north of the Oostanaula to reinforce General John Hood's corps. Upon arriving at their new post, Major Capers receives orders to place the Cadet Corps behind a split rail fence beyond a thicket of woods, joining battle-tough veterans. The Cadets quickly take their places behind the fence with the soldiers already there.

With a nod to the nearest private, Norman hurries into a spot and motions for Paul to join him. Lieutenant James Oaks of the 9th Illinois Mounted Infantry takes note of the cadets in uniform coming out of the woods from the direction of Resaca as they line up behind the rail fence.

Paul is practicing aiming his musket. He stares down the sights, catching view of several
opposing forces located not too far away. "The Belgian Muskets will work great in this nice weather, Norman."

Keeping his eyes toward the enemy, Norman shifts his position slightly and flashes a grin at his friend. "Surely will and my powder is dry and ready."

Major Capers, behind the fence, is in front of the cadets giving orders to Captain Austin and Captain Victor Manget for the proper placement of each company. Not taking the cadets seriously, the 9th Illinois charge the cadets. On command the cadets give a loud yell. "Come on, you dirty Yankees!" Determination and courage that belies their young age, they launch a volley of fire killing several of the charging Union soldiers on horseback. After recovering from the surprise, the 9th Illinois launches a full Union-mounted regiment up the slope toward the cadets. Against heavy odds, the cadets keep firing as several more of the 9th fall from their saddles. The 9th again retreats into the dense woods for cover and safety. As the battle ebbs, and the whiz of the bullets fade away, the cadets take count. Not a single cadet has received a wound. Continuing to retire deeper into the woods, the cadets are soon withdrawn from the line of battle for some unknown reason.

The cadets are jubilant. Major Capers praises them for the exceptional valor while under fire for the first time. "You all knew the elements of the tactical routine. All of you followed orders without hesitation. This shows GMI will graduate the future military leaders of our country. Congratulations! You exhibited the quality of the corps well in one of the first battles of
Resaca."

The morning of the 14th, General Sherman orders an attack at General Johnston's center with a division of General John Palmer's XIV Corps. General Palmer's Corps attack across Camp Creek Valley towards the crest held by General Hardee's Corps. There, General

Sherman's army confronts devastating infantry and artillery fire. The picture of the first battle for Legare and Rooster is powerfully dramatic. The battle brings to life the reality of war.

Rooster turns to Legare. "They want to kill you as badly as you want to kill them. Capture never enters their mind."

Legare nods in the aftermath. War becomes a game of survival. Grape and canister fly into the ranks. Bombshells burst overhead and the fragments fly on all sides of Legare. A dozen or so of his comrades lay nearby, wounded and screaming or dead. A strange, involuntary shrinking nearly overpowers Legare. He can neither advance nor retreat, but is frozen by his emotions, by his humanity. His cheeks blanch, his lip quivers, and he hesitates to look upon the human carnage. This has nothing to do with the boastful bravado, the boisterous talk the men shared as they spoke longingly of fighting for the Confederacy. Legare thinks of Mia and Joshua. He wonders briefly if he'll ever see them again, of how they'll manage without him. He recalls his last night with her, her tender kisses. Suddenly he straightens and glances around.

He must survive for his wife and son . . he must. He swallows hard and inhales the odors of gunpowder and blood. Legare faces the field with new resolve.

Successive volleys of artillery strike the ground and tree limbs upon which the soldiers lie. The Yankees mass their troops eight deep and advance under a heavy fire of double charges of grape and canister. Soon, the Yankees come within range, and the 63rd renders an incessant volley of musketry. Legare picks out a moving blue target and opens fire against the Yankees in a visible and audible defense. His aim is true and his target falls, as does the soldier Rooster fires on. With his first shot, Legare transforms from a young man in to a soldier. Fear no longer exists. No longer mindful of themselves or their orders, the Yankees spring forward in full assault, swarming into the open. Legare, Rooster and the soldiers of Company A receive the advancing Yankees with broad sheets of musket balls, striking the charging and unprotected Yankees with deadly effect. The artillery resounding on both sides joins the battle complementing the rattle and roar with deep, earth-shaking explosions. The air continues to swirl with storms of screaming grape. The trees splinter, splattered with blood on both sides. Hesitation gives way to an uncontrollable desire to rush into the thick of the battle. The dead and the dying comrades serve only to stimulate Legare's revenge. He grows cool and deliberate as the cannon balls pass by him and rake murderous channels though his friends.

No mortal man can stand the Confederate fire. Then, over the battlefield, a bugle call is heard, ordering a retreat for the beaten Yankees. Only the sound of scattering musket shots and the moaning of the distant wounded lying upon the battlefield remain. The noisy voices of the cannons are now still, and the dusky pall of sulphurous smoke rises above the fields. Legare slowly stands. Unnerved and silent, he looks upon the form of a fellow soldier, who only a few minutes ago, stood in the full flesh of life and happiness. Human brains splashed about, bodies without limbs, limbs without bodies, disfigured faces and a headless corpse.

The ground is ploughed up and stained with blood. Now come the bloody litter bearers with their woeful burdens. Wounds of every conceivable and unimaginable character. Right arms torn off, not cut off, like a bird's wing with all the muscle and organs closely connected with it. A deadening sensation, thank God. The skull over the cerebellum blown completely away and yet the poor man still lives. There are few groans, except from men unconscious, or from men injured by concussion. Legare begins to comprehend the horrors of war. Quietly he whispers a silent prayer for his fallen comrades.

The various Confederate units are directed to areas of encampment for supper and picket duty. Gradually in the distance, Legare and John McCurdy see what appears to be a different type of men in uniform. There are shiny buttons glistening in the near noontime sun, a different style cap, and the unit seems to be well organized in their march.

"I've never seen a unit like that before, Legare.

"Me either," replies Legare. "Who could they be?" After a moment Legare excitedly turns to John. "I think they might be the Cadets from Georgia Military Institute! I need to find out! If they are, Norman is here, I'm sure!" Legare turns to Rooster, "Is it all right if I find out if that unit is from GMI? If they are, my brother-in-law might be with them!"

Rooster replies, "Go ahead, but make it quick. We will be moving out in about an hour."

Legare rushes the hundred yards down the wagon trail to where the Cadet corps has halted to eat their rations. Approaching the bivouac, Legare asks, "You're the GMI cadets, right?"

"Yes, sir, we are," replies one of the cadets. "My brother-in-law is Norman Jernigan." Legare's heart begins to race. "Is he with you?"

What seems like an eternity transpires in a few seconds when the cadet answers and points. "Yes, he should be over there, about twenty-five yards or so on the left side of the trail."

"Thanks! "Legare turns, stirring up dust as he rapidly strides toward the area where Norman is taking rations. Stopping at the area of the trail where Norman should be, Legare begins to scan the cadets. Most of the cadets have found newly leaved-shade trees and are just settling down and taking rations from their haversacks. Others are already eating and chatting. Legare spots someone who bears a resemblance to Norman, tall, lanky, yet more mature and masculine than he had remembered. "He has to be Norman!"

Legare's heart is still racing with excitement and his mouth even begins to dry as he quietly approaches Norman. Legare smiles and kneels in front of the man. "Hello, Norman!"

The cadet looks up. "Wrong person, Norman is

over there!" He points to another cadet several yards away. Legare is somewhat embarrassed. "I'm sorry, I haven't seen Norman in several years and thought you were him."

"Don't worry about it." The cadet shouts, "Hey, Norman, there's a fellow over here looking for you!" Legare stands, turns, and recognizes Norman at about the same time as Norman recognizes him. "I cannot believe this is happening!" Norman tells Legare as the two meet at the halfway point.

They shake hands and then tentatively embrace. "Ma and Pa wrote me about their surprise visit over Thanksgiving and Christmas. They told me all about little Joshua and their visit with you in Savannah. Then I got the letter from Mia. She told me how happy the two of you are. I couldn't have asked for a better brother-in-law."

"Thanks, Norman. I can still call you Norman?"

"Sure, all my friends at GMI call me that."

"You know I have loved your sister since I first saw her."

"She has loved you as well, Legare. I knew it but the folks had their mind set on Buster. The power of true love cannot be conquered. You and Mia proved that! Come and sit down. I want you to meet my roommate, Paul Goldsmith." Norman and Legare walk together to where Paul is sitting and eating his hardtack. Paul, having been observing Legare and Norman, stands as they approach. "Paul, this is my brother-in-law, Legare Hill. Legare, this is Paul Goldsmith."

Each extends his hand and they shake. "Paul's cousin is James Goldsmith in Stone Mountain."

"I know Mr. Goldsmith. He's the railroad agent at the depot."

Paul motions to Legare. "Have a seat and let's have supper together. Looks like you could use a little food."

"I've lost a little weight over the past few weeks. Got some bad meat at Thunderbolt, but I am doing much better now."

The three find comfortable spots in the May sunshine. Legare opens his haversack and retrieves his rations for the day. While eating, their conversations run from Legare's experiences in Savannah to the boys' experiences as cadets. Norman and Paul listen to Legare's stories intensely and express their delight in coming to Resaca to fight the Yankees along with their discontent about not being involved in more military operations.

The hour passes by fast and the buglers sound assembly. Legare stands and takes his scarf from his neck. "Your sister embroidered this for me for Christmas. See here, she embroidered this heart, little Joshua, Mia, and Legare. I want you to have the scarf to wear from the three of us."

He hands the scarf to Norman. Not knowing what to say, Norman holds the scarf in his hands and gently touches the material. "I really can't take this, Legare. Mia made it for you."

"Mia will be glad for me to share our symbol of family with her brother, for we are one family. I must go now. My unit is waiting for me."

Shaking hands, farewell, Legare bids goodbye to Norman and Paul. "God's speed to both of you." Then Legare turns away, waves and double times back to his unit.

Taking ranks with his company, Legare is asked by John, "Were you able to find Norman?"

"Yes, and all is well. I gave him the scarf Mia made for me."

Paul and Norman prepare to board a southbound train back to the institute on the morning of the 15th. The train includes several hospital cars. Before boarding, Paul and Norman are assigned to assist the wounded soldiers on board. Upon arriving in Marietta, Paul and Norman dutifully and solemnly assist with the removal of the wounded soldiers from the hospital cars. They assist by gently placing the wounded in the hay wagons which take them along dusty clay roads to the hospitals. Paul, Norman and the rest of the Corps did not have long to gloat.

They now must serve provost duty to protect government and private property for the next week.

During the evening of May 18, General Johnston's army arrives in Cassville. Behind breastworks and under the light of the nearly full moon, Legare and Rooster's conversation is overheard.

Captain Buster Phillips has recognized the familiar voice of Legare Hill. Buster positions himself to see the two and hear their conversation without becoming suspect. To him, Legare appears a trifle more mature than when he vanished from Stone Mountain three years ago with "his" Mia. Otherwise, Legare had little change in personal appearance. His face, bronzed by exposure to the elements, wears what appears to be a pensive look as Buster eases closer to hear better. With hatred in his heart, Buster considers a plan to kill Legare and involuntarily draws his pistol. With his eyes focused on Legare, his Sergeant taps him on the shoulder. "Sir, the battalion commander wishes to see you right away."

Coming to his senses, Buster returns his pistol to the holster and departs with his Sergeant. Rooster continues carrying on the conversation. "You're in my neck of the woods now, Legare! Did you know that at one time, Cassville was the largest city between Savannah and Nashville? It still is the largest city in North Georgia. The citizens of Cassville have changed the name of the city to 'Manassas' and the county from 'Cass County' to 'Bartow County.'"

Legare responds, "I heard about the name changes, but not about the population. Is this the railroad station where Andrews stopped to get water, wood and a train schedule during the Locomotive Chase?"

Lying on his back, Legare looks at the stars and thinks of Mia and little Joshua. He confides in Rooster, "In all these years the people of Stone Mountain have not drifted out of my milieu."

The moon is brighter and her rays are just lighting the mountains. Rooster answers, "Look at those mountains. There are Yankees somewhere out there, probably behind earthworks just like us. Their possessions and our possessions will become a bitter dispute tomorrow. Over yonder lay our father's people. For though you're true to the land of your birth, you're but half Southerner by blood. I sometimes wonder how a Southern grandfather could have given his fairest daughter in marriage to a coldblooded, New Englander Yankee. I don't doubt that our noble ancestors have turned in their graves many times since the outbreak of this war."

Legare replies, "A little more common sense would greatly help the blood of the South. It is too hot, and it needs cooling."

"You're right. It's too rash, and needs tempering. We should rely upon the Yankee background of shrewd common sense, patience, judgment and endurance."

"The Yankees have not shown any of those qualities as far as I am concerned when it comes to state's rights." Rooster continues, "Still, if we would graft the qualities of heart and mind of the North and the South, we would have a combination the world would envy. Right now we stand to lose everything."

"The best Southerners do not yield to anyone in their devotion to the South."

"And the Northern instinct provides me with a clearer insight into the tendencies and inevitable conclusion of this fratricidal clash of minds and material," Legare answers back.

"I have never doubted for one moment that the South will meet defeat, but I don't exactly freely give my life to the cause. If only the Lord would bid this carnage to cease and let the banner of peace be again unfurled."

Legare's tone becomes very melancholic. Rooster looks at him sharply. "It's unlike you to be so despondent."

Exhausted and weak, Legare responds, "My thoughts come from no lack of courage, but I feel I might not survive tomorrow's fight."

"Turn in and sleep off this nonsense. Your mind is as tired as your body!" Rooster wraps himself in his section of carpet and, bidding Legare a courteous good night, stretches his form upon the gathered hay, which softens the ground beneath, and is soon in a dreamful sleep.

Legare cannot refrain from thoughts of his Mia and little Joshua. They weigh heavily on his heart and mind. He closes his eyes and can feel Mia and little Joshua's presence as she walks among the gardens and parks of Savannah. Legare knows Mia patiently awaits his return to be united with her and their son. He smiles within as he sees his Mia easily adapt to the exotics of the Savannah social atmosphere.

These reflections come to Legare as he sees his wife and realizes that what should be an episode in both of their lives, could be fermenting to become a tragedy. His thoughts stray doggedly to Buster Phillips and attempts to formulate what Mia's life could have been if she had loved and married Buster instead of him. Legare struggles not to imagine that he may, on the battlefield, leave his wife and child to the dependency of their relatives. Frightened by these sad images, he takes paper and pencil and by candlelight writes a letter to her.

His heart feels lighter once his thoughts and feelings are penned. He folds and places the letter in his pocket next to his heart. Exhausted by these conflicting emotions, he lies upon the hay and slips into a heavy slumber under his overcoat.

At dawn, May 19, there's no time for Legare to consign his letter to the safe keeping of Rooster.

The sharp jangle of the muskets and the drummers calls him to duty. Quickly Rooster and Legare gather their equipment and prepare to take their positions on the emplacements. General Johnston's aspirations are as elevated as if he is perched high on his horse. He expects a decisive victory by the Army of Tennessee from General Polk and Hood's ambush against General Sherman's army.

General Johnston issues an order to be read to his army, "Soldiers of the Army of Tennessee, you have displayed the highest quality of the soldier: firmness in combat and patience under toil. By your courage and skill you have repulsed every assault of the enemy. By marches you have defeated every attempt upon your communications. Your communications are secured."

General Johnston continues, "You will now turn and march to meet his advancing columns. Fully confiding in the conduct of the officers and the courage of my brave soldiers, I lead you to battle. We may confidently trust that the Almighty Father will still reward the patriot's toil and bless the patriot's banners. Cheered by the success of your brothers in Virginia and beyond the Mississippi, our efforts will equal theirs. Strengthened by His support, those efforts will be crowned with the like glories."

The 63rd Georgia Regiment on the front line of General Hardee's rear guard, becomes actively engaged in a light skirmish with General Thomas's division. Pvt. T. F. Burbank is lying adjacent to Legare behind the breast works. A musket ball penetrates the earthworks and shatters Burbank's shoulder. Screaming, Burbank reels over toward Legare. Legare lays down his weapon and moves to assist Burbank. He lifts Burbank from the ground and moves toward the rear line.

Captain Buster Phillips, Georgia 52nd, Company "I" of the 25th Alabama Regiment and a company of the 22nd Alabama Regiment, occupies the area through the cemetery along the graves and tombstones. Orders are given, "To throw up earthworks as rapidly as possible for protection and if necessary remove any monuments or tombstones which might hinder the construction of the earthworks." The 63rd is also forming a line inside the cemetery. One grave, which has been walled in with brick about two feet high, has a large marble slab covering the grave. The smell of bacon is apparent. When John Dent and Alonzo McCurdy of the 63rd remove the slab, they find a lot of flour and bacon beneath the slab. John and Alonzo leave the contraband food, replace the marble slab and continue to throw up earthworks around the grave. The Union forces post their batteries west of town on a hill and begin an unrelenting fire. The town of Cassville is now directly between the contending armies.

Chapter Twenty-seven
The Bear Hunt

Around one o'clock there is a knock on Buck's front door. He looks at Betty Gail as he pushes back from the table and states, "I wonder who that might be? He goes to the door and looks out of the window before opening the front door and sees Isaac. Opening the door, Buck greets Isaac and invites him in. "Eaten yet, Isaac?"

"Had a late breakfast, but thanks. Jus' got back from checking on de cows and it appears that uh black bear killed one of de calves. Left lot-a tracks and all. Buck runs his hand through his hair on the top on his head.

"Haven't had any bears through here in a while. I guess we best try and track him down before he comes back and gets another. Let me finish dinner while you get the horses and rifles ready. I'll have Betty Gail pack us up some food to take along. Better bring your rifle and pistol."

Returning to his dinner he tells Betty Gail about the dead calf and that he and Isaac are going to try and track it down.

"It's spring time and bears are really hungry this time of year. You best be careful," replies Betty Gail.

Isaac goes to the barn, saddles the horses, loads his rifle and pistol and waits for Buck, who arrives in about half- an- hour. Isaac sees Buck approaching and mounts his horse. When Buck arrives, he slings his rifle across his back and mounts his horse. "Let's go bear hunting, Isaac. Show me where the remains of the calf are and let's start tracking."

Upon reaching the site, Buck and Isaac dismount and tie their horses to the fence. Looking over the remains and then the footprints, Buck tells Isaac, "looks like a pretty big one by the size of the prints. He wasn't in much of a hurry since he ate most of the calf here.

Isaac walks over to the fence and removes some fur. "Looks like he climbed da fence here. There's paw prints on da udder side. Seems like he has been makin' a trail through the woods fer some time."

Buck and Isaac mount their horses. "Come on, Isaac. Let's go through the corner gate and start tracking. Maybe his trail is clear enough to lead us to him or his den. Didn't see any cub tracks so I don't think it's a mother bear. Just a hungry and mean ol' papa bear." Once through the gate, Buck and Isaac quietly place their rifles in their hands. Rather than riding through the thick woods, they elect to walk as quietly as possible. Buck and Isaac spot fresh skat on the ground as they follow the obvious path of the animal.

Buck and Isaac have been walking and tracking the bear for over four hours as the sun gets lower in the sky and the shadows grow longer. It's still early spring as the air become chilly and the sky begins to get cloudy. Buck looks up at the sky and whispers to Isaac, "Might get a little rain."

Isaac muffles his reply with his hand partly covering his mouth, " Sure hope not 'cause the trail is still mighty hot."

Suddenly Buck and Isaac turn looking at each other. "Was that a scream, Isaac?" Buck whispers. Standing still and holding their breath so as to listen better, they hear a gunshot and another scream in the neighboring woods! Not knowing if someone had shot the bear, was injured by the bear or both, they hastily tie their horses to a tree and rush the thick woods toward the screams and gunshot. Unfortunately it begins to drizzle. The closer the pair gets to the locus of the screams they hear what appears to be angry men's voices shouting obscenities.

Buck's military training taught him to slow down a bit in order to get a better perspective on the situation as he approaches. He and Isaac listen more intensely and it definitely appears someone is in dire distress.

Suddenly there are no more screams, yet Buck and Isaac can see horses about twenty-five feet away. Easing even closer, Buck and Isaac sight two Negro men tied to a tree, and another Negro man lying face down on the ground. There are two white men, both strangers to Buck and Isaac, each on top of the two Negro women.

One white man has a pistol held to one of the women's head and the other white man has tied the arms of the other Negro woman behind her back. His rifle is laying on the ground a couple of feet away from him.

Isaac whispers to Buck, "What's we gonna do?

Silent for a moment, Buck whispers back, "Think about it for a moment, Isaac. Our first option is not a good one at all. If we capture them we will have a huge problem mainly because they are slavers and have captured five runaways." Isaac continues to listen intensely. "If we turn them over to the sheriff probably nothing really will happen even though they raped the two women and killed one Negro. That is just the culture of our times. Also our identity will be revealed and we could become suspects as abolitionists, by interfering with the slavers."

"De hunter become de hunted so to speak," whispers Isaac.

Buck continues, "We have two other choices. First, we can silently sneak away and forget that we ever saw this ugly scene or second we can kill the two white guys and save the Negroes." Buck hesitates a moment thoughtfully and realizes what they have to do. "I don't think we have a choice. We need to save the Negroes."

Isaac breathes heavily. "I never killed before, Buck, but I can't let this go.

Buck looks sternly at Isaac. "Okay," Buck points to one of the white men. Isaac you shoot him. I'll take the other one with the pistol. Buck takes his index finger and places it between Isaac's neck and his shoulder. "Approach him from the side, quickly place your rifle here pointing toward his neck and shoot through his neck. Let nothing else enter your mind. Tell me when you are ready."

Isaac nods resolutely.

"Okay, let's ease as close as we can get. This rain will really help. Watch me and I will give the signal to move in on them."

Buck and Isaac are able to get within ten feet and one of the Negro men sees him. Buck places his finger over his mouth to indicate they are there to help. The two white men are concentrating on the women and are unaware of Buck and Isaac's approach. Buck gives Isaac a nod and the two rush the men. Within a matter of a few seconds Buck and Isaac almost simultaneously place their weapons and fire. The two white men did not have time to blink before collapsing on top of the women. The women begin to scream and cry as they begin to struggle from underneath the weight of the two dead men. Buck and Isaac drop their weapons and drag the men off of the hysterical blood-soaked women.

"Isaac, help the women while I untie the men.

Isaac, confused, is too deprived of emotion and physical feeling for the two perpetrators to even give them a second thought. Buck dashes over to the two Negro men, removes his knife and sets them free. Without saying a word they bolt to the women clutching them in their arms. In the meantime, Buck attends the fallen Negro. He turns him over on his back. The poor fellow had been shot in the chest and was dead. Isaac is with the four Negroes and begins talking to them as they all walk toward the dead man. They kneel beside him and rub his arms and chest. One of the women kisses him gently and lovingly on the forehead.

It is now raining heavily. Buck is silently contemplating the grimness of the situation, not only for him and Isaac, but for the survivors as well. Buck finally speaks, "What's going on here?

One of the Negro men begins by telling Buck, "We

are runaways from south of here en those slavers caught us at de creek. We's trying to get to da Union lines and head north to da River Jordan. Tis my brother they killed. He takes Buck's hand in both of his and begins to sob. "I cannot thank ye enough or we's all would be dead."

Buck peers at Isaac and tells the group. "We must leave all of the bodies and horses here or else stand getting into deep trouble. Take nothing from here except what is yours. Isaac and I will get you to a safe place that works with the Underground Railroad. From there you will shepherd north. The foursome study Buck and Isaac for a moment.

Isaac gains their confidence and tells them, "Look around. You have to trust us. They all nod their heads in agreement.

Buck tells the group, "This rain and nightfall is from heaven. All traces of us will vanish quickly. We must go a little more than a mile from here to the station. Isaac, help them gather their belonging, while I get our horses. Hopefully no one is out in this pouring rain. If you see anyone, jump into the woods. We must move quickly." Soon the group is on the road with their meager belongings, heading toward the Presbyterian Church and freedom.

Buck tells Isaac, "You go ahead and let the Reverend know what's going on so we do not have to hesitate at his door. If there is a problem rush back and let me know."

As the group reaches the Presbyterian Church, Isaac is waiting nearby for them. He approaches Buck, "All is clear. Take them to the back basement entrance and he will closet them in the secret room until arrangements can be made. Food and dry clothing will be there.

Isaac and Buck lead the group to the back of the church basement. Buck takes each of the Negro's hands and says, "Godspeed. One of the men replies, "We does not knows who ye are, but God Bless ye." The other three embrace Isaac and Buck as they enter the basement.

Buck tells Isaac on the way home, "The reason I

wanted you to shoot the slaver through the neck is so when they are found no one will suspect murder because there are no bullet holes in the skull. Hope they stay there four or five days and by then the coyotes, bears and turkey buzzards would have done their job."

Isaac replies, "I know, we had no other choice. Silent for a moment, Isaac continues, "Buck, did you ever think about sin?"

Buck replies, "I think about it all of the time. Why do you ask?"

Isaac continues, "Sin is man-made. It sure would be a nice world if'n man did not sin."

Buck looks at Isaac, "Never thought of it that way, Isaac, but you are absolutely correct." Buck and Isaac continue their rainy journey home as each of them reflects silently on their harrowing experience. Finally reaching the barn, Buck tells Isaac," Go ahead and take care of the horses. I'm going to tell Betty Gail and Sally we are home so they won't worry. Isaac asks, "What you gonna tell them why we are so late? I'll say, "Didn't want to give up. We almost had that bear in a corner until the rain started, but the rain and the bear won out this time."

Several days later the sheriff comes by while Betty Gail and Sally are on the porch. "Hello Sheriff. What brings you to these parts today?" asks Betty Gail.

"Where's Buck and Isaac?"

"Setting bear traps on the back side. Bears been getting some of our calves.

"Just wanted to let you know two whites and a Negro man were found dead on the other side of the mountain at the creek. Look like the bears got them-- animal tracks everywhere. Only one shot fired from a rifle. Horses dead too. Found the bodies from the turkey buzzards circling overhead. Seems like you already know about the bears. Keep your eyes open."

Giving a concerned look, "Anybody we know?" asks Betty Gail.

"Strangers in the area as best I can tell from the remains and saddle bag contents."

"Thank goodness and thanks for coming by, Sheriff, I'll be sure and let Buck and Isaac know of the tragedy.

Chapter Twenty-Eight
The Messenger

Congressman Joshua Hill and Emily are at their home in Madison in mid-June, when there's a knock on the front door. Upon answering the door, the butler finds a wounded Confederate soldier supported with a homemade crutch. Accompanying the soldier is a man and a woman. All of whom are strangers. "Kin I'se help ye?" asks the butler.

The older strange man asks, "Is this the home of Congressman Hill?"

"Ya'as, sah. Dis 'uz ez hones'." [Yes, sir. It is his home.]

"We have some information we must share with Congressman and Mrs. Hill regarding their son, Legare, if they are available."

"Yo name, sir?"

"I'm Rooster."

"We are Mrs. Mia Hill's parents."

"I'se git 'im. Wait 'lease."[I will get him. Wait please.] Shortly the butler returns, "Pleas' cum in."

As they enter, Congressman and Mrs. Hill are rushing to the foyer to meet their in-laws and Rooster. Congressman Hill and Emily immediately observe the heartbroken human forms entering their foyer. Buck and Betty Gail with a disconsolate demeanor look at their friends Joshua and Emily. Emily places her hands over her cheeks and mouth and begins to sob. "Please don't tell me my baby is dead! Please tell me Legare is alive."

Joshua draws Emily close and is unable to speak. Betty Gail walks to Emily and Buck extends his hand to

Joshua and clasps his hand in his own. Then in a soft, reverent voice, Buck breaks the sad news to Joshua and Emily, "I wish for all of us that I could turn the clock back. Legare is gone."

Emily begins to tremble, nearly falling to the floor. "My boy. My baby boy is gone! Dead. Killed by the Yankees!"

Joshua and Betty Gail assist, Emily to the couch in the parlor with Rooster and Buck following close behind. The butler, also in tears, retires to the kitchen and returns immediately with water. Emily takes several sips and begins to somewhat compose herself.

"When did this all happen, Buck?" Joshua sounds as if he's nearly overcome with grief. Joshua closes his eyes briefly before turning back to his friends.

"Rooster came by early this morning and told us the terrible news. We immediately went to the depot and boarded the train for Madison." "Please, Buck, you and Rooster have a seat. Rooster please tell us . . tell us everything, where Legare was killed and what happened."

Holding tightly to his crutch, Rooster clears his throat as best he can, lowers his head for a moment, and then looks at his friend's parents. The words momentarily stick in his throat as he fights to control his own emotions. "Well, sir, Legare died like a true patriot at the hands of our enemy. He was killed instantly and suffered no pain. It happened above Cass Station on May 19." He pauses for a few seconds to regain his composure. "He was a true friend and a true patriot. I'll sorely miss him just as you will." Joshua holds Emily closer. "Thank you, Rooster. We appreciate the effort it must have taken for you to get here with this news." Stricken with sorrow, Emily erupts into wails of anguish.

With tears on his cheeks, Rooster remorsefully says, "Congressman and Mrs. Hill, I'm deeply sorry."

Rooster reaches in his shirt pocket and hands Joshua a sheet of paper and three small envelopes. "I removed these buttons from the uniform you made for Legare. His wedding band is in the other envelope along with several locks of his hair. This last one is a letter he wrote to Mia the night before he was killed. It was ready to be placed in the mail. I thought about bringing a handkerchief

Mia made for him, but I know he would want to be buried with the handkerchief next to his heart. That is where I placed the handkerchief . . right next to his heart." Rooster struggles to maintain his composure. "Legare had given the beautiful scarf Mia made for him to Norman Jernigan. They accidentally met in Resaca at the Oostanaula River. Shortly after that, Legare was killed while assisting a wounded comrade to the rear . . the only person killed near Cass Station that day. It was when our unit was in retreat to Cassville on May 19th. We did not have time to properly bury Legare in the cemetery due to our orders to immediately withdraw to a new position."

"On that sheet of paper I have written down where McCurdy and some other soldiers and I placed his body. John Dent and Alonzo send their deepest sympathy as well."

"Congressman Hill, if there's anything I can do for you or your family please let me know. My address is also on the paper showing you where we placed Legare's body." After pausing several seconds, he says, "I must go now."

Betty Gail stands and walks over to Rooster. "Our home is your home, Rooster. Your thoughtfulness for our breaking hearts will never be forgotten." She kisses him on the cheek. Buck shakes his hand tightly and squeezes his shoulder with the other hand. Joshua stands, with pain in his eyes and unable to speak, he likewise takes Rooster's hand and places it between both of his and nods.

Rooster hobbles over to Mrs. Hill and takes her hand, "God bless you all, Mrs. Hill. My heart and sympathy is with you."

The butler escorts Rooster to the front door and hands him a sack containing several biscuits and ham.

"Good day, sah, bless ye en be safe," says the butler as he opens the door.

"Thank you." Rooster makes his way down the stairs with his home-made crutch, biscuits with ham and limps away.

"Buck, if you don't mind, come with me to my study. I suggest we depart on the first train in the morning for Savannah."

"By all means. I checked the schedule and the earliest one leaves at 8:35 in the morning."

"If you will bear with me a few minutes, I may need your help. I must write to James R. Crews, the Superintendent of the West Point Railroad." In a broken voice, "He can assist me in locating my son's remains. We want him buried in our family plot in the cemetery near our home."

Taking a pen and paper, Congressman Hill writes, "You have doubtless heard of the cruel affliction this abominable war is bringing to my hearth stone. I can't help thinking this is more than I merit. My poor boy met his death on Thursday morning, the 19th of May, as I am informed, about 2 miles above Cass Station." He pauses and glances up at Buck. "Buck read me the note from Rooster and I will write the specifics in the letter."

Buck takes Rooster's note and reads, "He was killed beyond Ben Johnson's house on the road leading from Cassville to Kingston, about one half mile from the road."

Changing the wording slightly, Congressman Hill continues, "He is said to have been brought by some of his comrades nearer the Railroad."

Then Congressman Hill continues with the directions as Buck reads, "His body is left by the side of the public road, somewhere about or near a deserted cabin or perhaps nearer still to a small frame house near the Railroad. No one else was killed."

In closing, Joshua writes, "His name is Hugh Legare Hill, age eighteen years with a fair complexion. His hair is light brown and thick and inclined to curl a little but was thin. He is about 5 feet 8 1/2 inches in height, trim, erect figure, eyelashes long and dark. He had been sick and was rather thin in flesh, clothing all marked with his initials and name, thus 'H. L. Hill,' dark gray Jeans, new (nearly) and lighter gray jacket, plaid domestic shirt-name on the front. His death wound was received in a retreat and entered at the back of his head." As he writes, tears drop from his eyes and stain the letter. He takes his handkerchief to soak the moisture from the paper. "I write these particulars in the hope that, with the shifting scenes through which we are passing, you may see some chance to ascertain the fate of my son's body, whether it was interred by some kind human or was left to waste away by the action of the elements. My object is to recover his remains as perfectly as may be. Should any opportunity offer for you to obtain for me this covert information, I know you will take pleasure in receiving it for me. Respectfully, Joshua Hill."

Joshua leans back in his chair. His eyes and nose are red and damp.

Then he leans over and adds a postscript, "I forgot to state that my son had a beautiful set of regular and white teeth." He seals the letter in an envelope and hands it to Buck. "Please have the butler take this to the post office right away."

Buck, Betty Gail, Joshua and Emily arrive at the Savannah depot around two o'clock in the afternoon. Buck arranges to retrieve their baggage and procure a carriage. When all the bags are loaded, he gives the driver directions to Mia's house. Emotionally exhausted, Emily and Betty Gail are clutching handkerchiefs in one hand and holding tight to their husbands' arms with the other.

"Our biggest concern is whether or not Mia will be home when we arrive," Buck says. "If she is, poor Mia will know why we are here." Buck stares at the passing scenery a moment.

Joshua nods distractedly. "I hope she is home too and, like you said, she's bound to know why we're here."

For the first time in his life, Buck dreads seeing his daughter. Being the bearer of the bad news of Legare's death would be one of the hardest tasks he'd ever done. The news will break her heart.

The carriage ride proceeds toward Mia's for what seems like an eternity. As the driver maneuvers the last turn in the road, Mia's house comes into view.

Approaching the turnabout, Emily and Betty Gail begin to feel the emotional strain of their grim duty. Tears flow from their swollen eyes when they see Al in the front yard working in the small flower garden. As the carriage enters the turnabout, Al stands to see who might be approaching. He finally recognizes it is the Hills and the Jernigans and rushes to the carriage. "Mornin', Mistuh Hill, Ma'am Emily. Mornin' Mr. Jernigan, Ma'am Betty Gail. Miss Mia no says uh comin'."

"She isn't expecting us." Buck jumps down from the wagon, his hat in his hand. "Is she, home, Al?"

"No, suh, Jess, Miss Mia en baby at de hospital. I tink be bac' soon."

"Where might Tot be?"

"Tot in bac' workin' herbs."

"Take the luggage inside, please, and fetch Tot."

Buck and the family follow Al as he takes the luggage inside. Then he goes to the back to get Tot. Al expresses his concerns to Tot. This visit has to do with a major crisis, and he suspects it has to do with "Mistuh leGree." Hastily Al and Tot enter the parlor. Tot, looking somewhat puzzled, says. "Mornin'. Wehkum. Eb'rt'ing al' right?" [Good morning. Welcome. Everything all right?]

Attempting to hold back their emotions, Emily and Betty Gail walk over to Al and Tot and Betty Gail explains, "We have sad news for Mia and you, but we will wait and tell you the news when Mia comes home."

Nervously, Tot answers, "Yaas, ma'am. Uh want tea or coffee, suh, ma'am."[Yes, ma'am. Would you like some tea or coffee, sir, ma'am?]

"Thank you, Tot. We will have some sassafras tea," replies Betty Gail. Buck looks at everyone. "I believe I will go outside and wait for Mia. It will be better for her to see me when she arrives rather than when she opens the door and finds all of us inside. When she arrives and I speak to her a few minutes, then y'all come outside." Not waiting for a reply, Buck departs and nervously sits on the stairs and begins his painful wait.

He watches a bright redbird scratching the leaves in the fresh flower garden looking for a quick meal. Suddenly he sees a familiar carriage heading in his direction. It's Mia, little Joshua and Jesse. Buck's eyes begin to fill as Jesse points toward him and looks at Mia. Mia stands in the carriage as Al rushes the carriage to a stop in front of the house. Buck walks slowly down the stairs and stands next to the carriage as Mia leaps to the ground.

Buck grabs Mia and hugs her with all his might! "I'm sorry, honey. I'm so sorry, honey." They both begin to weep.

"I know why you are here, Pa. I see it in your eyes. Legare is gone! I haven't heard from him in weeks. My letters go unanswered. I hate Joe Brown! I hate Joe Brown! He ordered my dear husband to his death! He killed my husband!" Mia begins to sob even more deeply. Betty Gail, Congressman Hill and Emily emerge from the house and come to Mia's side.

Emily and Betty Gail embrace Mia. Betty Gail whispers, "I love you." Betty Gail, then unable to speak, whispers, "All of our hearts are broken."

With tears on his cheeks, Joshua embraces Mia. "We've both lost a dear person, Mia. Our hearts have been ripped from our chests. We must remember he died as a true patriot, a soldier and a very loving husband and father. Your memory of our son and your husband will always be one of youth. He will never grow old in our memory or yours."

Jesse is holding little Joshua, who is becoming very upset. He breaks away from Jesse and rushes to his mother. Tugging at her dress, he looks up to his weeping mother, "Mama. Mama, why you crying?"

Mia picks up little Joshua and squeezes him tightly. In a choking voice, Mia whispers in little Joshua's ear, "Daddy is gone to heaven. Your sweet daddy has gone to heaven."

Al and Tot are watching from the front door. Tot takes her apron, wipes her eyes, takes Al's arm, and says to Al, "Oh, no, Mistuh leGree dead. Oh, leGree dead! Oh poor Miss Mia. Her man is dead." Tot and Al go to Mia. Tot also embraces Mia, "Muhself don' kno' wah fuh to say, Miss Mia. Muhself sad wid you. Muhself en Al h'aa't' bauk'up fuh." [I don't know what to say, Miss Mia. I am as sad as you are. My and Al's hearts are broken too!]

Joshua turns to Jesse, "Go and tell Richard and Josephine that we are here. Avoid telling them our cause.

Just say we must see them."

Jesse wipes his eyes. "Ya'as, shur, Mistuh Hill."

Mia looks around at the beautiful day. "The birds are singing, the bees are busy with the flowers, the air is calm . . I feel like the angel of death is no longer waiting to deliver me a message. Let's go inside."

Emily offers to take little Joshua from Mia, but he reacts to the disturbing emotional event, turns away from Emily and clings to his mother.

Several days later, Buck, Emily and Joshua are on the train returning to their homes. Betty Gail is staying with Mia and little Joshua for the time being. Buck reminds Joshua, "When you hear from Mr. Crews, remember I'll be honored to assist you in any way to recover Legare's remains."

"I will call on you, Buck. Thank you."

Soon the Hills are standing alone on the train platform in Madison. Buck sees the attendant summon a carriage for them as he watches from the passenger car. The train slowly pulls away and heads toward Stone Mountain. Buck hopes tomorrow does not bring him similar news of Norman since he hasn't heard from him for some time.

Buck's first stop on his rounds in town is at the Post Office. Thomas Browning, the Postmaster, sees him coming and retrieves a letter. "Looks like a letter from your son."

Buck rushes forward as Thomas gladly hands him the letter. "Thanks, Betty Gail is back home from Savannah and is anxious to hear from Norman." He opens it and begins to read,

"The hot and humid days of June are somewhat less bothersome than normal since we are camping on the river. We have plenty to do at West Point, Georgia. We still train soldiers in the camps, instructing the same as at Camp McDonald. The entire corps are taking care of the horses since there are no stable hands with us at West Point. The horses are as important as our weapons. We walk and exercise them every day, and the artillery units are drilling every day. Once the soldiers in the Confederate camp learn the basic drilling and manual of arms, the best ones begin training in the use of artillery.

"The locals are very nice to us. They allow us to sleep in their sheds if it is raining. Most of the cadets are able to ask their families to send or bring a waiter. However, there is now a chance they'll escape to the Yankees. None has left yet, but if the Yankees get too near, I think they'll escape to the Yankee side. Tomorrow, I think I'll be able to do a little fishing in the river. Any word from Mia? Love, Norman."

"How is he?" asks Thomas.

"Everything is good," replies Buck as he tips his hat and smiles. He folds the letter, rushes to his wagon, takes the reins of the horse and heads home so Betty Gail can read that their son is doing well.

Chapter Twenty-nine
Good Samaritan's Work

Dr. George Washington Maddox is in charge of Dr. Hamilton's hospital in Stone Mountain, next to the railroad depot. More sick and wounded soldiers arrive daily for treatment. Dr. Maddox is also using his home as a hospital. It is located a couple of blocks away from the Georgia railroad. Betty Gail and the ladies of the churches are getting busier since soldiers are retreating from General Sherman's army.

Fresh vegetables are delivered to the depot by the women from their farms and divided into baskets of fresh vegetables, berries, peaches, apples, and sweet potatoes. Then they depart for one of the three churches in Stone Mountain – the Baptist, the Methodist and Presbyterian – and the hospitals.

The doctors direct the ladies to treat most of the illnesses with one of the sovereign panaceas, either whiskey, quinine or turpentine. As each patient finishes his meal, an orderly changes the stained and ill-smelling dressings. Even with their best attempts, wounds continue to sour– growing more painful and the moans become louder. Betty Gail and the young house maidens are the only blissful respite to these miserable conditions. Only those who are unable to awaken cannot consume the nourishment and comforting smiles from the young maidens. With tenderness, they cleanse the wounds of the ailing and dying.

A dying young soldier takes Betty Gail's hand, "Please, ma'am, I know I'm dying. My pa is dead from the war. I don't want my ma to be lost and not know where I am.

Please write her for me and let her know where I'm buried so she will not be lost as well."

"I'll fetch a pencil and paper and you can write her and I'll mail it for you."

"I can't write and ma can't read or write. Just put her name on the envelope and mail it to Dalton. She'll get it and have someone read it to her."

Betty Gail writes as the dying soldier speaks his last loving words to his loving mother. She lays the pencil and letter aside. Then she holds his hand until she can no longer feel his pulse, and the dying young man slowly drifts into a peaceful and eternal silence.

In the rear of Dr. Maddox's hospital is the whiskey still for the three hospitals. The slaves are distilling whiskey by the barrel. The fires are ablaze day and night, producing a good barrel daily of either peach brandy or corn whiskey.

The shrill whistle of the train signals that passengers, freight, wounded, dying and dead are arriving at the depot. As the train stops, the hospital staff is somber, afraid that loved ones or neighbors may be among the casualties. Most of the wounds involve the head and the upper limbs. Climbing on board to assist the wounded, Betty Gail fortunately finds no dead among this transport. As the aids unload the hospital car, she looks out and sees a wagon approaching the hospital carrying several more wounded soldiers. She hurries to meet the wagon as the horses are tied down. Soldiers with bloody bandages fabricated from their torn clothing cover the gashing wounds. Several slaves come out to transport the sick and wounded into the hospital.

Betty Gail holds the door open as four slaves carry the poor dead soldier to a waiting wagon for transport to the local cemetery. The soldier still has the horrible-smelling bandage with dried blood covering his wound. Betty Gail nods a "Thank you" to the local preachers and a burial group which accompanies him to the cemetery and then walks over to the post office to mail his letter as she had promised.

"Good morning, Mr. Goldsmith."

"Good morning, Hiram and Martha. I see you are on

time as usual to sort out the vegetables and meat for the hospitals." James looks out the window toward the wagons outside.

"Yes, sir," replies Hiram. "Folks around here have been very supportive of the hospitals. Fortunately, the crops are plentiful and the livestock healthy." Hiram and Martha Tweedle are in charge of separating the food which is delivered to the depot. The community trusts them to allocate the supply to the churches and hospitals for the staff and the patients.

After breakfast the next morning, Buck and Betty Gail are sitting in front of the fireplace. "Buck, the news from Norman is not coming as often as it used to. I worry about his getting involved in this war as a cadet with the state militia."

"I worry with you and without you. Paper is in short supply, and I know he's going to get involved in more than training soldiers, especially since they had that skirmish in Resaca. And Mia is in Savannah alone and does not want to come back home right now. Sometimes I think maybe we should move there with her, but I know she won't stand for it." Betty Gail puts down her mending, pulls her chair closer to Buck and places his hand in hers.

"Buck, she's always been independent minded. Her last letter said she is doing fine. It seems Richard is taking good care of her. Tot, Al and Jesse are loyal to her as well. Fortunately, Legare left her means of support and she has a good house in which to raise our grandchild. We just have to pray for both of them. I've grown older quicker since Legare got killed." Betty Gail begins to cry and takes her apron to wipe her tears away.

Buck squeezes her hand tightly and he turns to hug and comfort her. "My mind is spinning with the same thoughts. We just have to hope and pray that there are no further tragedies in our family."

Betty Gail regains her composure and begins to stare at the edge of the fireplace, "Buck there's a gap forming between the edge of the fireplace and the fake wall." Buck gets up from his chair and walks over to the area Betty Gail points to. She follows close behind. They inspect the gap closely. "If someone else notices that gap it may give them a clue that something's not right," she says.

"Yep, the wood has dried from the heat of the fire and shrunk back. I've got some more of the same wood in the barn. "Running his hand along the wall, Buck makes a decision, "I'll make molding to cover the gap from the floor to the ceiling on both sides then go over the mantle and down the other side and tie it all together. I'm glad you saw that. It could have gotten worse with time. Also, I know you won't forget, but remember if something happens to me, I buried our gold at the bottom of the fourth fence post to the left of the back gate. Just the two of us know about where it is buried. I know our valuables and canned goods will be safe behind these two fake walls. I'll find Isaac and get started on repairing the gap."

"Well, we are at war and the war is gonna get closer to us."

"Yep, I'm already worried about killing and burning. Governor Brown needs to come to his senses and make peace. There's no way to hide the livestock."

Betty Gail nods in agreement and starts to go back to her mending. Suddenly, she looks up at him. "Probably the best approach is to turn them loose in the woods. Our county voted against secession, so maybe the Yankees will appreciate us even more since we are flying the Union flag. Sally and I are canning more of our vegetables and fruits today and tomorrow."

"Isaac and I'll try to find another good hiding place for the extra. Don't offer any extras to the church or neighbors. As far as the meat goes, there's plenty of wild game, squirrel, rabbit, deer, and a few bear. Meat's no problem. In the fall we'll have plenty of pecans and chestnuts and wintertime, we can grow greens."

Later in the morning, Isaac and Betty Gail are in town purchasing canning supplies while Sally is at the farm preparing the food for canning. "Best git mo' powder des in case bandits cum 'round. Des a worsen den de Yankees."

Betty Gail replies, "We are going to do our best to

survive this terrible war. If it takes hiding food and killing bandits, that's what we will do. They best not come around our place!" Isaac loads the wagon with several large bags of flour, corn meal, canning supplies and grits, and they head home.

The next day, Buck, Betty Gail and Isaac load the wagon with fresh vegetables and fruits for the hospital. On the way to town they pass some cavalry of Colonel Dibrell, who are their way to Yellow River. Buck and Betty Gail pull over to the side of the road so the cavalry can pass. One of the officers sees the wagon load of food and brings his mount to a stop next to the wagon.

"Have any extra you can spare for us?" asks the officer.

"This wagon load is for the patients in the hospital, but take a bushel of apples and a couple bushels of corn. I can get more in a day or so from my farm." The officer signals for a supply wagon to come over and load the corn and apples. "What's the latest on the approaching Yankees?" asks Buck.

"They are all around McAfee's Bridge. The Yanks are taking over Cross Keys to Pinckneyville, Lebanon Church and all the way to Warsaw. We have run them off from Yellow River. Those Yankees have been trying to destroy the railroad from here to Augusta while we have been trying to cut the railroad north of McAfee to keep them from getting supplies. You best be prepared in case they break through here. We don't have enough cavalry to do both operations. Stone Mountain is right on the railroad to Augusta." Buck steps from the wagon and begins checking what food has been taken.

"Take several more of the watermelons. More will be ripening in a couple of days."

"Thank you Mr. . what's your name?"

"Jernigan. Buck Jernigan. This is my wife, Betty Gail."

The officer tips his hat with his fingers. "Thank you, Buck and Mrs. Jernigan."

The officer shouts, "Move out!" and the wagon and troops soon disappear towards Yellow River.

Buck leaves Betty Gail and the wagon at the

hospital. "While you have the wagon unloaded, I'm going to the depot and get the latest report on our men."

Betty Gail goes inside, finding two orderlies, "There's food on the wagon. How about taking it to the cook house for me."

"Yes, ma'am."

Buck walks up to a small group of his friends who are looking at the roster. "Good morning, Jesse. Good morning, William." Jesse Lanford and William Nash return a good morning to Buck.

"Looks like George got wounded. Read here, Buck."

"George Riley Wells wounded in the wrist on May 15 at the Battle of Spotsylvania Courthouse and sent to a Richmond hospital. Isaac Pope, slightly wounded on June 7, at Cold Harbor."

"Said the Yankees are all around trying to destroy bridges and the railroad. Best start hiding your food and goods."

Jesse continues, "We're hiding everything we can. Looks like Ransom is going to be a prison guard at Camp Sumpter near Andersonville."

Buck then cautiously moves over to the "Deceased" roster. "The only new addition is Pressley Lanier. Buck reads, "Killed at the battle of Spotsylvania Courthouse."

Pointing to Pressley's name, William Nash says, "Preston was in the same unit as George Riley Wells and look here on the captured list. John McClelland was captured on May 10. I almost hate to ask you, Buck, but how is Mia doing in Savannah and how about Norman?"

"Mia wants to stay in Savannah in her and Legare's house. Her slaves are still with her and Legare's Uncle Richard checks on her daily. It's just a terrible thing. Poor Legare was against the war and the war took him anyhow. He truly loved my daughter. Congressman Hill is trying to get through the lines to recover Legare's body." Solemnly, his two friends listen. "A cannon ball through our hearts could not do more damage than that sad news from Rooster. Norman is probably going to wind up fighting with

GMI as a State Militia. I just pray we don't lose another."

Chapter Thirty
Bewildered Citizens

From his headquarters on Sunday July 17th, General Sherman issues Special Field Orders No. 36:

"The operations of the army for tomorrow, Monday the 18th of July will be as follows:

"1 Major-General Thomas will move forward, occupy Buck Head and the ridge between Nancy's Creek and Peachtree, also all the roads toward Atlanta, as far as Peachtree Creek.

"2 Major-General Schofield will pass through Cross Keys and occupy the Peachtree Road where intersected by the road from Cross Keys to Decatur.

"3 Major-General McPherson will move toward Stone Mountain to secure strong ground within four miles of General Schofield's position, and push Brigadier-General Garrard's cavalry to the railroad and destroy some section of the road (railroad), and then resume position to the front and left of General McPherson.

"4 All armies will communicate with the neighbors. The general-in-chief will be near General Thomas' left, or near General Schofield.

By order of Major General W. T. Sherman"

A courier delivers a message to General Wheeler from Colonel Dibrell stating that the Yankees are at Buchanan's and heading for the railroad and the Stone Mountain Depot. General Wheeler gets word to General John Kelly to send a regiment to the depot for protection.

Around one p.m., about six miles beyond

Buchanan's, the Federal advance guard reaches Browning's courthouse in Tucker. They are ready to turn onto Fellowship road at Browning's Courthouse and proceed to the City of Stone Mountain.

Approximately fifty Confederate cavalry surprises the advance guard of the Union Army. General Garrard has information from a Confederate deserter that in fact it is General John Kelly's cavalry.

The sun is slightly past noon on Tuesday as General Garrard's troops reach the end of Fellowship Road and approach the railroad about three miles west of the Stone Mountain Depot. The other troops dismount and, once the rope corral is secure, they tie their horses along the circular length of rope. Next, the men go to the supply wagon and obtain the tools and fuel to begin the destruction of the railroad ties and tracks. Captain Dartt discusses the task at hand with the men and instructs them to begin and work and head directly toward the Stone Mountain Depot. The men take off their shirts and line up along the tracks. Soon the first section of track is separated. Soldiers drag the ties and place them in a pile. Another soldier pours fuel on the ties and with a "swoosh" from the ignition the ties begin to burn, sending a rising stream of smoke into the July sky.

When the large force of troops arrives at the railroad, Colonel Miller and Colonel Minty find Captain Dartt's troops are already hot, sweaty and stinking from the July heat and humidity and are taking a short break. They confer with Captain Dartt and he informs the two Colonels about the rumors of a large Rebel force in the area. "We have a strong advance guard to protect us from a surprise attack. So we are moving with great speed, no matter how hot and humid the day."

"Thank you, Captain Dartt, for the briefing."

"No problem, sir." Captain Dartt salutes Colonel Minty and departs.

Colonel Abe Miller's Indiana troops lack experience in the mechanics and art of rail and tie removal. General Garrard arrives and orders the Hoosiers to tear down nearby fences and builds large fires at the end of each rail section.

James Milliken, a local farmer, wonders where all of the slaves are and notices several heading in the same direction away from his place. He mounts his horse and follows a good distance back. Appearing slightly over a ridge, to his astonishment, is a large group of slaves talking with the Union Army! There are thousands of troops. He turns, and in a full gallop notifies as many neighbors as possible. A Union guard notices James Milliken's sprint and chases for about one mile before stopping and returning to his unit. James continues to head to Stone Mountain to warn the citizens about the large Union force heading in their direction. Riding into Stone Mountain and stopping at City Hall, he relays to the clerk what he has seen.

The clerk immediately rings the bell at City Hall, which beacons to the locals to gather for an important announcement. The little town of Stone Mountain becomes a beehive of activity as the city clerk announces the news of the approaching Union forces. The stores close and people head for their homes, hoping no foragers arrive at their doors. The hospital makes plans for more wounded and dying to arrive. Very few of the populace have ever been in direct contact with a Yankee military force.

Yet the seriousness of the situation overtakes any concept of panic at the hospital. Yankees are known to take over Confederate hospitals and even burn them down. The staff hopes that its work with Union patients, as well as their own, might spare the hospitals. "We must continue our work in an orderly fashion if the Yankees make an appearance at the hospitals," says Dr. Maddox.

Buck and Isaac are tending the fields as Jesse Lanford and Mark Beauchamp arrive at his farm simultaneously. It is one of those July days when the air is still, the bugs are plentiful and the dust is thick. Even in the shade, there is no comfort from the searing heat. Mark dismounts and walks to the farm bell in front of the house. He grasps the long rope and begins to toll the bell. Buck is on the far corner of his farm as the bell sounds. All of the slaves and Buck mount their wagons and horses immediately and head for the house at full gallop.

Arriving in a matter of minutes, Buck sees Mark and Jesse standing by the farm bell. Jesse and Buck rush to meet each other. "What's the matter, Jesse?"

"The Yankees are at the end of Fellowship and are tearing up track on the railroad. There must be 5,000 Yankees, some heading to Decatur and some to Stone Mountain."

"How about the ladies at the hospital?" asks Buck.

"None wants to leave. They say their duty is there and ours is to get the crops hid before the Yankees steals 'um!" retorts Jesse.

Mark, somewhat unsure, says, "Buck, the Yankees are not known to bother women and children except for taking their food. Y'all best get and hide your stock."

Buck removes his hat and wipes the sweat from his brow. "I'm grateful to both of you for the warning."

Buck sends Buster Phillips' slaves back to their farm and directs them to secure all belongings and to hide food. Once they are out of sight, Buck and Uncle Isaac enter the house. Sally stays outside with Old Charlie to watch for any signs of humans, friend or foe. Fake walls have been built on each side of the massive fireplace inside the parlor. Shelving is within the walls from floor to ceiling. The walls match the old decor of the house perfectly and are undetectable. Each wall is divided into three horizontal sections that are easy to remove.

The Jernigans' table and storeroom have fifty or sixty jars of freshly canned vegetables. Removing one layer of the horizontal fake wall, Buck and Uncle Isaac begin placing the jars on the shelves. The uppermost shelves contain the family heirlooms, extra clothing, bedding and cooking utensils along with ammunition and weapons. They complete their task in a timely manner and set the wall in place without any sign of disturbance. Several canning jars of vegetables remain on the tables in case Sherman's bummers show up demanding food.

Sally hurries inside. "Mars Buck, I seed dust yonder and don't know who hit be!"

"Stay calm, Sally, it's too early for the Yankees. They gotta get to the depot first before they head out here," replies Buck.

A wagon comes to a halt in the yard. William Sheppard jumps out. "Have you heard about the Yankees?"

"Sure have! How about town and the hospitals?" asks Buck.

"The stores and hotels are closing but all is well at the hospitals. There's no worry for their safety. Mrs. Jernigan said to let you know she is gonna stay the night either at the hospital or the church. She sends me here to bring in some fresh corn. They need more corn silk for stomach broth and corn to feed the patients."

The people of Stone Mountain are exceedingly nervous. What few women are left feel helpless with most all of the men gone to war. The shocked women try to find hiding places for their few, yet precious heirlooms. Some use the chimneys as a secret storage space. The horses and livestock are turned loose in the woods and the chickens are set free from their enclosures. The women gather the children in their homes and lock the doors. Betty Gail has all of the food brought into the hospital. She instructs her assistants, "Do not leave any food outside. Take the horses and hide them over the hill. Nobody knows how long these Yankees will be here. There are some commissary supplies at the depot." She informs one of the assistants, "I'll take two or three slaves and get whatever I can from the commissary car at the depot and bring them here for safe keeping." A few citizens have an old musket and with such a small population and with most of the men in the army, the only defense the city can depend on is General Joe Wheeler's forces.

Hastily, General Wheeler orders Colonel Dibrell's cavalry force to the Stone Mountain depot. They arrive and wait for the Union advance into the city of Stone Mountain. Colonel Dibrell orders his men to take cover in the buildings and surrounding woods. Colonel Dibrell arrives at the depot and sees Betty Gail unloading the commissary car. "Ma'am, I suggest you get back to where you came from for now. The Yankees are coming into town."

She points to the hospital. "Colonel Dibrell, I am in charge of the hospital over there. Just trying to save as much of these supplies as we can for the army."

"It's just too dangerous right now. You don't need to get shot."

"We'll take what we have and get on back to the hospital," Betty Gail says.

Colonel Dibrell has already directed his commanders to their positions for a surprise attack on the Yankees and has his aide rush to alert the bugler of the plan, "When the last Yankees pass our position at the edge of town, man, sound charge and our forces will open fire at once." Colonel Dibrell takes his place in the woods with his staff and observes the Union force. Leaving their horses behind so as not to be detected, they become alarmed at the size of the Union force. Colonel Dibrell begins to wait for the last of the Pennsylvania and Ohio troops to pass. Soon he realizes that the lead column is probably already at the depot while the end of the Pennsylvania and Ohio are not even in sight. His bugler points in the direction of the depot. "Look, sir, something is burning near the depot."

"It must be the depot and water tank." Realizing what is happening, Colonel Dibrell orders his bugler to sound "charge." The firing commences and surprises the Yankees. Dibrell's forces have the advantage and charge the Yankees. Numerous Pennsylvania and Ohio soldiers fall wounded or dead from their mounts. Some of the wounded remain in their saddles, slumping and trying to find their way to the rear. Several Yankees had dismounted outside of the hospital when the attack begins. Unable to get organized against Dibrell's cavalry, the Yankees, thoroughly disorganized and unsure of the number in Colonel Dibrell's cavalry, hastily mount and escape from town. The battle is over in less than five minutes and Colonel Dibrell's cavalry suffers no losses.

Betty Gail opens the front door to the hospital and observes the water tank as two of its support legs are roped to six cavalry horses. With a smack from the Union riders, the horses tear away the legs and the water tank falls to the ground splashing its contents along the tracks. She observes another group of Yankees throw fiery torches onto the roof of the depot. Slowly the flames begin to grow larger and spread across the roof.

Twisting her apron in her hands she sternly tells her assistant, "Nothing we can do about the depot fire. Just have to let it burn itself out. It's mostly granite except for the roof. We need to gather the wounded and bring them here. Send for the horses so we can hitch them up."

Her assistant rushes out and disappears over the hill. She returns inside and begins checking on the patients. Many are aware of the skirmish, yet many are so sick they are unaware of their surroundings. She and the nurses attempt to calm the wounded and sick, reassuring them that the Yankees will not harm soldiers in hospitals.

Betty Gail sees the slaves hitching the horses and mules to the wagons. She goes outside with several of her nurses. "Go with the wagons and bring back the wounded. Bring back both the Yankees and Confederate wounded and dead."

Without discussion, the nurses climb onto the wagons and begin the search along the dirt road running along the railroad tracks.

A train on its way to Atlanta stops at the Stone Mountain Depot. James Goldsmith runs out to speak with the engineer. "Yankees tore up the tracks about a mile from here."

The engineer asks, "Why didn't you telegraph us?"

"There are no working telegraph lines along this stretch of the Georgia Railroad," remarks the nervous station agent. In the meantime, he places the station clock on the wall, which he had escaped with as the Yankees came into town on the previous day. The townspeople and Confederate military alert the engineer that the tracks were destroyed during the day by Union General Garrard's troops. The agent directs the engineer on which side of the track to park the freight cars with the cargo. Moving the freight cars to the sidetrack, the train begins a long backward journey to Lithonia, where there's a turn-around, and heads back south.

Chapter Thirty-one
Saving the Hospitals

On July 18, General Garrard decides to send Colonel Abe Miller's command and Lieutenant George Robinson's 2nd section of the Board of Trade Battery on the road to Stone Mountain around noon. Captain Adam Pinkerton's 72nd Indiana Company is the advance guard.

Colonel George Dibrell's Tennessee Mounted Infantry are lying in wait for the 72nd Indiana as they approach the picket line at Browning's Courthouse. Colonel Dibrell's forces launch a surprise infantry attack from the woods. Captain Pinkerton's Unit dismounts and forms a skirmish line. There's now a thin line of Gray and Blue, soldier against soldier, Yankee Spenser rifles against Rebel muskets.

Both Union and Confederate are equal in courage and self-reliance. Moreover, they are zealous in their cause. A Confederate officer instructs his men from the skirmish line, "Just sight the location of one of the Yankees from a puff of smoke from his weapon. That's how to locate him."

Each side firing, the Gray advances and then the Blue advances. Both sides gain and lose a few yards. A Confederate soldier dodges from tree to tree to protect himself. Out of breath, he drops to his belly upon the ground. He peers cautiously just to find a rise or an advantage ditch so he can take aim upon a Yankee. His eyes are always to the front. He strains his vision as he scans the battle for the slightest motion, hopeful to deliver his gift of death to a Yankee. The Confederate soldier never exposes himself. He loads his weapon as if it is an unconscious act. He bites his salty paper cartridge and drives the charge home with his ramrod, primes his weapon with a percussion cap. Seeking and finding his target, he fires at the enemy, three shots per minute.

The Yankee cavalry has a great advantage. The Yankee soldier simply loads his metal case single round into the rifle chamber and fires. His weapon carries a bullet further and faster than that of the musket. The bullets whiz by the Confederates as commands are shouted. He hears his wounded comrade moan and sees his dead friend lay silent. The Confederate raises his hat as another comrade looks for a Blue to take the bait. The Yankee does. The Confederate aims and fires a shot and watches the enemy fall as his crimson blood flows from his mortal wound. The two Confederate soldiers congratulate each other and continue to tease and seek out another Yankee.

Captain Pinkerton cannot hold his line and anxiously requests reinforcements from Colonel Miller. Colonel Miller orders the 17th Indiana, the 123rd Illinois and Lieutenant Robinson with his two Parrott cannons to reinforce Captain Pinkerton's precarious unit. Lieutenant Robinson fields the Parrott Battery and opens fire. The Confederates witness a sudden rattle, a whoosh of air passes overhead and the shells begin to explode. The solid shot sings as it passes through the trees. The Confederate soldiers hug the ground as huge branches are torn away and without mercy descend upon them. "Aim lower. Aim at the earthworks," shouts Lieutenant Robinson. Suddenly the Parrott Battery fires and destroys the earthworks.

Bits and pieces of mutilated Confederates fly from the path of the cannon balls. The noise of the cannon fire is that of an exploding volcano. The Confederate soldier is deafened and cannot hear the orders from Colonel Dibrell. He turns to look for his leader and disappears from another blast of the Yankee cannon. The Confederate advantage is quickly reduced. Colonel Dibrell's unit hastily withdraws through the tall timber. The Confederates are able to get to the railroad where the 4th Michigan's destruction of the railroad ended the day before. General Wheeler's

Confederate Cavalry, under the command of BG. John H. Kelly, covers their withdrawal.

General Kelly orders snipers to take refuge in and around the houses along the railroad track at the city limits of Stone Mountain. With the provident eye of the majestic granite mountain in the background, the sharpshooters take their position. With his telescopic rifle, each Confederate sharpshooter sights along with the infantry and commences firing from the upstairs windows.

Parrott cannons of Lieutenant Robinson, artillerymen arrive and open fire against the Confederate sharpshooters.

The initial cannonball rips through the second floor of the house. Crashing into the front room, several inches above the floor, the cannonball knocks the chair out from under the owner. Terrified, the owner hastily exits through the hole produced by the cannon ball in the far wall. The shock of the cannon fire again disrupts the Confederates and the sharpshooters rapidly abandon the house. Colonel Miller's men charge. As the Parrott guns continue to fire, General Kelly's Cavalry are in full retreat with Colonel Miller's in hot pursuit through the woods surrounding Stone Mountain.

The roar of the nearing cannons signals the citizens that the war is coming to Stone Mountain. Then the rifle and musket fire draw closer, louder and sustain longer. Betty Gail locates a large white sheet she and Bennett Jeffares had stored. On the sheet in large print is the word 'HOSPITAL.' She and Bennett go outside and tie the sheet across the front of the hospital. Betty Gail checks the tie-downs to be sure the sheet can withstand any strong winds. "I hope the sheet will send a message to the Yankees that this is a hospital and should not be disturbed," she says. "Maybe they will leave the patients alone."

"It just depends on which Yankee shows up from what I understand. Some good and some bad. I've heard that some of the Yankees come in and steal from the patients," replies Bennett.

The hospital staff, standing in front of Dr. Hamilton's hospital, located across the railroad track from the depot, turns their attention to the distant sound of horses' hoofs and clouds of dust which appear over the tree line. Betty Gail fears the Yankees are close by, but she is surprised when the retreating Confederate cavalry rush and scatter through town. Soldiers on foot follow behind. Some stopping, taking cover, loading the clumsy musket, firing and retreating. Betty Gail and the nurse dash inside and observe from a window. In horror, Betty Gail sees one soldier fall. Then another falls. Then four more poor soldiers surrender their lives.

An orderly taps Betty Gail on the shoulder. "Miss Betty Gail, some of the patients are trying to scramble out of here." She leaves the horrific view from her window and begins to visit and reassure the patients that they are safe but panic breaks regardless. Even the most critical vainly attempt to escape.

"The Yankees will not harm you!" exclaims Betty Gail over and over as she attempts to comfort the patients. She sits beside a critical soldier and holds his hand and tries to reassure him that the Yankees are not going to harm him. At that instant a stray bullet breaks a window and some of the shattered glass falls on the suffering soldier. Startled, with his eyes wide open, he tries to raise his head and speak. Betty Gail can feel his rapid pulse and suddenly she feels no pulse and hears a long shallow relaxing exhaling of his last breath. She releases the soldier's hand and quietly says a prayer for him. Then she gently pulls his sheet over his sleeping face. Bennett Jeffares is standing nearby and witnesses the soldier's demise.

"I'll take him to the cemetery when the town settles down, Mrs. Jernigan."

"Thank you, Bennett."

Betty Gail hears the front door open and is concerned that someone is trying to leave. She hurries to the front and finds James Goldsmith, the station agent holding a large wall clock under his arm. "Hello, Betty Gail. Sorry to disturb you, but the Yankees are nearby, and I only had time to get the wall clock out of the station and run over here."

"That's fine, James. You can help us comfort some of the

nervous patients."

"I'll be glad to help. General Kelly told me he has instructions for his cavalry to burn the provisions at the depot if they are unable to beat the Yankees back."

"Just put the depot clock under the sofa," said Betty Gail. "And go to one of the rooms and sit with some of the patients."

He places the large clock underneath the sofa in the front room and goes to one of the patient wards. Betty Gail smells smoke through an open window and hurries to see where it's coming from. Dr. Maddox opens the front door and Betty Gail and he see smoke surrounding the depot across from the hospital. "Not looking good, Dr. Maddox. Looks like General Kelly is burning more provisions at the depot." She shakes her head sadly, understanding the implications. "Not a good sign, I'm afraid."

"I suppose we best prepare for a Yankee visit," replies Dr. Maddox. "And hope that they're compassionate."

Colonel Dibrell's Confederate forces set fire to two hundred bales of cotton, thirty-five hundred bushels of corn and three freight cars of commissary goods before continuing the retreat.

The Yankees arrive close behind the retreating Confederates.

Now they have orders not to pursue the Rebels beyond the depot. The woods are too dense and it's getting late. Yankees begin to forage against the flames and set fire to the depot containing quartermaster commissary supplies.

Colonel Abe Miller, accompanied by his staff and guards, enters the hospital. He glances at the assembled hospital workers. "Who is the Doctor in charge here?" shouts Colonel Miller.

"I am," replies Dr. Maddox, as he approaches Colonel Miller.

Betty Gail inhales deeply and steps forward. She looks directly into the eyes of Colonel Miller. "We have critically wounded and sick soldiers here, from both the north and the south, sir. A kinder and mellower voice would be appreciated." The nurses and orderlies are quiet and continue the routine of caring for the patients.

Hesitating for a moment, the Colonel replies, "Show me the Union soldiers, Ma'am."

"This way, please," says Betty Gail as she motions with her head. "We treat whoever needs treating, without regard to their loyalties."

"May I return to my patients?" asks Dr. Maddox.

"You may. Go with him, lieutenant," retorts the Colonel as he follows Betty Gail upstairs.

As they enter room number two at the head of the stairs, Betty Gail informs the Colonel, "Here they are. Four of your Union men along with twenty-four Confederates. One private is recovering from a scalp wound. Another private has severe chest wounds with complications of high fever and delirium, the third an amputated foot."

They move among the patients as she points them out to Colonel Miller. He hesitates a moment at each bed and looks at the patients. At the bed of the amputee, he looks more closely at the bandages. Betty Gail waits until he catches up to her.

"And, the fourth is this Sergeant, who is recovering from malaria," says Betty Gail, pointing to the Sergeant.

"I see you're caring for these soldiers as if they are your own kin." Removing himself from the room, he asks, "What is your name, lady?"

"Mrs. Betty Gail Jernigan."

Colonel Miller moves toward his adjutant. "Bring all Confederate and Union wounded to this hospital immediately." The Adjutant salutes, removes himself to execute the Colonel's orders. "Mrs. Jernigan, generally we take over hospitals, especially those on the railroad or else we burn them to the ground. I am aware that DeKalb County voted against secession. This is but a small hospital and since you have obviously shown compassion for federal troops, I am placing an order on the door that this hospital is to be spared by all federal troops passing through."

"Thank you, Colonel, but there's an even smaller hospital two blocks from here and a Wayside 'round the

Mountain. Could you render the same courtesy to those as well? And allow us to keep one horse and one mule at each hospital?"

"I see no problem with your request, after I examine the other hospitals. Show my Sergeant where the hospitals are and, if it is as you say, I'll direct my clerk to draw up the two other orders," states Colonel Miller.

"Thank you, sir. Now, may I go to attend the wounded?"

"In a few minutes. Where is the calaboose?"

"There, by the depot and all of the doors are open. Nearby where your men are fighting the fire to get the commissary goods from the freight cars," replies Betty Gail.

"You may return to your patients now." Colonel Miller begins talking to Dr. Maddox while waiting for the Sergeant to return with his report.

"Sir, I checked the hospital across the way and I'm certain it would meet with your approval. The other one the lady mentioned is far around the mountain. I hesitate to go there with the thick woods, sir, unless you feel it is that important."

"Thank you, Sergeant. If the other hospital you inspected is as this one, I feel comfortable in signing an order for all three. Send my clerk in here, Sergeant."

"Yes, sir" Colonel Miller directs his clerk to draw up the orders to spare the hospitals and the Wayside and grant the right to keep one horse and one mule at each location. He signs the documents, gives them to Dr. Maddox and Betty Gail and then departs.

The Yankee ambulance Corps moves into town and begins to recover the mortal casualties. The Union's wounded refuse to enter Dr. George Washington Maddox hospital for initial treatment and are taken to the Union field hospital instead. The conscious Union soldiers thank Betty Gail and the other ladies for their kindness as they board their ambulance and head to the federal field hospital.

Colonel Miller reports to General Garrard. During the course of Colonel Dibrell's withdrawal, Colonel Miller's men recovered a battle flag belonging to Colonel Dibrell's unit. General Garrard is content to continue the railroad track destruction up to the depot and orders the complete destruction of the remaining supplies at and around the depot.

As the sun is beginning to set on this hot, humid and indelible day in Stone Mountain, an urgent report is given to General Garrard. The report contains intelligence information that General Wheeler is ordering reinforcements for the retreating Confederates. Due to the time of day, General Garrard orders his army to fall back to Browning's Courthouse.

The two academies, one common school, three churches, sawmill and cotton gin are intact as the Yankees depart, but eighty Confederate soldiers, mostly unknown, lay dead. The local preachers pray for their souls as Bennett and his helpers bury the dead.

At sunset, Buck peers up the narrow dirt road in search of Betty Gail. Concerned for her safety, he heads out to determine what has delayed his wife. Isaac watches as Buck departs and then continues to feed the chickens, ducks and hogs. His last chore before dark is to secure the horses in the barn.

Monday, July 19, 1864
"HEADQUARTERS CAVALRY DIVISION, General Garrard files his report to General McPherson.

"GENERAL: I have to report that, owing to the appearance of the enemy in this vicinity last evening, I sent a regiment to the Peachtree road, one to McAfee's Bridge, and ordered Colonel Long, with his two regiments, up; also, that trains, stragglers, etc., constantly passing along this road, I did not feel justified in moving forward until all was secure.

"This delayed me till 12 m., when I sent the Third Brigade, Colonel Miller commanding, toward Stone Mountain. They met strong opposition just outside of my pickets, and had heavy skirmishing

to within a mile of the depot. I then moved up Long, and we went into the town. We fought two brigades, but the country being so unfavorable for cavalry, I was unable to reap the fruits of the victory gained by my dismounted men. We captured no prisoners, but captured one set of colors, which they dropped in their hasty retreat. The depot, containing large amount of quartermaster and commissary stores, was burned, also about 200 bales of cotton, also the railroad as fast as we advanced. The delay caused by skirmishing prevented me advancing beyond the mountain, and I have just reached my camp of last night. These two brigades came in last night, and I have no doubt that it was in view of saving the Government property in the depot. The rebels set it on fire after we reached the edge of the town. We had to use artillery to drive them out of the houses.

"I could only spare five regiments for this duty, and if I am to guard such an extended flank it will be impossible for me to do anything else.

"I would suggest the destruction of McAfee's Bridge, and that my line be contracted. I then can be of assistance to you and guard the left.

"Very respectfully, your obedient servant,
"K. GARRARD
Brigadier-General, Commanding Division"

Following the railroad eastward, the 98th Illinois Mounted Infantry arrives shortly at their objective, the 555-foot trestle spanning Yellow River. Several old men and boys guard the wooden span as well as a wagon bridge several yards downstream. Their weapons consist of ancient muzzle-loaders and shotguns. One of the young boys, acting as a picket, sprints toward the bridge and shouts, "There's a bunch of Yankees heading this way."

"Take cover boys and get ready."

Everyone deploys to an advantageous location

against the approaching Yankees. The picket arrives quickly and finds a spot among his friends. When the Yankees appear, a man anxiously fires the first shot at a distant Yankee and misses. The surprised 98th returns the volley with their Spencer rifles. The man is shot and killed. Realizing they are about to suffer the same fate, the others run for their lives and disappear in the woods.

The Yankees approach the east bank of the bridge. One of the soldiers confirms that the old man is dead, "Shot right through the chest." The commander of the 98th has a detachment set fire to the Wagon Bridge and trestle. A short distance downstream, there's a large flour mill containing 8000 bushels of corn, a large quantity of flour and the house of the miller. Unmercifully, the Yankee torches the bridge.

Chapter Thirty-two
Local and National News

During the afternoon of July 25, 1864, William Sheppard rides around the mountain, seeking his pal, Buck. Appearing very distraught, he dismounts and hurries over to the porch where Buck is securing food to be hidden from the bummers of Sherman's Army. "What's wrong, William?" Buck asks anxiously. "Is your family okay?"

Yes, they're fine and all went to Athens two weeks ago. Have you heard about our friends Presley Jones and George Daniel? Both have been shot and killed!"

Buck is stoic. "Have a seat, William. Have some sassafras tea with me." Buck pours a cup of tea, hands it to William as he settles into a chair next to Buck. He leans back and takes a sip. Buck continues, "I heard of the awful clubbing and shooting of Presley after the Yankees captured him for shooting two of their comrades."

Williams leans forward, "Yes, but even more awful is after all that the Yankees shot him in the head in front of his daughters and began to make fun of his daughter's tears!"

Buck shakes his head in an attempt not to visualize such a scene. "Did the Yankees do any further harm to his daughters?"

"Just walked away laughing at his distraught daughters while pointing at Presley."

Buck grunts in disgust and exhales deeply. "Bless him, too old to be a soldier but not too old to fight. What about our friend George? How was he involved in this matter?"

"George chanced to be home on furlough for

several days from his Confederate quartermaster unit. He happened to take his gun with him to meet his daughter at the depot, who was returning from a visit in Conyers. When the Yankees saw him armed, they were still upset from their comrades' deaths so they arrest him."

Buck drops his hand and pats Charlie on his head. "What happened next?"

"You won't believe it, but the Yankees had what is known as a drumhead court martial. They charged him as a 'suspect of resistance' and in a matter of minutes sentenced him to be shot."

Buck stands up quickly, looks straight at William and shouts, "Shot!" William drops his head, "Yep, and took poor George to the grove north of Colonel W. W. Clark's home and shot him." Unable to believe what he has just heard, Buck paces for a moment. Turning to Williams, he raises his fist. Another victim to the inhumane influence of Northern civilization. The Yankee officers have no control over their men.

"Many more are gonna die cause this war was lost before it started!" Changing the subject to clear his mind, Buck asks, "How were you able to keep your buggy and horse?"

"I had them hid deep in the woods. Around midnight, I was able to sneak out on the trail by the creek. There were no Yankees camping there."

"You see, the Bluebellies came through here, tearing up the railroad and burning the depot and got everybody scared in town. Did you stop by our friend Thomas Maguire's place and see how he is doing?"

"Sure did. He said the Yankees hit his place around midnight on the 21st. They came in force and held his family at gunpoint. Soon his house was filled with the thieving Yankees. They robbed them of everything they could carry off. He and Mrs. Maguire said they busted open the trunks and threw all of the dresser drawers on the floor. Finally, the Yankees left around 8:00 in the morning on their way to Covington and Social Circle with some of his runaway slaves. From what he could find out, the Yankees circled back to Lawrenceville and Monroe. Some others went by Durand's

Mill and set Rockbridge on fire. He's pretty shaken up."

"Stay for dinner, William. We'll eat early and then you can get on the road."

"Thanks, but I need to git." William is somewhat rested but still visibly upset. "I got a few more stops before I get home."

"Just be careful. There's still some Yankees in the area. Last I heard, the folks in Gwinnett caught some lone bummers and strung 'um up."

"Serves 'um right," replies William as he waves good-bye to his friend Buck.

Buck and a few friends meet at the depot to study the war roster of the citizens of Stone Mountain. "James, I dread coming here more and more every day."

"It's not pleasant at all, Buck," responds James Goldsmith. "All of us are really suffering emotionally. I got this old newspaper from the North from a soldier who passed through last night. Listen to this news, fellows. Those Copperheads may save us yet!" Buck, along with William Jones, William Camp, Benjamin Woodsen, and John Fowler sit on the steps of the loading platform and begin to listen.

"This old Northern newspaper states the Copperheads of the Democratic Party held their convention in Chicago, August 29-30. Former Congressman Clement Vallandigham, a vehement opponent of President Lincoln, operated behind the scenes and influenced the adoption of the Copperhead platform. The Convention was full of criticism of President Lincoln, especially for issuing the Emancipation Proclamation, the military draft, the use of black troops and his violation of civil liberties."

Buck and his friends chuckle as Buck says, "Keep on reading, James!" "Roddy goes on to say 'he blames the abolitionists for prolonging the war and denounces the government as increasingly despotic.'" Continuing, James reads, "Listen to what this Ohio editor has to say. 'He can see no reason why anyone should be shot for the benefit of niggers and Abolitionists!' Marcus Pomeroy of the Wisconsin newspaper calls Lincoln 'fungus from the corrupt womb of bigotry and fanaticism, and a worse tyrant and more inhuman butcher than has existed since the day of Nero the ruler.'"

"Here's a new word for us—'miscegenation.'"

"What the devil does that mean?" asks Buck.

"Here the article says 'miscegenation' means a marriage between two different races and this is what President Lincoln and the Republicans want."

"Don't believe a word of it myself !" retorts John Fowler.

"So, what is the Copperhead platform?" asks Benjamin Woodsen.

Reading silently for a moment, James Goldsmith finally says, "Their proposals for a cease-fire and negotiated settlement with the Confederacy were ratified by the delegates and incorporated into the official party platform."

Buck shakes his head and tightens his jaws. "Sounds like there could be two separate countries yet!"

"Well, who did the Copperheads nominate to save the South?" asks William Camp.

"The delegates elected General George B. McClellan, a War Democrat, and gave him an anti-war platform. When General McClellan accepted the nomination, he rejected the peace plank, guaranteeing in its place to bring the war to a conclusion with more skill and energy than President Lincoln."

"Who's the Vice President for the Copperhead Democrats?" asks Buck.

"It says here a Peace Democrat, Ohio Congressman George Pendleton, was elected as the Vice President Nominee."

Buck stands up and stretches. "Never work! One for war and one for peace. They are already fighting each other! We're no better off ! Time for me to get."

Later that afternoon, Buck returns to the depot to catch the latest news as the telegraph begins to click. James sits down by the keypad and happily says, "Looks like we are hooked up again, at least for a while." James begins writing with Buck watching. "Mayor Calhoun surrendered Atlanta today. Stop."

Buck and James look at each other in wonderment. "I don't find that to be a big surprise. Do you, James?"

"Surely don't. What's next for us? We got nobody in town."

Buck responds while shaking his head, "We're at the mercy of the thieving Yankees. I best git on home. The Yankees 'bout cleaned us out, and I'm sure they'll be back for more."

Buck and Isaac are checking the fences when they spot about a dozen Yankees rapidly approaching. Stopping the inspection, they watch the Yankees as they pull up next to the split rail fence.

"Hey, Mister," shouts the lieutenant who is leading the scouting party for General Garrard, "What, the best way to get up this mountain?"

Buck spits his tobacco over the rail and looks at the lieutenant. "Walking."

"We need to take our horses up."

Buck looks sternly at the lieutenant, "They can walk with you. The mountain is solid rock. Lots of good places for a horse to break a leg."

Getting somewhat irritated, the lieutenant remarks, "You best tell me which way is the easiest route if you want to keep your fences."

Buck points. "Yonder way is the most gentle slope."

"Hey, darkie, you know you are free. Do you want to go with us?"

"No, sah."

The lieutenant jerks his horse's reins and directs the members of the scouting party to follow him.

Buck takes his handkerchief and wipes his forehead and looks at Isaac, "I bet you those Yankees are looking to establish a signal post on top."

Chapter Thirty-three
Colleagues for the Union

The butler delivers the daily mail to Congressman Hill. Joshua looks through the mail and hurries to find Emily. Holding the letter in his hand, "I have a reply from our friend, James Crews."

She eagerly rushes to Joshua's side and looks at the envelope. "Open it and find out if he has any news about our son." Joshua takes his fingers and separates the seal then he begins to read. "Dear Joshua and Emily, I have been fortunate to locate the body of your late son. . ."

Emily begins to cry and holds Joshua closely and whispers, "We can bring him home now."

"Yes, we can, I must telegraph our dear friend, Congressman Nathaniel Foster. He can help me get through the Union lines." Joshua summons his driver and carriage and goes to the depot. At the depot he instructs the railroad agent. "Send the following message to Congressman Nathaniel Foster."

"Yes, sir, Mr. Hill." The agent takes a seat at the telegraph desk and Joshua begins to dictate the message. "Nathaniel, I received word from James Crews that he has located my dear son's remains. I would appreciate you going to assist me in arranging a meeting with General Sherman."

Together Joshua and Nathaniel Foster approach the picket line of General Sherman at Decatur. They identify themselves to the picket. Joshua glances around briefly. "We are former members of Congress and particular friends of General Sherman's brother, John Sherman. We are requesting to speak with General Sherman if he is available."

The guard has the two former Congressmen escorted to the Duty Office. Upon arriving, the picket introduces Congressman Hill and Congressman Foster to the Duty Officer.

He shakes their hands. "Have a seat, Gentlemen, and I will have General Sherman informed of your wishes."

Joshua quietly confides in Nathaniel, "I hope General Sherman will extend us a visit."

"I feel that he will, especially since we are Union supporters. Besides, he's probably very curious to know why we are requesting to meet with him."

The Duty Office returns. "General Sherman has approved your request. Please follow me."

Joshua and Nathaniel breathe a sigh of relief, smile at each other, and the Guards escort the pair to General Sherman's headquarters.

As Joshua and Nathaniel enter, General Sherman comes forward, extending his hand in greeting. "Welcome to my headquarters, Mr. Hill, Mr. Foster. I have heard my brother speak fondly of both of you and I know both of you were against secession. I suspect you have something of importance to discuss with me is why you requested this visit."

Joshua shakes Sherman's hand. "Thank you for honoring our request, General."

"Please have a seat around the conference table, gentlemen. Captain Dayton, my Aide-de-Camp, will join us." General Sherman opens a box of cigars, "Would either of you care for a fresh cigar?"

"Thank you, General, if I may," replies Nathaniel as he removes an aromatic cigar from the box and passes it beneath his nose.

Joshua hands the box to Captain Dayton, who returns it to General Sherman. "No thank you, General. I'm not a smoker."

General Sherman removes a cigar for himself and

he and Nathaniel light up. General Sherman places his cigar in the ash tray and leans back in his chair. "To what do I owe the honor of your visit today, gentlemen?"

Joshua clears his throat. "My main purpose for our visit today is to seek your permission to recover the body of my son, Legare."

General Sherman blinks surprisingly and, again extending his hand, nods slightly. "You have my deepest respects, Mr. Hill. Where was your son killed?"

"Legare was killed as General Hardee's army fell back somewhere near Cassville. My friend, James Crews, with the railroad, located his burial site. I am simply asking your permission to go through your lines."

"Again, Mr. Hill, you and Mrs. Hill have my regrets for the loss of your son. I will gladly grant you permission to go by rail to the rear. Captain Dayton, have the clerk write a directive to the commanding officer, General John E. Smith, at Cartersville. Instruct him that he is required to furnish Congressman Hill and Congressman Foster an escort and an ambulance for the purpose of recovering his dear son's remains."

Joshua stands. "Thank you, General. Thank you not only for me, but for my wife, daughter-in-law and from all our family members."

"You are quite welcome, sir."

Captain Dayton proceeds to the clerk with his instructions. "Gentlemen, please accept my invitation for dinner at the officers' mess."

"Thank you kindly, General. We will be glad to accept," replies Joshua. He can't help but notice General Sherman's careless dress, which affirms the rumors he has heard. Sherman is physically spare and of good height. His hair is not unpleasantly red, his forehead is very fine, and his eyes clear and restless. Sherman impresses Joshua as a man with an active temper with a somewhat dyspeptic facial expression and views him as an ordinarily kind-hearted individual. However, he has heard that when the General becomes aroused, he is severe and utterly unrelenting. His manner is very frank and outspoken. Joshua has been told

General Sherman possesses extraordinary mental power and is blessed with an abundance of nervous energy.

During dinner, General Sherman tries to make conversation easy for his guests. "Atlanta was the industrial center for the Confederacy. The factories produced large quantities of mortar shells, pistols, saddles, brass buttons, clothing, and torpedo fuses. Thousands of tons of steel have been forged as armor plate for ironclad ships in Atlanta. You have seen a part of the country over which the Union army has passed. I can easily apply the same measure of desolation to the remainder of the State if necessity should compel us to go ahead to Augusta."

Nathaniel asks, "General Sherman, what is it you would request us to do? Vice-President Stephens is our best hope for peace."

"Governor Brown should fully realize the dangers and that further resistance on the part of the South is madness."

"We agree with you whole-heartedly on this subject, General," replies Joshua.

"I hope your governor will so proclaim that fruitless efforts on his part will lead to the destruction of the entire state. The governor can withdraw his people from the rebellion in pursuance of what was known as the policy of 'separate State action."

Joshua replies, "I only see Governor Brown burying his head in the sand."

"If you see Governor Brown, please describe to him fully what you have seen. Please attempt to enlighten the Governor that if he remains inert, that I will be compelled to go ahead and devastate the State in its whole length and breadth."

"We will be glad to be your emissaries to the Governor, General.

"Also relate to the Governor, there's no adequate force to stop us. Ask him to issue a proclamation withdrawing his State troops from the armies of the Confederacy. If he does this I will spare the State, and in the passage across Georgia, the Union troops would be confined to the main roads."

"We will talk with the Governor and give him your

message," replies Joshua.

"Also assure the Governor, the Union army would moreover pay for all the corn and food it needed. Then invite Governor Brown, in my name, to visit Atlanta. I will give him safeguard if the Governor wants to make a speech; I will guarantee him as full and respectable an audience as any he has ever spoken to."

Joshua looks into Sherman's eyes and with a stern, yet disheartened look. "Your offer to discuss the fate of our State is very amiable, but frankly I don't believe the governor will accept your invitation or offer. However, you can count on us to do our very best for the sake of the people of our State and for the Union."

"I have also sent similar messages by Judge Wright of Rome and by Mr. King, of Marietta to Governor Brown, hoping for a response through them."

At the conclusion of the dinner Joshua rises to take his leave. "Thank you again, General, for your consideration of my request. My family will always remember your gracious act of compassion. Nathaniel and I will do our utmost to convince Governor Brown to consider your offer to visit with you."

As they depart the general's headquarters, Joshua remembers his conversation with Buck. "Nathaniel, I must telegraph Buck as soon as we arrive home. He offered to accompany me to recover Legare's remains."

At Legare's graveside at the Madison, Georgia cemetery on September 23, the preacher concludes, "For Thine is the Kingdom, the Power and the Glory, forever and ever, Amen."

Buck, Betty Gail, Uncle Isaac and Aunt Sally stand along with Mia, little Joshua, Congressman Hill, Emily and their children. Uncle Richard, Aunt Josephine, Tot, Al, and Jesse stand on the opposite side of Legare's casket as it is slowly lowered into the ground.

Motionless, Mia clutches the gold necklace Legare gave her at Christmas. On the necklace is a button from his overcoat and a locket containing a strand of his hair.

Joshua turns to his daughter-in-law. "My dear Mia Emily and I love you as a daughter and will always think of you as such. We have a sealed letter for you from Legare, given to us by Rooster. I thought maybe you would want to read it at his graveside alone." Lips quivering, Joshua reaches into his pocket, removes the sealed letter and presses his hands to Mia's with the letter.

She acknowledges Joshua's gesture with tight lips, a simple smile. Tears stream down her soft cheeks. Little Joshua is standing by his mother's side and holding tightly to her black dress.

Buck slides his arm around his daughter. "I love you, Mia. Will you be all right?"

Betty Gail wipes the tears from her own eyes and then Mia's. "I love you, Mia. God rest his soul." She kisses Mia and little Joshua.

Mia resolutely nods.

Emily moves closer to Mia and little Joshua. In tears, she kisses Mia then kneels to the ground to bid her son farewell. Mia holds her hand and they give each other comfort in their grief.

Joshua helps Emily stand. "We will go to our carriages and wait for you, Mia. Please be in no hurry to depart."

Mia, all alone except for little Joshua, sits on the soft grass next to Legare's open grave. The gentle breeze and beautiful fall foliage divulge nature's own story of the cycle of life. Mia tenderly pulls little Joshua into her lap and draws him near. Almost as if afraid, she opens the last letter she'll ever receive from her husband.

"My Dear Mia,

"I sleep with you and our child at my side every night and we walk together every day. I feel your breath and smell your sweetness even when you are not with me as I sleep. You are a true jewel of our Southland, a Cherokee rose in full bloom. You have the inherent beauty of mind, of soul, and

of character. These three qualities lift you as an icon to a higher power and give you exquisite charm.

"You possess the Spartan traits of the South . . endurance, fortitude, courage, and superiority of mind. These compel respect, even from Aunt Josephine, and these traits will inspire leadership in our child.

"My dear precious one, you furnish the golden urn in which my heart is enshrined. You hover over me as I sleep in this bivouac as if you are making the sentinel rounds of my tent. You have made medicine for and have bent over the wounded and dying in the hospital. I only hope God continues to make me worthy of your gentle love and sweet loyalty.

"My reverence will forever linger at your altar. Kiss our son each day that I am away.

"With an abundance of love I can only describe as infinity plus one,

Legare

The following day, Buck and Betty Gail accompanied Mia and little Joshua to the Stone Mountain depot. Bidding each other a sad goodbye Mia and little Joshua board the train. As the train departs little Joshua is waving and smiling to his grandparents who are saddened to see his and his mother depart. As the train pulls out of sight, Buck turns to Betty Gail and confides in her, "I wish Mia had stayed with us in Stone Mountain for a while longer. I truly worry about that girl and grandson of ours."

"She's independent just like you, Buck. She's got her mind set on working at the hospital. She feels she owes it to Legare. Besides, it keeps her busy and helps clear up her mind from this awful tragedy."

"Here we are at the Madison Station. I see Joshua got my telegram. His driver is waiting for us." After supper, Joshua and Buck retire to the parlor. Joshua informs Buck, "I have just written a letter to my friend, James Crews, in West Point. I would like you to read it and give me your opinion."

"Sure."

"I saw a great deal of Atlanta — houses and people. There has been no wanton destruction of property to any extent beyond fencing and outbuildings, which in some parts of the city has suffered. If I could see you I could tell you much more than I can undertake to write. I can say of a truth that General Sherman was right in his arbitrary order to evacuate Atlanta. Those who remain are generally in a pitiable condition with small available means and, with no market, they are faring badly . . I was treated with marked kindness wherever I went. I spent a week nearly about Cartersville and Kingston and several days at Rome. From Kingston to Atlanta, the country as far as the eye can reach is one prolonged scene of desolation. The silence that reigns is only broken by the sound of movement . . men, teams of wagons, squadrons of cavalry and occasionally a railway train. I wish it could be seen by every war man in Georgia. But I doubt if it would do any good, so visionary and fanatical have our leaders grown."

"I think you define the situation very accurately," says Buck. "Is this also a draft for the Governor?"

"I'm not sure what I can do about the Governor, especially since I ran against him. But for Georgia and our good family and citizens I will do my best. I have a meeting scheduled with General Sherman on the 28th."

Joshua Hill and Nathaniel Foster, along with Judge Wright, arrive at the appointed time at General Sherman's headquarters.

"Gentlemen, I want you to understand that President Lincoln appreciates any effort you can afford to bring this conflict to a close. You have his full support and I will provide any assistance you request to this end." During the course of the meeting military statistics, army strengths, munitions, and the general morale of both sides are compared. At the close of the meeting, General Sherman says, "Gentlemen, please do your very best to persuade Governor Brown to abandon his crazy vision and save the lives of an untold number of young and energetic men. Thank you for your support of the

Constitution and the Union. Go in peace."

On the same day, General Sherman receives a telegram from General Halleck regarding the evacuation of Atlanta.

Chapter Thirty-four
The Yanks Arrive

The inclement weather of October has given Colonel Robinson an extra degree of surprise. Buck is unaware of the Yankees' presence. He and Isaac are up early making the rounds to the fields, checking the Irish and sweet potatoes on his farm and at Buster Phillips' place. Charlie barks loudly as a large force of Yankees on wagons appears suddenly on his property.

Buck and Isaac rush to the house and prepare to meet the riders. Betty Gail is standing on the porch wiping her hands on her apron. The Yankee units consist of ten wagons and at least one hundred soldiers. He begins to wonder if these are the dreadful bummer troops coming to steal their belongings.

Buck has his Union flag flying. Soon, the wagons appear at his front and he realizes his fears are turning into reality. Betty Gail steps from the porch and clutches Buck's arm. Now standing face to face, the bummer rides up asks, "Do you own this place?"

"It's mine all right," replies Buck.

"I see you're flying the Union Flag at your place. That means a lot to us. But nevertheless, we need food for our troops. We are part of Colonel Robinson's unit and have orders to take whatever food we need. Just don't interfere and you'll be okay. Sergeant, take two wagons and begin loading what you can find from those two barns. Corporal, take another wagon and dig and load the potatoes from that field." The wagon drivers snap their reins and hastily move to the barns and the fields. "Lieutenant, post guards along the trails to this place. We have already had enough encounters with the Confederates."

Peering into the bummer's wagons, Buck sees a rocking chair, a baby carriage, and several large trunks stacked together with stolen rations from other farms. The bummer then orders two Yankees inside to take whatever they can find. He orders the other to gather the chickens, turkeys, ducks, and hogs. Buck turns and starts into the house behind the invading Yankees.

"You just stay where you are, mister, and everything will be okay. Lady, you take a seat in that rocking chair on the porch."

"I'd just as soon stand here with my husband, if you don't mind, lieutenant!"

"I'm going to ask you one more time nicely, to kindly take a seat in that rocking chair on the porch."

Buck pushes her along toward the porch. "Best do as he says, Betty Gail." With a determined frown, Buck continues, "As for your supplies, since I don't have a choice, I suggest you help yourself. Your friends at the signal station on top of the mountain come by here regularly and help themselves just like you."

Soon, the bummer comes out the house wearing Buck's old tri-cornered hat and carrying Buck's Masonic plaque. "Not much in this place, already been cleaned out. Just a few eggs and some greens as far as food and this here squirrel rifle. Don't have any use for it." He throws Norman's rifle to the ground.

"You best leave the Masonic plaque," retorts the commander. "Several of the generals are Masons and they will take serious offense if you have it in your possession." The Bluebelly throws the Masonic plaque onto the porch.

"Check the cookhouse and smokehouse and bring back all the meat you find. Hey, darkie, where's all the food?"

Isaac replies, "Dun all gone! Yankees on da mountain gots it de other day." Soon the Yankees bring out the horses from Buck's and Buster's barns.

The other cavalrymen are rounding up the cattle from the pastures and driving them to the road. The lieutenant shouts to one of his men, "Get that mule lying on the ground over there."

Isaac steps forward, "Jus' gots one ole mule, it gots bads tail en jonts. Layin' yonder 'n da pastur 'bout to die."

The lieutenant looks at Jack and sees his gray whiskers. "We'll leave the half dead mule, one cow and one hog since you're a Mason and flying the Union Flag. I see you have chickens."

Buck looks at the lieutenant. "I appreciate you leaving the ole mule sir. He's just a pet." The officer pays little attention to his thanks and hastens his men to claim the chickens and kill and dress the hogs. Shots ring out, and the hogs fall one by one to the ground.

"Hang those hogs by their hind feet. Then slice their throats and let the blood run or the meat will sour. If it's a boar, cut his testicles out to save the meat from spoiling." The Yankee shooter takes his knife and runs in under the dead hogs' chins. He backs away and watches the blood ooze slowly from the still animal. "Round up the rest of those cows. We'll bring them with us. Burn his cotton gin and sorghum press!" He turns his attention to Isaac. "You know, darkie, you're a free man now. You can leave this place."

"I'se knows!"

"Who lives there?" He points to Buster Philips' place.

"Mars Buster, he's gone!"

Where is he now?"

"Off a-fighting, but my people's livin' dat house."

"Have all of the darkies move back into their places. Sergeant, take a couple of men and get that house cleaned out and set it to blaze." The Yankees go into Buster's house and carry off all the household supplies. Soon, smoke and flames begin churning from the windows.

In the meantime, the lieutenant orders some of Buster Phillips' Negroes to begin cleaning and dressing out the hogs. The bummers chase the cackling chickens down one by one. They tie the chicken's legs together and toss them in the wagons. The cattle are herded together.

Two hours pass and the bummer orders all of the Negroes to gather 'round his horse. "If you tell me where the rest of the food is hidden I'll give you a nice reward and allow you to come along with us. If you know and don't tell me, I'll burn your house down! So, where is the food buried or hidden on that mountain?"

Standing quietly, some simply shake their head. "Ain't no more food. Blues gots it all."

Suddenly, one of the bummers turns the corner of Buck's house shouting, "I've found the cellar, but nothing there—no apples, peaches or pears!" "Mister, you're lucky you're flying the Union flag or I would burn your house to the ground just like your neighbor's!" shouts the lieutenant.

Buck doesn't respond. "Who lives down that road?"

"Just the Wayside. When Colonel Abe Miller was here in July, he left orders not to disturb the Wayside. Otherwise, nobody else now. All the men are in the war!"

"Why aren't you fighting?"

"Too old and got a bad hand." Raising his hand, he continues, "Lost these fingers in the war with Mexico."

The Yankee commander of the bummer ignores Buck and orders the darkies to place the dressed hogs in the already overloaded wagons. Then the Yankee orders, "Burn all of the buildings on that Confederate's farm, except where the Darkies are living. Leave them some food, but get all the potatoes." Offering a few indignities to the slaves, the foraging party begins driving the livestock away from Buck's farm.

Loaded down with the day's bounty of poultry, meal, meats, sweet potatoes, honey, and sorghum and without having room for any more provisions, the Bummers organize the wagon train and watch the flames for a while, then head back toward Colonel Robinson's main unit.

Betty Gail leaps from the porch as Buck, with a steaming temperament, turns and picks up Norman's squirrel rifle. Betty Gail picks up the Masonic plaque and simply hangs it on a nail on the porch wall. "Those bummers are nothing but a band of marauders,"

Buck mumbles to himself. "There's no need to fight the fires at Buster's place, Isaac. The buildings are already too far gone. Just let them burn out. Those Yankees are mad because this particular farm is not the land of milk and honey they are accustomed to!"

Buck and Isaac enter the house and find the place has been ransacked. Broken furniture, cut-up bedding, turned over tables and upset vanities litter the floors. "Isaac, it appears bummers feel free to take what they can carry away and what they cannot carry they spoil and destroy. Just mind your tongue and we will survive this ordeal, the Lord willing and the Creeks don't rise. The pecans will be coming in soon. It'll be a good source of food for all of us. We've got rabbit boxes, deer and squirrels, too."

Looking over at Buster Phillips's place, Buck notices that the wood shed, gin house and silo are burning. Buster's barn doors are smoking but the fire did not take to the structure for some reason. Some of Buster's slaves are already throwing water on the doors as he and Isaac rush over to assist them. Reaching for the sledge hammer, Buck knocks the hinges loose and the two sizzling barn doors fall to the ground. The slaves lash the doors and drag them into the dirt away from the barn. Buck thanks the darkies for being alert. "Lucky day, these doors are fresh green wood. Probably why they didn't catch."

Betty Gail is still standing on the porch when Buck returns. Looking at the ruins of Buster's place, she tears up and leans against him. "There's not much left for Buster now. His heart, soul and property . . mostly gone." Taking her apron, she wipes her tears away and sits in the rocking chair and begins weeping out loud as Buck comforts her.

Chapter Thirty-five
Preparation

On Tuesday, November 9, from Kingston, Georgia, General Sherman meets with his commanders. "The election is over, whether for good or evil to the South. Lincoln has won."

Some of the state counts are delayed due to severe storms, but the results become clear that President Lincoln is re-elected with 55% of the vote. Electoral vote for President Lincoln 212, for General McClellan 21." All of the commanders and personnel present stand and give cheer and applause. It appears the National Union Party also gains seats in Congress to retain unassailable control, 149 to 42 in the House. The National Union Party now controls the Senate, 42 to 10. The Party also takes back several state legislatures and lost only the governorship of General McClellan's home state of New Jersey."

Again, the commanders and other personnel stand and applaud. "After this meeting is complete I have some very fine wine for us to offer a toast to the President, but first let us finish the campaign.

Later in the afternoon General Sherman issues Field Order No. 120 which details the Left and Right wings, responsibilities on his Savannah Campaign.

Buck, Jesse, Betty Gail and William Sheppard visit with James Goldsmith at the Depot to get the latest news. James asks, "Have you heard the latest? Looks like Lincoln and Johnson are in."

"Not much we can do about it one way or the other.

We got no say-so in the matter," replies William.

"You're right, no say-so at all. The South is on the edge of a steep cliff. I just hope we can back off before we fall or get pushed over," interjects Jesse. "There were some more people coming through Saturday night from Atlanta. They said the last train for the north leaves the morning of the 13th, which is tomorrow. They hear rumors that Union soldiers are scattered along the railroad a hundred miles north, and as soon as that train passes, the work of destruction will commence. The railroad will be completely destroyed and every bridge burned."

"The refugees think General Sherman is getting ready for some kind of a march because the Union armies are assembling in Atlanta. They hear rumors that, after destroying the city, the Union army will commence to march." Buck angrily says, "They are gonna steal and destroy everything in their path. I fear their track will be one of desolation no matter where they go."

James continues, "One fellow said he had been to the railroad depot for the past three days several times and had a conversation with General Slocum. The General told him that he had witnessed many sad and some ludicrous scenes."

"Such as?" asks William.

"General Slocum went on to say that all citizens, white and Negroes, are beginning to apprehend that something is about to happen. The few white people remaining after their families were sent away are alarmed. This is the reason he and many are leaving the city, giving up horses, lands, furniture, Negroes and all. He said the Negroes want to go north and the Train Car House is surrounded by them."

"Let'um go and live with the abolitionists," retorts Jesse.

"He nods his head in agreement with General Slocum as General Slocum told him that hundreds of cars are literally packed with Negroes and their dirty bundles, inside and outside. He said the sight is pitiful, old toothless hags, little pickaninnies, fat wenches of all shades from light brown to jet black, are piled up together with their old bags, bundles, broken chairs and whatever else they could carry. Some of 'um gnawing old bones, some of 'um squatted by cars making hoecakes, some of 'um crying for food which the Union cannot supply."

William says, "Why, I read that Sherman said he would feed those who wanted to go north. Just another Yankee lie."

"What else did the man say, James?" asks Buck.

"General Slocum points at the rail cars and tells the old fellow, "Many of the white people are as anxious to get north as the darks. They even gladly accept a place in a rail car reeking with the odor peculiar to the 'American of African descent.' It is a sad sight and I anticipate seeing many such before spring."

Buck asks, "So what was the final outcome of his conversation with General Slocum?"

The General pats the old fellow on the shoulder and tells him, "I wish for humanity's sake that this sad war could be brought to a close. I must go and write my wife about what I have seen. While laboring to make it successful I shall do all in my power to mitigate its horrors."

Buck shakes his head. "He's not the only one. Let's git, Betty Gail. I'll drop you off at the hospital and then check the mail to see if there's a letter from Mia or Norman."

Monday, November 14, General Sherman's 56,204 marching troops, 5,063 cavalry and 1812 men with 65 artillery pieces, 2,500 wagons, and 600 ambulances arrive at or near Atlanta. Each infantryman carries 40 rounds of ammunition. The wagon train holds another 200 rounds per man.

From his headquarters at the Neal House, General Sherman orders, "Remove all of the sick, lame, non-combatants and those that may falter from your commands. This action is imperative in order for this army to maintain momentum and mobility. The composition of the army must be men whose bodies will endure hardship and disease without consequences."

Chief Commissary Officer Colonel Beckwith submits his final report to General Sherman. "Sir, there's a 20-day supply of rations, which is approximately 1.2 million rations in the possession of the troop. We have a good supply of beef cattle on the hoof which will accompany the two wings. Additional rations are plentiful along the route of the march for both wings."

Under a full moon on that November 14th night, Colonel Poe pays a visit to General Sherman at the Neal House. "Have a seat and a cup of coffee, Colonel."

"Thank you, sir. Just wanted to report that my staff of engineers has been busy all day preparing the material for the complete destruction of the list of properties which you have listed. You will be able to watch the fireworks from your headquarters later this evening, sir. Sit back and enjoy the show. I just wanted to double check the list to be certain you did not want to add any other building."

"I believe the list is complete, Colonel, so proceed with your orders."

"Yes, sir, on my way."

Colonel Poe's large force begins its destructive mission. First, there are scattered levels of a red glow as the great depot, the roundhouse, and the machine shops of the Georgia Railroad are reduced with explosives and then set ablaze. One of these machine shops is used by the rebels as an arsenal, and in it are piles of undetected shot and shell, some of which proved to be loaded. General Sherman is watching the growing flames of the night when a hideous bursting of shell fragments come uncomfortably near. General Sherman dashes inside, "That was a close one. I almost didn't get to leave Atlanta for Savannah."

He takes another cigar from his humidor and lights up. Returning outside, he and his staff take chairs and scan the skyline as the flames reach the block of stores near the depot, then more to the heart of the city, where two thirds of the trees, the theaters, jail, slave markets and fire stations begin to turn to ashes.

General Sherman is going over orders again with Major Audenried. General Sherman's eyes become strained. He lays his pencil down and looks out of the window, "Colonel Poe has orders to leave the courthouse and the great mass of dwelling houses. Maybe Governor Brown can see the flames in Milledgeville or at least smell the smoke tomorrow. His entire state is going to look like this if he doesn't come to his senses."

Chapter Thirty-six
Atlanta Torched

Betty Gail and Buck are home, sitting by a small fire after dinner, reading *The Bible* when Isaac rushes in, pointing to the sky exclaiming "It's on fire!"

"What's on fire?" Buck asks as they rush outside behind Uncle Isaac. Looking southwest from Stone Mountain, the Jernigans view the full moon against an eerie red sky. Becoming anxious, Buck remarks, "My gosh, I think Sherman is burning Atlanta!"

Betty Gail takes Buck's arm. "How could he do such a thing?"

"Don't rightly know, but let's climb the mountain to get a better view. Isaac, stay at the house and keep all the lanterns lit and wait for us to come back home." Just as Buck and Betty Gail begin their climb, they hear the sound of horses rapidly approaching. Buck places his lantern on the ground. He and Betty Gail back away so they can see who the riders are as they come closer. Buck recognizes the riders as they approach under the full moon. "It's Jesse Lanford and James Goldsmith."

"I guess you see the flames from Atlanta," asks James, dismounting. "Surely do! We're going to the top to get a better view. Want to come along?" asks Buck.

Jesse shakes his head. "Better not. I hear there are some bandits in the area."

"I'll climb with you. My wife is staying with my cousins," says James. "Here's a lantern for you." Buck passes the hissing lantern to James.

With his musket in hand, Buck leads the group up the moonlit gray sentinel.

Steadily they climb, making their way over the familiar bulging boulders. The night is cool from the mid-November breeze. Quietly, they pass the abandoned and disintegrating saloon the Dents built.

At the last steep barrier, negotiating the remains of the stone wall, Buck stops as Betty Gail takes a moment to catch her breath. As Buck looks toward Atlanta he turns, gasps and points. Without saying a word, he is stone-faced and silent for a moment. Then he shouts, "Look there! Atlanta is burning!" Betty Gail jumps to her feet.

She places one hand over her mouth and takes Buck's arm with her other hand. "Oh, my God."

Buck stands in awe, viewing a sight none has ever seen before and one he hopes never to witness again. The heavens seem to burst with huge, dark clouds of smoke. Roaring flames follow with finger-like projections pointing to the moon. Thundering sounds of the distant explosions boom in the air, followed by more dense, black smoke and fireballs. Blown by the wind, huge walls and massive balls of fire race from the south of Atlanta to the north.

Buck looks up at the moon as it pales from the smoke, and their path becomes darker. "Let's get on to the top for a better view." He takes Betty Gail's hand as they climb to the highest point of the mountain where they witness the flames becoming more aggressive and intense. Although they cannot feel the heat, Buck feels the flames charring deeper into his heart. He begins to sneeze as the night breeze brings the remaining ashes of Atlanta to his eyes and nostrils. Finally, before daybreak, Buck is sitting next to Betty Gail and they silently observe the raging inferno that sinks from the sky. The blazes are no longer aggressive and the angry, startling waves of flames no longer roll as high. The color grows paler and slowly fades with the sunrise.

Buck looks over his shoulder as the morning sun peers over the horizon and the sky regains its natural blue color. The stillness of the morning air is eerie. An umbrella of dense black smoke isolates the circle of annihilation and the whispering remains of smoldering ruins. The smell of smoke is strong on top of the mountain. Buck takes Betty Gail's hand, nods somberly to his friend, and the three of them proceed slowly down the mountain.

Standing on the porch of the Neal House on a chilly Tuesday morning of November 15th, General Sherman confides in Major Dayton, "Today we march and the march from Atlanta to the sea begins. Generals Oliver Howard's XV and XVII Corps, is the right wing. By now he should be departing down the McDonough Road to follow the Macon and Western Railroad southeast to Jonesboro."

On her way to the hospital, Betty Gail senses a loneliness in her little hamlet. It is now practically a ghost town. She is exhausted from her previous night on the mountain watching the destruction by fire of Atlanta.

She waves at a neighbor as she rides through town, where most of the buildings are still standing. She prays General Sherman does not burn the town as he did Atlanta, especially since it is maintained by the women and small children. Betty Gail stops at City Hall. Buck had asked her to deliver some chestnuts to Mayor Browning.

Around nine o'clock a.m., Clarissa McCurdy, wife of the late Robert McCurdy, and her daughter, Agnes, are heading out of town in their buggy when they witness the clouds of dust brought on by the approaching Yankees. They stand up in the carriage to confirm their sighting.

"Those are Yankees, Agnes! Sit down and hold tight. We've got to warn the folks in town." Clarissa hastily turns the horse and buggy and rushes back into town. All is quiet until they thunder in as the Paul Revere of the South. "The Bluebellies are coming!" She stops in front of City Hall and shouts, "Mayor Browning, Bluebellies are coming!" Mayor Browning and Betty Gail rush out of City Hall. "What did you say, Clarissa?" asks Betty Gail.

Clarissa points toward Fellowship Road, "Hundreds

and hundreds of them! Yankees heading our way. Coming from Fellowship Road. I got to go and warn my folks." She snaps the reins and speeds off toward south. Betty Gail and Mayor Browning look around and see the few men in town run out of their stores. Clarissa is very clear in her vivid detail of the Yankee column as she spreads the word of the approaching Yankees. Panic sets in as the store owners attempt to load wagons and flee with their belongings before the Yankees arrive.

Mayor Browning mounts his horse. Betty Gail shouts to Mayor Browning, "Wait, I'll ride with you. Less chance of your getting hurt with a woman along."

"You best stay at the hospital, Betty Gail. I am going to introduce myself as the Mayor of the town to the Yankees." He heads toward Fellowship Road to confirm the sighting of the approaching Yankees. Mrs. McCurdy's last stop is at the hospital and she hurries to inform one of the attendants of the approaching Yankees. Then she continues her escape to the south of town. The nervous attendant rushes inside and informs the staff what is happening.

In a short time, Betty Gail arrives, and, as she enters the front door the excited attendant runs to her, "Miss Betty Gail . . Miss Betty Gail . . 'em 'ankees a comin! 'em 'ankees a comin!"

"I already know that. We have a duty to care for our patients regardless of the chaos outside."

Confirming his worst nightmare, Mayor Browning stares at the approaching advance guard of Colonel James Selfridge and waits. Well in front is a small detachment of six mounted infantry. They hold their reins in one hand while resting their carbines across the pommel of the saddle. They usually move at a faster pace than the main army to investigate any suspicious activity or circumstances.

The detachment of the advance guard sees the lone rider and approach as they point their weapons toward the Mayor. "What is your mission, mister?" asks the squad leader with a snappy voice.

"I am Thompson A. Browning, the Mayor of Stone Mountain. I would like to speak to your commanding officer."

"Do you have any weapons?"

"Not on me or with me at the present time, sergeant."

"Anybody else with you or hiding to bushwhack us?"

"As far as I know, I am alone. One of our lady citizens was riding this way and saw your column. She returned to alert us that you were heading in our direction."

"If you're lying you'll be shot! Wait here. Corporal, stay with the rest of the squad and guard Mr. Mayor while I talk with Colonel Selfridge." The sergeant reins his horse, kicks up dust and heads back to meet the column of Yankees.

The sergeant salutes Colonel James Selfridge as he comes closer. "What did you find out, sergeant?" asks the Colonel.

"The man says he is the Mayor of Stone Mountain and his name is Browning. He would like to speak to you, sir. The squad has him under guard."

The colonel and sergeant return to the location of the advance guard, where Mayor Browning waits. "I am Colonel James Selfridge. I understand you're the Mayor of Stone Mountain. What can I do for you?"

"Yes, I am Mayor Thompson Browning. There are no Confederate forces in our town. We only have forty male citizens remaining. Ten are youth ages sixteen and seventeen years old and thirty are men in their forties and fifties. We have three hospitals in town and one Wayside 'round the mountain. We have nothing with which to defend ourselves against you and only ask that you pass through and leave us be."

"If your people do not brother us, Mayor, my soldiers will not bother them. You may go back to town and relay my message."

Mayor Browning aims his mount toward town and gallops away. As he comes close to the cemetery, the grave diggers are preparing to bury another unknown casualty of the war. Halting at the cemetery, Mayor Browning passes on to the diggers part of his conversation with Colonel Selfridge. "I have just spoken with the commander and he told me if we bring the Yankees no harm, they'll bring us no harm."

Appearing more at ease, one of them comments, "After what they did to Atlanta last night, Mayor, I don't trust them!"

"We really don't have a choice right now, just pray all goes well for the next couple of days. I need to get on into town."

Around ten o'clock, the Union advance guard draws near to the cemetery. The grave diggers appear uneasy as the advance guard approaches. "Hold up there, you digging that grave. We want to check that coffin!" shouts a lieutenant in the advance guard. The two white and two Negro diggers stop and lean on their shovels or spades. The lieutenant rides closer with his sergeant and several other troops.

"Sergeant, open the coffin and any others which are recently buried. "The Sergeant and two men dismount. They direct the diggers to get crow-bars from the wagon. Doing so, they hand the crow-bars to the sergeant and his men. They commence to pry open the coffin.

"Nothing in here, sir, except a dead rebel!"

The Yankee sergeant points his pistol at the grave diggers, "Uncover those four graves with the fresh dirt." Soon four more coffins are unearthed and the sergeant and his men take the crowbars. Exposing just the top of the next three coffins, the sergeant jumps in the hole alongside, prying the top off of each one of the coffins.

"More dead Rebels, sir!"

Then he observes the fourth coffin. As the sergeant and his men approach it, the diggers back away toward the wagon. Noting their behavior, the sergeant looks at the diggers and says, "So this is the one with the bounty, huh?" The lieutenant draws near on his horse and the sergeant and his men take the crowbars and hastily rip its top off. The lieutenant is thrown from his horse, the sergeant and his men turn and retch uncontrollably at the extremely nauseating odor and sight. Inside, there are at least a dozen decaying amputated limbs. Covering the blood-stained rotting flesh are maggots and oozing sour fluids. Pale and struggling to catch their breath, the soldiers leap from the hole and fetch canteens from their mounts.

Once the lieutenant regains his composure, he says, "Okay, diggers, rebury your dead. You darkies are freemen now and can go wherever you like. Sergeant, bring the wagon and let's get on up the hill to meet Colonel Selfridge at the depot."

Taking the mule straps, the sergeant mounts his horse, tugs at the mule and points the team up the hill. Once over the hill, he views the town. All the sergeant encounters is plenty of dust from the other members of the advance guard, but not any obvious panic or disruption by the civilians. The town appears ghostly. The other members of the advance guard are scouting the surrounding area and buildings to ascertain if any Confederate sharpshooters are in position or in hiding.

Unable to locate any Confederate troops' presence, the Yankees go to the roofless depot to remove what supplies would benefit their army or their personal needs. Colonel Selfridge arrives to investigate the hospitals and the jail for wounded or imprisoned Yankees. Mayor Thompson is at the hospital with Betty Gail, standing in front. Betty Gail is clutching the orders of Colonel Abe Miller. Colonel Selfridge approaches her with several of his troops. "Step aside, Ma'am, we are here to remove any Union wounded and to take the able Confederates as prisoners."

"Before you make any hasty decision, Colonel, I suggest you read this order from your Colonel Abe Miller." She deliberately unfolds and presents the document to Colonel Selfridge. The Colonel appears somewhat surprised by the document. As he finishes reading the orders he says, "Do you have any Union soldiers in either of the hospitals?"

"No, we do not. I don't know if you have been in a hospital before but I'll be glad to take you on a tour if your stomach can bear the sights and smells, Colonel!"

"Please do. What is your name, Ma'am?"

"Mrs. Betty Gail Jernigan"

"May I ask where your husband is?"

Betty Gail inhales deeply never taking her eyes off

the colonel. What should she say? She chooses honesty, feeling that, perhaps, this Yankee will not be like so many who have come before. Sternly staring at the colonel, she responds, "Working on the farm 'round the mountain. I'm sure your foragers will pay him a visit before the day ends!"

The colonel motions for two of his troops to follow him inside and the others are to stand guard outside. As they enter, a sense of nervousness appears on the faces of the soldiers. Although it is November, there has not been a real cold snap and flies are everywhere. Placing a handkerchief over his nose, the colonel passes several soldiers who are gasping, their eyes heavy-lidded. The lady members of the churches sing quiet songs, while others read from *The Bible* to comfort the patients in their remaining hours of life.

"Colonel, these soldiers are preparing to meet their maker. Some of them have names, but many do not. These poor souls will never hear again the cry of 'Charge' or the smell of the sulfurous air from the discharge of gun powder. Look at their pale lips as they struggle hopelessly against their mortal pain."

Without acknowledging her comments, the colonel begins climbing the stairs to the second floor. The moderate November weather makes the stench even stronger. In room number two, the colonel finds twenty-six wounded soldiers, each with crimson-stained bandages, crowding in the twelve-by-twelve room. He sees no flag, no bayonet, no plume, no lance and no gun. Just fading human shadows conveying more than tongues can speak. None of the soldiers is moaning—just quiet human forms with empty expressions on their war-torn faces.

"I've seen enough, Mrs. Jernigan. I certainly will respect Colonel Miller's order and leave the hospitals as is. Please direct me to the other hospitals so that I may inspect them."

"Over yonder." She points in the direction of the second hospital. "They'll direct you to the third hospital from there. We also have a Wayside 'round the mountain. They also are protected by this order."

Colonel Selfridge turns and departs and meets an

awaiting Sergeant who informs him, "Colonel, we just took this wagon from the grave diggers, what do you want us to do with it?"

"Return it to the grave diggers. There are orders not to disturb the hospital, the Wayside, its patients and its contents or supplies. Post a guard as well to ensure the orders are obeyed."

Appearing puzzled, the sergeant replies, "Yes, sir." He snakes the team about and heads back to the cemetery. Once there, the Yankee sergeant pulls up and shouts, "Here's your wagon and mule, boys! You're lucky to keep them. But keep digging 'cause there will be plenty more Rebels for you to bury! "He details a private to stand guard to inform the passing troops to leave the wagon and mule alone. He slaps his horse and gallops back towards town.

Shortly the Pioneer Battalion appears. They begin passing by the depot and hospital. Betty Gail observes some of the wagons are full of Negroes. Others are full of rope, chains, block and tackle, saws, shovels, picks and spades. Betty Gail turns to the Union guard, "What do the Negroes do for your army?"

"Their job is to keep the roads clear of fallen trees, remove traps set by the Rebels and fill gaping holes on the roads. In other words, to keep the army moving."

"They look like slaves."

"No, Ma'am, they are former slaves, freedmen we have hired."

"I see. And where is your army going?"

"No one really knows, but we all suspect we are on the march to Savannah, ma'am."

"Savannah!"

"Yes, Ma'am, Savannah!"

Betty Gail turns and walks away in shock. Her heart suddenly beats faster and she feels a lump in her throat as she becomes emotional. She takes her handkerchief from her cuff and wipes tears as she walks to the back of the hospital to regain her composure. She knows Mia is safe for now, but what about Norman. "Where is my boy? We haven't heard from him lately. I can only pray he is safe."

Around one o'clock the dust cloud begins to build. The thunder of hooves and foot soldiers shakes the ground as the Bluebellies pour through town. Suddenly a Yankee commander shouts, "Halt," and the troops slowly come to a stop. "Take a dinner break."

The men begin moving to the sides of the road, finding places in the shade whenever possible. Betty Gail watches many of the soldiers retrieving hard tack and pork from the knapsacks. Then, without warning, many of the Bluebellies embark on the besieging of houses and businesses. She observes soldiers emerge from doorways and backyards, bearing quilts, plates, poultry and pigs, attacking beehives, honey in the hands and besmearing the faces of the boys. Several of the soldiers come near the hospital while swarms of others poke hundreds of bayonets in the corners of yards and gardens after concealed treasure.

"Why is this happening?" she wonders and wipes her tears on her apron. Standing on the front porch, she sees a Bluebelly running across the railroad track proudly raising his shining silver candle-holder prize.

She witnesses the shouting and scrambling and how the Yankees exchange their spoils for another with their comrades. Betty Gail silently prays, but her quiet beseeching prayers go unheard.

As she and the hospital staff look helplessly on from across the road, the Yankees amuse themselves in their folly of robbery and destruction. She watches as the town and its surroundings become victims of the Yankees' foraging parties, who break into the stores and buildings. In about thirty minutes any item of value is on the Yankee wagons or on their person.

Buck is making his rounds in the fields, checking the cabbage and lettuce crops on his and Buster Phillips' place, when Charlie begins barking. Buck and Isaac hurry to the house and prepare to meet a rider who is thundering down the road. Malcolm Hamby, a local wagon maker, rushes to Buck's place. "Yankees heading your way!"

Buck hollers, "Is Betty Gail all right?"

"Was when I left." He departs hastily at the same breakneck pace as he arrived.

Malcolm is no sooner out of sight, than Buck can see the Union column heading in his direction; the Union Flag is being held by a soldier on the head mount. From his vantage point, he can't determine how many soldiers are in the detail. But one Union soldier is too many in his opinion.

Buck slaps his hat against his leg. "Isaac, looks as if the bummers are here again!" The Union flag still flies in front of his house, so he feels less uneasy than he might otherwise. The Captain in charge of the expedition canters up to Buck. "I assume this is your place, mister?"

"That's right, I own the place . . or what's left of it."

"Why are you flying the Union flag?"

"That's becoming a good question after what we've been through with you Yankees, but I still believe in the Union my forefathers fought for, those who believed in Thomas Jefferson. Take what you can find. Another expedition was through here on the 27th of last month . . cleaned us out and burned my neighbor's buildings except for his barn and slave quarters."

"Where is your neighbor now?"

"Off fighting for the Confederacy." Buck glances over to the wagon train. "Looks like you have had a good day so far. Your wagons are nearly full of Georgia grown and Georgia raised."

The captain replies sarcastically, "We've got a large army to feed and we appreciate you folks raising the food for us! Take that barking hound and sit over there by the fence."

Buck takes Charlie and he and Isaac find a comfortable spot by the fence. Realistically, there was nothing he could do except watch. He was thankful the captain wasn't a more violent man. The captain gestured toward the out buildings. "Check the house, barns and cellars. Bring all the cows here. Kill and dress the remaining hogs. Then load all the corn, hay and syrup on the wagons."

The troops snap the reins and the wagons move toward the barns. Other soldiers follow the now familiar routine of checking for buried goods while others invade the house. Sally stands silently on the porch as the Bluebellies rush by her. The captain looks toward her and the Masonic Plaque catches his eye. He rides over to Buck. "I see you're a Mason."

"That's right. I am a Third Degree Mason." The captain sees Jack lying in the pasture. "Is that mule dead?"

Buck knows Jack has a mind of his own when it comes to strangers. Hoping for the best, he answers the captain, "Almost. Got struck by lightning and has bad joints. Lays down most of the time and can hardly walk."

"Sergeant, see that mule over there? See if you can get him up." The sergeant climbs the wooden fence and goes over to Jack, who lies still as the sergeant begins to examine him. Jack lifts his head and neighs heavily as if saying to leave him alone.

"Looks pretty bad, sir. Even his tail is messed up! Do you want me to shoot him?"

Buck looks alarmed and begins to stand up, but the captain waves him off. "Save your bullet for a Rebel!"

Buck resumes his position as if he is getting more comfortable. Two Yankees bring the only cow left on the place and tie her to the back of one of the wagons. A pig squeals and a shot rings out. Then silence.

The captain orders the sergeant, "Gather all the darkies and bring them here."

The sergeant takes several other soldiers with him as the captain dismounts and climbs the steps to the porch as the slaves gather around. "Listen to me." All of you are free now. You can go anywhere you want to go. However, for the time-being, General Sherman recommends that you stay on the farms and draw wages for your work. There really is no other place for you to go right now." He looks directly at each individual. "I'll give you a reward if you show me where any food is hidden."

One of Buster's darkies steps forward, holding his hat in both hands, "New greens growing now. Blues gots it's all utter day."

"Okay. Sergeant, I see all of the wagons are back.

Set that rebel barn on fire and burn this man's gin and smokehouse. I know he is hiding food somewhere!" In a few minutes, Buster's barn is ablaze. Buck's smokehouse and gin are set to flames. The captain watches as the smoke begins to climb, then orders his foraging expedition to depart.

Buck and Isaac go to the house entering with Sally. "Looks like the Bluebellies tore everything up again. You and Sally get it together, and I'll see what I can do about keeping the fires from spreading with the other hands." Buck goes outside. He and the other hands extinguish any grass that begins to burn around the smoke house and the cotton gin.

There's no rifle or cannon fire this time in town only troops and more troops. Approximately 15,000 Yankees, 625 supply wagons and 150 ambulances on this day alone pass through the once prosperous tourist town. The Yankees peer at the burnt-out granite hull of buildings. They pass the lonely hospital, sitting next to what used to be the main depot and a main Confederate railroad supply line for troops, munitions and commissary provision.

General Ward points out several locations to his Adjutant, which Colonel Miller had told him about during his skirmishes in Stone Mountain in July. As General Ward approaches the partially burned depot, he notices it is pretty much still functional. He looks toward the hospital. "See the hospital there? I think that's where the Union soldier was being cared for." General Ward instructs his second in command, "Stay with the troops while I visit the hospital." He and his Adjutant rein up to the front of the hospital, the guard snaps to attention and salutes. General Ward returns the salute and the guard opens the door for him. "I am General Ward. Is there still a lady in charge of the hospital?"

"Yes, sir. I believe the lady I have been talking with is in charge."

"What is her name?"

"I heard her say Mrs. Jernigan, sir."

"Where is she now?"

"She said she was going to the cookhouse out back to begin preparing the supper meal, sir."

"Thank you," replies General Ward. Then the General and his adjutant enter the hospital. He passes through the ward and the smell of rotting flesh to the rear of the buildings. Standing in the door he asks, "Are you Mrs. Jernigan?"

Betty Gail, not recognizing the General's voice, turns with a mighty surprised look. "Yes, General, I am."

"Colonel Miller spoke highly of you and asks that I stop in for a visit to ensure that his orders not to disturb this place are still being carried out."

"So far, General Ward, there have not been any problems. A Colonel Selfridge came by earlier and I told him we have no Union soldiers here at this time. I showed him Colonel Miller's order and he informed me that he would have it verified."

"I'll remind Colonel Selfridge that I am familiar with Colonel Miller's order and I will also endorse the order today. You'll be fine, Mrs. Jernigan. Your thoughtfulness in treating any soldier is a blessing to all of these poor dying and sick soldiers."

"To you, sir, I will offer a cup of tea and some corn bread." Betty Gail pours a cup of tea for the General and his adjutant. She places them on a saucer along with a small piece of corn bread on the side. She walks over and hands the tea and cornbread to the two soldiers.

"Thank you kindly, Mrs. Jernigan. I do hope your family is well. I know this war is devastating to both sides. Maybe by the first of the year this dreadful conflict will end." He raises his cup and takes a sip. "What kind of tea?"

"Sassafras. Made from the root of the sassafras tree. You can identify which trees are sassafras because their leaves are the first to change color, sometimes as early as late July. It's a popular tea in Georgia. I hope you enjoy it." Then she pours a cup for herself.

"Again, Mrs. Jernigan, don't worry. I'll inform Colonel Selfridge not to disturb these hospitals and Wayside around the mountain. I just wanted to stop by and say hello and thank you again for caring for the wounded Union soldiers. I must get back to my command. When the war is over, maybe our families can become friends. Just for your information, tomorrow the soldiers are going to destroy the rails on the road. One of those unfortunate events of the war." They set their cups down. "Thanks for the tea and corn bread."

"Yes, thank you, ma'am," says the adjutant.

General Ward takes her hand in both of his. "God speed, Mrs. Jernigan."

"Thank you, General, for your kindness to these soldiers." Betty Gail watches them leave and returns to her duties in the outside kitchen. She ponders what will become of him before the war ends.

The General and his adjutant turn and depart. Outside, the General instructs the guard to inform Colonel Selfridge that he has been here and Colonel Miller's orders stand.

"Yes, sir" replies the guard. He retrieves the General and the Adjutant's horses. They mount and gallop away to return to the head of their column.

The guards at the hospitals change about every hour. Every so often a band comes by. Some bands play marching music while other bands carry their instruments. There is always the sound of beating drums and occasionally the sound of a fife. Sometimes, she peers out of the window to view the never-ending column of Bluebellies. Having seen enough of the Yankees, she continues to assist with preparing supper for the patients: corn bread, pork and pumpkin pie.

Now the bummers appear up the road from town to the area of the cemetery. The grave diggers are placing their shovels, picks, and spades in the wagons preparing to go back to the hospital. The officer in charge of the bummers stops and asks the diggers, "What's in the coffins?"

"Here we go again!" mutters one of the grave diggers and he sternly replies, "The dead!"

"Dig them up and take his wagon and mule, Sergeant!"

At this point, the Yankee guard approaches the commander of the bummers, salutes and says, "Sir, we have orders from General Ward and Colonel Miller not to disturb any property, any food, or any animals with the hospitals in this area. Also, sir, these coffins have been dug up and all is clear there, sir. The orders are at the hospital by the depot, sir."

The lieutenant, with a look of disgust barks, "General Ward and Colonel Miller must have relatives here to give them all of this protection!"

Suddenly, a herd of about two hundred mooing and belching cattle begin passing the cemetery. All anyone can do is wait. Cows running through the cemetery, cows spooking the mules, cow plops all along the way and more dust.

As the last of the cattle and drivers pass the bummers fall in behind the herdsman. The grave diggers sit on the wagon and wait until the bummers are over the hill and out of sight. Then, they snap the reins and direct their mule and wagon to the hospital. "I sure would like to dig just one grave and put a thousand dead or alive Yankees in it."

"Make it one hole and two thousand!" replies another of the diggers.

Even the Yankee invaders wear red cloths over their faces. Although she knows they are wearing kerchiefs over their mouths and noses, Betty Gail ponders how the men in the column can handle all of the dust accumulating on their clothes, skin and in their lungs. By the end of the day, the red dust is so thick that the patients watching the parade near the railroad track have covered their faces to filter the air and keep from turning red from the dry dust. Even the hospital has a red hue on the walls. Never has so much dust been stirred up in one day in this once prosperous village.

"I figure if all of the provision wagons and ambulances alone were lined up, they would stretch from Stone Mountain, up Fellowship Road and almost to Brown's Court House." Betty Gail sighs and starts to return to her work, but another sound catches her attention. She places her finger to her mouth motioning to be quiet. "Do you hear cows?"

"Me's do." replies the kitchen assistant and they rush to the front of the hospital. Several stray cows rush past the depot from the herd. One of the drivers chases and turns them back to join the herd.

Betty Gail turns to the guard. "Wonder who you stole those from?" The herd rumbles through town and will eventually end up in the bellies of the Yankees. As the herd passes through, she sees the bummers with their wagons full from their ritual of marauding excursions. "I wonder if they went by our place again?" she murmurs, fighting the urge to go home and check on Buck.

Soon, all is quiet as the last of the cattle mosey through town. Shortly, supper is ready and the attendants file in to eat early. Then they begin feeding the soldiers. Tables are set for the few who are able to walk while the others are having the staff encourage them to slowly sip and eat as much as possible. Betty Gail is about to fall asleep on her feet in the kitchen, but she sees the inviting chair near the fireplace. She wearily drops into the comfortable seat. Taking her shawl from the chair, she wraps it around her shoulders and falls into a deep sleep almost instantly.

Chapter Thirty-seven
Without Resistance

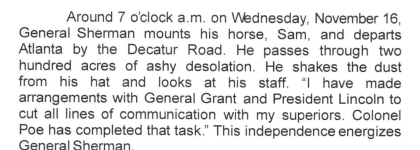

Around 7 o'clock a.m. on Wednesday, November 16, General Sherman mounts his horse, Sam, and departs Atlanta by the Decatur Road. He passes through two hundred acres of ashy desolation. He shakes the dust from his hat and looks at his staff. "I have made arrangements with General Grant and President Lincoln to cut all lines of communication with my superiors. Colonel Poe has completed that task." This independence energizes General Sherman.

Accompanying General Sherman is his personal staff and a company of 1st Alabama cavalry under the command of Lieutenant Snelling. A company of 9th Illinois Mounted Infantry under the command of Lieutenant McCroy guards the General's small supply train forming the rear guard of the XIV Corps. The marching men and wagons of the Fourteenth Corps are under the command of Major General Jefferson C. Davis.

The Third Brigade of the First Division of the XX Corps takes their respective position along the railroad. Beginning at the Stone Mountain Depot, the 82nd Ohio Regiment is in place at the three-mile mark and the other five regiments assemble up to the five-mile mark. This gives each division around two miles of track to destroy before eventually reaching Lithonia. One of Colonel Robinson's Regiments remains in the city to destroy several hundred yards of the spur track to the quarry works before beginning their mission of destruction of the main road with the other units of the Third Brigade. Slowly, the ransacked City of

Stone Mountain is awakening to the Yankees' movements as they prepare to destroy the railroad.

An orderly shakes Betty Gail gently. "Wake up, Miz Betty Gail. Them Bluebellies 'uz back. Lookin' dey ready ter destroy de road."

Betty Gail opens her eyes. "My goodness, it's daylight! I don't even remember getting in this rocker, much less falling asleep. Did I hear you say the Bluebellies are about to destroy the railroad?"

"Yes-um, looks yonder. Seed dems all in line."

Betty Gail stands and goes to the window. "Look at those Bluebellies. Lining up toward Rockbridge Road as far as you can see. We just about had the road repaired and now they're tearing it up again. I don't understand why that Yankee General Sherman doesn't use the road to move his troops about. Just does not make any sense . . but again, I'm not a general." Trying not to dwell on this disturbing subject, she continues, "It looks like the oatmeal and grits are ready for the patients. I'm sorry that I didn't wake in time to help you with breakfast."

"No worry, ye tired fum yistiddy!"

Once the fire begins and all of the soldiers are on the west side of the road, they march to the new location and fall in line behind the section one soldiers. The commanders of section two also fall in behind the commanders of section one, who are preparing to repeat the process.

The section three commanders take the place of the section two commanders and the one thousand destructive Yankee soldiers wait for the rails to become red hot. Then, one of the captains, lieutenants, or sergeants will supervise the bending and most importantly, the twisting of the rails. The Bluebellies bend and twist the rails around trees and posts. They call them "Sherman's neckties." Particular attention is also given to the glass insulators on the telegraph poles, which are broken by the section two soldiers. The entire operation of rip and burn is a festive occasion for the Bluebellies, especially since there is no threat from the Confederate Army.

Other Yankees follow each of the three sections. Some are on horseback tugging on a line of horses that the laboring Yankees rode into town. Others slip away and break into homes or stores. One smiling thief comes out, holding his bounty of sterling silver in the air. "Look what I got. They had it hid in the chimney!" He laughs and brags as he places the stash in the saddle bags.

A few others have live rabbits from pens and traps. "Gonna make a good supper! "Tying the back legs of the squirming rabbits, the Yankee places them on the commissary wagon. Other men are trotting all over the streets in town, peeking, looking and exhibiting greed as if their mission is on the order of Holiness.

Around 9:00 a.m., General Sherman approaches the hill near the Howard House, close to the intersection of Moreland and DeKalb Avenues, the Confederate defense line of July 22. He pauses and turns to reflect upon the scenes of the past battles. "Major Dayton, we are standing upon the very ground whereon the bloody battle of July 22 was fought. "I think there is the copse of wood where McPherson fell. He was a much better General than I. "Major Dayton quietly listens. "Behind us lies Atlanta smoldering and in ruins. The black smoke is still rising high in air. It hangs like a pall over the ruined city."

"Yes, sir, it does General."

Off in the distance on the McDonough Road, is the rear of General Howard's column. The gun-barrels are glistening in the sun. The white-topped wagons stretch to the south. The Fourteenth Corps is immediately behind him. The troops are marching steadily and rapidly with a cheery look and swinging pace. It seems to make light of the thousand miles that lay between the Union army and Richmond.

General Sherman turns his horse's head to the east. Atlanta is soon lost behind a screen of trees. It becomes a thing of the past. In his mind, that city clings to many a thought of desperate battles of hope and fear that now seems like a memory of an almost forgotten dream. The day is extremely beautiful, clear sunlight, with bracing air. An unusual feeling of exhilaration and things to come, vague and undefined, still full of adventure and intense interest, seems to pervade all minds. The general sentiment is that the Union armies are marching for Richmond. There, the war should end. The marching soldiers do not seem to care about their destination or the progress of the war. They neither measure the distance nor count the loss of life. They do not bother their minds about the great rivers to cross or the food for man and beast which must be gathered on the way. There's a "devil-may-care" feeling pervading the officers and men that made General Sherman feel the full load of responsibility, for success would be expected as a matter of course, whereas, should he fail, this march would be adjudged.

For each division of the XX Corps to cover their two miles on the road, about six separate applications of rip and burn will be required. The commissary wagons follow each section, furnishing fresh water as needed. For dinner, they'll provide potatoes and beef, along with hard tack that is always presented.

By two p.m., the destruction of the road to Lithonia is complete. The men return to camp and move out down Rockbridge Road to Yellow River. The XX crosses Yellow River and sets up camp for the night on Thomas Maguire's Promise Land Plantation. Here, the XX Corps wait for the supply trains to close up on the main body.

Buck and Isaac try to replant some greens for the winter from his store of seeds. They are returning to the house when Buck notices a cloud of dust coming from Tower Road. Again, straining his eyes, he is able to distinguish it is the same bummers who paid him a visit yesterday. He goes calmly to the gate with Isaac to meet the foragers. When the lieutenant reaches the gate, only the wagon and the lieutenant stop while the other soldiers scatter across his place. "We thought we would pay you a surprise visit today to determine if you were lying yesterday. For your sake, I surely hope everything is the same. What did you have for dinner, mister?"

"I had a hare from the rabbit box over yonder and the ginhouse is just as you left it!" Buck forces himself to remain calm and spits his chew toward the lieutenant's horse. Yet he realizes these men are very serious, but he isn't willing to compromise his dignity to preserve the ego of this arrogant officer.

Peering over at Buster Phillips' barn, the lieutenant is surprised to find it is still standing. "We set that barn on fire before we left. I see it did not burn so we will give it a better start today!"

Behind Buck, one of the horsemen rounds his house and dismounts. Throwing the door open he enters saying, "Everything is the same as yesterday, lieutenant!"

"Go look in the cellar you found yesterday," orders the lieutenant. The bummer dashes to the back of the house and finds the door ajar, just as yesterday. He checks the cookhouse and the crib. They are also as they were the previous day. He reports back to the lieutenant. "Everything's the same, sir."

"Corporal, we did not do a complete job on the barn yesterday. Seems like it did not want to burn. Get those darkies to gather up plenty of wood and straw and set the Confederate barn to a good blaze this time."

"Yes, sir." The corporal mounts his horse and rides to the other side of Buster Phillips' house where the darkies are. They had not seen the bummers arrive at Buck's and become anxious as the corporal approaches. He reins his mount to a halt. "You darkies get all the wood you can carry and head to the barn. We got some cooking to do!" says the corporal with a smirk.

"Cookin'?"

"That's right . . cookin'," replies the corporal.

The darkies deliver the kindling to the barns nervously. In the meantime, another Yankee adds several piles of straw in the inside corners of the barns, as well as in the loft. "Set that wood on top of the straw in the corners inside, and you," pointing to a younger darkie, "Get a big pile in the loft on top of the straw. Get a move on it! We are in a hurry to see this place burn!" exclaims the corporal.

"Burns dat barn?" asks one of Buster's slaves.

The Corporal replies angrily, "That's what I said. Set it on fire now."

The darkies look at each other more nervous wondering exactly what the Yankee meant about cookin'.

One of Buster's darkies' eyes grow wide and whispers to another darkie, "He's ain't gonna be cookin' me's." He throws down the kindling and makes a dash for the woods. They are out of sight before the Yankees realize what has happened.

"Let 'em go. Just stack the wood and torch this place. We need to get back to camp with our haul," orders the Corporal. By the time he and his squad return to the lieutenant, the barn is smoking with flames emerging from the hay door.

"See you around, mister!" shouts the lieutenant as he snaps the reins on the wagon teams and heads toward camp.

After a couple of hours in hiding the Negroes emerge from the woods as Buck gives them an "all clear" shout.

General Sherman surveys the surrounding terrain from his horse. "Major Audenried, that must be Stone Mountain looming in the distance. Send my headquarters staff to the XIV Corps camp site. I want to see this monolith up close. On my maps, sometimes it's called New Gibraltar and sometimes Stone Mountain. We will take the wagon trail along the railroad to get there. This way I can inspect the road destruction first-hand."

Before reaching the roads, tall columns of black smoke climb into the sky and eventually drift back together, forming a long stream of darkness.

"The results of the cross-tie burning and rail twisting, I hope," says the General. Upon reaching the road, he brings his horse to a stop. Looking in both directions he studies the destruction of the road. There are only a few mounted infantry patrolling this stretch of devastation.

He views the piles of cross-ties, some smoldering, some still in full blaze. The rails are now around trees twisted and shaped into his namesake. The General smiles. "Perfect, not a straight rail in sight. I expect no less from General Slocum!"

Approaching the town, Colonel Spencer, the Commander of the 1st Alabama Cavalry, sends a scouting party to town. They are to determine the best direction to the mountain. The advance party stops and asks Colonel William Cogswell of the Second Massachusetts Volunteer Regiment for directions. "General Sherman is on his way to view the mountain, sir. Which is the best way to the mountain, clear of any rebels?"

"The only Rebels here are in the cemetery, the hospitals and the Wayside. They've all lost their will to resist. Most of them are just waiting to die. The General will be safe here. Just turn right at the end of this block. The wagon trail name is Tower Street and it will take you to the mountain. We are to destroy all public buildings and other structures that might benefit the Confederates this afternoon. We will wait until the General returns from the mountain, just in case we run into any hidden explosives," explains Colonel Cogswell.

Soon the 1st Alabama, General Sherman and his headquarters guard, the 7th Ohio Sharpshooters, enter town. Colonel Cogswell greets him at the depot. "All is clear here, sir. For your safety, I'll wait until you return from the mountain before we set fire to a couple of other buildings."

"That will be fine, Colonel," replies General Sherman. Sherman and his guard pass several double log houses in the midst of large oak groves with autumn leaves on their branches. The cabins rest upon the gentle hillsides of Tower Street toward the Wayside.

General Sherman observes many Confederate soldiers at the Wayside from a distance. "Major Dayton, Instruct Colonel Spence to investigate that location."

Rushing inside and seeking to find Mary Hamilton, Joe the attendant shouts, "Miz Hamilton! Miz Hamilton! Yankees! Coming down da road." Mary Hamilton places her hands on Joe's shoulders and takes a deep breath. "Calm down. It won't do us any good to panic. Let me think."

"Yez'um," he says, gulping for air.

"You go through the wards and quietly and calmly tell everyone what's going on." Joe hesitates and glances down the road at the approaching dust cloud. "Go ahead, Joe, and urge the patients to remain calm no matter what because I have a copy of orders from Colonel Miller to leave us alone. We should be fine."

"I'se not sure. Dem last Yankees didn't wanter leave us be."

"We're not looking for trouble, Joe." She turns toward the door and prepares to face the coming confrontation.

Many of the patients become extremely nervous. A few who are able leave by the back door to run to hide in the woods. Mary retrieves Colonel Miller's order and dashes outside. She is waiting as Colonel Spence appears with his horsemen. By now, most of the wounded Confederates have withdrawn to the interior of the Wayside and are peering out of the windows and around the front while others peep from behind trees and bushes at the rear of the Wayside.

"Madam, is this a Confederate hospital or what?" inquires Colonel Spence. "This is a hotel built by my father, Andrew Johnson, but now is a Wayside for the wounded and sick soldiers who are returning to their homes. I have a copy of orders from Colonel Miller. When he was here in July he issued orders to not disturb this place and these orders have recently been endorsed by General Ward." She hands him the copy of the order. With a surprised look, Colonel Spence takes and reads it. "Are there any Union soldiers here, madam?"

"None at all, Colonel."

"I still must inspect this facility, madam." He summons a Captain and explains the order from Colonel Miller. "Give this place the once over, but do not disturb or remove anything. If you find any of our men, bring them with you. Do not take any prisoners unless there's a confrontation."

"Yes, sir, Colonel." The captain explains the orders to a lieutenant, who, in turn, takes his platoon to inspect the site as quickly as possible. "Stay with me, madam," directs Colonel Spence.

The lieutenant sends two squads on horseback to check the woods and two squads to inspect the interior of the building. Going from room to room, the Yankees find nothing unusual. One Yankee goes through the kitchen and grabs a handful of fresh cornbread. "Sure is fresh and hot! I bet that good looking lady who takes care of you could be just as fresh and hot as this here cornbread!" He laughs, grabs another hand-full of cornbread and departs by the back door.

In about ten minutes the platoon is back together. The lieutenant reports to the captain and colonel. "There are no Union soldiers in the Wayside but we did find several wounded Confederates in the woods. Evidently, they were frightened and were hiding."

Colonel Spence orders the men back to the column. He acknowledges Mrs. Hamilton and dismisses her at the same time.

By now, General Sherman is taking a squad about a hundred yards up the mountain. Colonel Spence rides his horse and reports to General Sherman that the hotel is a wayside for wounded Confederates returning home. He informs the general that in July, Colonel Miller wrote an order not to disturb the Wayside or hospitals in the town. The order has also been recently endorsed by General Ward. It said he had found Union soldiers at the hospital and they were being treated as well as the Confederate soldiers.

"Fine, let's travel on and see if we can ride all of the way around this large pebble," General Sherman advises Colonel Spence. They rejoin the column and head East on Tower Street.

Chapter Thirty-eight
Tête-à-Tête

General Sherman and part of his guard proceed to the steep side of the mountain. Once they come to a clearing, they see the smoke from Buster Phillips' farm and Buck's place. General Sherman directs Colonel Spence to send a platoon forward to reconnoiter the area. As they wait for the results of the scouting mission, the other troops spread out to ensure General Sherman's safety. Betty Gail Jernigan approaches the column. As she rounds a bend in the road, she is taken by surprise by several of the Yankee soldiers.

One has his Spencer rifle pointing directly at her. "Get off of your horse!" shouts a sergeant. "Where are you heading?"

"I live just a stone's throw from here and my husband is expecting me."

The sergeant walks up and grabs the reins from her. "Mighty fine mount. Might just keep it for myself. You best follow me."

"You best check with General Ward before you make that decision, mister! I have an order from him stating I can keep this horse. Where are you taking me?"

"You'll see," as he leads her and her horse toward the area where General Sherman is waiting for the return of the scouts.

Colonel Spence sees the two approaching and meets him part of the way. "Sir, this lady was riding through and we stopped her. Says she lives not far from here."

Betty Gail sees the smoke coming from the area of

their farm. Lunging forward in a panic, she shouts, "That smoke is coming from our place! What have you done to my husband and home?"

The sergeant and a corporal restrain her and she renders a good kick to groin of the corporal. He grabs his crotch and falls to the ground. The sergeant yanks a handful of her hair, pulling her to the ground face first. As Betty Gail falls to the ground, the sergeant takes his foot and places it firmly on the length of hair and near her skull so she is unable to move. Betty Gail screams from the pain as the hair is pulling from her head. Attempting to scratch the sergeant's legs, she reaches but cannot get to an area above his high boots.

"Calm down, lady. We've done nothing to your place and I have sent some scouts there to find out what's causing the smoke." The corporal, still rolling and moaning, slowly rises to his feet and moves away to sit in the shade of a nearby a tree. "I'll tell the sergeant to let you up, but another scene and we'll have you in ropes. Do you understand?"

Silent for a moment, she responds with a definitive "Yes. Let me up and let me go to my husband and my place."

"Just hold her there a few more minutes, sergeant, and then let her up. If she gives you any more trouble, bind her."

"Yes, sir."

In about fifteen minutes, the scouting party returns to report to Colonel Spence, who is at the side of General Sherman. "A barn is burning and some small out buildings have been burned. There's a Union flag flying on the porch next to the burning house!"

Colonel Spence orders the lieutenant, "Go to the rear and bring me that woman whom the sergeant is restraining." The lieutenant departs as the colonel describes the incident about the woman to General Sherman. The lieutenant reaches the sergeant and gives him the orders from Colonel Spence. By now Betty Gail is sitting up. "On your feet, woman! We are going to see Colonel Spence and General Sherman." Betty Gail is still so mad she does not comprehend what the sergeant has said. She stands up and they walk the fifty or so yards to General Sherman.

"Ma'am, I'm General Sherman and would like to know who lives in the house with the Union Flag out front."

Still upset and now taken back by who has just spoken to her she says, "That is our place and it seems as if some of your abominable Bluebellies have lived up to their reputation. I would love to give you the same compliment that I just gave to your corporal!"

Ignoring her statement, General Sherman asks, "Who lives there with you?"

"My husband and some darkies!" she replies in a stern voice while looking directly into the General's eyes.

"Colonel, send in several platoons and secure the entire area. I want to go in and talk with Mr. . What is your husband's name, lady?"

"Buck Jernigan, General!"

Buck, Isaac and Sally are cleaning up the ashes and cinders from the gin fire when Isaac sees the approaching Yankees. "Here's day com' agin'," shouts Isaac.

Buck wheels around as the column approaches. He, Isaac and Sally begin to spread out in both directions as they are surrounding his place. Buck says angrily, "Another two hours in hell is coming our way again!"

The lead horses approach and the Yankees dismount. "We are here to inspect your house and out buildings, mister. You're about to have an important visitor. Anybody in your house?"

"No, look for yourself," Buck looks surprised and expresses his feeling to the lieutenant, "I don't need any important guests around here. I just need you Yankees to leave us be."

Soon, the lieutenant returns and details a couple of privates to stay with Mr. Jernigan. He rides to Colonel Spence and informs him of the all clear. Colonel Spence turns to Betty Gail tells her to mount her horse and says, "Come along, Mrs. Jernigan." The sergeant releases the horse's reins to her, and they gallop up to Buck's unbelieving eyes. The two privates salute Colonel Spence. "Mr. Jernigan, I believe," says the colonel.

"That's me all right!" replies Buck as he races to Betty Gail, who leaps from her mount and runs to him. They embrace momentarily and Betty Gail moves to his side. Turning slightly sideways, she places one arm under his arm and the other hand on his shoulder.

"They stopped me on the way home, but I'm all right now."

"What's going on here?" Buck asks the Colonel.

"We are the rear guard of the XIV Corps and General Sherman is with us. He is curious about the Union Flag flying from your porch and would like to talk with you."

"If it's truly General Sherman, bring him in, there are a few things I would like to say to him as well. I'll be waiting on the porch, but don't expect any tea from us!"

Colonel Spence rides to get General Sherman. Buck and Betty Gail go to the porch, where she relates her harrowing experience with the Bluebelly sergeant.

Isaac is on the porch the entire time pressing his straw hat close to his chest with both hands. "What them Bluebelly want, Mars Jernigan?"

"Don't reckon I know yet, Isaac, but we'll find out soon enough. Bring a couple more chairs over here."

Isaac brings two more chairs from the other side of the porch and puts them near where Betty Gail and Buck are sitting. The sound of horses approaching becomes more distinct as General Sherman, Colonel Spence and six other Yankees approach the porch. As soon as the group brings their mounts to a halt, a Sergeant jumps from his horse to take the reins from the General as he dismounts.

General Sherman looks around a moment and admires the Union flag. He climbs the several stairs leading up to the porch where Buck, Betty Gail and Isaac are waiting. "I'm General Sherman and I am curious why you're flying the Union flag."

Buck stands. "I'm Buck Jernigan. This is my wife, Betty Gail, and my farm hand, Isaac. Have a seat, General." Observing the manner of dress of General Sherman, Buck snaps, "You dress as shabby as everyone says! Don't your troops call you Uncle Billy?"

Suppressing a smile, General Sherman replies, "Yes. That's one of the better ones. My manner of dress has followed me all my life. At West Point, I had the grades but I did not get above the rank of private because of it." While taking his seat, he repeats, "I'm curious about the flag."

"Simple, we are Union people and did not endorse the secession as did most folks around here. My neighbor signed up for the Confederacy. Our son is somewhere with the Georgia Military Institute--- Lord knows where. My family fought to form the Union and I fought in the war with Mexico. Your foraging party was here yesterday and again this morning. For no reason other than my neighbor's being in the Confederate Army, they set fire to his barn and out buildings. Even though the darkies were living in the main house, they set to blaze just like you burned Atlanta." Buck turns and points to the top of the mountain. "If you wanted to see hell, you could've seen it from the top of the mountain as Atlanta was burning Monday night." He points to the Masonic plaque hanging on the porch wall. "One of the bummers brought out my Masonic plaque and showed it to the lieutenant. According to him, that saved my house from his match. I obeyed every request, gave no resistance and still lost nearly everything."

"We are at war and I must feed my army," responds General Sherman. "The foragers are under strict orders to leave food for the citizens. If Governor Brown had accepted my invitation to discuss peace, then the burning of Atlanta would not have occurred."

Buck vigorously responds, "The Constitution is the Constitution. The Constitution, Independence and States Rights, is what our forefathers fought for. Do you think there would've been a war if the North seceded?"

"Probably not. But States' Rights and constitutionality is not a good reason for slavery," responds General Sherman.

"Remember, 'Uncle Billy,' the antislavery movement began in the South although slavery was just as common in the North. Thomas Jefferson led the emancipation effort. When Oglethorpe settled Georgia, the

Charter of 1732 said, that all and every person who resides within Georgia shall be free. Georgia was the only colony of the thirteen which did not allow slavery."

General Sherman leans back. "I did not know this about Georgia. So how did Georgia become a slave state?"

"Reverend George Whitefield, by 1748, had Negro slaves caring for his Orphan House at Bethesda, near Savannah," Buck began. "He and the Honorable James Habersham had a great influence with the trustees of the Charter. Mr. Habersham asserted that the Colony was unable to prosper without slave labor. Reverend Whitefield based his support for slavery on philanthropy. He boldly declared it would be of great advantage to the African to be brought from his barbarous surroundings and be among those that are civilized and Christian."

"So when did slavery become legal?" asks Sherman.

"In 1749 the trustees in London came to the conclusion that it would be better to permit slavery. Then the colonists of Georgia were able by law to own and use slaves and the article prohibiting slavery was repealed."

"Seven Northern states abolished slavery because it was not profitable," retorts Sherman.

"Yes and they sold the slaves to the Southerners. There were plenty of white men, women and children slaves in those days. And there are a great number of free Negroes in Georgia today. I just read that Virginia has about sixty thousand free Negroes. Alfred Cuthbert, a former Representative and United States Senator who also was a prominent planter, emancipated his slaves and paid their passage to Liberia."

"What do you think makes slavery so profitable, Mr. Jernigan?"

"See the pile of ashes over there?" Pointing to the remains of his cotton gin and sorghum press. "In the South, cotton is king. The invention of the cotton gin in Savannah, by Eli Whitney, is how the South makes slavery profitable. Cotton cannot be profitable without the cotton gin and slaves are not profitable without cotton. They more or less hold hands. All other crops are secondary. The cotton gin machine can clean more seeds from cotton in one day than one hundred hands can clean in several months. From what I have read, cotton exports went from around 400 bales in 1800 to 82,000 bales in 1810."

"So where did the farmers come from and why to Georgia to grow the cotton?"

"General, I think you are giving me a history quiz."

"Maybe so, Mr. Jernigan. The last question might just be a bonus question."

"Georgia population began to increase with families moving from Virginia and North Carolina. What caused this migration, General, is that neither the soil nor climate in Virginia and North Carolina are suitable to grow cotton. Slavery came to Georgia as the families from Virginia and North Carolina brought their slaves with them to work the cotton fields. Crops are more profitable and the surplus cash is used to buy more Negroes."

"Just good simple economics, Mr. Jernigan. With the increase in the population, cotton cropland became more valuable. The cotton gin not only increased the demand for Negroes but also the demand for land."

"Right, General. The cotton gin was one of the most important inventions ever made. It gave and still gives to the commerce of the world a staple commodity which is in universal demand and it gave to the people of the South our most valuable and important crop . . cotton. The gin has proven to be practicable, except when you see it smoldering in ashes like that over there," he said, rolling his head again in the direction of the gin house. "So, General, would you feel it safe to say that the cotton gin is the root cause of this Civil War?"

Raising his eyebrows and tightening his chin, General Sherman ponders over the last statement. "Not so much the cotton gin. It's just the catalyst for the greed and profit that enslaves humans. I am not an abolitionist and I certainly do not believe in Negro equality."

"Impressive statement, General. Then why are you here?"

"I am a soldier fighting to preserve the Union!"

Buck observes the general for a moment "Lord Macaulay said Eli Whitney did more to make the United Sates powerful than Peter the Great did to make the Russian Empire dominant."

"Very true," replies the General. "I hate to see it fall apart in the South."

"Well, General, you and your bummers come through here and steal our livestock, our vegetables, our poultry, our cotton, our tobacco, and our family valuables, then burn what's left. But just think, when all of the food is eaten, either by you or us, it's gone. Won't have a new crop for one year. Guess what, General? You cannot beat us economically in Stone Mountain."

"Why do you say that, Mr. Jernigan?"

"Because we have the granite. You cannot burn it, eat it or take it away. We can harvest granite twelve months each year. The granite is not a seasonal commodity. It does not depend on the weather or the plow. Anyone who wants a job in the quarries has a job. It's the big plantation owners who are going to suffer from the economic impact of the Emancipation Proclamation, including your bummers. Our granite quarries will rebuild the South!"

"Do you have children, Mr. Jernigan?"

"We have twins, a boy and a girl. Least ways, we still hope we have two. Like I said, my son is a cadet at GMI and Lord knows where he is now. I read where you had the honor to burn the GMI campus as well. Our daughter eloped with Joshua Hill's son, Legare. You Yankees killed him. Nonetheless," Buck said, fighting to contain his emotion. "I must thank you for allowing Congressman Hill to recover Legare's body."

Taken aback by this statement, General Sherman cuts his eyes to the colonel and then to Mrs. Jernigan. "Your family certainly has my condolences, as do all of the families on both sides of this conflict who have lost love ones. I am a soldier as are your generals. We have a duty to do. Mine is to restore the Union." He stands and surveys what's left of the Jernigan farm.

"I know about war. I lost these fingers in the Mexican

War. Joshua Hill is a great man for our state. He should be the governor, not the secessionist, Joseph Brown. If Joshua was Governor you probably would not be on my front porch today!"

General Sherman nods in agreement. "Mr. Hill is one of the men I met with and asked to deliver a message to Governor Brown. I offered to meet the Governor and hopefully sway him from entering the war and avoiding the ultimate destruction of your beautiful State. From current events, you're aware, he turned my invitation down. You have noble men fighting for the Union, the likes of Alexander Stephens and Robert Toombs. Combining Robert Toombs' powerful and sometimes reckless character with his articulate English makes him a natural leader in truth.

"There's also Herschel V. Johnson and Benjamin H. Hill. All good men who favor the Union."

Betty Gail shakes her head. "The newspapers attempted to portray Toombs as procession, but he came home and quickly let it be known that was not the case. He stated that a call for the state convention to consider secession had brought dishonor to the state. He urged everyone to stand by the constitution. The convention met and The Georgia Platform was adopted. The Platform says Georgia holds the American Union secondary in importance to the rights and principles of Georgia. That Georgia will resist any act prohibiting slavery in the Territories or a refusal to admit a slave State into the Union."

"That's right," says Buck. "Then there are the crazy abolitionists. The pitiful old man John Brown, who worked himself into a frenzy and attacked the federal arsenal at Harper's Ferry in Virginia. He was going to use the weapons to start a war and to free slaves.

General Sherman nods. "An unfortunate choice."

"One of his sons and twelve men were killed plus several darkies. Your people of the North think he gave his life for a just cause and is some kind of a martyr. Under normal social conditions his act would probably have gone mostly unnoticed. He deserved to be hung. He is regarded as a murderer by us. You sing his praise: 'John Brown's body lies a-mouldering in the grave, his soul goes marching on!' We sing to the same tune, but different words, 'We'll hang John Brown on a rotten apple tree, as we go marching on.'"

"When President Lincoln issued the Emancipation Proclamation, the Italian General Giuseppe Garibaldi hailed President Lincoln as 'the heir of the aspirations of John Brown,'" remarks General Sherman. "Personally, I regard slavery as being an indispensable part of the Southern economy and it does me no good to judge slavery's morality. I strongly believe in the Union. So what was your reaction to the Proclamation?"

Buck pauses for a moment. "First, the freedom the Proclamation promises depends upon a Union military victory and this gives the war two goals: keeping the Union united and freeing the slaves. The North has more than just territory in mind. They want more voters for their party's perpetuating power."

"What might that be, Mr. Jernigan?" asks General Sherman.

"Why, the loss of the Southern States means loss of ninety percent of the tax revenues from the tariff, like the Morrill Tariff, which burdens the Southern economy."

"You must admit, realistically, it appears the Union shall prevail."

"Most probably," retorts Buck looking directly at General Sherman.

General Sherman, still standing, looks earnestly at Buck. "Since the Proclamation was issued on January 1, 1863, the Negro enlistments have approached 200,000 men. However, the Proclamation's impact on the military has had some units near mutiny and desertion, while inspiring other units to focus not only on reuniting the Union but to fight for liberty as well. It is apparent as the slaves become free your Confederate war engine slows, cracks and begins to fall apart. No longer are slaves producing and preparing food, serving in hospitals, making uniforms, working on farms, building fortifications and rebuilding railroads. Freedom has taken its toll on the South."

"What do you think will happen to the freed slaves?" Buck leans over and spits a stream of tobacco over the porch rail. "I support Governor Brown on one item concerning the freeing of slaves. First, most of the former slaves will remain in the South since some of the Northern States have laws prohibiting former slaves from settling in their states. Second, the wealthy land owners instead of buying slaves will buy land for cultivation. Now, the poor whites and the poor freed slaves will become tenant farmers. With no land and no money, they compete as day laborers of the land owners. And finally with a large paid labor force, the wages of the poor whites will equal the lower wages of the poor free slaves. Discontent by the poor whites with this intrusion will lead to more conflict."

General Sherman takes a drag of his cigar. "If your true conservative disposition had prevailed under the flag you're flying, I think you could have had the support of that large and influential body of Northern men who were and still are sincere to have the elements of the Constitution fulfilled. So how did Georgia end up with Joseph Brown?"

"By hook and crook! The people of the mountains are extremely independent and overwhelming in favor of the Union. Joe Brown is the exception. The mountain folk have few slaves. The battles in Congress supporting the protection of slavery in the Territories are of no interest to them. Lucky for the mountain folk, Joe Brown is Governor or there would be serious trouble between this Union part of the State and the State government. The State militia would hang us all for flying the Union flag it had not been for Joe Brown."

"What about his character?"

Buck gestures as to describe the physical being of Joe Brown. "Joe Brown is angular, awkward, cold and determined. He has a simple and homely style and applies common sense to problems. This trait is common among the Puritans who live in the mountains of East Tennessee and North Georgia. This makes Joe Brown, whose nickname is 'Old Judgment,' irresistible to the people of Georgia."

Still dragging on his cigar, General Sherman nods. "My army has had some experience with the mountain population and recognizes their feelings. We saw a great many Union flags in the mountains. I would like to know more about your governor."

"The year of his second nomination in 1859, John Brown made that preposterous raid. Joseph Brown supported the indignation created by John Brown's raid. People remember the horrors of the San Domingo slave rebellion spread fear that the Northern abolitionists were going to send agents to Georgia and the South to organize a Negro insurrection. Sectional feeling began running high over the incident."

"Exactly how does the South describe an abolitionist?"

"In the South an abolitionist is one who favors emancipation and is an infidel, a murderer, a thief, a ravisher, an incendiary plus all of hell's accumulated horrors which are not otherwise appropriated. This led to the emotionally active movement which led to secession and to you, sitting on my porch." leaning forward, Buck looks very serious. "Uncle Billy."

"I look around this area and see only women and children and only a few men older than you. Where are all of the men of the state?"

"You know where they are. Out there staining the ground red. By the time the war was going good, Georgia had given one hundred-twenty thousand soldiers to the Confederate armies."

"Yes, but what I see and hear, Joseph Brown's Home Guard turns out to be nothing more than official murderers and horse thieves. From my officers, understanding from the mountain people, the Home Guard has the authority to obtain draft animals and supplies and to deal with draft evaders and deserters. Their tactics include executions without trial and torture in retaliation against friends and families of confederate resisters."

"Kinda reminds me of similar traits of some of your Union soldiers, General."

Colonel Spence intercedes, "Watch your tongue, Mr. Jernigan."

"Let him speak, Colonel."

"Yes, sir." replies the red-faced colonel.

General Sherman continues, "I sent Union troops to Pickens County and several other places to rescue families and to suppress your Home Guards. In return for the protection by the Union, many of these mountain folks gave me their assistance as spies against the pro-Confederate families. What is your feeling about the Conscription Act, Mr. Jernigan?" "The Conscription Act which crearted the draft is the most demoralizing piece of legislation ever contrived and passed by the Confederate Government. It is a dim-witted piece of legislation and its passage has cut into the zeal of the people at home as well as those in the army. This law is a slap in the face on the patriotism of the entire Southern population. Just like the one Lincoln had passed. I read it caused riots in New York."

"Didn't Joshua Hill run for Governor in '63?" asks General Sherman.

"Surely did and got beat. The majority did not want a Union supporter in office. Although he tried to act as if he supported the Confederacy, he did not convince the voters. Joseph Brown got more than fifty percent and beat Joshua Hill and Timothy Furlow. Timothy Furlow is a passionate supporter of secession."

The General turns toward the late afternoon sun. "Colonel Spence, have my clerk write an order over my signature for the protection of Mr. Jernigan's place as well as a script for one thousand dollars to replace his property."

"It has been an interesting conversation with both of you, Mr. and Mrs. Jernigan. I hope this war can come to a sensible conclusion soon and all of us return to normal for the good of the United States." General Sherman walks over to the remains of the cotton gin. In his mind he visualizes the entire destruction of the Southern economy as nothing more than a larger pile of ashes after the war.

"Why are you studying my burned down ginny, General? Your troops have burned houses, barns, and feed bins for the pure pleasure of seeing smoke and flame."

General Sherman lights another cigar. "Care for a cigar, Mr. Jernigan?"

"Don't smoke. Just chew." Buck turns and spits on the ground.

"Mr. Jernigan, I admit a lot of mischief goes on during a war. However, my orders are to destroy structure and machinery which is of value to the Confederate war effort. I decided to base this decision on my experience when I was the military administrator of Memphis on July 21, '62. I found the place dead. No one doing business, the stores closed, churches, schools and everything shut down. The people were all more or less in sympathy with our enemies and there was a strong prospect that the whole civil population would become a dead weight on our hands. Inasmuch as the Mississippi River was then in our possession northward and steamboats were freely plying with passengers and freight, I caused all the stores to be opened. Churches, schools, theatres and places of amusement, to be re-established and very soon Memphis resumed its appearance of an active, busy, prosperous place. I also restored the mayor, whose name was Parks, and the city government to the performance of their public functions and required them to maintain a good civil police.

"Soon I began to receive reports that citizens were giving secret support to the Confederacy. So when a party of guerrillas in the town of Randolph, north of Memphis, fired on an unarmed Union steamboat carrying civilian passengers, I ordered Randolph burned, stipulating that a single house be left standing to mark the place."

Buck listens anxiously. He and Betty Gail are appalled. Neither had heard the story. General Sherman walks back to the porch and takes his seat. Major Dayton offers him a cup of water. As the general finishes his last swallow, Buck can tell that General Sherman is still upset by the events of Memphis. After lighting a cigar and taking a few drags, he leans forward in the rocking chair, "Mr. Jernigan, when one nation is at war with another nation, all the people of the one are enemies of the other. Then the rules are plain and easy to understand."

"That's pretty much true, General."

"Most unfortunately, the war in which we are now

engaged has been complicated with the belief all of the Southerners are not enemies. It would have been better if, at the outset, this mistake had not been made."

"So the acts of the citizens of Memphis set your mind to the destruction of property?"

"It would have been wrong to continue to be misled by compassion of my Southern countrymen. I had to proceed on the basis that all in the South are enemies of all in the North. Not only are they unfriendly, but also all who could procure arms now bear them as organized regiments or as guerrillas. There was not a Union garrison in Tennessee where a man could go beyond the sight of the flag without being shot or captured."

"In all due respect, General, you would react the same way if your city was occupied by Confederates."

"Probably so. But it so happened that the people had cotton and whenever they saw our large armies move, they destroyed the cotton in the belief that we would seize it and convert it to our use. They did not and could not dream that we would pay money for the cotton. It had been condemned to destruction by their own acknowledged Confederate government. The cotton was therefore lost to the Southern people. It could have been, without injustice, taken by us. We could send it away, either as absolute prize of war, or for future compensation.

"But the citizens turned to the commercial enterprise of the Jews. The Jews soon discovered that ten cents would buy a pound of cotton behind our army. That four cents would take it to Boston where they could receive thirty cents in gold."

"I think the citizens of Memphis had rather sell it cheap on the black market to whoever wanted to buy rather than surrender it to the Union," replies Buck.

"But at that time the Union was willing to pay for the goods. Nevertheless the opportunity was too tempting and it spread like fire. When the Jews discovered that salt, bacon, powder, firearms, percussion-caps, etc., etc., were worth as much as gold, they sold these goods as well for a huge profit; and, strange to say, this traffic was not only permitted, but encouraged. Before we in the interior could know it, thousands of barrels of salt and millions of dollars had been disbursed. I have no doubt that Bragg's army at Tupelo, and Van Dorn's at Vicksburg, received enough salt to make bacon. No other way could Bragg and Van Dorn have moved their armies en mass. When from ten to twenty thousand fresh arms and a due supply of cartridges were also obtained, I knew what was happening. As soon as I got to Memphis, having seen the effect in the interior, I ordered my own command that gold, silver and Treasury notes, were contraband of war, and should not go into the interior, where all were hostile."

"I guess you could call the Jews 'War Brokers,' but I know there were Union sympathizers in Memphis," says Buck.

"So, what was the 'gold' rule all about?" asks Betty Gail.

"Every gold dollar that was spent for cotton was sent to the seaboard to be exchanged for bank-notes and Confederate scrip, which would buy goods in Memphis, and was taken in ordinary transactions. I therefore required cotton to be paid for in such notes, by an obligation to pay at the end of the war, or by a deposit of the price in the hands of a trustee, viz., the United States Quartermaster. Under these rules, cotton was being obtained about as fast as by any other process and yet the enemy receives no 'aid or comfort.' Under the 'gold' rule, the country people who concealed their cotton from the burners and who openly scorned our greenbacks, were willing enough to take Tennessee money, which bought their groceries. Then that trade was encouraged and gold paid out. I admit that cotton was sent in by our open enemies, who can make better use of gold than they can of their hidden bales of cotton.

"I wrote my brother and told him that the entire South, man, woman, and child, is against us and that the South's fighting spirit has to be extinguished. Civilians as well as soldiers have to be regarded as enemies, thus making the war terrible even against some who are personal friends."

General Sherman's clerk interrupts. "Sir, here is the order you requested."

Buck clears his throat and moves close to Betty Gail. Looking at Betty Gail, he simply raises and lowers his eye brows. He isn't certain what to expect from the General.

General Sherman continues to drag on his cigar as he reads the contents, signs the order and the script, stands and hands them to Buck.

Buck accepts the documents.

"I very much enjoyed our conversation and if I should see Joshua Hill, I'll give him your regards, General. Again, I thank you for allowing us to recover Legare's remains."

There's no offer of either's hand in this departure. The sergeant brings General Sherman's horse to his side and the general readily mounts. Betty Gail whispers to Buck, "That's the sergeant who threw me to the ground and held me there with his foot on my hair."

Buck walks over to the sergeant. "Excuse me, Sergeant."

"Yes?"

"Just one thing, Sergeant. If we ever meet again on equal terms, I would suggest that you have your head shaved." Buck then spits a wad of tobacco on the Sergeant's boot.

The Sergeant's face turns beet red and gives Buck the "I'm ready now look," takes to his mount and then snaps his horse around.

Colonel Spence orders the bugler to "sound assembly." He and General Sherman turn-about and the column moves toward town on Tower Street. Soon, the last of the Union troops are out of the surrounding woods. General Sherman gives his horse the rein and canters away towards town with that easy, swaying seat, so characteristic of a leisurely, well-to-do general.

Colonel Spence, riding adjacent to General Sherman, smiles and says, "That was a slick interrogation, General. That farmer had no idea you were extracting information from him."

General Sherman grins. "A very interesting man, that Mr. Jernigan. Knows his history. I wonder what his two children are like. His daughter is the widow of Joshua Hill's son and Jernigan's son is a cadet at Georgia Military Institute."

"Well, Colonel, the Union has won this war. We just need to reach Savannah."

"A very interesting man indeed," answers the colonel.

Buck and Betty Gail observe a piece of history disappear as the afternoon shadows grow longer and the last Yankee horses round the bend where they appeared earlier. Buck comforts Betty Gail. "Good or bad, failure concerns General Sherman as much as success. He's not afraid to take a chance to succeed. He's a General for sure."

Chapter Thirty-nine
Passing Through

Major Capers looks down the rows of the GMI cadets. "I have sad news this morning. On Sunday, November 13 and 14, General Sherman was in Marietta reviewing General Kilpatrick's Cavalry Division. According to the news, Marietta, along with the Georgia Military Institute, was burned. Gaunt chimneys and the superintendent's quarters are the only reminders of the proud school."

Sadly, Norman asks Paul, "Do you think we will ever rebuild?"

Rubbing his forehead, Paul looks despondent to Norman. "Only if we win this war."

On Saturday, November 19, General Wayne receives a report from General Johnston, "General Sherman's army is heading for either Macon or Augusta." General Wayne issues an order to move six hundred troops, the cadet corps and Robert Guards, consisting of 150 convicts on parole who promise to fight, to Gordon.

Although Norman and Paul are still recovering emotionally from the news of the destruction of the GMI campus, they and the cadets are eager for battle, maybe even more than before. Norman and Paul are greasing the wheels on the caissons and cannons. Norman sits on the cannon brace. "I guess we are preparing our last two brass cannons for the movement to Gordon. That major railroad center seventeen miles from here needs a good brass cannon to protect it from the Yankees."

Upon arriving in Gordon, the cadets build breast

works and set up the artillery before dark and the garrison is able to light some camp fires.

Sitting by the campfire, Norman says, "Feel the moisture in the air, Paul? Looks like the weather is about to change to bitter cold with rain or snow. Best bundle up good tonight."

The next morning, Sunday, November 20, 1864, General Wayne and Major Capers are attempting to telegraph Macon. General Wayne briefs Major Capers, "The lines have been cut by the advancing Yankees. I'll send a scout to determine the location of the Federal forces."

Major Capers replies, "There's a soldier named James Rufus Kelly, who is home after losing one leg. I know him and he was a great scout."

"Fetch him for me."

James Kelly is located and reports to General Wayne. "I understand you're looking for me, General"

General Wayne studies Kelly standing there with one leg missing and being supported by a forked branch for a crutch. He is slender in frame, but mighty gritty looking and appears to be full of spunk. "I need a scout to find the Yankees. Can you help?"

"Glad to, General, I need to work on my score sheet." So Kelly volunteers and is on horseback to spy on the advancing Yankees for General Wayne.

"Major Capers, attach five passenger cars and three flatbed cars to the best locomotive out of the nine at the Gordon depot. Pick the best of the one hundred and fifty railroad cars as well. We must reposition to the east as soon as possible."

James Kelly returns from his scouting mission and reports to General Wayne, "The Union forces are heading directly for Milledgeville."

"I've been trying for eight hours and I am still unable to reestablish communications." General Wayne studies his maps for a moment. "We will abandon Gordon. It's a non-essential military position. Order our command to withdraw to the important Oconee Central Railroad Bridge. We can better defend the bridge against the Yankees rather than defend Milledgeville. Stronger units can defend the Capital."

The following morning, Friday, November 22, General Wayne's and General Caper's small command begin the series of loading the cannons, horses, and troops. The cadets direct the men of Roberts Guard in loading their cannon, caisson and limbers. Cannons will be able to fire from the flatbed cars when necessary.

In a low voice, Norman says, "Paul, Clayton, keep a close eye on these guys, they don't even look like their mothers can trust them."

"You are right about that," replies Clayton. "Several of them tried to slip out of camp last night. When the guards challenged them, their reply was 'we just want to pee.' Some others said they wanted to help the guard on duty. No matter what, they were ordered back to camp."

By four o'clock p.m., all of the provisions and troops are on board the train when Rufus Kelly returns on horseback from Macon. He reports that a large Union force is just outside of Gordon. General Wayne informs Kelly, "We are going to defend the Oconee River Bridge."

Kelly, visibly upset, becomes incredulous and curses the general, "You're a white-livered cur with not a drop of red blood in your veins... well, you damned band of tuck-tails, if you have no manhood left in you, I'll defend the women and children of Gordon!"

The entering Union forces fire shots at the train as it pulls away from the station. The cadets prepare for a fight, but the train roars out of range quickly. Kelly and one other townsman by the name of Bragg begin firing on the Yankees with their new Henry repeating rifles. One Yankee bites the dust and the others scatter. For nearly one hour the two men keep the Yankees at bay.

Kelly says, "The whole world is turning to Yankees."

Kelly retreats to the Solomon Hotel. Inside, Mrs. Solomon is very aware of the skirmishing on the street. She sees Kelly high-tailing towards her hotel in his attempt to elude the Yankees. All he has is his pistol and crutch. As he rushes into the hotel, Mrs. Solomon yells at him, "Rufus, throw your crutch toward the back and get over here quick."

Kelly hurls his crutch toward the back door and heads for Mrs. Solomon. "Get under here quick and be very still" she directs Kelly as she lifts the bell of her hoop skirt. Kelly, somewhat hesitant and with an astonishing look asks, "No offense, Mrs. Solomon, but, did I hear you right . . did you say get under your hoop?"

"If you want to live, that is what you best do, and do it now!" whispers Mrs. Solomon.

Kelly, too nervous to be embarrassed, ducks under the bell of her hoop skirt. The Yankees burst into the hotel lobby with guns and swords ready. Mrs. Solomon is standing and waiting for their grand entrance into her hotel.

"Where's that rebel that came in here?" demands a lieutenant after jerking open the door of the lobby.

Placing her hand upon her bosom and the other on her forehead, Mrs. Solomon says "Yonder through the back door-and . . he nearly caused my death!"

By now, other Yankees are arriving. The lieutenant directs some of them to search the entire hotel. He and several others rush out of the back door in search of the elusive Kelly. In the meantime, the other rebel, Bragg, escapes into the thick woods.

Shortly, Mrs. Solomon sees that the area is clear and informs Kelly, "All of the Yankees are out of sight," and she lifts her bell again and he emerges timidly.

"I truly wanna thank you, Mrs. Solomon. You saved my life. "Now get and go kill them Yankees, Rufus!" directs Mrs. Solomon.

Kelly slips around from the back of the hotel to the woods near the area where the Yankees entered town. There, he finds one rifle on the ground near where he shot a Union horseman earlier. He launches a surprise one-man assault on the Yankees. This time, after killing and wounding several more Federals, he runs out of ammunition. The Federals surround and capture him without any further resistance.

The Yankees force Kelly to witness the burning of the depot, railcars, and locomotives, as well as the destruction of the railroad tracks. The lieutenant does not order the burning of the Solomon hotel. He remembers seeing a Masonic plaque in its lobby. Being a Mason, he questions Mrs. Solomon concerning the plaque. She proudly lets the lieutenant know that her late husband was a Mason.

That evening, a Union court martial finds Kelly guilty of murder. He receives a sentence of death and is to die the following day. However to his benefit General Sherman arrives and orders his troops not to try another soldier in uniform doing his duty. Kelly is jailed but later escapes.

Chapter Forty
Surrender or Die

On the morning of December 6, 1864, Jesse knocks loudly on Mia's door. "Miss Mia, 'e might be dane'gus fuh go tuh town teday. People duh hurry 'cross de ribbuh tuh Kahlinuh. Deh plennie uh bad tings gowin on een town."[Miss Mia it may be dangerous to go in town today. People rushing across the river to Carolina. There are a lot of bad things going on in town.]

They're fleeing before Sherman marches into town," replies Mia. "Reverend Blount told me the white scum of the city are out of their dens like nocturnal beasts to the work of pillage. Mainly men, women and children force open doors like hungry dogs after a bone, each for himself, indifferent to the property or the rights of others. They grab, smash, pull, tear, anything, everything, shoes, meat, clothes, soap, hats, whatever comes to hand. First they take, then run to hide their spoils in some place, only to return and swell the crowd at some other point."

Tot wrenches her hands. "Me's scared fer you, ma'am Mia."

"Most citizens are probably leaving today, but I must stay and care for the wounded and sick. If you want to go, Tot, you, Jesse and Al certainly are free to do so."

"No, ma'am, I's stayin' wid you Ma'am Mia."

"Gather everything we need and put it in the carriage. Load and bring the two pistols as well." She and Tot begin packing bags with cloth and food supplies. When each piece of baggage is full, Jesse puts the baggage in the carriage. Mia sends Tot out to the carriage with little Joshua and returns inside. She opens the secret closet and carefully places some of the valuable items inside. Mia secures the wall and checks to be sure that it is undetectable. She exits the house and does not lock the front door. When she boards the carriage, Tot says, "Ma'am, you don' lock de door."

"If the thieves want to come in, the door is open. That way we won't have to replace it. Besides, Al will be here." Tot hands Mia the two pistols and she places them under her lap blanket.

"Les' tek de long road to de town, Ma'am Mia. I tink 'e gwoin saffuh since de murderas deh een de town now." [Let's take the long road to town, Miss Mia. I think it will be safer since the marauders are mostly in town right now!]

"Okay, let's git!" exclaims Mia.

Jesse heads the carriage toward the round-about road to the hospital. The ride is uneventful until they near the first row of houses in town. Just as they approach the homes, two bushwhackers on foot jump from the bushes. One grabs the bridle and pulls the horse's head as low as possible. The other bushwhacker circles the carriage. Mia pulls back the hammers of the two pistols and whispers, "Stay calm, Tot!"

Tot draws little Joshua closer to her. The green eyes of the white scum are flashing as he approaches. His hair is long and full of tangles. He has an ugly and dirty face with a few black teeth on bottom and bare mouth on top.

He shouts, "You, with the kid, get out now! Pretty lady, you stay put! We's taking this here carriage and I'm gonna take you with me!" He reaches for Mia.

Tot pulls Joshua even closer as Mia jumps up. Her blanket falls to the floor of the carriage. Simultaneously, she takes aim and fires into the chest of the bandit. The force of the bullet sends the bandit to the ground flat on his back. With a single spasm, his body goes limp as blood begins to seep through his filthy clothes.

The horse recoils from the sound of the shot and throws the second marauder to the ground. Nervously, Jesse steadies the horse. Pulling the hammer back, Mia jumps from the carriage bypassing the dead bandit. She approaches the other marauder as he is getting up from the ground. He has his back to Mia. While on the ground, he gathers a handful of sand and fully realizes that his pal is probably dead.

"Stay where you are or I'll shoot ya!" shouts Mia.

Pretending not to hear Mia, he stands and turns toward her. He smiles as if to show off his single, rotten front tooth. As Mia begins to talk about sparing his life, he throws the sand in her face and lunges for her. Mia realizes her peril and quickly forces her eyes open long enough to fire both pistols. He is within one foot of Mia. One bullet strikes him in the groin, and the second bullet strikes him in the left side of his neck. He grunts and with his eyes wide open, he reels to his left as he falls to the ground. Blood erupts from the artery covering his neck and chest. Holding the reins of the nervous horse, Jesse jumps down to comfort Mia. They walk and stand over the second dead bandit as he takes his last breath. Her pistol is still smoking as his body falls still and silent, blood slowly oozing deep in the sand. Jesse assists Mia back to her seat in the carriage. Little Joshua is still clinging to Tot.

Tot gets water and pours it on Mia's eyes. Softly, Jesse utters, "I een kno' wah fuh say Miss Mia! You look moh cahm 'dan me." [I don't know what to say Miss Mia! You appear calmer than I am.]

Although her son is too young to realize what is happening, Mia reaches for little Joshua and hugs him tightly.

"Wah we do wid de boddie, Miss Mia?" asks Jesse.

"Leave them to rot! Let's get on to the hospital." Onward to town, they pass homes and businesses with broken windows, doors open and goods scattered all about. People are running in all directions with arms full of bounty. Another bandit attempts to stop the carriage, but this time Jesse snaps the reins nearly running him over and speeds past him. Soon, they are in the safety of the hospital. Mia instructs Tot, "Take little Joshua to Madame Cazier's office and stay there. I'll file a report about the shooting with Dr. Blair."

On December 20, 1864, General Beauregard

receives orders to take charge of the troop withdrawal from Savannah, across the Savannah River."

"The withdrawal begins at dark and the first across the bridge will be the light artillery, Field Batteries and supply wagons. General Wright, your division should begin crossing around 9:00."

"Yes, sir."

"General Lafayette Mclaws, your Militia will march behind General Wright's division."

"Yes, sir."

"Around midnight, General Smith, your Militia will follow."

"Remember the pontoon bridge might be somewhat treacherous, so take each movement slowly."

"Colonel Clinch."

"Yes, Sir."

"The GMI cadets will act as rear guard. The rear guard of the forces is composed of Companies A, B, and K of the Sixth Regiment, Confederate Reserves, commanded respectively, by Lieutenant Bilboe, Captains W. M. Davidson and J. R. Johnson. This battalion is under Major Cunningham as provost marshal and is composed of cadets with a few men to fill out the ranks. To these boys was paid the compliment of the post of danger which is the post of honor: to protect the rear of Hardee's corps and guard the city until the last minute and only to leave when the enemy is within half a mile of their position.

Before the rear guard passes, set fire to the *Isandiga*, the *Firefly* and the new gun boat *Milledgeville* and blow up the floating battery *Georgia* at her moorings. I have discussed these plans with Mayor Arnold and he fully understands my decision to withdraw from Savannah. Any questions? Dismissed."

The evening turns to a cold, dark and foggy night. There appears to be no rhyme or reason in the chaotic movements of humans or animals. Random Confederates fire their weapons into the air, cursing and chasing after the nymphs of the night in a last call for glory and love.

Obeying orders, the men burn campfires

continuously to give the concept of a strong defense. The withdrawal begins once darkness falls completely on the river. Starting with the light artillery, the Field Batteries and supply wagons, the well-ordered withdrawal proceeds slowly, dictated by the instability of the road across the boats and pontoons. Around 9:00 p.m. General Ambrose Wright's division crosses.

At 10:00 p.m., Cadets Frank, Goldsmith, and Norman are given an order. "Spike the cannons and join the army in the retreat back."

Through foggy Savannah, the cadets prepare to spike the cannons. Cadet Loftin hesitates and places his hand on one of the cannons. With tears in his eyes, he grasps his tattered GMI cap and places it next to his chest. Overcome with feeling, he utters in a broken voice, "To spike these faithful cannons is to place a spike into the soul of the Cadet Corps and the spirits of our faded cadets: Anderson, Alexander, Baker, Jordan, Mabry, Mcleod Smith and Marsh."

Norman feels the transfer of Frank's emotions. They remove their worn caps as their eyes also swell and tears begin to flow. All four, silent, quietly back away. The cloudy moon light glistens brightly from the frost on the cannon barrels as if to say "Thank you" from their fallen comrades. The cadets regretfully depart leaving the cannons intact.

They know that the war is nearing the end. They prepare to become the rear guard of the retreating Confederate army. Reuniting with the Cadet Corps, the Cadets march just over three miles back to Savannah and form the Confederate Army's rear-guard between the Louisville Road and the Savannah River.

Company A, under the command of Lieutenant Bilboe, Company B, under the command of Captain W. M. Davidson and company K, under the command of Captain J. R. Johnson of the Sixth Regiment, Confederate Reserves, and the Cadet Corps compose the rear guard under the command of Major Cunningham.

Near midnight, all Confederate shelling ceases. Slowly, the Federal troops begin to emerge from their damp, cold and slimy earthworks. Taking over a more dry area, most sleep through the night.

As the cadets enter Savannah in the early morning, they set fire to their remaining supplies. Norman and Paul are given an axe by Colonel Clinch's engineers. "Hold on to these. We will need assistance in releasing the pontoon bridges." Norman holds the axe in one hand and his musket in the other. Explosions are not only heard, but felt as the ships in the navy yard and Savannah Harbor are also being blown apart.

"Our orders are to protect the rear of General Hardee's Corps and guard the city until the last minute. We are to leave Savannah only when the enemy is within a half mile." As Norman and the Cadet corps march along they can hear the roar of the robbers and the breaking in of doors, which, with the click of their heels on the sidewalks, made melancholy music, the only music in that sad hour by which to keep time.

Every arrangement had been made for the removal of the army from Savannah. Those who are familiar with the location of the city know that it is built on the south side of the Savannah River with Hutchinson Island in front. North of that island is also another river which has to be bridged.

Paul looks around at the dark and weird surroundings, "Norman, I don't think we have to worry too much about the Yankees bothering us tonight."

"I doubt it as well. I just hope Mia is in Stone Mountain. She does not need to be here with the Yankees just around the corner. I have worried about her the whole time we have been here."

"Yes, I know. Surely she has returned to Stone Mountain by now."

"There goes the rockets signal for the completion of the crossing."

"Let's move out," shouts the provost guard.

The cadets begin crossing the bridge. Though they are the last to cross of the rear guard, they present a pitiful sight. Their uniforms are shaggy and the temperature is cold and damp.

"Paul, look at us. Any person seeing us in this silhouette of the light from the fires at the east of the bridge would consider us an immense funeral procession stealing out of the city in the dead of night."

Looking toward the flames, Paul nods. "Yep. You're probably right. These immense flames no doubt produce a morbid backdrop."

"Take your axes and cut the bridge loose from the docks," shouts Colonel Clinch to his engineers. Paul and Norman move to the edge and back of the pontoon bridge. With simple, yet determined strokes, the ropes are cut and that portion of the bridge slowly pulls away from the Savannah side of the river. The flats, which form the pontoon bridge, are set on fire after the army crosses the river. Some are entirely consumed, others drift and lodge against the bank on Hutchinson Island. Some are still linked together and are burning fiercely. Others float down the river like huge torches.

Norman stands silently and observes above the Habersham Rice Mill at Krenson and Hawks Shipyard, a number of unfinished gunboats for the Confederate government all on fire below the city. Other gunboats are also in flames at the Willink's Shipyard. Norman points up the river and tells Paul, "Look, the only war vessel saved from the flames is the *Savannah*. It's just there gleaming in the light from the flames."

Leaning on their axe handles after cutting the third portion loose and as the last of the rear guard, the Corps of Cadets reaches the sandy hills of South Carolina.

"What's next, Norman?" asks Paul.

"Where to from here, Paul?" asks a weary Norman as their feet touch the South Carolina shore.

In the dim light he taps Paul, "Look, there's General Hardee standing with his staff under the Confederate National Flag. The river breeze has her really flying tight."

"Maybe she's happy that we are all still alive," retorts Paul.

Mayor Arnold and the city aldermen remain at the

Exchange throughout the night and they finalize plans for the surrender of the city to General Sherman. Arrangements are made for horses and carriages to transport the mayor and aldermen and some prominent citizens to the front lines under a flag of truce. The city clerk comes into city hall and the Mayor asks, "Are our hacks ready?"

"Well, Mayor, seems that General Wheeler's men took the hacks except one and left all the carriages." He looks at his watch. "It's 4 o'clock and the sun will be coming up soon. Let's load the one carriage and head out to find General Sherman and surrender the city before we are under assault."

Proceeding down the Augusta Road, General Geary's advance guard spots Mayor Arnold near the intersection of the Charleston railroad and Augusta Road with the white flag of truce. The officer in charge of the advance guard sends a rider back to inform General Geary. "Sir, the Captain thinks that Mayor Arnold is up ahead."

General Geary rides forward and shortly he meets the Mayor, pulls his mount to a stop and leans forward and says, "Mayor Arnold, I presume."

"That is correct. I am Mayor Arnold."

"I am General Geary. I understand you desire to surrender the city of Savannah."

"Yes, Sir. The city of Savannah was evacuated last night by the Confederate military and is now entirely defenseless. As chief magistrate of the city, I respectfully request your protection of the lives and private property of the citizens and our women and children."

General Geary replies, "I accept the Mayor's surrender of the city and grant your request." General Geary turns to his Chief of Staff, "Immediately issue the following orders which will bring the city under martial law."

Returning his attention to Mayor Arnold, he tells him, "Mayor Arnold, lead me to the Exchange Building."

Before the sun can rise at 6:00 a.m., General Geary leads a division under the command of Colonel Henry Barnum of the XX Corps into Savannah at early dawn and before the sun first glides the morning clouds, the National colors, side by side with the colors of General Geary's division are unfurled from the dome of the Exchange and over the U. S. Customs-House. As the Union troops enter the city, the majestic ancient oaks give a more surreal sunrise with their great branches, some as large as the trunks of mature trees with boughs, hang flowing with tender drapes of Spanish moss. The gentle ocean breeze produces a caressing flow within the moss in contrast to the night, when the waving moss appears, as the spirits of lost hopes.

All is not quiet however. Anarchy is the rule of law. Buildings are burning. Slaves and poor whites are fighting over supplies of food. General Geary immediately issues orders. "Guards are to be posted at every building and warehouse immediately. Colonel Barnum, you are to take a brigade and begin patrolling the city. Arrest any person who violates your orders to restore peace."

"Yes, sir."

General Geary sets up headquarters and his Adjutant delivers him a copy of the *Republican* newspaper dated December 21. General Geary takes the paper and reads the front-page article by James R. Sneed, the Editor. "To the Citizens of Savannah. Under the fortunes of war, we today pass under the authority of the Federal military forces."

Up nearly all night at the hospital, Tot continues to keep the fire glowing in the stoves and watches over little Joshua as he sleeps. The Mayor has heavily armed police surround the hospital during the night to ensure the safety of the staff and patients. Tot hears the sound of slowly moving horsemen and awakens Mia. Tot hurries to the window and moves the curtain back. She turns to Mia with her hand on her chest and says, "Oh, Ma'am Mia, yar come de Yankees. Dem thick iz bees."

Mia jumps up and feels the shaking from the tramping of the horses. Looks like the city is safe from attack. The mayor kept his word and surrendered."

By noon, the Union forces have restored law and order and are in total control of the town. Mia meets with Dr. Blair. "Could you please summon a policeman so I can file the report of the shooting?"

"Sure. I'll get the officer in charge of the hospital guard to come in and take your statement." Mia meets the policeman in Dr. Blair's office, and he interviews Mia, Tot and Jesse.

His last question is, "What did you do with the bodies, Ms. Hill?" asks the officer.

"Let them lay where I shot 'em. If the rats and buzzards haven't eaten them, they're still there!"

Dr. Blair snickers to himself.

The policeman, somewhat red-faced with her blunt answer, clears his throat. "That will be all. If I need any more information, I'll contact you." He departs.

The hospital is operating normally and Mia is anxious to return to her house on the river. "Dr. Blair, do you think you can contact the police chief and ask him to give us an escort home and maybe post a guard for a day or so?"

"Don't mind at all, Mia." Shortly thereafter, Mia and Tot gather their belongings and they load the carriage.

"Without warning, the city has become the Mecca for the thousands of Negroes who are following General Sherman's army. They are stampeding and overrunning the city and adding greatly to the confusion. They have joined in the ruthless foraging for food and valuables," remarks Dr. Blair.

"I still have my pistols with me. If anybody enters this hospital in a threatening manner, they will meet their match. Do you want to carry one on you, Dr. Blair?"

"Wouldn't mind at all, Mia. Never thought you would ask. Mine are at home."

"The other one is in my bag." Mia reaches under her coat and retrieves one of her pistols. She holds the pistol around the cylinder and hands it to Dr. Blair. "Take this one. I get the other one. But when I'm ready to leave I would like to have this one back."

"General Geary is sending patrols through the

streets to break up the lawlessness," Dr. Blair continues. "I was by the Masonic Hall this morning where guards are posted and they were hauling off the thieves trying to steal the valuable mementoes of the lodge."

They walk outside. Black smoke rises into the sky from several directions. Mounted Union soldiers are with Union foot soldiers guarding groups of the lawless poor whites and Negroes who are caught pillaging and setting fire to property. "I suggest you wait until later or even tomorrow to go to City Hall to talk with Mayor Arnold about a guard," Dr. Blair says.

"That's probably the best idea. I'll dispense medicine in the meanwhile. I'll be in the herbal medicine room if you need me," replies Mia.

"I think your house is far enough out of town to be safe."

"Hope so." She turns her attention to Tot, who is standing nearby, "Remove the baggage from the carriage and return to Madame Cazier's office. We're staying here a while longer."

Within an hour, General Sherman has taken up quarters in Mr. Green's house, when a Mr. Albert G. Browne of Salem, Massachusetts, the United States Treasury agent for the Department of the South, asks to meet with him. "Come in Mr. Browne. What can I do for the Treasury Department?"

"I know you are very busy, General, and I will get right to the point of my visit."

"What point, Mr. Browne?"

"I am here to claim possession in the name of the Treasury Department of all captured cotton, rice, buildings and commissaries forthright."

General Sherman takes his cigar from his mouth and walks from behind his desk and stands directly in front of Mr. Browne. "Forthright you say." Raising his voice, he points his cigar toward Mr. Browne. "How dare you come into my office ordering me around? I take my orders from the President, the Secretary of War and General Grant, not from some underling of the Treasury. My army has use for these articles and this army has fairly earned the use of them. In no uncertain terms, neither I nor any of my staff will surrender the quartermaster's possessions unless so ordered by my superiors."

Frightened by General Sherman's attitude, Mr. Browne says, "My mistake, General Sherman. I am following my orders from the Treasury Department and hope to be of assistance to your army."

"You, sit down. I'll tell you what I'll do and what you can do."

Mr. Browne nervously takes a seat and General Sherman returns to his desk, lights a cigar and takes a deep drag. He blows smoke rings and watches them disappear. Then he leans over his desk, "After the proper inventories are completed, if there remains any provision for which the army has no special use, I'll turn them over to the Treasury." Colonel Dayton is standing nearby. "Colonel Dayton, get me the latest inventories on the captured commissary supplies." Sitting and waiting for Colonel Dayton to return, General Sherman continues to indulge in the silent pleasure of his cigar, while Mr. Browne devises a shrewd and clever plan to better himself with General Sherman.

Colonel Dayton returns and hands General Sherman the report. He studies the report and advises Mr. Browne, "The preliminary inventory so far shows that in the warehouses there are at least twenty-five thousand bales of cotton. Also, in the forts, there are at least one hundred and fifty large, heavy seacoast guns. This belongs to my army until further notice."

"Very well, General," pausing and standing, Mr. Browne approaches General Sherman, "General, there's a vessel that is preparing to sail for Old Point Comfort. If she has good weather off Cape Hatteras she'll reach Fortress Monroe by Christmas Day."

Then, appealing to General Sherman's ego, "If I may, I would like to make a suggestion, General,"

"Go ahead. I hope it is better than your last one."

Clearing his throat, he states, "General, I would like

to suggest that you send a telegram to President Lincoln giving the President Savannah as a Christmas gift."

General Sherman thinks, "No doubt something like this is what this little weasel Treasury guy had in mind for himself."

Mr. Browne continues, "The President would especially enjoy such a pleasantry."

General Sherman immediately answers back. "Good suggestion and a great idea. Have a good day yourself, Mr. Browne." Colonel Dayton escorts him from General Sherman's office.

Taking to his desk, General Sherman sits down and writes on a slip of paper to be left at the telegraph office at Fortress Monroe for transmission, the following:

"SAVANNAH GEORGIA,
December 22, 1864
To His Excellency President Lincoln, Washington, D.C.

"I beg to present you as a Christmas-gift the city of Savannah, with one hundred and fifty heavy guns and plenty of ammunition, also about twenty-five thousand bales of cotton.

W. T. SHERMAN, Major-General

Chapter Forty-One
Reflections

Mia is up early on Friday, December 23 with the security of her house on the river foremost in her mind. She tells Tot and Dr. Blair that she is going to visit Mayor Arnold to seek protection of her home. Mia feels somewhat safe as Savannah is much quieter and guards are visible in all directions. Putting on a heavy coat, she departs for the mayor's office. She walks by several Yankee soldiers, who acknowledge her passing with a bob of their heads. A slight breeze stirs the fog as she reaches Mayor Arnold's office. When she enters City Hall, Mia finds Mayor Arnold's staff busy talking to the Yankees about the locations of the food, cotton and military supplies. Mayor Arnold is standing in the conference room as Mia pokes her head around the corner.

"Hello, Mia. What brings you here this morning?"

"Dr. Blair said since I am working at the hospital that I could ask you to send a policeman to my house to keep it secure."

"General Sherman and General Geary have already established security around town and at private homes as well. You'll need to talk to either General Sherman or General Geary about placing a guard at your home."

"Congressman Hill gave me a letter of introduction to General Sherman. He said I might need it someday. He is a good friend of General Sherman's brother. He met General Sherman in Decatur when Legare was killed in Cassville," replies Mia.

"That's great!" Pausing and turning red, Mayor

Arnold continues, "Excuse me, Mia, I mean it's great that you have the letter."

"No bother, I know what you meant."

The mayor continues, "General Sherman is meeting with citizens and city officials, so let's go over to Mr. Green's house while I have time." Once outside the office, the mayor suggests that they walk since Mr. Green's house is not far away. "You know the war is basically over. What are your plans?"

"I'll stay in Savannah in memory of my husband until the war ends and the patients at the hospital no longer need me to make medicine. Then I'll return to my family in Stone Mountain at least for a while." Mia wipes at a tear that slips down her check. The wound to her heart from Legare's death still hurts. "Jennifer told me about a GMI cadet dying at Guyton Hospital. My brother is a cadet at the Georgia Military Institute. Evidently, the cadets were conscripted into the Georgia Militia by Governor Brown. Jennifer also told me the GMI Corps was not too far from Savannah when the cadet came to the hospital. He never regained consciousness and died within a day of his arrival. I just pray that Norman is okay. I went to the Confederate garrison and wrote him a letter. The sergeant said he would send it through the Confederate mail right away. I know if Pa or Ma told him I was in Savannah he would try to find me."

"You and the women of Savannah have kept this city alive during these dark days. Although Savannah is the same externally, she is bleeding internally. All of you ladies set the example of loyalty to the cause. You rose to the demand of the moment with such a noble spirit, as if inspired directly by God. Of course, some say that if the women had not encouraged the war, it is possible it could have never come about!"

"I don't think I exactly fit in that mold." She attempts a smile, but it never reaches her eyes.

Approaching Mr. Green's house, she sees a long line forming. As the mayor passes, many of the citizens standing in line acknowledge his surrender with gratitude. The mayor and Mia approach the guard at Mr. Green's front door.

"I am Mayor Arnold, and this is Mrs. Mia Hill. Mrs. Hill would like to speak with General Sherman if he is available."

"One moment, sir." The guard enters the house and returns shortly. "Step inside and the orderly will escort Mrs. Hill to General Sherman's office."

"Follow me, Mrs. Hill."

Mia precedes the mayor into the house and an orderly comes out of one of the rooms. "General Sherman can see you now, but only for a few minutes."

The orderly knocks on General Sherman's office door and from the other side a voice says, "You may enter." The orderly opens the door, and Mia enters, looking directly at General Sherman as he stares back at her. "What is it I can do for you, young lady?"

"General, my name is Mia Hill. I believe you know my father-in-law, Congressman Joshua Hill."

General Sherman pushes his chair from behind his desk and stands. "Please take a chair, Mrs. Hill. Yes, I do know your father-in-law. He is a strong Union man and after meeting your mother and father, I find them to be strong Union people as well."

Mia's eyes widen and her heart races. "You know my Ma and Pa?"

"Yes, I do. I had the pleasure of accidentally visiting your family farm while viewing that big pebble you call Stone Mountain." He laughs. "Your family is doing fine. I left them a letter of protection before departing. Your father, mother and I had a long discussion about this unfortunate war and this great union."

Mia clasps her hands together. She never realized she would hear this from General Sherman. "Thank you kindly for that, sir."

"You Southern women are the toughest I have ever known. You've thrown yourselves body and soul into this war. I believe the men would have given up long ago but for the women. You'd keep the war going for thirty years, if you had the power."

"Yes, General, most of the Southern women have the virtues of heroines. They are more firm, courageous and patriotic than I even thought I could be. Yes, I'm a Union supporter like my family, but I must stand by the South." Mia continues, "Mr. Hill told me of your kindness concerning my late husband. I can only say thank you." Mia's voice begins to tremble a little as she composes herself.

General Sherman understands her feelings and he attempts to mask his. She unknowingly reflects the same emotions as General Sherman. His son Charley was only ten months of age. He died on the fourth of December of 1864. He never saw or held Charley.

After a moment of reflective thought, General Sherman returns his thoughts to the present. "If there was a way to turn back the history of this war and have a peaceful nation, I would be the first to reverse this painful conflict. I am sorry for the loss of your husband, Mrs. Hill. This war is a huge cost to every family of this country, North and South. Our nation is going to lose fully two percent of her population."

Regaining her demeanor, Mia softly replies, "Thank you for your kind thought and kindness toward my family, General Sherman. I have but one request."

"What is it, Mrs. Hill?"

"Could you please post a guard at my home on the river? I work at the hospital formulating herbals for the patients. Usually, I leave Tot there with my son, but with the marauders and bandits about, I'm afraid they may damage the house and harm Tot and little Joshua."

"I can certainly take care of that matter for you. Do you plan to return to Stone Mountain?"

"As soon as the war is over and the patients' crisis is over, I'll take little Joshua and Tot and go back home at least for a while. Our child was born here and I last laid eyes on my husband here. So my heart is in Savannah and I can never remove Savannah from my soul."

"I will have an order written for your protection as long as you remain in Savannah. Also, the order will have a provision for an escort for you back to Stone Mountain, no matter how you travel. Is there anything else, Mrs. Hill?" Mia rises and extends her hand in gratitude, while crying on the inside.

General Sherman softly takes her hand as if to comfort not only her soul but his as well. While holding her hand, he escorts her to the door of his office. He instructs his orderly to obtain Mrs. Hill's address.

"Thank you again, General Sherman." Mia gives the orderly directions to her house and then meets Mayor Arnold in Mr. Green's library. The mayor and Mr. Green are engaging in a general conversation as she walks into the library. "Hello, Mr. Green. It has been a while since I last saw you."

"Good morning, Mia. It has been a while. I hope General Sherman was able to comply with your request."

"Yes. He said he'll post a guard at my house as long as I am in Savannah." Mayor Arnold conveys to Mr. Green and Mia, "We must get along now. I think it smart of you to have General Sherman as your guest. Like you say, Charles, extending such a courteous gesture will hopefully preserve your estate."

"Just as good a move as yours, Mayor. Saving Savannah from the torch and more human suffering takes a great statesman. I hope you and General Sherman have a constructive meeting this afternoon. You and Mia have a good day."

They bid each other farewell and depart. Once again on the way down the path from Mr. Green's house, some of the citizens recognize the mayor and greet him, while others reach to shake his hand. The early morning sun is climbing in the sky and the moist winter air hints of heat as the mayor and Mia head toward the hospital and City Hall.

Chapter Forty-Two
Christmas—1864

Mia and little Joshua awaken on Christmas morning to the warm aroma of Tot's breakfast. Mia hears Joshua squirming in his crib next to her bed. She gets up and sees his sweet smile. He catches his mother's eyes and begins kicking his feet and hands joyfully. She gently picks up the little boy and gives him a big hug and kiss. "Merry Christmas, my little angel. This kiss is from me." She kisses him again and begins to cry. "This one is from your father. I know he is looking at you right now and wishing you a merry Christmas." She lies on the bed clutching little Joshua and begins to sob heavily. She thinks about her wonderful Christmas the previous year and wonders about her family. *How are Ma and Pa, Isaac and Sally? Where is my brother? Is he still alive? How I miss them and dream of my home and my family in Stone Mountain. Hopefully, there will be peace soon and the poor soldiers will suffer no more wounds or die.*

There is a knock on the door. She hears Tot's voice, "Miss Mia, I had Massuh little Joshshuh, bottle ready."

"Come on in, Tot."

Tot enters and sees Mia on the bed holding Joshua. Looking somewhat puzzled, "You 'n Massuh all right, Ma'am Mia?"

"It's just Christmas Day away from home and my loved ones. It would not be so bad if I could find out about my brother. Not knowing about him, that is the hard part." Tot hands Mia the baby bottle and she sits up in bed. Little Joshua kicks his feet and grasps the bottle. Mia holds Joshua close to her bosom, rocks slightly and whispers a song.

"Muhself cook good Chris'mus brekwas fur you and mistuh Joshua."

"Sure does smell good, Tot."

Soon little Joshua finishes the bottle and Mia takes him and goes to the table. "What a great Christmas breakfast! Fresh eggs, rice grits and ham! When we finish, you need to have Jesse to fetch the carriage so we can go to the hospital. I'm sure you made some breakfast for him as well."

"Yass um, membuh you tell me las' night fuh mek 'nuff so 'e kin hab some too. 'E got um 'n 'e happy. 'E kno' you prob'ly want fuh go to de hosbiddle, so 'e 'hab de carriage ready fuh you." ["Yes, ma'am, remember you told me last night to make enough so he could have some as well. He already got his and is happy. He knows you probably want to go to the hospital, so he will have the carriage ready for you."]

"Let the guards outside know we will be going soon, so one can follow us. You can give them a respectable meal. After all, it is Christmas."

As they go through town on the way to the hospital, most all of the women are wearing black as they walk to and from their homes and church. Passing by the Union camps on the various squares in town, Mia cannot help but see the small trees sticking up in front of the Union tents. They have hardtack and pork dangling from the branches instead of the traditional cakes, oranges and candy.

For the most part, it is a very somber day. When Mia, Tot and little Joshua reach the hospital, Mia turns to the Union escort. "I'll be ready to head home just before dark. Please have someone here to escort us."

"Yes, Mrs. Hill, and thanks once again for the piece of Christmas ham."

Tot takes little Joshua and goes to Madame

Cazier's guest quarters. Tot is to keep little Joshua away from the patients for fear of contagious diseases. Mia goes to the herbal medicine supply room and checks on the supply. She finds a sufficient amount on the shelves. There appear to be fewer sick or wounded soldiers arriving. She decides to visit with patients. Comforting the dying on Christmas Day is very difficult. Mia meets Madame Cazier in the ward. They hug and wish each other a Merry Christmas.

Mia watches the near empty hallway a moment, "Today, life's blood curdles in my heart. The awful shadow of this fiend war is all around us." Madame Cazier replies, "Yes, my blood curdles as well, Mia. These poor soldiers hear our voices with tears and reply with a grateful smile. Yet their lives are like a giant pine tree shattered by a lightning strike." The two continue going from bed to bed, comforting and feeding some to recovery, some to the hereafter.

Buck and Betty Gail are not fairing quite as well as General Sherman. Christmas Day is gloomy and cold. The smoke from the chimney rises straight into the sky. Entering the house, Buck gives a few vegetables to Betty Gail. "This is about all the greens Isaac and I can find this morning. We did find a fat rabbit in the box. I think he's probably full of greens."

Standing over the stove with Sally, Betty Gail replies, "Well, a fresh pecan pie along with two chickens and some fresh greens will do us for Christmas dinner. We are lucky to have this much left between the Yankees and those State Militia coming through here stealing whatever they want."

Betty Gail begins to cry and goes to Buck. He takes her hand and walks with her over to the warm fireplace, fresh and glowing in the crisp winter air. "Our souls and spirits are empty. We haven't heard from Norman or Mia. Governor Brown putting those Cadets in the Militia to fight is not right. His son is still with the cadets, I suppose. I pray every night for their safe return. I check their rooms every morning, hoping to see our sweet children and grandchild sleeping in their beds, hoping the war is just a bad dream."

"Lord knows where the cadets are. I don't think the military really knows where all of our soldiers are located," replies Buck.

Taking her apron, Betty Gail wipes tears from her eyes. "For fear I might hear the worst."

Buck bends over, picks up a log and throws the wood upon the hot cinders. He places his arms around her and pulls her close. "I know how Mia is and when she gets ready to come home, she will. I miss them more than even you can imagine." Buck's eyes swell with tears. "She's always been an independent gal and knows how to care for herself. Norman has good sense and thinks things through. Now that Sherman has Savannah, the war is over for Georgia. Brown just needs to wake up. Enough is enough."

Suddenly, Ole Charlie begins barking. They rush to the door to see what excites him so much. "It's Rev. Moss. He must be coming to get some of his chickens or livestock. Got his goat pulling a cart. Good morning Rev. Moss"

"Good morning to the two of you. I hope you're having a fair Christmas Day. I know it's hard on all of us not knowing where our loved ones are," says Rev. Moss as he ties the goat to the fence. "Looks like we got a break from all the rain and sleet. Worst winter ever, I believe."

"Very true, cold weather and cold hearts. No word from Norman or Mia. Sure would make our Christmas brighter if we only knew that they were safe," replies Betty Gail.

"Just trust that God's watching after them, Betty Gail. Well, I've come over to get a couple of guinea hens or a couple of the Plymouth Rock chickens for supper."

Buck replies, "Several of the neighbors came by yesterday and got some turkeys and chickens. The whole flock has done well since the neighbors brought in one or two each. They're breeding and laying good. Everybody around here should have a decent supper for Christmas with the Yankee bummers gone! I'll give you a hand catching those guineas. They're pretty fast."

"Thanks, Buck." Buck climbs down from the porch and they head to the chicken pen.

"Some of Governor Brown's Militia came through the other night looking for conscripts and deserters. They talked to me and Betty Gail for a while, checked the house out. Wanted to know why we had so much livestock and poultry. I just told them that all the neighbors got together thinking the more we put together the better the breeding. I didn't say anything about Sherman's orders. They shot one small pig and took the eggs. They searched our barn looking for evaders and then decided to stay on and camped out on our place for the night. Mean looking bunch. They came back the next morning and took more eggs and some chickens and turkeys before leaving."

"Who were they looking for?"

"Never did say. Just asked questions about who's been coming and going. Wanted to know where Norman was and I told them. No need to try and catch the guineas running loose in the yard." Buck opens the gate to the chicken pen. He and Rev. Moss chase a couple into the laying boxes. Reaching in, they pull the squawking guineas with their wings flapping out of the laying box and tie their legs.

Laying the chickens in the cart, he unties the goat. Let me get on to the house. Thanks for everything and I hope you and your family have a blessed day. Buck climbs onto the porch. He and Betty Gail go inside and are greeted by the smell of the warm pecan pie. The crackling fresh logs send a warm glow throughout the room.

Betty Gail looks around. "Feels like the fire is talking to us. Letting us know the kids are all right. Do you feel their warmth coming from the fire, Buck?"

Buck again holds Betty Gail tight. "There's something special about the fire today and that must be what it is. We need to keep it burning as long as possible, especially today."

The back kitchen door opens suddenly. Isaac and Sally come in from the cookhouse. The aroma of the two chickens sizzling and ready for the table overpowers that of the pecan pies. Sally places the chickens on the table, while

Buck and Betty Gail gather up the greens from the hearth and place them on the table. "Well, let's all sit. Isaac, you and Sally join us like you always have for the holidays." Sally and Isaac render their usual smile and set a place at the table.

"Today, instead of prayer we will listen to the spirit of Christmas coming from the glowing fire in the fireplace," says Betty Gail as her voice trembles.

"The chil'ens gonna be all right Miss Betty . . I knows it," says Sally as she touches Betty Gail's hand. The crackling fire and its warmth embody the thoughts of Betty Gail and Buck during their quiet dinner. Buck, Betty Gail, Sally and Isaac take their seats at the small dining room table. There are four other plates set, and Buck looks to those four empty seats and offers his Christmas prayer. "God guide and protect our children and grandchild." His voice somewhat cracking, Betty Gail reaches and takes his hand and squeezes it gently. Let your eternal love bring peace to this land. Amen."

The cadets have an exhausting and strenuous march in South Carolina. They pass through Hardeeville, finally reaching the railroad in Bamberg on Christmas Day. Hungry, dirty, unshaven and a long way from home, they are unrecognizable and demoralized from the recent events as they gather around the stove in the depot. Some of the cadets' feet are in a terrible state as a result of blisters from the long march from Savannah. Paul, Norman, and several other cadets are given permission to go hunting for squirrels and rabbits.

Upon returning from their hunt, Norman and two locals skin and clean the kill quickly and set them to roasting. Other residents sing Christmas carols. They sit and talk to the cadets, curious about their service in the Confederacy. Some even take notes for an article in the newspaper. After the meal, the cadets join in singing. Finally, a little after dark, the cadets grow tired. They graciously thank the citizens for sharing Christmas and food with them. Slowly, the citizens depart and the cadets are left with only three of the cadets' parents: Calhoun's, Breeses, and Hills.

Cadets Calhoun and Breese are from South Carolina and decide to join their state units. Cadet Lieutenant Hill is being transferred to General R. W. Carswell's staff. He has been assigned as Assistant Inspector General for the First Brigade of the Georgia Militia. "Farewells do not come easy," Norman explains to his comrades.

Paul whispers, "This is the last time all of us shall be together," as he embraces his three departing comrades. They quietly leave the depot and board the carriages with their families. The Corps stands outside, and waves until the light falling snow muffles the sound and sight of the departing coaches. Returning inside the depot, each cadet finds a spot and falls into one of the deepest and safest sleeps they have experienced in a long time. Norman wraps the scarf which Legare had given him around his chilled neck, re-reads his letter alone and drifts off to sleep, still clutching it tightly in his hand.

Chapter Forty-three
Segregated Emotions

Saturday, April 15, 1865: J. W. Goldsmith enters the depot and notices his clerk at the telegraph hastily taking down a message. Looking over the shoulder of the clerk, he reads the message: "Last evening, April 14, 1865, Good Friday, while attending a special performance of the comedy, *Our American Cousin*, President Abraham Lincoln was shot in the back of the head. Accompanying him to Ford's Theater were his wife, Mary Todd Lincoln, Major Henry R. Rathbone and other dignitaries. As the play was in progress, a figure with a drawn derringer pistol stepped into the presidential box, aimed, and fired. The president slumped forward."

Shock and chills fill J. W.'s body as he reads as fast as the message is put to paper. "The assassin has been identified as John Wilkes Booth. Booth dropped the pistol and waved a dagger. Major Rathbone lunged at Booth and, though slashed in the arm, forced Booth to the railing. Booth leapt from the balcony and caught the spur of his left boot on the flag draped over the rail. Upon landing on the stage, Booth shattered a bone in his leg. Though sustaining an injury, Booth rushed out the back door and disappeared into the night on horseback.

"A doctor in the audience immediately rushed upstairs to the box. The bullet entered through Lincoln's left ear and lodged behind his right eye. President Lincoln was paralyzed and barely breathing before being transported across Tenth Street to a boarding house opposite the theater. All of the doctor's best efforts failed to sustain the President. The President was pronounced dead at 7:22 a.m. on April 15th. Vice-President Andrew Johnson to be sworn in as President at eleven o'clock today at the Kirkwood Hotel by Chief Justice Salmon P. Chase. End of message."

Grabbing the message, J. W. rushes outside shouting, "LINCOLN KILLED! SHOT!" Rushing to the hotel across the street, J. W. swings open the door and repeats his message to the few early morning patrons. Those on the street follow him inside. Everyone gathers around anxiously waiting for the telegram to be read.

J. W. hands the telegram to a hotel patron. "You read it, sir. Too much for me right now!"

The patron takes the telegram and reads the contents to the assembly of citizens. When he finishes, some of the citizens take the telegram and read it again in dismay while others flee to spread the word. J. W. takes the telegram back to the depot and makes a copy. He takes the hand scripted copy and posts it on the depot bulletin board for the citizens. In a short time, the few people remaining in town begin to assemble and read the frightening news.

Betty Gail and Buck leave the farm for town around noon. Betty Gail has a basket of spring lettuce, cabbage and spinach. The hospital staff and church members are gathering food for Easter Sunday for the patients.

The town is slowly rebuilding. Saws and hammers sound throughout town as Buck and Betty Gail round the corner of Tower Street and Main. Looks like we are going to have a beautiful, but cool Easter this year, Betty Gail."

"We had a decent crowd at church last night. Lots of crippled and disfigured men were there. Wish you could have come along, Buck. It was a beautiful service."

"Lots of thieving still going on. Can't leave the place at night. Buster's place is nothing but ashes. Gotta get that ground turned since we bought it from him. Gonna miss him as a neighbor, but it's probably for the best since he will never be happy living in Stone Mountain."

Stretching to see the crowd at the depot, Betty Gail peers at the throng. "Wonder what the excitement is at the depot? Lots of people reading the bulletin board."

"Must be some important news for that many folk to be hanging around this time of day." Buck reins in the buggy and ties the horse to a hitching post. Walking to the depot, Buck asks a passerby, "What's all the excitement?"

"Haven't you heard? Lincoln's was assassinated on April 14th, at the Ford Theatre while attending the *American Cousin* stage play! Assassinated by a fellow named Booth! "

Taken by surprise, Betty Gail's hand flies to her mouth and she gasps. She and Buck hurry over to read the telegram. They read the second telegram: Vice-President Andrew Johnson sworn in as President at 11:00 a.m. on the fifteenth after the President dies.

The new President states, "The course which I have taken in the past, in connection with this rebellion must be regarded as a guarantee for the future."

"This is unreal! Killed the President! Those Radical Republicans and abolitionists are probably going to make life tough on the South. At least President Lincoln opposed that radical meanness. Johnson is gonna be much harder on us, just because he's one of us!"

Ten days later, another telegram divulges the sad story, "On April 26, 1864, General Joseph Johnston surrenders just seventeen days after General Lee surrenders at Appomattox ." The terms of General Johnston's surrender are analogous to those which General Lee signed at Gettysburg. General Sherman then orders his generals to extend the same conditions of surrender to the Confederates in their area of military operations.

Upon awakening on Monday, May 1st, the cadets receive new orders. They are to return to Augusta and guard the arsenals and government stores from looting.

Norman reads the Special Order and hands it over to Paul. "I guess we are heading for provost duty again in

Augusta. At least it will be warmer than it was in January. I just hope the citizens understand that we are here to keep the peace and to protect their property."

"We have nothing to cheer about except that we're still alive and pray that our families are all well. At least we have warm clothes and boots. We started out protecting our state against Yankee invaders. Now we are protecting our state against our own people," replies Paul.

After a few short hours on the train, the Corps arrives at Augusta City Hall. The scene in Augusta is not much better than Milledgeville. Thousands of ragged, skinny, veterans with wounds, with disease and missing limbs pass through the town.

Governor Brown receives a letter from General Wilson on Tuesday, May 3rd. The letter extends to the governor the same honorable terms of surrender which had been granted to General Lee and General Johnston. General Wilson also states that he'll accept the surrender and that of his officers.

The war in Georgia is over.

The Cadet Garrison is able to maintain the peace and protect the stores until May 20, two days after the Federal Troops, arrival in Augusta.

During the midmorning of the 20th, the Yankee garrison is to relieve the Georgia Military Institute Corps of their provost duty. The cadets return to City Hall and turn in their weapons and tents. In formation, with most of the cadets in GMI uniform, they are waiting command for dismissal. The Yankee commander orders the color bearer to turn over the Georgia Military Institute colors to him. Cadet Coleman, the battalion's color bearer, removes the colors from the flag staff, walks to the Yankee commander and plants the flagstaff at the feet of the Yankee Officer. Cadet Coleman places it under his shirt then buttons his vest. Returning to his post he shouts, "Damn the man who unbuttons this vest!"

The Yankee commander angrily leaves his post and approaches Coleman as if to confront him. The corps of cadets watches this event with a keen eye. Suddenly, as with a single mind, the entire Cadet Corps breaks ranks and encircles the Yankee Commander and Coleman.

Realizing the gravity of the situation and not desiring to instigate any confrontation, the Yankee Commander hesitates. Biting his lip and twitching, he taps his finger on his hat brim, "The flag is yours to keep!"

He then sharply turns about as the cadets cheer and make an opening for the Yankee to pass through. Returning to the reviewing stand, he directs Major Capers to dismiss the Georgia Military Institute Corps of cadets. "The final fight is yours, honorable cadets. You are dismissed to return to your homes."

Suddenly the war is over.

The boy soldiers of GMI are the last to do duty in the cause of the Confederate States of America east of the Mississippi. It is now time to head home to rebuild an uncertain South.

Norman asks Paul, "Do you realize that on May 14th of last year we were at Resaca? Now we have one mission left and are lucky to be alive to complete it!"

"Yep! For 371 days there was glory in hell!" Paul replies.

"Remember what we discussed the other night about our next mission?"

"I certainly do, Norman."

"Are you still up for it?"

"We've been through too much to separate now. Although I miss my folks as much as you do, this needs to be done. I'm with you because I know you would do the same for me."

Norman and Paul are among those waiting to board a train. They are now a part of the mass of skinny, demoralized soldiers gathered at the depot. They board the train. The whistle blows and with the jerk of the engine, the war is left behind. The train is loaded with passengers, military cargo and Union soldiers. The worn and tattered gray uniforms match the disheartened and torn souls of the defeated Confederate soldiers.

After a two-hour ride, the train reaches Norman's

and Paul's destination. The platform is busy with loved ones looking for a special person as the solemn, rag-draped soldiers disembark from the passenger cars. Many of the soldiers spot their families and rush into each other's embrace. Some soldiers can only stand on crutches and wait with anticipation of the forthcoming welcome. The crutches drop on contact as their emotions carry them into the loving arms of their children, wives, or relatives. Smiles mix with tears, compassion with gladness, but most of all love and brotherhood.

Federal troops begin unloading commissary box cars. Several other passenger cars have Federal soldiers to reinforce the garrison already occupying the town. In a short time, the platform gradually clears. Arm in arm, many of the Confederate soldiers scatter with their families and friends to places unknown to Norman and Paul. A few rag-clad Confederate soldiers remain on the platform standing alone, looking about in hopes of discovering a familiar face. Finally, realizing that there's no one seeking their presence, the disheartened Confederates join together and walk without a purpose toward town.

Once in town, Norman points out, "Look at those freedmen. Don't they look dazed, like they don't know what to do with their newfound liberty? Some of these darkies must have followed Sherman here. They are just wandering aimlessly everywhere."

Paul replies, "One fact for certain, the darkies may be poorer than their late masters, but they are better prepared for poverty. They have been accustomed to want, exposure and toil. Slavery had been a hard school but the darkies have learned more than one lesson. The lesson we are learning is the darkies will endure the present better than their old masters' families. Also, they never learned to dread the future."

Norman looks around. "From what I remember, we need to head in that direction. It should take us about forty-five minutes or so to get there."

Paul looks at the position of the sun for the time of day. "That has to be in the right direction. Let's start walking."

Slinging their haversacks and knapsacks over their thin shoulders, the two GMI Confederates begin their mission. The mid-afternoon sun gleams down, filtering through the trees and the two comrades proceed along the dusty, dirt wagon road. "Seems a little different from when we were here last time."

"Surely not as cold as before. I can still feel that bitter cold whenever I think about how miserable we were," replies Norman.

About thirty minutes into their walk, the pair stops by a local store and asks for directions. The store clerk looks at them suspiciously and questions, "Why do you want to know?" Norman explains who they are.

Upon further questioning, the clerk is satisfied with their answers and steps outside with them. "Go about a mile, then take a turn to the left. It will be the second wagon trail. Then take the first wagon trail to the right. It will be the first on your left. Can't miss it."

"Thank you very much." Norman and Paul shake the clerk's hand and proceed to their final destination.

Walking at a quicker pace, they pass the first wagon trail. Gazing ahead on the trail, Norman says, "Look, there's the second trail the clerk was talking about." His heart begins to beat a little faster as the object of his and Paul's mission draws nearer. Rounding the corner of the second trail, the pair strains their eyes to find the next turn. By now, they are in a double-quick step. Nervous, Paul and Norman begin to breathe heavily.

Norman shouts, "Look! There, one hundred yards ahead! The next turn is there! I can see the roof through the woods!"

"I see it! I see it!" shouts Paul.

The two begin running as fast as their weary legs can move. Dashing around the last turn, they spot the building not more than another hundred yards away. Slowing down a bit, Norman draws his canteen from his side. Still walking rapidly, he takes a mouthful of water and then hastens his pace again. Finally, reaching their destination, they stop in front.

One of the Federal guards notices the two Confederate soldiers, "Halt and stay where you are. Do not move. Put your hands up!" Approaching Norman with his Spencer rifle, the guard demands, "What are you two Rebels doing here?"

Norman, nearly breathless from his dash, explains and asks the guard to please confirm his statement with the owner. "Keep your hands up." Then the Federal guard instructs his partner to notify the occupants that there's someone out here they need to identify. The second guard proceeds to the door. When the door is opened, he gives the butler a message. The butler looks beyond the guard and sees the two Confederates with their hands high in the air. He closes the door and the guard waits for the owner to appear.

"I wonder if she'll know me. It's been nearly four years." Soon the door opens and a radiant young lady steps out. Norman sees his sister and shouts to the top of his crying voice, "Mia, it's me! Norman!"

Placing her hand over her mouth, Mia screams, "Oh, my God! It's my brother! He's alive! Norman, it's really you!" Mia begins to sob uncontrollably, leaps past the guard and rushes to her brother. The other guard moves aside. Norman drops his arms and dashes to meet Mia. Meeting near the foot of the steps, Mia and Norman embrace and boldly sob with raw emotion.

Paul witnesses a truly awe-inspiring moment and sits. He places his face in his hands and begins to release all of his emotions. Paul looks toward Mia and Norman, then to the heavens and swallows the lump in his throat. "This war is over! This war has ended for all of us!" Paul begins to stand and the nearby guard offers him his hand in assistance. Paul accepts the help, "Thank you." Picking up his and Norman's belongings, Paul walks to where Mia and Norman are standing. Mia turns to Paul, wipes the tears from his red eyes and hugs him dearly.

"Hello, Paul. Welcome." Then Mia stands between the two friends and places her arms around their necks. Mia draws their cheeks to hers and together they walk to the house.

Entering the house, Mia introduces Norman and Paul to Al, Tot, and Jesse. "They were slaves of Legare's uncle and aunt. Now they work for me and live in the quarters in back of the house. You two look very tired. I know you would like a hot bath."

"That would be the greatest!" responds Paul.

"Al, you and Jesse get hot water going in the tub downstairs and upstairs. Tot, how about preparing something for Norman and Paul to eat while the water is getting hot."

"Yaas, Ma'am," reply Al, Tot, and Jesse.

Mia, Norman, and Paul take a seat in the parlor. "Why the guards, Mia? Are you under some type of house arrest?" asks Norman.

Sitting next to Norman, Mia laughs, "You won't believe the whole story, but General Sherman met Ma and Pa in Stone Mountain, and General Sherman's brother is a good friend of Congressman Hill. Congressman Hill gave me a letter of introduction in case I ever needed one, so I presented it to General Sherman and asked him for a guard at the house. He ordered the guards posted as long as there is Union presence in Savannah or until I feel I no longer need it."

"Whoa!" responds Norman. "Tell me more!"

"There's plenty of time to talk later. Right now let me show you to your rooms. I still have Legare's clothes here . ." Mia is silent for a moment. "I know he would be glad for you and Paul to wear some of them. Oh, I hear your nephew waking up! Let's go get him!" Norman and Paul follow Mia to the bedroom. Little Joshua is standing in the crib. Mia picks him up and turns to Norman. Looks just like his handsome pa, wouldn't you say, Norman?"

Norman responds, "Exactly! Come see your Uncle Norman!" He reaches for little Joshua and the tot throws his arms toward him. Norman takes his nephew in his arms and heads to the parlor. Mia's chin begins to quiver, seeing Joshua in the arms of her brother.

They have an early supper and invite the two

Federal guards to join them. Tot prepares fresh fish and rice with spring greens and beets. After supper, Mia takes Paul and Norman to the dock. Norman carries little Joshua on his shoulders until they reach the end of the dock. The four sit down and Norman holds Joshua in his lap.

"If you ever want to relax, this is the place. Right here on the end of the dock. Just lay back, and at night you can see every star in the universe."

Norman sighs and stares at the river for a moment. "Paul and I came to Savannah to check on you, but also to find out if you're ready to come home with us, at least for a while. Ma and Pa would love your visit."

"I know. I'm ready to visit for a while, but this is my home now. Legare and I lived here and Legare still lives in my heart. Our child was born here. I can never leave this place." Mia begins to cry a little. "My heart will always be here."

Norman moves closer to his sister and takes her hand. "This place is beautiful, Mia, and I truly understand why it is your home now."

She looks toward the house. "Legare's spirit circulates throughout this dwelling and through me every day. I still climb to the cupola and fish from this dock with him. Legare will never grow old. He will always be young and debonair." Norman squeezes his sister's hand. "The war's over now. Let's send Ma and Pa a telegram that we are safe and healthy."

"I tried to send one a week ago and the lines were still down then, but let's try again."

"You and Paul rest for a couple of days, then I'll go to Stone Mountain with you. Tot's family is from Decatur and I promised her that I would take her with me when I visit my family, the Hill's and Legare's grave in Madison. She would like to try and find some of her family."

"I'll go to the telegraph office, Mia."

During the next several days, Norman and Mia talk about their experiences. Norman shares with Mia the details of his brief meeting with Legare. "I have the scarf in my haversack you made for him. He insisted that I take it. I wore it around my neck during the cold spells and always thought of the three of you. I was really proud to have him as a brother- in-law. Are Jesse and Al going to stay and work for you, and watch your house while you're away?"

"Yes, I pay them one dollar a week, plus give them a place to live and food to eat. They both know they're free to leave whenever they want to but they're very old and have no family."

Paul asks, "What tongue do the darkies speak in Savannah?"

"It's Gullah. From what I understand, the Gullah language is a Creole blend of Elizabethan English and African languages. It was born of necessity on Africa's Slave Coast and developed in the slave communities of the plantations of the Southern coast. It's difficult to understand unless you listen closely. When Tot was given to us by Legare's Uncle Richard, it took me a while to understand her."

It is apparent to Norman that his twin sister's heart and mind have matured even more rapidly than her person.

Chapter Forty-four
Homeward Bound

Early in the morning, several days later, Mia, little Joshua, Norman, Paul and Tot prepare to board the train for Stone Mountain. Mia looks at her loyal servants. "Jesse, I'll be back around the middle of July. You and Al take care of the place for me. You shouldn't have any problems while I am away. Here is a letter to show anyone who questions you. The guards will still be at the house. See you in a month or so." Jesse takes the letter and tips his hat.

"Mia, I'm going inside to send a telegram to let Pa and Ma know we will be there on the afternoon train. I wrote them from Augusta and told them Paul and I were going to bring you home, so they are expecting us."

The conductor shouts, "All aboard!" Norman is carrying little Joshua in his arms. Tot, Mia and Paul are following behind. The conductor takes Tot by the arm, "To the rear car!"

Norman stands eye to eye with the conductor and levels a stare that rises from the maturity he gained as a soldier. "She is the nanny for our child. She is going to be with us."

Begrudgingly, the conductor says, "The darkie will have to sit with one of you! Get on board!"

The clack-a-de-clack of the train mesmerizes little Joshua to sleep in his uncle's lap. Norman gazes silently as the train nears the Oconee River. All through the countryside the scars of war unfold before his eyes. The forts, earthworks and stockades are still standing, as if waiting for soldiers. Army wagons, ambulances, dead mules and horse skeletons are scattered everywhere. The odor of decaying animals fills the passenger cars as the train flees past the gruesome sights.

Norman sits quietly most of the trip. He is touched by the gloom that covers the face of the land. Reflecting on the scenes at the various depots along the route to Stone Mountain, the returning of the brave brings them home with mixed emotions to the loving hearts that sent them forth. Friends and comrades died on those battlefields\, and these men are changed forever.

These scenes pierce Norman's thoughts, "Nay, their very presence kept alive the chagrin of defeat. Instead of banners and music and happy greeting, there's only silence and tears to welcome the defeated home. Not only for the dead are these lamentations, but also for the living. If the past is sorrowful, then the future is scarcely less so. A piece of cornbread, with a glass of milk, and a bit of bacon, is perhaps, the richest welcome-feast that family love can devise for the returning hero. Time and the scathing results of the war have wrought ruin in his home state. A part of the reunited country is in light and the other part in darkness and between the two is a zone of bloody graves." Lithonia is the last stop before Stone Mountain. "Wonder how Mr. Maguire survived the war, Mia?" Norman asks.

"We'll have to ask Ma and Pa. Hopefully, he didn't lose too much." Shaking his head, Norman replies, "Wouldn't count on that."

Mia leans over and tells Tot, "You want to get off in Decatur. Either one or two stops after Stone Mountain. The conductor will announce the station. Here's four five-dollar gold pieces. This should take care of you for a while. If you can't find your kin, come back to Stone Mountain and talk to the railroad agent, Mr. Goldsmith. He will get you in touch with me. Also, here is a letter explaining that you work for me and I gave you the money. Show the letter in case you run into any problems. Good luck on finding your family."

Little Joshua is wide-awake taking in all of the scenery and talking very well. "Uncle Norman, Uncle Norman, look!" He points to a small lake. "River!'

"That's a lake. You can walk around a lake but you can't walk around a river."

In a short moment the landscape becomes familiar. Norman stands little Joshua on the floor. "Mia, hold him for a minute. Paul and I want to look ahead."

Getting up from their seats, Paul and Norman go to the rear of the passenger car and look out over the half door. The whistle blows and the train begins to gradually slow down. They see people standing along the wagon trail next to the railroad. Some ladies use their hands to block the afternoon sun as they strain to recognize a loved one who might be on board. A few older men raise their hats and wave as the train slows down.

Young children run along the wagon trail trying to keep pace, but gradually give up their quest to beat the train to the depot. Mia gets up and makes her way to the back of the swaying passenger car. Norman can see the engine passing the depot and listens to the steam being released from the engine boiler in preparation to come to a stop.

At an instant, and to their overwhelming joy, Betty Gail, Buck, Uncle Isaac, Aunt Sally, Turner and Maria Goldsmith, J. W. Goldsmith and his wife, Lucretia, come into view. The conductor quickly opens the door panel and descends the steps. Norman leaps to the ground, followed by Paul. They rush to greet their families. The conductor places the lady's stepstool and helps little Joshua and Mia also to the ground. Tot follows behind closely. Though her heart is still dark and empty, Mia is consumed in tears as she witnesses the joy and happiness of loved ones reuniting.

"All aboard!" shouts the conductor. Mia immediately recognizes Chip as one of the conductors on the train when she and Legare eloped.

"You better get on board, Tot, before the train leaves. You have the money and letter. If you need me, you know how to find me." Tot turns to board the train.

Chip stands in front of the door to the passenger car and points to the rear car. "Sorry, darkies ride in the last car."

"Come, Tot, I'll walk there with you," says Mia. "There is no use arguing right now."

Saying nothing, Tot tearfully hugs Mia and little Joshua, boards the train and the conductor closes the half door. Finding a seat next to a window, Tot waves as the train slowly pulls away.

Mia walks alongside of the train until she reaches her family. The train picks up speed and disappears around a curve heading toward Decatur.

With emotions beginning to wane, Buck turns his attention to Mia and little Joshua. Mia kneels down next to little Joshua. "Remember the stories about Granny and Papa, Uncle Isaac and Aunt Sally. This is your Papa who came to visit you last Christmas. Over there is Granny, Uncle Isaac and Aunt Sally.

Buck bends over and lifts Joshua. He pats Buck's face and says, "Papa, I love you." These are the first words to come out of Joshua's mouth as he continues to rub Buck's strained, yet smiling face. Soon, the rest of the group gathers around Mia, talking all at once in their excitement at being re-united.

Facing each other, Norman places his hand on Paul's shoulder. "Well, Paul, we made it home despite all odds." The family members become quiet as Paul and Norman say their farewell.

Hesitating, and finally speaking with a broken and emotional voice, Paul grabs and embraces Norman tightly. "Yes, we did Norman! We survived!" The two comrades embrace as their families watch, filled with joy, love, admiration and deep respect for their two soldier boys.

Little Joshua and Papa are quickly becoming big buddies. Each day, he and little Joshua walk around checking on the hired help. Buck decided to convert Buster's cornfield into a pasture. The hired help is rebuilding the split-rail fence around it. "Little Joshua, let's go over to the fence. I'm gonna show you how to inspect a split-rail fence." Walking around the fence, Buck looks at the manner in which the split rails are interlocked. "See here," Buck places his hand between two rails and tries to pull the rails apart. "This is what you call 'hog tight!' Stick your hand in between the rail and see if you can lift them."

Little Joshua bends over and finds a little space to put his hand. He pulls and pushes. "Can't, Papa!"

Buck smiles. "I guess it's 'hog tight' then. Now, we have to get the rails high enough. The rails should be 'horse high'. That's about here on me." Buck places his hand across his collarbone. "Now, in your case, your collar bone is not tall enough. Stand next to me. See? You're about knee high. Let's fetch that new horse I bought from that farmer in Elberton to measure the fence." Buck and little Joshua walk over to a hired hand working the cotton. "How about bringing that horse over to the fence? Little Joshua needs to be sure the rails are high enough."

The worker positions the horse close to the fence. Buck picks up little Joshua and moves so the horse is between them and the fence. "Now, look over the horse's back." Little Joshua lifts his head and peaks over the big animal. "See how high the fence is? Just about as high as his back. That makes it just right!"

Little Joshua nods his head in agreement and says, "Big horse and big fence, Papa. Little horse, little fence."

"You are absolutely right! You kinda sound like your Uncle Norman! Let's go over and check on the sorghum press. Isaac should have some new oak rollers cut today."

Betty Gail summons the family for dinner. Once at the table, Buck asks little Joshua, "Would you like to say the blessing for us?"

"Yes, Papa." Everyone bows their head. "Dear God, thank you for this day and my family. God, take care of my pa, I love him very much. Amen."

Mia leans over and kisses little Joshua on the forehead. Buck begins passing the chicken.

"We turned all of our chickens loose in the woods so the Yankees couldn't have them. So we're having left over Yankee chicken," says Buck.

"This is about the only meat we have to eat right now. Yankees got most everything else. We have plenty of spring vegetables so help yourself to whatever you want."

Buck begins to discuss the purchase of Buster's farm and then his selling it to Uncle Isaac for the same price. He goes on to tell Norman and Mia that Isaac and Sally took their money and now have over five hundred acres. "They are going to divide it into small tracts for freedman to buy.

"Isaac will hold the deed until the freedman pay off the mortgage. Hopefully he will be able to buy more land and repeat the project. As you know they are still living on our place and will do so as long as they want. "

Norman replies, "I am very proud of them and whatever I can do to help with that noble project, just let me know."

"Just one other matter, Mia, I am more than glad that you did not marry Buster. He was not the right man for you. You are a better judge of character than I am or was. Please forgive me for being such a hard nose at that important time in your life."

Everyone tears up a bit as Mia rises from her chair and sits in her father's lap. Hugging him around the neck she tells him, "I love you, Pa, You are the best father anyone could ever hope for." She kisses him on the forehead.

Buck goes into town the next day to purchase grease for the newly constructed cotton gin and sorghum press. The town is rebuilding slowly.

Not many newcomers yet. Noticing Jesse Lanford, Isaac Nash, Mark Beauchamp and some other friends in a crowd in front of the hotel, he decides to stop and chat a bit. As he approaches the crowd he can hear there's a hot debate going on about the consequences of the war.

"Afternoon."

"Afternoon, Buck."

"Good afternoon, Isaac, I'm glad to see that your wrist amputation has healed."

"Yes, I'm thankful. After that wound I got in Gettysburg and that ordeal with gangrene in the hospital in

Winchester, Virginia, I'm feeling lucky to be alive."

Buck asks, "Who is this fellow?"

Jesse replies, "It's Joe Livsey stopping for dinner on his way to Rockbridge."

"My goodness, haven't seen you in quite a few years," replies Buck. He listens as Joe becomes very vocal and holds up a Northern newspaper, "This is the Northern idea of the freedman. Here's what they have to say, "The Negroes are free now, and must have a fair chance to make themselves something. What is claimed about their inferiority may be true. It is not likely to be proven, but true or false, they have a right to equality before the law. That is what the war meant and this must be secure to them. The rest they must get as they can or do without as they choose."

Buck listens to the conversation. Joe lays aside the newspaper. "Slavery might be ended as a legal status by proclamation, but as a living fact, it cannot be. The slaves' hands can be unshackled by a constitutional amendment, but on the other hand, the heart and brain must have an opportunity to expand before the freedman can be capable of automatic liberty."

Jesse becomes somewhat upset at the agitating, "Joe, the North has nothing to fear, because we have lost our slaves, our bank stock, everything by the war. We have been beaten and have honestly surrendered. Slavery is gone."

Joe looks towards Jesse, responding, "The slave is now free, but he is not white. We have no ill will towards the colored man as such and in his place, but he is not our equal, cannot be made our equal. We will not be ruled by him or admit him as an equal with the white race in power. We have no objection to his voting so long as he votes as his old master or the man for whom he labors, advises him, but when he chooses to vote differently, then the Negro must take the consequences."

Buck decides it's time for him to intercede. "The Northern man feels now that the Negro could be a voter. The Southern people will have to treat him well because we of the South will need his vote. You can count on the Negro to remain true to the government and party which gave him liberty in order to secure that party's preservation. Enough of our own Southern whites will go with the Negro for the sake of office and power in order to enable them to retain permanent control of those states for an indefinite period."

John Rankin raises his voice to be heard, "The Northerners think the Negroes will go to work and things will gradually adjust themselves. The Northerners think we would have the Negroes as slaves just to keep the country in constant turmoil for the sake of slavery."

Isaac Nash lifts his handless arm and shouts, "The Northerners blame the South for bringing on the war and killing a million men. Now the Northerner says we cannot complain if the very weapon, referring to slavery of course, by which the South held power is turned against us. Supposedly this justifies the means of righting the wrongs which the North says we have created."

Again, Joe Livsey retorts, "I think I can speak for most Southerners. I feel the Negro is will be made a voter simply to degrade and disgrace the white people of the South. The North cares nothing about the Negro as a man, but only enfranchises him in order to humiliate and enfeeble us. Of course, it makes no difference to the people of the North whether he is a voter or not. There are so few colored men there. That means there's no fear of one of them being elected to office, going to the Legislature, or sitting on the bench. The whole purpose of the measure is to insult and degrade. But restored, with the Blue Coats out of the way, we will show them their mistake."

Buck hears enough. He looks at Jesse Lanford and John Rankin.

"Listen up, folks." The crowd directs their attention to Buck. "You must remember that neither the nature, habits of thought, nor prejudices of men are changed by war or its results. The institution of slavery is abolished, but the prejudice, intolerance and bitterness that it has fostered and nourished are still alive. These prejudiced feelings will live until those who have been raised beneath the glare of this war have moldered back to dust. Joe, you are making yourself sick. States' Rights were defeated on the battlefield. Now the legal structures of the Constitution to resist tyranny and despotism are no longer strong. The executive, judicial and congress who are the ultimate guardians of liberty, the Tenth Amendment and States' Rights are now tied up and choked. The war is over. Pick up the pieces and start over. Try living in peace for a while!"

Buck, Jesse Lanford and John Rankin walk away from the small gathering.

"Do either one of you need a lift?"

"We're good, Buck. Came together."

Disgusted, Buck gives a goodbye wave and directs the horse homeward.

When Joshua wakes the next morning, Mia brings him to the breakfast table where his Papa and Uncle Norman are waiting. When he sees his grandparents and uncle, he tears away from Mia and rushes over to the table. "Good morning, Papa. Good morning, Granny. Good morning, Uncle Norman." He gives everyone a big hug and kiss. Betty Gail displays a grand smile. "Looks like we all got our warm-up kisses for the day!"

"Can't ever get too many from this little fellow. Now, little Joshua, right after breakfast we have a surprise for you. So let's eat."

"Okay Uncle Norman. What's the surprise?"

"Can't tell you, I have to show it to you. So eat all your breakfast." Mia helps little Joshua into his chair. He quickly finishes his breakfast of child-sized portions of eggs, grits and a small hoecake. Little Joshua looks at Uncle Norman. "All through! All through!" He tries to lift the tray attached to the high chair.

"Mama will help you get down." Mia wipes his face and hands. She lifts the tray over his head and to the back of the high chair. Norman gets up and takes little Joshua's hand. Buck follows right along.

"What's the surprise, Uncle Norman?"

"It's in the yard next to my room."

Betty Gail, Mia, Buck, Norman and little Joshua depart by the front door, go down the porch steps and head around the house to Norman's bedroom window. When they round the corner. "Look, little Joshua. See that box? The surprise is inside. Come on over and listen." Little Joshua stares at the box as they walk quietly so they can hear. Norman gets on his knees and puts his ear to the box. "Put your ear here like mine and listen, Joshua." Little Joshua gets down close to his uncle and puts his ear close to the box. "Can you hear that scratching?"

Little Joshua's eyes get big with excitement. "Yes! See?"

"I'll open the box and take the surprise out for you. Sit right here in front of the box."

Mia sits next to little Joshua. The boy anxiously watches as Norman gently lifts the front of the box. Cautiously, he slides his hand under the trap door and takes hold of the occupant. Suddenly, a baby rabbit appears.

The child's eyes light up with delight. "Look! It's a baby rabbit," explains Mia. "Uncle Norman pets the baby rabbit to calm him down."

Norman gets on his knees. "Here, Joshua, you pet the baby rabbit while I hold him." Little Joshua cautiously feels the soft fur.

Gleefully he responds in the emerging voice of a three-year-old child. "Nice rabbit, Uncle Norman. I want to hold him."

"Let's go inside the chicken coop just in case he tries to run away."

Uncle Norman and little Joshua go inside the chicken coop and begin playing with the rabbit.

Buck follows them in. "While you children are playing with the rabbit, we are going to pick some fresh vegetables for dinner. I'm going to check out the watermelons. Betty Gail, you and Mia get some greens and carrots and whatever else you want for dinner."

"After little Joshua and I get a little house for the baby rabbit, we'll be out there to help," says Norman.

Mia and Betty Gail pick up a basket on the way to the back garden. As they walk down the rows of tomatoes, Betty Gail notices Mia appears to be holding back tears. Betty Gail waits for Mia to catch up, "What's bothering you? We can talk if you would like."

"Yes, I know, Ma. It's just that . . over there at that window in Uncle Isaac and Aunt Sally's cabin is where they wished me and Legare the best when we eloped that night." Mia begins to weep and Betty Gail puts her arms around her daughter's shoulders. "It seems like it was yesterday. I can see them now. 'Bless you both!' they whispered to us as we disappeared into the moonlit night. Time is such an illusion." Betty Gail rubs Mia's back a few short minutes. "Let's cut greens and pull some carrots, Ma."

Soon, the two women begin the harvest joined by little Joshua and Norman. Getting on his knees, Norman demonstrates for Joshua the technique for getting the carrot out of the ground. "Watch me. Put your hands around the bottom of the green leaves and pull up real hard . . "Like this." Norman pulls the carrot out of the ground.

"Let me try, Uncle Norman!" Mia and Betty Gail laugh and watch Norman give Joshua a helping hand in pulling up a carrot on his own. Finally, with a stubborn jerk, the carrot pops out of the hard ground.

"Look, Mama! I got me a carrot!"

Mia kneels down and gives him a hug. "Good work. You're going to make a great farmer."

Betty Gail sees Buck in the nearby watermelon patch, "Let's go find out if Papa found a ripe watermelon. It's July and some of them should be ripe."

The weather is very warm, almost hot in fact. The sun shines bright, so Buck's forecast for a blistering day appears to be coming true. Buck sees his family heading in his direction. "Found the first ripe melon of the season.

Come on over here, little Joshua. "The family gathers around Buck.

He has one knee on the ground as he takes his handkerchief and wipes the sweat from his brow. He pulls little Joshua close to his side. "There's no watermelon better than a good, ripe, Fourth of July, Georgia watermelon. Why, a ripe Georgia watermelon is sweeter than a hogshead of sorghum syrup."

Pulling Joshua closer, Buck points to the brown stem on the watermelon. "First, my boy, you've got to find a brown stem, just like on this watermelon. The next thing you do is thump the melon. If it thumps like your forehead, it's not ready. But if it thumps like your belly, it's right as rain." Buck thumps little Joshua's belly and watches him jump away and giggle and rub his belly.

Buck and little Joshua take turns thumping the melon, listening for the right sound. "Let's cut it loose. We can take the watermelon and put it in the creek to cool before dinner. What do you say about that?"

"Pull it, Papa!" says little Joshua jumping up and down.

Buck reaches and pulls the melon from the vine. He grins and stands up with his prize. Everybody chatters about the melon as they start to walk toward the creek. Everyone but Buck. His face takes on a strained appearance. He doesn't move or talk for a few seconds. Suddenly, he drops the watermelon. It bursts and scatters on the ground. Buck slumps over and falls. For a fleeting second, nobody moves.

"Buck! Buck!" screams Betty Gail. Mia and Norman rush over to him falling to their knees.

They find their father motionless. He has no color in his lips. His skin color is fading. His eyes are looking upward with the pupils fixed. He is no longer breathing.

"Oh, Pa!" Mia takes his hand and clutches it to her breast. She's seen death too many times not to recognize it. "No. . ."

Betty Gail falls to the earth next to her beloved husband as she tenderly raises Buck's head, holding his face gently in her hands. Her eyes seem to penetrate through his lifeless eyes into his soul. She had visited this place so many times before, but now all she sees is sadness and uncertainty. "Buck! Buck!" she wails.

"Don't leave me! Please don't leave me!"

Mia is holding her father's hand against her heart while sobbing uncontrollably. Little Joshua is frightened and clings to his mother's skirt hiding his face from the tragic scene which he doesn't understand.

Norman kneels between his sister and mother. He does not want to believe what he sees unfolding before his eyes. He closes his eyes willing the scene before him to dissolve into what he hopes is a nightmare. When his Ma reaches out to him with her trembling hands he realizes this is no dream. His Pa is dead, and his Ma needs him. Norman places one hand across his mother's back and with his other pulls his sister close. His chin begins to quiver as tears stream from his eyes.

Betty Gail hugs Buck around his neck while quietly assuring him, "I love you, Buck. I love you, Buck."

Dismayed little Joshua utters, "Pa Pa, Ma Ma!" His mother places her other arm around her son and gazes intently at him through her tears. "Papa has gone to join Daddy in heaven. We're not ready for him to leave us, but he has just the same." She removes her father's hand from her chest. "Kiss Papa goodbye, little man. He wants to take your kiss with him to your Pa."

Little Joshua looks at his mother and kisses his Papa's lifeless hand. Then Mia gently caresses little Joshua's cheek with his papa's hand. Mia reflects upon Legare's birthday when their family was once again united.

How her father had always been her hero. How he loved her mother and her brother and his grandson. What's going to happen to all of us . . to Ma, Uncle Isaac, Aunt Sally and our family . . now that Pa is gone? Her tears increase as her heart silently wails in pain. She returns her dear father's hand to her heart.

Norman's mind flashes back to the time his pa bought Jack for him, when his pa gave him his first squirrel gun and the joy of their trips to GMI. He has always loved his pa for the strong foundation he made for their family. He was a large chunk of granite standing in their midst. Now, what would they do?

From a nearby field, Uncle Isaac and Aunt Sally bear witness to the tragedy. Assuming something terrible has befallen Buck, they harness a horse to a wagon and rush over to the sad scene. The family is unaware of their presence as they stop nearby. Betty Gail, Norman and Mia are deaf to the entire world until Isaac and Sally step forward and kneel on the other side of Buck's still and lifeless body.

Norman looks up from his somber daze. His heart is aching and he is afraid Ma and Mia can hear it breaking inside his chest. He must be strong for them. As he gulps in a deep breath of air, Norman reaches across his lifeless pa's body and takes Uncle Isaac's hand. "Pa's gone, Uncle Isaac, Aunt Sally, Pa's gone."

Uncle Isaac places his other hand on Buck's arm, "We's so, so sorry Mars Norman. God bless 'im," replies Isaac with a strained voice. Aunt Sally stands and in what seems to her as slow motion, walks around to kneel next to Mia. Tears spring from her eyes and glisten on her dark cheeks in burning streams. There is no comfort now, only sadness and heartfelt pain. Filled with emotion, she is unable to speak. Mia embraces Sally. "Pa loved you and Uncle Isaac. You raised and cared for us as if we were your own children. We love you as much as he did. What are any of us going to do without him?"

Norman places his hand on his ma's shoulder. "We've got to get Pa to the house, Ma." Norman stands up and takes his mother's arm.

"Come on, Ma."

Betty Gail slowly releases Buck. She stands and places both hands over her face. She looks at Buck praying he would stand up with her. After all four rise, they embrace, and in their deep dark sadness they comfort each other.

Norman steps away. "Uncle Isaac, help me put Pa

on the wagon." Isaac releases Buck's hand. He walks over to the wagon and takes the reins of the horse. Quietly, he moves the wagon close to where Buck's body rests so unnaturally still. Betty Gail, Mia and Sally wipe their tears away as they watch Norman and Uncle Isaac gently placing Buck's body in the wagon.

Norman helps his grieving mother and sister onto the wagon. Betty Gail eases close to Buck and places his head in her lap. She looks lovingly at him and caresses his face. Mia clasps her pa's hand. Norman holds little Joshua in his lap. Uncle Isaac and Aunt Sally slowly walk with the wagon as Norman drives the team that carries Buck home from his final trip to his watermelon patch.

Uncle Isaac halts the wagon at the front of the house. Norman silently gets out and places little Joshua in Sally's arms. Proceeding to the rear of the wagon, he studies the scene of his mother and sister beside Buck. They both look so lost.

His thoughts reflect, "A love lost forever."

"Ma, let me help you and Mia down. Uncle Isaac and I will take Pa to the bedroom where he and Sally can prepare him." Betty Gail tenderly lifts Buck's head from her lap. She kisses him on his forehead and hesitantly slides away from his lifeless body. Mia kisses his hand again as Norman helps them from the wagon. Aunt Sally hurries inside and brings a sheet to Norman. He and Uncle Isaac prudently wrap Buck's body in the sheet. In the meantime, Sally is dressing the bed properly with additional sheets in preparation for her and Isaac to bathe and clothe their former owner.

Betty Gail, Mia and little Joshua follow Norman and Isaac to the bedroom where they place Buck's body. Norman gently takes his ma's arm. "Ma, you and Mia come on in the dining room. Aunt Sally will fix you something to drink." Betty Gail and Mia gaze at the white sheet and feel even more grief-stricken. Norman sits with his Ma and sister and in the deafening silence as they clutch one another's hands hoping for strength.

At the cemetery, Reverend Moss, is standing next to the Jernigans. He departs their side and moves forward to deliver Buck's eulogy. "Dear friends, I talked with Betty Gail last evening and asked her what she would like for me to tell you about her late husband and to give a short eulogy because everyone present already knew Buck's virtues. First of all, today, July 4th, was Buck's favorite day. He was a patriot inside and out." Reverend Moss fixes his eyes toward Betty Gail and her family.

"She told me, if I said nothing else, just be sure and let everyone know what a great person Buck was. And that he was! Today is the Independence Day of America. Buck was against secession and proudly flew the Union flag during the conflict. His devotion to his God, his country, his family, friends and neighbors in war and peace was always the same. Put them first. Protect and love them. This he did until he passed."

Reverend Moss signals Dr. Goldsmith to proceed with the Masonic service and then returns to his place next to the Jernigans.

The Granite Sentinel glistens from the morning rays of sunshine as she peers silently over the solemn gathering on a hillside in the Stone Mountain cemetery. The Masonic Brothers of Stone Mountain Lodge 111 have gathered to perform a funeral service at the grave site of their departed brethren, Buck Jernigan.

They end the service:

For as much as it has pleased Almighty God to take out of this world, the soul of our beloved brother, we therefore commit his body to the grave. Earth to earth, ashes to ashes, and dust to dust . . Sleep on, my brother.

"Would everyone join us in the model prayer?" Everyone recites the Lord's Prayer. "Amen." All Masons quote together, "So Mote it be!"

The day after her Pa's burial Mia wakes early. After breakfast and helping clean the dishes, she lays the dish towel on the sink. "I think little Joshua and I'll go to the cemetery this morning and place some flowers on Papa's grave. She remembers the Fourth of July was always such a special day for him."

Norman responds, "If you can wait until later in the day, Ma, and I'll go with you. Got a few chores to do around here first."

"Actually, I kinda want to be alone for a while, but would be happy to go back with you this afternoon."

Norman winks. "That's fine."

Around ten o'clock, Mia has finished helping her mother gather eggs, feed the chickens and harvest a few beans and squash for dinner. Before she and little Joshua depart for the cemetery, they walk through the small flower garden to select some fresh summer flowers. She points to yellow daises. "Joshua, Papa would really like these." They cut a few to place on his grave. When they are ready to leave, Norman has their wagon and only horse ready for Mia and little Joshua. As they board the wagon, Charlie gives out a weak howl indicating he'd love to ride along. "Come on, Charlie. I'll help you onto the wagon." Norman gingerly scoops up the dog and places him in the back of the wagon close enough for little Joshua to pet. As they approach the cemetery all is quiet and serene. She and little Joshua tie off the horse near her father's final resting site.

Charlie lifts his head, and gives a happy yap as they approach. Little Joshua pats him on the head which elicits a whine for even more attention.

Mia rubs the old dog. "Be back in a minute then we will head home." She and little Joshua walk the short distance to her father's grave. They kneel and lay the flowers across the simple plot. "I see Papa smiling at you, little Joshua. He must have delivered your kiss to your Pa."

Mia points to a songbird in a nearby tree. "Hear that bird singing?

Your grandpa sent him to tell us that he is in heaven with your Pa and that he appreciates that little kiss you sent."

Little Joshua smiles at his mother. Then he notices a stick on the grave. He picks it up and tells Mia, "Mama look, a stick on papa's grave. What is it? Mia takes the stick from little Joshua and studies it for a moment. "Why it looks like a wagon wheel spoke with a little red paint on it. Ignorant of the signifiance of the red spoke to her beloved father's courage she hands it back to little Joshua. He studies it a bit further and asks, May I take it home ma?" Mia gives a gentle smile with an affirmative nod. "It would be a nice memento from your papa's grave."

Suddenly, Mia is startled as a shadow appears over her right shoulder. She takes little Joshua's hand stands and turns in the direction of the looming shadow. Before her about ten feet away is a man in a suit holding his coat over his arm. Mia stares into the glaring sun and studies the figure. He is aged and slender, yet has a familiar face.

"Hello, Mia. I was passing through on de train. When I went by to see your folks, dey said I could find you here. I am truly sorry 'bout your pa. I jest want ta say hello."

Mia pulls little Joshua close as her eyes widen. She murmurs with shock, "Buster, is that you?"

The End

Epilogue

William Still (October 7, 1821 – July 14, 1902)
Was an African American abolitionist in Philadelphia, Pennsylvania, conductor on the Underground Railroad, writer, historian and civil rights activist. He was chairman of the Vigilance Committee of the Pennsylvania Anti-Slavery Society.
Often called "The Father of the Underground Railroad", Still helped as many as 800 slaves escape to freedom. He interviewed each person and kept careful records, including a brief biography and the destination for each, along with any alias adopted. He kept his records carefully hidden but knew the accounts would be critical in aiding the future reunion of family members who became separated under slavery, which he had learned when he aided his own brother Peter, whom he had previously never met before. After the Civil War, Still published the secret notes he'd kept in diaries during those years, and his book is a source of many historical details of the workings of the Underground Railroad. He is one of the many who helped slaves escape from Confederate America.

William Still forged a connection with the family of John Brown. His network to freedom also included agents in New Jersey, New York, New England and Canada.
Conductor Harriet Tubman traveled through his office with fellow passengers on several occasions during the 1850s. He was instrumental in financing several of Harriet Tubman's trips to the South to liberate enslaved Africans.

Harriett Tubman(c 1822-March10,1913)
Was an former Africian American slave who became a famous "conductor" on the Underground Railroad, leading

hundreds of slaves to freedom. Harriett Tubman became famous as a "conductor" on the Underground Railroad during the turbulent 1850s.

Tubman had made the perilous trip to slave country nineteen times by 1860, including one especially challenging journey in which she rescued her seventy-year-old parents. Of the famed heroine, who became known as "Moses," Frederick Douglass said, "Excepting John Brown -- of sacred memory -- I know of no one who has willingly encountered more perils and hardships to serve our enslaved people than Harriett Tubman. John Brown, who conferred with 'General Tubman' about his plans to raid Harpers Ferry, once said that she was "one of the bravest persons on this continent."

The slave quilt code is the idea that African American slaves used quilts to communicate information about how to escape to freedom. The idea was introduced and popularized throughout the 1990s. Most quilt scholars and historians consider the "code" to be completely lacking any basis in fact. After the Civil War, quilting became a method for freed slaves to commemorate their methods, routes and symbols of escaping slavery.

Proof

Made in the USA
Charleston, SC
12 November 2015